AT THE END OF IT ALL

RAE LYSE

RAE LYSE BOOKS LLC

Cover Design

Rae Lyse

Editing

Jenine Corneal of @imajinconsulting

For Granny J.

CONTENT NOTE

This is a standalone new adult contemporary romance that contains mature themes and subjects that may be disturbing to some readers.

"This one's for my lil' nigga, Ace. I pray you find the home you told me you were searching for when we talked on that yacht in Malibu. You still one of one for an eternity, Kid. "

DOMINIC "DOUGH" DEBLANC | 2022
GRAMMY ACCEPTANCE SPEECH FOR BEST
RAP ALBUM

PART 1

THE LAST DAYS OF SUMMER

CHAPTER ONE

Ace

Houston, TX
August 2022

I'm addicted to reporter's voices.

The tone.

The bravado.

"After several months of speculation, we can confirm that NBA Hall of Famer and Lakers head coach, Ason Williams, has decided to lend his talents to HBCU Lockwood State with his son Ason 'Ace' Williams Jr. in tow as a walk-on. You might recall that Williams Jr. was on a fast track to the NBA and predicted to be the number one overall pick in the 2020 draft. Many are skeptical of this move after the UCLA Bruins suspended the former baller indefinitely during his freshman season amid allegations of—"

The fucking *nerve*.

The audio from the video cuts out and my eyes snap over toward Pops in our backseat next to me.

"I was listening to that," I mumble, leaning into the back passenger door.

Pops stares down at his phone, swiping at the screen while we inch forward in traffic. "You shouldn't consume junk media so early in the morning."

"But you were just watching it."

"I was and now I'm not. Drive yourself to practice and you can listen to whatever you want."

His driver, Gus, presses the screen on the radio and soft jazz pulses through the truck's speakers. I turn back to the window, looking for the rolling hills I left in LA for good this time.

There's no hills in Houston. The city is flat and full of suspect bayous. Their version of the Hollywood sign is a raggedy message a graffiti artist painted above I-45. Its style changes depending on the city's mood, but the underlying message is always the same. I swear every time Gus rolls under it, Pops says the same ole' shit.

"Man, oh man." He sighs. "Be someone. I hear that and I receive it."

Today's no different.

"Find your purpose and *be someone*. Don't I always tell you to find purpose in what you do? That's what my buddy Ma—"

"Marshall used to say." I cut him off, tearing my eyes away from the message painted above the highway. "He told you that the night you got drafted."

Pops starts talking over me, drifting off on a tangent about his dead best friend who only exists in anecdotes and way back when stories.

A drawl coats each of his words because Houston is *his* home. It's the only city him and Mom swore they'd ever love because it's where they met the summer Mom turned eighteen and it's where their favorite people existed. People like Marshall who ended up playing ball at Lockwood and his wife CeCe, who was supposedly Mom's good girlfriend.

Mom and Pops locked eyes at the Fondé after he beat Marshall in a pickup game CeCe dragged her to. She used to call it an "H-town love story"—some real corny shit. But I liked the way her face lit up when she talked about the day she saw Pops cross Marshall over better than Allen Iverson.

"Damn. That's why you back home for good?" I ask, interrupting his fake sermon that Gus nods at. "Still searching for your purpose at forty-two? Sticking it to the man?"

I pump my fist up with a smirk, but he doesn't smile at my pathetic attempt to lighten the mood.

He hadn't smiled at my jokes since he quit his job. I don't blame him. Shit, my jokes hadn't hit the same since I woke up without Mom's reassurance that he'd laugh with me one day—even if I didn't make it to the NBA.

He stares back at me with hard, brown eyes that don't look like mine, because I look like Mom in every way. He says we even think the same.

"Nah." He shakes his head. "We here because I've obviously been doing you a disservice for the past two years."

"A *disservice?*"

"This ain't so much about me as you think. You need to learn some things and you ain't gon' learn them in that cushy condo in Westwood Angie convinced me to let you buy."

I shake my head at the thought of my "cushy" condo

with a motherfucking yuppie as a tenant. They'd have a perfect view of Century City from the balcony where I used to take shots of 1942 to the head while chopping it up with my friend Cree after visiting Mom.

"You exactly where you need to be," he adds.

I doubt that. Houston's not the same place without Mom. The air's muggier, Mom's condo is quieter, and their H-town love story doesn't have that same corny appeal to it. It's different.

Gus pulls into one of the staff parking lots on campus and my stomach turns.

Lockwood State ain't shit like UCLA, but walking around and seeing a sea of brown and black faces always makes my turning stomach calm—even if they look at me like an alien half the time.

My hand dangles on the door handle as Pops takes a deep breath. "It's gonna be a good day. I'm claiming it."

Yeah, good for him. He's the respected one. He's Coach Williams. I might as well be his lackey because the worst thing I lost in this whole *thing* those reporters like to yap about was my name. It didn't matter if I was back at UCLA or here at Lockwood, on both campuses I'm nobody but Ason Williams' fucked up son.

"Yeah... a'ight," I mumble, pushing out of the truck.

The heat hits me as soon as my slides touch the cement. It spreads from the ground and climbs up my body so tight it's suffocating. Sometimes I can't breathe when I walk outside here and I don't think it's the heat that steals my breath.

I toss my backpack over my shoulder and walk off, leaving Pops to collect all the bullshit he totes to practice in this new weird midlife crisis he's having.

Mom said he'd been having midlife crises before he

even hit midlife. There was always someone to mold, a cause that needed his attention, and a game that needed winning. His last crisis was after my suspension. Now he's going through another. This one's impulsive and has him doing shit people never expected him to do—like quit his job and move back home.

———

"HOLLYWOOD!" LaQuan reaches his hand out for me to slap when I walk into the locker room. "The man of few words."

We lock hands and he wraps me up in one of his extravagant ass handshakes.

Even in the locker room, nobody calls me by my name—I'm Hollywood or *Cali* if my accent shifts too much.

"What's the deal, brodie?" I ask.

"*You*, nigga. You still ain't fucked with me and we been teammates for two weeks now. You got something against big dudes?"

I snort. "Nah... you know better. I just ride dolo."

"Man, fuck that dolo, shit! Come fuck with me. I told Coach Williams I'd keep your ass outta trouble."

I nod and toss my backpack in my locker while his words run together in my head. "Oh, for real? *You*, keep *me*, out of trouble?"

LaQuan Jenkins is a center and my neighbor in the locker room. We don't have shit in common besides our lockers being next to one another and the fact that we been playing ball on the same team for two whole weeks. He's from Opelousas, has a different handshake for every dude on the team and likes to ask me about the snow bunnies in LA as if I needed a reminder about them.

"I know you older and all mature now but that don't mean you can't parlay with us. The baddies still love you."

My stomach turns again and I regret not throwing my headphones on before I walked into the locker room. "Oh, for sure."

"I'm for real! We two weeks in and I ain't seen you out nowhere. I know you gon' be at Splashtown! You gotta be."

My eyebrows wrinkle. "The water park?"

"No." He tosses his hands up in frustration. "The last party of the summer."

"Never heard of it."

"See! That's why you need to get up with a big dude like me. I can show you the wild ways of these down south hoes—"

"He don't wanna hang out with your country bumpkin ass, Quan," my other neighbor Bryson chimes in.

"Why you all in our conversation, bro? This between me and Hollywood. Not your 'freshman—can't even get a bitch to sneeze his way—don't know if you wanna be Mexican or black—forever in the friend zone head ass.' So stay out grown folks' business."

"Got 'emmm!" the rest of the team wakes up from their afternoon slumps to chime in.

It's not justified, but then again, it kinda is, because every nigga had to know his place in the locker room—especially the young ones. It's the pecking order, and one thing about pecking orders is that they don't happen overnight. Bryson Sanchez is at the very bottom because he's a lame freshman with a big mouth. What's even worse than him being a lame freshman is that he has my spot on the team because Pops doesn't believe in nepotism. He says it was created for untalented white kids—not me.

"Man, fuck you!" Bryson waves his hand.

LaQuan pulls at the spiry twists on his head and looks at me with his lips cocked to the side as if to say, "anyway" but I'm already fishing my headphones out of my backpack and fumbling with the power button.

"Guys, guys, settle down," Marquise Brown, a small forward, mocks in his most proper voice. "If we don't stop, Bryson's gonna tell his girlfriend on us."

"Girlfriend?" LaQuan howls. "That boy don't even know what pussy smell like."

That one makes me chuckle while I press the side of my headphones.

"Nah... he knows what it smell like 'cause he got one. That's why his girl don't want to give it up. She know she might as well be scissoring another bitch."

I toss the headphones on top of my head and kick my slides off while glancing at Bryson and his tomato red cheeks.

I can hear that shiny court begging for my sneakers through the locker room's double doors because I'm still trying to make up for the time they spent apart. In the HPE at Lockwood there's no avalanche of blue with people yelling my name at the top of their lungs, cardboard cutouts with my face, or space. It's quiet and little with broken equipment, but I can't trip about it. It's the last court Marshall hooped on and another place Pops thinks is his, so he's obsessed with it and all the people it comes with.

"Aye!" I cut in, shoving my feet in my sneakers.

Their rumbling laughter creeps to a stop, and I feel their eyes piercing into my body as I pull my phone out of my pocket. "Ya'll shut the fuck up. Let homie breathe."

LaQuan smacks his lips, and Marquise stifles a laugh after glimpsing at Bryson.

"A'ight, *Cali*," Marquise mutters. "We coolin'. We coolin'."

They can finish getting on Bryson's head when I finish making love to Marshall's old court with Dough blasting through my headphones, because lately he was the only one that got me.

CHAPTER TWO

Lourdes

"Come on, Phat. Ask Marcus again," Chelsea begs, leaning in so close, her hot breath touches my ear.

Sneakers squeak against the freshly polished gym floor as the boys' basketball team trots out.

I scoot forward and search for Bryson's wild hair on the court. "I asked him this morning, and the answer was the same as it was yesterday. I ain't asking again."

She smacks her lips. "What if this is the last line they have until we graduate? I can't cross without you."

"A—you don't even know if you're going to make it past the interest meeting, let alone cross. B—you don't even know where that shit is. You heard a rumor about where it might be."

"I heard from a reliable source!"

Bryson's curly mop comes into my line of vision and I scoot forward again, digging my elbows into my thighs. "Some random girl's tweet ain't a reliable source."

"She's not random. We're lab partners in chemistry. How you even think I started following her?"

I roll my eyes.

The random girl *was* random and I know Chelsea didn't strike up a conversation with her outside of the internet. She's too shy to do anything as brave as that.

I whip my head from Bryson as he jogs past our spot in the bleachers. "Are y'all really lab partners or do you just stare at her from across the room during lab because she's Greek?"

Her glossy lips droop, her cheeks get flushed, and she confirms what I already know—she's still a nobody, just like me. But my brother Marcus told her that our freshman year in college was about reinvention, so she hangs onto that because she thinks everything that comes out of his mouth is gospel.

"All I'm saying is, you got a job at the bookstore. You can pay Marcus back."

"Off $7.25 an hour?"

She lifts her red-tinged cheek and shrugs.

Four-thousand dollar dues to pledge a sorority won't fly with Marcus. There are too many other things he can do with that money. He can replace the catalytic converter on Mama's car so she can stop taking Ubers to her doctor's appointments. Shit, he can even knock out the balance on that loan he took out to fix the leak in the living room.

"When he said 'reinvention' he didn't mean spend a grip on doing it, Chels and he was really talking about you more than me—as in he wants you to meet *other* boys besides him."

"Whatever." She huffs, pulling away and giving me the space I'd been dying for since we sat down.

The boys dribble and laugh in their own world, waiting

for Coach Williams to walk out. Practices are closed, but no one cares enough to enforce the rule. Fraternities and sororities run the yard—not our mediocre basketball team.

"I thought you talked to him last week," Chelsea mutters, noticing the doubt in Bryson's steps. "I see him shaking from up here."

"I did. I'm not a psychologist."

The team isn't polished. It never was. Not even when my daddy played on it. We got the commits that almost made it to D1 schools—the boys who almost had the *it* factor but didn't have anyone to nurture them. My childhood friend Bryson is one of those boys. He was a good point guard in junior high and high school, but that was it. He don't have a daddy like Dell Curry to make him shoot threes until he gets dizzy. All he has is my brother Marcus and the old basketball goal that sits at the end of our driveway, but Marcus can't even turn good enough into great.

Coach Williams pushes out of a door from the back of the gym and Bryson's eyes jump around. I don't blame him. His good enough status as point guard is in jeopardy because of Coach Williams' sudden interest in our school.

"I can't believe President Bolden sold us out to an Uncle Tom and his Becky loving son."

I cut my eyes at her. "You really need to stop hanging out with your granny and her friends after church. You sound like her and Esther."

"Well, who else am I supposed to hang with after church? Ya'll ain't been in so long." She falls into a fit of giggles as Coach Williams shouts.

I read once that he never uses a whistle in his practices —not even when he coached the Lakers. He said the booming of his voice did the work a whistle did—it gathered the team, started and stopped drills, and it produced prayers for his players. That last part kind of fucked me up.

"My economics professor told us he wants to build a coliseum for a losing team. I even heard he paid off all them outstanding balances for the people that graduated over the summer. He thinks he can come in and wave his money around and we'll forget what happened at UCLA with his son. Typical," Chelsea says, gossiping like her granny, Mother Lenola.

His son is in his own world, dribbling the basketball between his legs with his front teeth digging into his bottom lip. Marcus called it a basketball quirk, like Steve Nash licking his fingers. I know all of Ace's basketball quirks because the Williams are a religion in my house even *after* what happened at UCLA. I never drank the Kool-Aid with Ace though. He's overrated.

"Maybe he's just a generous dude." I shrug, staring at Ace's honey-toned, corded arms.

He seems larger than the other boys, even though, as a point guard, he's one of the smallest. I can never figure out why he seems so big. I heard him talk for the first time last week. He came into my job and bought a fistful of Dum-Dums. He doesn't sound like his daddy. He has a laid-back Californian accent that makes him exaggerate the "ere" at the end of his words and makes me want to go lay out on a beach.

"It's hella hot in here. You ain't hot?"

That's what he asked my co-worker Brandy after pulling a Dum-Dum out his mouth and clutching a basketball at his side while she stared up at him.

He even dresses like he still lives in Los Angeles. He wears clothes like Fear of God Essentials and sneakers that cost more than our mortgage. When he swaggered out of the bookstore, Brandy told me they talked sometimes in her biology class and I wondered what they even had in common.

"He's such a fuck boy," Chelsea mutters.

He *is*, but he's a different type of fuck boy. One time Stephen A. Smith said he was a stain on the Bruins' reputation. Marcus said it was a fucked up thing to say about a kid who breathed basketball and had rappers like Dough naming mixtapes after him even after what happened. Dough said he came back from some shit most dudes don't ever come back from when a reporter asked him about their friendship. A lot's been said, but nobody really knows him except his daddy because the boy never even gave an interview before—not to Holly Rowe, Jim Nantz, or even a room full of reporters after hitting a buzzer beater against Villanova in the Sweet Sixteen.

"Definite toxic city boy vibes." I shake my head at the headphones over his ears.

The hairs on my arms stand at attention as Coach Williams gaits around in basketball shorts and a Polo. His eyes flutter up to me for a second and he gives me a slight smile, like he knows I'm one of the few people on campus that cares about his new losing team.

Maybe he can tell their squeaking sneakers make me warm inside and that this court was the last place my daddy touched before he died. I guess it's why he ain't kicked me and Chelsea out of his gym yet. I'm not Malika Andrews or nothing like that, but Marcus always tells me 'basketball' was the first word he taught me how to say. The second word he taught me was our daddy's name—Marshall. Mama claims Marshall knew Coach Williams. She says her good girlfriend Angie is the same Angie that married him because she introduced them to each other one summer at the Fondé. I don't know why Angie Williams would have ever had the time to bump her gums on the phone with Mama about "what the doctor said this week," but I never told Mama that. Not even when Angie stopped calling last year.

"Williams!" Coach Williams shouts as Ace dribbles past him.

Coach Williams snatches the headphones off Ace's head with a cool cat-daddy grin. "You know I have a zero-tolerance policy on headphones in my gym, young man. Get to the baseline and don't stop until I tell you."

Ace smiles and drops the ball. The back of my throat starts itching. I cut my eyes at Chelsea to see if she notices me scoot even closer to the edge of the bleacher to get another glimpse at that basketball quirk, but she's too busy stalking folks on Twitter for more clues to get her closer to pledging. When I turn my head back, Ace is gone.

Bryson says Coach Williams has a lot of zero-tolerance policies and he's sure nobody but Ace has the balls to break all of them and he was right. I try not to stare at him running up and down the court while the rest of the team warms up. Instead, I force myself to focus on Bryson.

"This boy hitting bricks," Chelsea says, looking up just in time to see Bryson miss another shot.

"Girl, shut up. Practice just started."

"I'm just saying. He's looking real looserish compared to baby Allen Iverson over here."

A loud cackle barrels out of my mouth as Ace runs past us. "That's fucked up."

"It's the truth!"

"Head up, Bryson!" I shout.

His head follows the sound of my voice and when we catch eyes, he's already frowning.

"Uht oh. Lover boy's pouting. I didn't know basketball could make one so angsty."

"Just as angsty as Marcus' new girlfriend makes you."

"Too far, Phat! Too dang far."

Our giggles blend with the bouncing balls and Ace's sneakers pounding the gym's floor.

"Alright, Williams. Strike one," Coach Williams waves his hand and then tosses the headphones on the bench below us. "Come on back."

When Ace stops, his skin is still dry. He nods with another breezy smile as if he didn't cross off one of Coach Williams' zero-tolerance policies in the first practice of the season.

The team huddles together except for Ace. He hangs beside Coach Williams, looking off across the court with a bored face while the staff focuses on the team. They're a mixture of white and black dudes who probably took this gig as a favor to Coach Williams. Marcus told me he brought them from Los Angeles too. I can tell from the way the fluorescent lights dance off the glittering watches on their wrists. They look like money.

"You guys look good. You look decent..." Coach Williams starts. "But good isn't enough for me. You should never want to be good *or* decent at anything you claim to love."

"Okay, Coach Carter." Chelsea snickers.

I dig my elbow into her bony side, making her squeal.

"I want great and a great team should tell a story. The film I watched from last season ain't told me a thing about y'all—not a story, a tale, nothing. All it told me is that I've adopted a bunch of little boys who don't know what characters they are on this court. Y'all don't know nothing about working together to resolve conflict in your story. I don't even think you know how to get to the end of a story."

Their faces scrunch into frowns, but after watching millions of Lakers games with Marcus, I understand there's a method to Coach Williams' madness.

"But that's alright, because I had a good friend that used to tell me that every main character has to overcome obstacles—internal and external ones because that's how we find our purpose in life. But the thing is, folks don't know what those obstacles are until something or someone brings them to the surface and today, I need them brought front and center so we can patch the holes up in this story we tryna tell as a team. So we gonna play some one-on-one with my lil' rusty storyteller here."

Everybody looks around until he picks up a ball from the court and tosses it at Ace.

"Alright, Brown. Come on." Coach Williams chuckles while Marquise grins at him with big eyes.

Ace bounces the ball with lax shoulders. His teeth push back into his bottom lip.

The thing I hate most about him and his fuckboyish ways are his handles. They're so smooth, he might as well be floating. Marcus always told me the easiest way to know if a boy had *it* was if the nigga looked like he was born with a basketball in his hands, but Ace doesn't look like he was born with a basketball in his. He looks like he came barreling out his mama with the world clutched in them— not a basketball.

"Dang," Chelsea hisses while Ace crosses Marquise and screws up that beaming smile he had on his face.

Dang is the only word to describe how Coach Williams uses Ace. The team isn't playing real one-on-one—they're playing one-on-Ace and by the time he gets to Bryson it's hard to understand why Coach Williams thinks he's rusty because he finds the holes that lie within each boy's game no matter the position they play just like Coach Williams wanted.

"Might as well be a one-man team versus a bunch of clowns. Yikes."

"This is fucked up." I groan as Bryson trots onto the court toward Ace. "He knows these dudes aren't on the same level as his son."

Chelsea snorts out a low laugh.

Bryson's loose shoestrings and crooked shorts look on par with her clown accusation. Ace swipes a tongue out, dribbling the ball and staring at Bryson as if they aren't teammates. He has this "me against the world" mentality and I guess I'd have the same way of thinking if I were ever in his shoes.

He doesn't talk until Bryson does something stupid, like having his arms too slack while he's supposed to be playing defense.

"Spread your arms," Ace says.

My knees throb from digging my elbows into them. I'm looking hard for the Bryson that gives Marcus hell in our driveway. He's not here though. Ace snatched all that confidence away. It's gotten lower each day he's been on campus. Now Bryson don't have anything left not even a voice because Ace's feet are too quick, his arms are too sturdy and his mouth is hot.

"Man, spread your arms," he says harder while spinning and driving past Bryson to the basket.

The ball goes in easy like all the ones he put up against the other boys.

Bryson tosses his hands behind his head instead of falling back into a defensive stance.

He's hiding. That's what Marcus calls it, but Mama says it's anxiety from all the pressure. Bryson told me he didn't know what it was. He just knows his brain stops working sometimes when niggas press him too hard on the court.

Ace dribbles between his legs and behind his back. His eyes lock with Bryson's and I can't hear him anymore. All I see are his full lips moving. They fold underneath his teeth and the nasty word flies out of his mouth.

P... U... S... S... Y.

The rest of his words trail behind it, but I can't make out what they are.

Bryson loses his footing and stumbles to the side while Ace drives to the basket again, finishing with a layup.

"Ohhh." I blow out a breath. "Bryson!"

"Phat," Chelsea hisses. "Hush."

"No, I know you saw what he just called him."

"Okay, but talk to him about it after. We'll get kick—oh shoot."

We're not invisible anymore. Ace dribbles in slow, fluid motions while staring at me. The itch I tried to stop in my throat earlier comes back even harder.

"This a weak ass nigga! Put your arms up, Bryson! He ain't even from here! How you let him hoe you like that?" I push the words out, hoping they'll satisfy the itching along the way.

They don't.

They just make Ace's handles more smooth than they were. The gym gets quiet except for the thumping basketball he keeps shoving against the court.

Bryson's arms fall and he's trying to crawl out of whatever hole his anxiety has him hiding in, but it's too late for that. Ace don't let dudes think on the court, and Bryson should know that. He's been watching him right along with the rest of America ever since we found out he was just as good as his daddy—maybe even better. By the time Bryson gets out of his head and tries to push his arms up to get out of that hole, the rest of the team howls out screams.

My brain has to hit rewind to breakdown what happened because it's too hard to understand.

There was Ace, a hesi, and a shot from half-court so smooth Dell Curry would've been proud. But most importantly, there a smile—at me—like I was the second coming of Jesus.

CHAPTER THREE

Lourdes

Low-key, boys give me hives. Not all boys. Just the boys I hate and like at the same time.

"So..." Bryson leans over the bookstore's counter, plucking my baggy smock.

"So?"

I think Bryson wishes he gave me hives. I don't hate and like him at the same time. I just like him. Not in a googly eyed childhood crush way—just a "damn, he looks kind of cute today" or "damn, those braces did wonders for lil' Bryson." He didn't look like he came barreling out his mama with a basketball in his hands and, according to his mama, Lucy, he didn't. He came out feet first, hollering so loud the doctors couldn't wait to shut his ass up.

"What you doing this Thursday?" he asks.

"Helping Chels finish setting up her side of the room before Blythe gets out of band practice." I flip through an *Essence* magazine I *borrowed* from the magazine rack next to the register. "Then I gotta go home and get Mama to bed for her appointment the next morning."

I skim over the "Instagram Style Watch" section, admiring a candid shot of Dough, his girlfriend, and her new softer body since he announced her new pregnancy in his last Insta post. She toted around a purse I didn't even know the name of, but I knew I liked.

I crease the edge of the page, waiting on Bryson to blurt out what he's been trying to ask ever since we graduated over the summer and my titties finally grew a cup size.

"Why? What's up?" I sigh, sucking the sugar out of the Bubble Yum I also *borrowed* from the candy display.

The question had been dancing at the tip of his tongue, but it wouldn't come out like he wanted it to. It's the reason my like-ometer hovered over "like" and veered no further than that. The nigga was too scary, *and* he had weak handles.

"Oh, nothing. That's cool," he replies. "Mama gon' let you move on campus next semester since she finally let you register for classes?"

I glance up, trying to contain my eye-roll.

Mama always told me as much as I rolled them, they'd get stuck.

"Maybeeee..." I drag out with a tight-lipped smile. "You gon' finally work on your defense this weekend?"

He scoffs, turning away from the counter and leaning against it. "It don't matter what I work on. That nigga is the coach's son. He'll always have the upper-hand. His daddy played with Kobe. He played for the fucking Bruins. Do you really think practicing gon' do me any good?"

See what I mean? I'll be cross-eyed before I hit thirty.

I slam the magazine shut. "Did I say anything about

what happened at practice yesterday? Did I even say anything about that boy?"

Ace is our new sore spot. Ever since he showed up to practice crossing dudes over and putting up one legged threes after a two-year hiatus from playing ball, Bryson gets salty anytime he thinks I might bring him up.

He shakes his head and looks out into the empty store. His leg bounces with all the pent-up energy he should've used at practice, but Marcus would get on my ass if I ever said that out loud to him.

I roll my eyes so hard at the back of his head that I see black for at least twenty seconds and when I open them, he's still pouting like the cry-baby he's always been.

I stare at the back of his curly mop and smile at the red tint on his bright cheeks. He doesn't give me hives, but he makes me smile... sometimes. The chain Marcus bought him for his eighteenth birthday dangles from his neck. I think I feel a hint of a butterfly tickling the insides of my stomach, but I'm not sure because boys never give me those.

I start to apologize until I hear *him* talking for the third time since the semester started. I guess he's on a roll now that the world don't care what he has to say.

"What's the deal, Brandy?" Ace asks from somewhere in the store. "What you got for me to snack on today?"

That hint of a butterfly I thought I felt comes back. It flutters at the entrance of the hole it came from as his voice booms from across the store. Suddenly, I'm in California on that beach with my toes in the sand. Bryson smacks his lips somewhere off in the distance and my eyes shoot around, searching for Ace.

When I find him, he's staring at the candy display with that basketball underneath his arm and Brandy standing next to him. He has the same smile he wore in practice when Coach Williams made him run suicides and when he heard me heckling him from the stands. His teeth are straight, white, and perfect like I imagine all boys in Los Angeles teeth to look.

For the first time since I met her, I realize Brandy talks with her hands. When she laughs, her hand hangs on Ace's shoulder and when she wants to show him something, she grabs his forearm and pulls him around. I finally understand what they have in common when her eyes sweep over his body from the tip of his soft curls to the Jordans on his feet: They're the same age.

They're older, and it shows in the way they're flirting. She isn't a lame freshman, and he isn't an insecure one. They both know what they want, and them prancing around the bookstore is just foreplay. According to Chelsea's roommate Blythe, Brandy was the first girl on campus brave enough to talk to him but Brandy left that part out of her biology hoe-tales.

"I can't even talk to my friends in peace without him slithering around," Bryson mutters, tossing an elbow on the counter.

I want to shush him because I'm trying to hear Ace's voice again. He tells Brandy that her hair smells like coconuts and asks how long it took her to twist her curls into the little mini-twists she keeps swinging around each time he smiles her way.

"Two hours? That's dumb long." He whistles. "Call me next time. I'll help you out—give your fingers a break and shit."

I'm sure there's a sexual innuendo hidden somewhere beneath his last comment, but I don't have Chelsea here to dissect it with me. My inner thigh itches where the tiniest welt pops up under my black leggings.

"Don't play." Brandy giggles, tilting her head to the side and looking up at him.

I don't hear his reply because I'm too busy thinking about the other welt on my inner wrist. I swipe it across the hard edge of the counter to stop its itching but it doesn't help and my thighs, *fuck*, they're on fire. I shuffle them back and forth against each other, praying I don't rub a hole in my leggings.

"Yeah... yeah. Phat can ring you up because I'm about to go on break. Hit me up this weekend like you promised."

Brandy's words sound like gibberish until Bryson interrupts my scratch-fest with a loud groan. "Do she really have to go on break right now? Ain't nobody even in this hoe. Bro... on my soul, I hate this dude."

And I do too.

I even hate the way he walks—pigeon-toed and confident.

Bryson glances at me over his shoulder like he did the first day we met in elementary school to warn me of the kid that had been messing with him at recess. But we're in the wild now, and Ace ain't a kid.

By the time he makes it to the counter, my titties that Bryson's been eyeing feel fuller and the rubbing I'm doing with my thighs feels *amazing*.

He drops a handful of Dum-Dums on the counter and I wait for him to say something to me—anything. Like ask me why I talked so much shit to him at practice the day before or for him to tell me he got me banned from Coach Williams' gym, but instead he just stares at my name-tag.

"*Lord*," he says while I zero in on his lips.

They're pink and big, and I wonder what they might feel like against mine. No one ever pronounced my name that way with lips like his and it makes the moisture in my mouth disappear.

"Your mom from France?" He tilts his head and grabs one of the Dum-Dums while I move on autopilot, ringing up the rest of the candy he slid onto the counter.

For the first time in my life, I think I understand what Mama means when she says I'll know the difference between a boy and a man.

"Boys let you run your mouth," she said, nodding and grinning. *"But a man gon' shut you right on up without even saying much."*

I feel Bryson staring at the side of my neck. Another tiny welt rises from my skin, snitching on me, and telling him that my virginal freshman ass encountered a boy I hate and like for real, but he doesn't get it.

Ace unwraps the sucker and pops it into his mouth while I try to remember all the reasons I was supposed to hate him—that *thing* that happened at UCLA, his daddy trying to hoe Bryson for the starting point guard position, the way he looked at me at that first practice, all the girls he was connected to that look nothing like me. There are so many reasons I should really fucking hate this dude.

"Or is she from Spain?" He tilts his head again, talking around the candy. *"Lourdes."*

He rolls the R in a way only a black boy can. It isn't obnoxious, but full of swag, like he picked up Spanish one summer from a Barcelonan nanny.

Mama's never been to any of those places he's talking about. The closest she's been to France is Baton Rouge, and she can't even point out Spain on a map.

"Nah," Bryson clucks for me like the duck he is. "Her mama from the Northside."

Ace smirks and pulls his wallet from his shorts while I fight to scream out "no shit, dumbass!"

He's talking about my name and wondering why my black ass mama named me after a French city when we've never been on an airplane. God, where is my voice?

"Right..." Ace nods, swiping a heavy black card from the folds of his wallet and sticking it in the card reader. "The Northside."

He lets the words linger while he punches his pin onto the keypad.

Ace

LEARNING women again is like rediscovering God. Not that I forgot God or anything like that. We were just beefing for a minute but we back cool—at least I think we are.

Yesterday, I realized that *this woman* is my reminder that Mom might've been right about God all along. She claimed he didn't make no mistakes but there's still a tiny problem with that. This woman isn't even a woman—she's just an immature freshman, and it has to be a mistake that her calling me a "weak ass nigga" makes my dick hard. LaQuan said she's Bryson's girlfriend "in his head" and he's like her yappy little guard dog all because I smiled at her while he tripped over his own ankles at practice.

"Yeah." Bryson frowns up at me. "Like I said...*the Northside.*"

"Cool." I nod at him.

Lourdes is the girl that won't give him any pussy and she sounds and feels like Mom told me all girls with her name should: *"They should sound and feel good. If you ever meet a girl with that name and she feels right...just know that's home."*

She didn't mention that they sounded just like her or tell me why she was obsessed with a name just because it was "so damn pretty," but I think I get it. Lourdes has a round face with cheeks that make me want to squeeze them between my hands, and she has braids that drape down her shoulders with baby hair swirled across her forehead. Her nickname fits her because all the best parts of her are grown woman *fat*—her thighs, her hips, her ass. I came across a lot of girls named Lourdes back in LA, but none of them ever looked or felt as good as this one. She's perfect, just like that name on her name tag.

The card reader beeps and I snatch my card out of it, waiting on her to bring the noise she brought in practice, but she doesn't. Her round lips fall open and she squints at me with cat-shaped eyes, like she's waiting for me to get on her for what she called me.

It doesn't matter if I'm at a PWI or an HBCU, all freshman girls are the same—desperate to find their place in college. Before my fall from grace, they were always at the *very* bottom of my to-do list. Shit, most of the time they weren't even on it and now God was spinning the block with his get back.

Bryson's eyes dance across the side of my face like he's waiting on me to challenge him to a pickup game in the middle of a fucking bookstore. He doesn't understand that yesterday didn't matter and no matter how many ankles I break or threes I hit, the starting position is still his. Nothing I said was personal. It was just basketball.

I take my time, sliding my credit card back into my wallet while he stares back and forth between the two of us.

I want to hear what names Phat will call me outside the

gym. The ones she called me inside were wild, but they were the type I expect to come out of her mouth because Bryson isn't the type of dude to teach his "girl" any better.

I don't think she's breathing until she takes a breath so deep, her tiny breasts push against the ugly smock she has over her clothes. She has skin like Mom's—smooth and brown. I can't see it, but I know she's blushing like immature little girls do.

Bryson smacks his lips as if he's signaling me to hurry my ass on while she's still there with an open mouth and pretty brown skin.

I grab the Dum-Dums off the counter. "I'll chop it up with you later, *Lourdes*."

CHAPTER FOUR

Ace

"Host families?" Bryson yelps from his seat in the back of the auditorium. "You must think we all poor."

I lean back as Pops paces at the bottom of the stairway.

We don't even have our own room in the HPE, so Pops holds team meetings in the cold, dark auditorium where my biology class is.

Goosebumps prickle my arms as my eyes shoot from Pops to Bryson—the fucking bozo. That's what I call him. When he really pisses me off, he's "Phat's bitch" because he does everything she tells him to at practice and he thinks he's going to fuck her. I saw it in his eyes when they danced across her breasts in the bookstore.

"You know what camaraderie is, son?" Pops places his foot on the bottom step and crosses his arms.

"Yeah, I know what that is," Bryson replies. "You think I'm poor *and* stupid?"

"No. I don't think you're poor or stupid."

"Then why you don't think I know what camaraderie is? I made it to college, didn't I?"

I've never played ball with a dude like Bryson. He's always angry about something—the professor pronouncing his last name as "Sanchez" instead of "Sahnchez," Phat leaving today's practice early, Marquise taking the last chocolate chip cookie in the cafe. All stupid childish shit.

Pops narrows his eyes at him.

Maybe he finally realizes the difference between coaching grown men and boys.

"Come up here," he says, waving his hand.

Bryson looks around.

"I'm talking to you, Sanchez. Come up here."

He pushes up from his seat with caution and bounces down the steps where Pops is waiting to deliver his third Marshall-influenced anecdote of the week. The first one blared out when he realized none of the boys on the team had scholarships and half of them worked part-time jobs to make ends meet. The second one came this morning when LaQuan found out his brother Keenan got locked up back in Opelousas. I'm surprised he hasn't run out of anecdotes over the past two weeks. I was just happy he wasn't delivering them to me.

As soon as Bryson gets close enough, Pops wraps his arm around his shoulders. The dim light reflects off his face. His eyes get big, like he's never been embraced by somebody other than his mom, or maybe Phat. They stand together and I hold in a laugh.

"Young men..." Pops starts.

That's what he calls all of us—especially me. I've been a "young man" since I was two.

"Mr. Sanchez seems to think that I think he's poor and stupid."

He lets the words settle in the air as he shakes Bryson by the shoulders and pulls him closer underneath his armpit.

"I don't think any of you are poor, uneducated, menaces to society..." His eyes drift to me and my chest burns. "Or dangerous."

"In fact, I think you're the richest bunch on campus. I'm not talking about monetary riches. I'm talking about rich in opportunity. Mr. Sanchez knows the textbook definition of camaraderie, but I don't want that definition. I'm talking about *my* definition of camaraderie."

I glance over at LaQuan in the desk next to me.

He's staring at Pops like he did this morning after Keenan called him from the St. Landry Parish jail and Pops told him that tough times built tough men. Afterward I gave LaQuan the crumpled wad of hundred-dollar bills stuck under the soles of the sneakers in my locker to put on Keenan's books because he said their mom had washed her hands of him. I couldn't imagine nobody's mom doing such a fucked up thing, but Mom used to say that not every mom was solid like her. I figured Keenan would make better use of the money than I would.

"I want you all to look around this room," Pops says.

They hesitate before their heads twist and turn to look at each other from their seats.

I heard this speech before when Pops coached one of my AAU teams back home. All the boys on that team came from different neighborhoods—Watts, Leimert Park, Compton, Crenshaw, Inglewood. I was the only one with a Kardashian as a neighbor, but Pops told me that didn't matter. We all bled the same and in America, a nigga was a nigga whether he was rich or poor, even though he always tells me I'm not rich. He and Mom are the only rich people in the family, so the Kardashian was *their* neighbor. Not mine.

"These are your brothers," Pops says. "Your lifelines on and off the court. I'm not here to tell you that you have to love each other. I'm telling you that you *must* love each other because in this world we live in, ain't nobody else gon' love my brother like I love my brother."

There's no talk about his three championship rings, his time playing alongside Kobe and Shaq, or that one time Jordan called him one of the greatest of all time even without that fourth ring. He's not a bragger and I don't remember a time he ever was.

"You have a community that wants to support you. Let them. Let them bring you into their homes and love on you like I love on you. Pick your brothers up when they're down." His eyes gloss over LaQuan and then me. "Stop harping on what you think I am and focus on what I'm trying to give you."

It's so quiet I hear Bryson's shallow breaths from the bottom of the stairs. I think I hate him a little less even if my reasons for hating him are stupid.

"I'm proud of you, Bryson Sanchez," Pops says.

"For what?"

"For showing up today. Ain't nobody ever told you they was proud of you for waking up this morning?"

I see the answer in the glossy coating in his eyes. My old friend Javier told me that Pops was the only man that had ever told him some soft shit like that and meant it. After that, I woke up wanting those words sometimes.

He nudges Bryson in the back. "Go'on and sit back down. Up in here asking me if I think you stupid. You a black man in America, boy. You'll always be the smartest man in the room."

Afterward, everybody gets quiet. There aren't anymore side conversations like before.

Pops snatches his phone from the podium behind him, frowning. He's hella deep in this new midlife crisis.

"Calloway..." he calls out. "The Brown family is eagerly awaiting your arrival for dinner this Thursday afternoon."

He keeps on—matching boys with families as if he's played personal matchmaker to pair everyone with the perfect family. LaQuan with the Andersons, Bryson with the Shafers, Marquise with the Taylors, Lucas with the Clarks.

Everybody comes out of their heads as Pops texts family contacts and dudes realize Mrs. Anderson works in the cafe and can whip up a mean gumbo, the music history professor Mr. Clark owns the original Screwed Up Records and Tapes off Cullen that DJ Screw used to record in, and Mrs. Taylor is the auxiliary squad coach so they'll get the scoop on the dancers. Everybody's got somebody.

"Aye..." LaQuan hisses from next to me. "You ain't got a host family?"

Well, everybody except me.

I shrug. "Guess not. Looks like I'm the only orphan around here."

"I mean, with a dude like Coach Williams as your daddy, it ain't like you need one." He holds up his hands. "I'm just saying."

I shake my head, looking down at Pops embracing another boy. "A nigga always need family, Quan."

He nods and I see the pity on his face. It's not the same expression I saw on all the white faces at UCLA. Those looks made my throat tight. It didn't relax until Mr. Palmer, the Title IX Director, told Mom it was best I left campus for good. She spent her last breath fighting him on it.

"Williams!" Pops howls from the front of the room, waving his hand.

He's still gripping that same boy from earlier and I realize that boy isn't a part of our team. His dingy white tee and steel toe boots give it away. Dudes are so excited about their *host families* I didn't even hear him breeze inside the auditorium because they're so loud hooting about "gumbo" and "baddies." When he opens his mouth, the lights flicker off his gold teeth. It's some real country ass Texas shit.

"Damn... that's yo host family?" LaQuan whispers as I push up from my seat. "Rest in peace to you, dawg. I'll save you a bowl of gumbo—looks like you gon' be needing it. He gon' have you eating sardines and fried Spam."

I smack my lips, but it isn't like LaQuan is fucking around. He *did* look like he'd smoke a blunt and then fry up a fire ass Spam sandwich. It would be too much like right if Pops gave me a real host family. He was always preparing me for the world where I'd be "a nigga" whether I was Ason Williams' son or not.

I jog down the steps toward them where Pops is still in his feelings with his arms wrapped around the dude, muttering into his ear.

When they notice me, there's no introduction between us. Instead, the dude pulls away from Pops and grips me around the neck in some type of post-prison embrace and I lose my breath for a second because I can't remember the last time somebody gripped me like this.

"Kid," he says, pulling me in close.

Not Cali or Hollywood, but *Kid*.

My breath comes back in a quick burst.

He pushes me from underneath his arm. "Coach Williams finally brought *The Kid* back home."

The Kid.

He holds his hand out, and I smack it. Our hands tangle in a dance.

"I'm Marcus," he says. "Me, Phat, and Mama gon' be yours while you home."

Hearing "Phat" and "yours" in the same sentence should've felt like a thorn going in my ass, but I felt the same way I did when I saw her flipping through that magazine behind the register at the bookstore—light.

"Phat?" I blurt.

Marcus' lips fall for a second and he narrows his eyes at me with a nod.

Pops laughs. "You know, the lil' chocolate drop with a mouth like her daddy's?"

He and Marcus hoot out similar laughs as if they've lived a life together I know nothing about and I'm trying to figure out who Phat is to both of them because it's the first time I've ever heard Pops say her name—even after all that clowning she did at our first practice. It's no use in me racking my brain because he's Ason Williams. Mom liked to say he was a man that knew the world and really she was a woman that did too. I still can't believe he didn't let all her friends say goodbye.

"Yeah." I nod. "I know who you talking about."

"That's my baby sister," Marcus replies. "She don't mean no harm."

"None! In fact, I think she make you go a lil' harder. You went a lil' stale today when she ran up out the gym." Pops laughs.

I didn't go stale. I went soft because her cat-shaped eyes were wild as she pushed out of the gym's doors.

"Well, I ain't have her there to remind me how much of a 'weak ass nigga' I am," I say.

That really makes them hoot—their Phat with her baby

face and chocolate skin calling me something she shouldn't have and me getting bored in a gym full of dudes when I realize I don't have her in my subconscious.

"Yeah, she had to go take care of something for Mama." Marcus slaps me on the shoulder, grinning. "Come by the house tomorrow night. She'll make it up to you."

Phat is Marcus' most prized possession. I see it in his eyes when he says her name. It's the same way Mom looked when Pops called me "junior."

He squeezes my shoulder with the strength of a man who's spent time in the gym and he's built like he played ball. His midsection pokes out a little like he had a beer on the way to campus, but he's still lean and looks the same age as me.

"Let me tell you something, young man." Pops cheeses at me. "This boy could've been a Splash Brother. I never seen nobody shoot a three like him—just *swish* nothing but net every single time. Just like his daddy Marshall."

My eyes get big.

Marcus' smile falls, and he squeezes my shoulder again. I can't focus on the fact that Marshall is real, and he's Phat's dad, because I know that smile on Marcus' face. It's the one I put on when people get comfortable and start talking about all the great things I *could've* done if I hadn't done that thing that has them talking in past tense about my talent.

Marcus nods. "Yeah...don't nobody have nothing on Daddy. He was the G-O-A-T."

"The GOAT of all GOATS! Nobody else like him."

My eyes hop back and forth between Pops and Marcus while they praise a man I was sure Pops made up until we got to Lockwood and I saw his name hanging in the gym. My gaze drifts past Marcus for a second and I catch Bryson hanging out by the entrance of the auditorium, staring at us with that same empty look he had after practice while complaining about Phat leaving.

"Like I said..." Marcus squeezes my shoulder harder. "Come by the house tomorrow night. We gon' put up some shots. Phat gon' cook us up something good, and I know Mama can't wait to see you."

When he drops his hand, his touch lingers with the only words I held onto—the ones about Phat being mine while I'm home.

CECE LOOKS LIKE MOM.

Her head is bald like Mom's was the summer she stopped leaving the house. I make sure my eyes don't widen at her clavicles jutting from her thin skin.

"You look just like your mama." She smiles, reaching up and smashing her hands against my cheeks as I stand in the front doorway.

I smile back because she sounds better in person than she ever did booming from the speaker on Mom's phone when Mom needed a pick-me-up from "CeCe back home." She has the same drawl as Phat and Mom, and I think I'm obsessed with it.

I close my eyes, inhaling the cognac from her breath. The smell makes my mouth water.

"I know," I reply.

The last time somebody told me I looked like Mom was on a yacht in Malibu, where we celebrated her forty-first birthday. I can't remember who said the words. I just remember feeling as good as CeCe after I heard it.

"Mama, you can't just be grabbing that boy face like that."

My dick jumps and my eyes pop back open.

"Oh hush, Phat," CeCe replies, pulling me into their house by my cheeks.

When she releases me from the shackles of her moist hands, my eyes find who they've been searching for since she ran out of practice to take care of that "something" Marcus was talking about. My chest has been as empty as those bleachers ever since.

Phat stares at me from the entryway in their tiny living room with her hands behind her back, like CeCe is conspiring with the enemy. She doesn't know whether she likes me or hates me and I ain't do shit to her, but Mom said that's how it'd be for the rest of my life.

"People who don't know you from a can of paint gon' hate you for whatever they think you did or didn't do," she said. *"Your response to that hate dictates the type of man you are."*

I don't know how to respond to a perfect girl that hates me and is curious about me though.

She rolls her eyes and my stomach jumps like my dick. She's not even dressed in anything exciting—just a black tank that shows the little curve at the bottom of her stomach and grey leggings.

"Ason, Phat in a mood 'cause she got another mouth to cook for."

It's been a while since anybody in Houston called me Ason just like it's been a while since anybody called me *The Kid*. Mom and Granny were the only ones that called me Ason here and when they left, I never thought I'd hear it in Houston again.

"Whatever," Phat replies. "I ain't in no mood."

I raise my eyebrow and stumble behind CeCe as she pulls me past Phat and deeper into their house. "If I knew I was gon' cause all this drama, I would've bought us dinner."

CeCe whips around with a grin and slaps my wrist. "You smooth like yo daddy, ain't it?"

"Nah... just trying not to cause more trouble." I chuckle. "Marcus here?"

"He ain't been here all day." CeCe grunts out a laugh and leads me into their galley kitchen while Phat's bare feet patter behind us, making Marcus' absence sting less.

The evidence of her cooking is spread around their kitchen—grease splatters on the stovetop, smoke floating from a skillet, and half-chopped vegetables. It don't look shit like the "something good" Marcus promised me because I don't think Phat knows what she's doing.

Mom would've called her a little lady. She used to tell me that little ladies weren't grown; they were trying to be, but that's what made them perfect. She swore I'd fall in love with one, just like she swore I'd fall in love with a girl with a name as pretty as Lourdes. Pops always told me not to believe her because she was a lame, hopeless romantic—especially when she got some wine in her system.

Phat shuffles in front of me and CeCe, easing back in front of the stove.

There's a wet spot on the back of her ass. It seeps through her leggings and shows the flower printed underwear she's wearing.

"C'mere, Ason. I wanna show you something." CeCe yanks my arm and pulls me toward their round dining table before I can get to know their house.

There was no gentle nudging to toe my shoes off at the

front door or the courtesy tour showing me the bathroom for guests, so I'm fumbling around like I been here before. It smells like a house that's raised generations and looks like the one Mom told me she grew up in.

Dust coated pictures and photo albums cover the table. She pulls a chair back, pushing me in it.

"Look... this me and Angie back in the day."

I don't have time to catch my breath before she shoves a picture in my face.

My heart slows as I stare at CeCe and Mom back when they looked less alike and more like themselves with straight-backs and bedazzled boot cut jeans on.

"When was this?" I ask, dragging a finger across Mom's almond eyes.

"Shit..." CeCe leans in over my shoulder. "We had to have been 'bout your age."

Her hand covers mine and we flip the picture over together.

"2001," we both read.

"She was pregnant with you 'round that time."

I squint at her flat stomach, searching for myself until loud clanking makes my eyes jump away from the picture.

"Dang it," Phat hisses. "Shoot!"

Bitter smoke drifts up my nose while CeCe reaches over me and shuffles through a stack of pictures.

"You got more?" I ask.

"Duh! Back before your daddy swept her away to LaLa Land, me and Angie was thick as thieves."

There's a dull ache in my chest. Her words sound like some shit Mom would say on her balcony over a glass of wine while we watched the sunset.

"She called LA that too." I chuckle. "She said it 'wasn't no City of Angels—'"

"'But a city full of devils *disguised* as angels!'"

Our laughter mixes and when she reaches over me to grab another picture, I smell Mom on her skin. I taste the metallic in my mouth and I'm fucking dying for something I promised Mom I wouldn't have at dinner. I told her I'd behave for her good girlfriend that she hadn't seen in so long.

CeCe jabs her boney elbow into my side while studying a picture of her younger self. "She might've been talking 'bout your ole' daddy."

I snort. "Shit... it wouldn't surprise me."

"Now, don't get me wrong, my friend loved Ason though. She loved him a lot even when he was a lil' devil."

When her words drift off, my sight goes with them and I lose her face because Mom's replaces it. For a minute, all the good feelings that come with seeing Mom after so long attack me—the stillness of peace that only her face brings, a swollen heart that grows too big for my chest when I hear her heckling me from the stands during games, and most of all contentment because I'm home.

"Yeah," I babble. "She loved him too fucking much."

CeCe's cheeks lift and her eyes scrunch so much I can't see the whites in her pupils. "How was the funeral? I wish I would've at least got a program."

"Quiet," I choke out with a swallow. "Real quiet."

Both sides of the family still hadn't forgiven Pops for it.

She taps the picture, shaking her head. "We all grieve in different ways, son. Go in there and have Phat fix you something to drink in one of my good glasses. It'll get you through dinner."

Phat doesn't hear us because she's too distracted, frowning at the sizzling mound of hamburger meat in the skillet.

I push away from the table and walk toward her.

The wet spot on her ass is even bigger and there's a matching one on the small of her back. She swipes a hand across her wet forehead when I ease next to her and I almost don't want to say anything because watching her is better sometimes.

I clear my throat, but she's still zoned into the over-cooked ground beef. "Hey..."

Her arm jerks and she drops the spatula in the skillet, and it's just like at the bookstore. She's staring at me with those big cat-shaped eyes like I'm the one that hates her.

"Your mom said to have you fix me something to drink." I nod my head to the opened bottle of Hennessy on the counter and I hear Pops talking about, "the lil' chocolate drop with a mouth like her daddy's."

It makes me smile and makes her frown harder.

She flings her braids over her shoulder and reaches up to open a cabinet.

"You forgetting something?" I ask, pulling the spatula out of the grease. "You trying to burn the house down?"

She whips her head back to me and the glass in her hand tumbles in a slow, fumbling motion, but she recovers and catches it.

"Phat, might be time for you to cut the burgers off, baby. Mama can't take all this smoke you got going in here!" CeCe yells from the table with her face buried in another album.

She's lost in 2001 while Phat's faltering in front of me because she's a little lady that doesn't know what to do with a man when her Mom's not watching. She doesn't know she's supposed to brush her arm against mine and I'm supposed to promise her a good time when the Hennessy knocks CeCe on her ass. Instead, she's a clumsy mess.

"I got you." I nod toward the bottle again. "Just fix me something to sip on."

I turn off the burner on the stove as she shuffles around and then sits a full glass of liquor next to me. It's too much, but I don't complain because thanks to CeCe, I'm searching for the one thing that always makes everything right.

I pick it up and after the first sip, my mouth leaks like a faucet.

"You got too much grease in the skillet," I mutter, scooping the burnt patties onto the paper towel covered plate next to the stove. "Go open the window for Mom."

The second sip makes those words come out because I want to watch her ass while she walks to the window and I don't know how to *not* call CeCe by the name that comes to mind when I look at her.

Phat gives me a double-take like she wants to say something, but nothing comes out. Her ass sways on her way to the window and my dick is happy to see those juvenile panties and her ass' natural curve at the bottom.

By the time I'm on my third sip, she's back in the kitchen without me having to tell her to come back, and that makes me take a fourth.

I swallow. "Come here, let me show you something."

The warmth from her body has my heart thumping and I need to stop sipping, but CeCe's frail body won't let that happen.

"Ground beef makes its own grease. You don't need this." I nudge the bottle of cooking oil away from the skillet. "And you don't need to cook it so damn high. What you in a rush for?"

She doesn't even give me a shrug, just a tilt of her head because she's curious, like I said.

"Listen to him, Phat," CeCe slurs, laughing. "That's a

good man right there. You ain't got to move so fast all the time. Life move fast enough as it is."

Those words make me guzzle what's left in the glass.

CHAPTER FIVE

Lourdes

There's a wet spot sitting in my panties. I felt it when Ace told me to fix him something to sip on and I saw it when I went to pee after Mama told me to fix his hamburger. It's still there after Ace asks Mama to explain what Zydeco is. The more he drinks with Mama, the lower his eyes get and the more they keep drifting over to me. He's doing that bullshit again—making my mouth dry, my skin itch, and my brain forget how to form words so I've been mute all throughout dinner and he probably thinks I'm touched.

I guess Mama was telling the truth about Marshall and Coach Williams. The dusty picture albums she made me pull off the shelf in the back of her closet yesterday confirmed it. Now I know the Angie Mama is always yapping about really is Coach Williams' Angie—the same Angie whose death they announced on ESPN and the local news last year.

"So it's like Cajun music?" Ace asks, swiping his tongue out to wet his bottom lip.

"Nah! That's for white folks. Zydeco is for us."

Mama's drunk already. She was drunk before Ace pulled up for dinner and she was drunk this morning after breakfast. I found the eggs I scrambled for her in the bathroom trash while I refilled her pill planner and she threw up a mouthful of Paul Masson before I left for class.

"Chris Ardoin, J Paul Jr, Keith Frank." She tosses her fingers out one by one and shimmies her shoulders.

A giggle almost slips out of my mouth until Ace looks at me again.

He knows she's drunk. It's in the tiny smile he gives me before he takes another swig of Hennessy.

My thighs are sore from rubbing them against each other. Every time I think that wet spot will dry up, he looks at me and I start rubbing them back and forth again. I don't know how long I can tolerate Marcus being his host nigga or whatever he is.

"Show me," he says, staring at me instead of her. "Play something for me, Mom."

Mama's so drunk she yanks her shattered phone out of her bra and swipes at the screen while Ace pushes back from the table.

In the two hours he's been in our house, Mama has turned into *his* mom, I finally know what Chelsea means when she says Marcus' voice makes her wet—ew, and Ace has taken over dinner. Now Keith Frank is singing, telling us to roll with him while Ace's caramel arm slides in front of me to take my half-eaten burger and steak fries.

"Come on, Ason!" Mama howls, tossing her bald head back.

Ace whistles back and my head whips around so I can watch him like he's been watching me. He grips the tulip glass in one hand and balances our plates with his other. He toed his Jordans off after I fixed his drink, and now he's doing what I'm supposed to be doing.

Before I can finish imagining what he might look like without clothes, he's already put our dirty dishes in the sink and stealing Mama's glass of Hennessy. He replaces it with a bottle of water and she doesn't notice because he pulls her out of her chair by her thin arm.

Her legs move and then her hips follow and he tries to do the same, but his legs won't cooperate. They're too used to Los Angeles. That giggle I tried to hide earlier comes out in an ugly snort while he dances just how I expect a nigga from Los Angeles to—stiff with his arms locked in front of him, doing an ugly ass two-step.

Mama shimmies around him. It's the most she's moved in a week. There's sweat prickling at the ends of her sparse eyebrows and the tight dress I picked out for her to wear bunches at the back. Ace grabs her between the folds and their feet shuffle together until they stop doing two different dances and their bodies sync together as one.

"He can move, can't he, Phat?" she yells over the music, chasing her breath.

"Yeah, Mama... he can."

They can't hear me over their laughs, the music, or Ace asking Mama if she got dressed up for him tonight.

I can't remember the last time Keith Frank played in our kitchen or a man held Mama at the small of her back. Her Miss Me Jeans are two sizes too big now and the cowboy boots me and Marcus got her last Christmas collect dust in the back of her closet. A month ago she told Granny she didn't think she'd make it to another trail ride, but somehow Ace changed her mind.

She laughs. "I'm taking you with me, Ason! I'd have to beat those bitches off you. You handsome thing you!"

The song ends and the wheezing from her chest grows louder.

"Okay, Mama. That's enough excitement." I push up from the table. "You ain't ate nothing for dinner."

"Yes, I did," she slurs, burying her head into Ace's t-shirt.

"Hennessy don't count."

"It do!"

If my eyes ever get stuck like she claims they will, her and Bryson would be the reason, and maybe Ace too, because he makes my body do weird shit.

I walk past them into the kitchen and fling open a cabinet to grab a plate.

"A'ight, Mom," Ace says. "I'mma chill outside and wait for Marcus. Let Phat take care of you."

It's the first time all night he's said my name, and it was worth the wait. He says it as if we're familiar with each other—like he comes to our house all the time for dinner to play mediator between me and Mama. He said it just like he said *Lourdes* at the bookstore. He says them like I'm his.

"Don't let her run you off," she whispers.

"She can't ever do that." He laughs.

I whip my head back from inside the cabinet I'm digging in, but he's already peeling Mama out his arms and grabbing his cup from the counter.

"Don't get lost in here," he says, shoving his feet back into his sneakers.

I think that was for me.

"MARCUS STILL NOT BACK?" Mama asks, stifling a yawn.

I shake my head and stare at Ace through the open blinds in our kitchen. "Nah. I called and he ain't answer."

"That knucklehead. He making us look bad. Got Ason outside by himself."

"It's nothing new. He ain't been home all week. Why you so concerned about how we look to this boy, anyway?"

The street light casts a glow on the glass of Hennessy in his hand. I roll my eyes at him dribbling Marcus' basketball against the driveway. By now, I've lost count of how many drinks he's snuck inside and poured himself while I cleaned the kitchen. They don't stop him from sinking a shot with his teeth digging into his bottom lip though.

"His daddy is a good man," Mama replies. "And Angie was a good lady."

"So, that's it? We supposed to treat him like he the president because his people is good peoples?"

"Yes."

"I guess." My eyes roll down to the soapy dishwater.

It's cloudy with Mama's tulip glass sitting at the bottom.

I swipe the dishrag against it for the hundredth time. "What about what he did?"

"What about it?"

"It was fuc—messed up. Don't you think? What does that say about us? Grinning with this boy that did something like that?"

Her sandals scrape against the floor behind me as I hurry and look away from him taking another swig out of his glass.

She bumps her frail body against mine, but I don't budge. "It says that we human just like he is. You should be kind to him because I didn't raise you to be hateful."

"I'm not being hateful. I'm being real."

"Were you at UCLA with the boy?"

"No, but I—"

"But nothing. You don't know shit about what happened." She swats my ass. "Stop making assumptions about people."

"Mama!"

"Mama my ass. Angie didn't raise a perfect man, but she raised a man with some sense."

The soap suds evaporate.

"What happened with his mama, anyway?" I ask, glancing back at Ace dribbling around in a circle under the moonlight. "How'd she pass? Don't seem like the world ever got an answer because of what... happened with him. Shoot, nobody even had time to grieve her."

A nasty leak of year-old police documents overshadowed the announcement of her death. Nobody cared to know what happened to Angie Williams anymore after that day—even if she was the original *it* black basketball wife our generation was obsessed with before the others came. Mama always said she walked so Savannah James could run.

"Why don't you stop staring and go talk to him? Maybe if you talk to him enough, he'll tell you."

I hold in a groan because Mama thinks she's Miss Cleo sometimes. If she finds out Ace gives me hives, she'll know about the secret in my panties.

"Whatever." I pluck the tulip glass from the bottom of the sink and rinse it off before walking out of the kitchen.

When I get to the front door, I hang behind it to steal a few more peeks before I get outside and things gets awkward. I don't have Bryson to talk for me or Mama as a buffer, and my head is still fucked up from all the times I heard Ace's voice throughout dinner.

"This glass not even clean!" Mama yells, making my stomach jump.

"My bad!" I shove the door forward and rush outside.

It's quiet except for the ball thumping against the pavement and the crickets chirping. He's on his own planet, just like at practice. It's just him, Marcus' ball, and his glass of Hennessy. I don't think other people exist on his planet sometimes.

Sweat leaks through his t-shirt and his earthy cologne floats in the air. I breathe in deep while another welt rises on my right inner thigh.

Sometimes there's this weird feeling I have for him and whatever happened back in Los Angeles. I'm split between him and the girl he left in shambles there. When I see him on campus, I don't know who I should feel sorry for—him or her.

"I thought you got lost in there," his deep voice rumbles. "What's wrong?"

My feet get stuck because apparently other people *do* exist in his world.

He doesn't wait for me to respond before he turns around and dribbles toward me. Sweat dances in his low curls and his eyes are even heavier than they were at dinner. He smiles like he can read my mind and another welt pops up on the back of my neck.

I want to tell him there's a lot of shit that's wrong: I'm sure Mama dumped her hamburger in the trash when I turned my back, Marcus won't stop disappearing, and I think I hate and like *him* at the same time.

Before I can try to say something, he pushes his glass of Hennessy to my lips. "Want some?"

The bitter smell makes me gag and I push it back.

"Oh." He smirks. "Mom don't let you drink?"

If she did, I would be as drunk and happy as they are and brave enough to stare into his eyes while he's towering over me.

I'm the closest I've ever been to him besides when we were in the kitchen and my body goes stupid. Welts, wet panties, and a mouth that forgets how to tell him that nobody in this house has ever let me sneak a sip of their wine, Hennessy, or Bud Light, no matter how many times I ask—but he already knows that. It's written on his face. And the only reason he's this close to me is because he's drunk. I'm not brave and chatty like Brandy. There's nothing about me that screams *interesting* or *interested*.

He clutches the glass with a smile that's always there—even when I see him eating in the cafe by himself and when he's wandering around campus in his expensive clothes with his blasé Californian attitude. Before I can try to talk again, he's back in my personal space with the glass of Hennessy.

He brushes my braids to the side and grabs my neck before I can freak out over him touching me. His hand lands right on top of the welt he caused. He scrapes his nails against it like he already knew it was hiding there and my knees turn into mounds of jello. I should stop him.

"You ever tell Mom about the shit you called me at practice that day?"

No, because she'd beat my ass. According to her, the only curse word I know *is* "ass" because it's in the Bible.

"Nah? I think you know better than that. I doubt she'd like the shit that comes out your mouth when she's not around."

I did, just like I knew better than to fight whatever hold he has over my body.

He swallows with a grunt. "*I* like the shit that comes

out your mouth though. I like the way it sounds. I didn't get a chance to tell you that because your lil' *perro* is territorial."

That wet spot turns into a lake even after his slug at Bryson. I *really* should stop him and whatever he's doing because tomorrow when he sees me on campus, I don't want to see the regret in his eyes. Guys like him are always regretful.

"Or maybe I just like your mouth." He chuckles, shaking his head.

He likes something about me? Scary me? Little ole' me that's never had a boy talk to her like this?

"Can you open your mouth for me?"

My lips fall open just like my legs moved to open that window in the kitchen. A quiet whoosh of air comes out of his nose as if he's breathing a sigh of relief that I follow his directions without questioning them.

He pushes the glass back to my lips, and I smell him on the rim.

"It's nasty," he mutters, tilting it up. "But it'll make you warm and make you never want to take another sip of it again."

When it splashes against my tongue, it doesn't taste as shitty as I expect, because he's still talking and soothing the welt on my neck with his fingers. The taste is bitter like his words, but his tone is soft and the flavor twirls across my tongue. My stomach cramps as he pulls the glass from my mouth just when my body warms up like he said it would. His finger replaces the glass, and he swipes it across my bottom lip like he's wiping away any evidence of what we've done.

"You warm yet?" He chuckles as if I'm the funniest girl in the world, even though I've never even talked to him directly. "Now you shouldn't be curious about it anymore. I took all the mystery away."

His voice jumps up and down like he's teasing me for being silly enough to think he would let me drink with him.

My limbs are loose from the tiny sip I took and I'm the true definition of a lightweight, or maybe I'm tipsy from him. Maybe this is life on his planet? Now I'm brave enough to oogle him like I see the girls on the yard do. He's fine and so drunk that I hear Los Angeles all up and through his words.

"You talk to everybody but me. That's bad hospitality, don't you think?" His fingers dig deep into my neck and I'm supposed to wince, but my body doesn't cooperate. "Tell me something good..."

He's so close I can see the layer of moisture on his bottom lip he's always biting. Tonight is the most I've ever heard him talk and I want more—need more—I'm craving more. I still can't believe he said he likes something about me.

"Or you too scared to do something like that, *Lourdes*," he slurs, swiping his tongue out like I knew he would. "You too scared to talk to me?"

I want to say something just as clever and sexy back. I want him to believe I'm as experienced as he is. I don't want him to know that the only boy I've ever kissed is Bryson, and *that* was an accident. I want to be audacious like Brandy and flirt without hesitating about how stupid I might look. There's so much shit I want to say, but, "she won't eat," tumbles out of my mouth in a clumsy hiccup.

She won't eat. *Mama* won't eat.

Damn, I fucked this moment up.

I step back to leave before Marcus pulls up, but Ace doesn't budge. He still has my neck locked between his fingers and I'm waiting on the pity to show in his brown eyes.

"Okay," he whispers.

"But—but you said to tell you something good an—and I —" I stumble over my words while he stares at me with the same expression he had when he scooped my burnt patties out of the skillet.

"And you did."

"No... that—that's not good. That's not good. Her *not* eating is not good."

I want a do-over. I want to try again. I want to take back my first civilized set of words to him. I don't know how to explain to him I'm not like any of the girls on campus. I can't have a dorm room with a roommate. I don't go to parties. I only take enough classes to keep my job on campus—

"Stop," he says.

"Stop what?"

"Stop thinking so much." He lifts the glass back to his lips and swallows. "Let me do that."

"Do what?" I choke out.

"Think for you."

"I don't know you like that." I frown. "How do I give my thoughts to somebody I don't even know, anyway?"

I thought I only asked in my head, but it came out after he swallowed another burning gulp of Hennessy.

"The same way you let me give you something you wasn't supposed to have that could've got you in trouble." His lips curve up. "Trust."

I'm even warmer now and his hand tightens around my neck. Everything bad feels good—even Mama not eating. My lips are loose and my voice is working and I'm already addicted to his voice despite the shit I talked about him when Marcus said he was coming over for dinner.

"Good and bad is all relative," he adds, shrugging. "One person's bad might be another person's good."

"And how did you decide *my* Mama not eating is good? Who said you could do that?"

My brain is on fire after being asleep around him for so long. I think I'm drunk for real this time, and none of my thoughts make sense. They're jumping all over the place from his perfect lips to my word vomit. Fuck, I sound my age.

He laughs and his finger swipes my bottom lip again despite there not being any extra liquid there for him to clean.

I think my lips are another thing he might like about me, but I don't want to jump to conclusions. I can't unsee the Twitter picture of him and the girl he took to his prom back in Los Angeles.

"You said I could decide when you opened your mouth for me." His finger falls. "Be careful of what you agree to do for men that just... ask."

"What's that mean?"

"You'll figure it out one day." He reaches up and catches my nose between his index and middle finger.

He doesn't let me sit in my embarrassing naivety for long before he drops his hand and starts talking again—slurring and moving his hands. The glass of Hennessy dances in my eyes under the moonlight while he raps to me about the laws that govern the planet he's always on by himself: Planet Ace.

"Our good is whatever you choose to tell me," he says, pointing from his broad chest to mine. "It's okay if Mom won't eat what we want her to eat. We just have to find something she likes, kid. You doing a good job."

Our. We. Kid.

Nobody ever told me I was doing a good job at anything.

He takes little sips of Hennessy between each of the words and his finger keeps lingering on my bottom lip to swipe away whatever he keeps imagining there. He's talking like he knows my life.

"We?" I blurt.

"Yeah... we. You never learned how to play follow the leader?"

That makes me laugh. "Is this the shit that drunk people talk about?"

"No, it's the shit me and you talk about. I want you on whatever I'm on," he says. "I gotta choose our vibe, so you gotta follow the leader. You feel me?"

I nod, because I get it. On Planet Ace, I'm his team and he's making sure I understand to fall in line like the good point guard he is.

"Yeah." I sigh. "I feel you."

He smirks. His eyes flutter against my moist chest and I hold my breath while I wait for him to get to my titties like Bryson does when we're about to leave each other, but he never looks down. He looks me dead in my face instead.

"And when I say I choose our vibe, I mean I choose it everywhere."

I blink hard.

I'm not sure if those words came out his mouth that way or if I imagined them. I think there's another sexual innuendo lurking in them, but it's no use in me dwelling on it because tomorrow, it'll be in a forgotten pile with the rest of the words he told me tonight.

Bright lights flash on us, exposing our closeness and my sweaty chest burns. Our bodies are too close, but he doesn't jump back. Music thumps from the car pulling into the driveway. I know it's Marcus and I know Ace can see that it's Marcus behind the wheel of his Buick, but he won't move his hand off my neck.

"C'mon." He pulls me towards the car, but just the thought of Marcus yanks me off his planet.

"Ace," I hiss.

"Phat," he hisses back, laughing.

"Go in the house with Mama."

He snorts. "Go in the house? You trippin'."

I'm back on Earth where Ace doesn't control the vibe and I remember the gun Marcus keeps in his middle console for boys like him because all the boys I ever liked were scared of Marcus—especially Bryson.

"Nigga, I'm tryna help you out."

Those words make his smile dip. Marcus' car beats behind us while we stand and stare at each other like we've been caught. Well, it's just me that looks like I got caught. Ace keeps holding my neck and the glass of Hennessy because it's obvious he hardly leaves Planet Ace.

I pull back, but he grips tighter. "Ace... for real. He's coming."

"And?"

"And you need to move or—or he's gon—"

Marcus' car door creaks. "What you on tonight, Ace?"

I wanna run.

"Shit..." Ace answers, staring at me like he did over dinner. "Mom got me on Henny. What you on, brodie?"

I try to look at Marcus, but Ace still has control of my neck, so I'm forced to stare at his lips while he talks for the both of us. Moisture pools underneath my armpits as

Marcus slams the car door and his sneakers scrape against the driveway.

"Shit... some drank," he replies. "Mama ain't no good. Got you assed out, knowing we 'bout to put that midnight work in."

Their conversation is so smooth it's like I'm invisible until Ace pulls me by my neck again as Marcus staggers closer to us. He pulls me so close I stumble and Marcus' contagious laugh rises above the chirping crickets.

Ace keeps soothing my irritated welt. His finger dances along it while he takes the last swig of Hennessy to the head.

"Hm. Here." He pushes the glass toward me, swallowing. "Go put some alcohol on your neck."

"What happened to your neck, fat girl?" Marcus asks, swiping a blunt from behind his ear.

My eyes bulge. I don't know how to tell him that Ace makes hives prickle my skin and they itch so bad and sometimes his touch makes them angrier.

"I—I uh," I stammer with a heavy tongue.

"You, *uh* what?" Marcus laughs, taking a sip out of the double cup in his hand.

It's like the calm before he realizes Ace lets me try his alcohol, makes my panties wet, and that I open my mouth when he tells me to.

"Mosquitoes," Ace replies for me, forcing our glass into my hand. "Go in the house with Mom 'fore they get worse, Lourdes."

And I think I want him inside of me despite what that white girl said he did to her back in Los Angeles.

CHAPTER SIX

Ace

"You fuck yet?"

That's always the topic in the locker room. There's no talk about the weak ass shots they put up or half the team's lack of endurance on the court.

Fucking is always what's most important.

Bryson snatches his wife beater over his curls and looks away from Marquise. "Man... come on. Fuck who?"

I nod my head while I tune in to their conversation. I have the volume turned down on Dough just enough to hear the one name I've been listening for since I touched her for the first time after dinner. It's a torturous way to get my fix since she stopped showing up to our practices.

"*Phat*, nigga," Marquise replies. "You said that was her name, right?"

"Oh my God." Bryson covers his face.

"'Oh my God,' you beat and the pussy was hittin' or 'oh my God' you still a virgin with no rizz?"

Their laughter rumbles throughout the locker room and

I don't find nothing funny about Phat's pussy being a part of today's hot topic. In fact, my neck heats like *my* pussy is the hot topic, but it's not even mine.

"Nah. Like 'oh my God,' get out my business."

"Bryson, Bryson, Bryson..." LaQuan cheeses. "Freshmans don't got no business, man. You a child."

"A wee lil' pipsqueak!" Marquise hollers in his best Scottish accent, inching behind Bryson and hooking an arm around his neck.

"Fuck outta here, man. I'm not telling ya'll shit."

Marquise cocks his head to the side. "So something happened?"

A simple sentence always opens the door for nosey ass dudes beating on it from the outside, but Bryson isn't old enough to understand that. He's exactly like Marquise described him—a pipsqueak.

LaQuan whips his head so hard his twists smack him in his beady eyes and the rest of the team inches closer to our lockers to get the CarFax on Phat's pussy—even Lucas Schmidt comes running and he's the only white dude on the team and speaks German.

"You hit it from the back or the front?" Marquise whispers with a grin. "Shit, was it bald or did it have peach fuzz?"

"Fuck that! Did you lick it and then stick it? That's what Keenan used to tell me to do. That shit made me a *God* in high school." LaQuan claps.

My stomach is in shambles and my neck is hot because I need to get *in* some pussy to get Phat off the brain, but I can't. LA won't let me and Phat's persistent, so she keeps popping in my head. I missed her voice today at practice, her mouth when I stumbled into Mom's after putting up shots with Marcus after dinner, and her smart ass mouth when I read Brandy's second thirsty text this morning.

I ease on the bench in front of my locker and push my right foot into my sneaker.

"Bro, get off me." Bryson shakes Marquise off his shoulders, but his lanky body doesn't move.

"Nah! Not until you tell us what it's hittin' for."

"Nah! Nah! Get off me."

"Come on...just tell us."

"Just give us a lil' hint. Was it good or not?"

"You bringing her thick ass to Splashtown?"

I've been in enough locker rooms to know how this will end. Niggas were straight vultures—especially ones that hardly got play from girls. The pecking order is at work again.

Bryson smiles, exposing every tooth in his mouth. "Shit, yeah."

"Okay." Marquise fans his arms out. "Clearly you hit if you bringing her on a date."

A *date*?

I roll my eyes over to Bryson in all of his red-faced glory.

They let out another round of howls like a sweaty ass fraternity party is comparable to a night out at Avra or Nobu in Malibu.

He grins wider and his next words come out slow. "A'ight... a'ight. I did. I hit it."

"Oh, shit!" everybody shouts but me.

My mouth gets dry while they shoot a million more questions at Bryson. Panties or no panties? From the front or back? Can she ride? And the worst: Did she swallow?

"Like a champ." Bryson gloats with bright eyes. "Like a motherfuckin' champ."

"Ooh-wee!" Marquise closes his eyes. "Oh, she definitely gon' be at Splashtown."

They're so impressed by what they think Phat did I hear the planning in their voices when they file out of the locker room and back onto campus.

When my left shoe makes it on my left foot, it's just me and Bryson. He was so into his newfound fame he couldn't even finish pulling his shorts up his ass, so he's stuck with me. Me and Dough are always the last ones in the locker room.

I fiddle with the laces on my sneakers even though they're already tight enough and pull my headphones off my head. Bryson has a tight smile on his face like he didn't notice Phat's absence again today at practice and after being her pet for so long, I'm sure he knows how frail CeCe is. He has to.

I swallow the ball in my throat. "Phat know you lie on her?"

He stops pulling at the strings on his basketball shorts and frowns. "Huh?"

"Do Phat know you lie on her?" I repeat, swiping my tongue out to taste her like I did on the rim of that glass.

"You calling me a liar?"

"I'm not calling you shit. I'm asking you a question."

"Yeah, a question I ain't answering. Just because they're your host family don't mean you know anything about her. You don't know nothing about me *or* Phat."

But I do.

Thanks to Mom, I know she's a little lady. Not just any little lady, but a perfect one with a perfect name and all the perfect features of a girl that shouldn't give Bryson or the rest of the clowns on our team a second look.

I know she can't curse in front of CeCe. I know she

never drank until she met me. I know she wears panties—girly flower ones. I know she doesn't know what it feels like to have any man behind her or in front of her. I know she's a virgin and when the day comes where she gets curious enough to swallow another man's seed, I hope she doesn't do something so precious with a lame clout chasing freshman like Bryson. Her lips are too pretty for that. I know too much about *Lourdes* and enough about Bryson to know that I hate him again.

I push up from the bench and grab my backpack from the floor. "You right. I don't know anything about you."

"Or her."

I chuckle. "Shit... thanks to you, I know a lot about her."

He inches forward and I do, too.

"I know she don't wear panties." I raise my eyebrow. "She likes it from the back... and she arched her back so good you didn't even have to show her how."

I raise my finger. "Oh... and she swallowed. That was my favorite part."

His nostrils flare. "So you eavesdrop all the time when you got them headphones on?"

"Only when it matters. Like when lil' boys find it necessary to cap for clout."

He laughs. "So what if I told a lil' white lie so they could get off my back? You ain't Mr. Perfect. Everybody knows what you did. You don't have room to judge nobody."

His words don't sting like he wants them to. The confused look Phat gives me sometimes hurts more than his weak comeback. I've been called worse by disgruntled Bruins fans, Black Twitter, and reporters. Shit, I survived a Lester Holt *Nightly News* report.

I study his face, trying to recognize the parts of him Phat might like. I want to ruin him for her and make his name taste bitter when she yells it out like she does at practice. But I don't. Pops' corny ass would call this a teaching moment.

"You just told thirteen niggas how good your girl's pussy is." I scoff. "Now they lusting over something that's supposed to be yours. Tighten up... *player*."

His eyebrows furrow, and he twists his mouth to the side.

I leave out the rest like how the teammates he's so desperate to impress will try to sample what's between Phat's legs because she "belonged" to a freshman and how I have this burning in my chest at the thought of them lurking between her legs when I shouldn't.

Lourdes

"IT'S KINDA like when Karrueche got with Chris Brown after Rihanna." Chelsea rips a piece of skin off the fried drumstick she's been gnawing on while glancing at Ace and Brandy. "Or—or any bobble-headed heffa that got with Bobby after Whitney."

Suddenly, my chicken tastes gummy because I catch Brandy running her fingers through Ace's short curls. They're bunched together at a round table in the back of the cafe and she likes him *real* bad. It's all on her face like Mama says about Chelsea when she looks at Marcus.

"Or it's even like Pavlov and his dogs. I swear I saw her drooling on the yard when one of those basketball dudes yelled 'Hollywood!' She hears his name, and she's foaming at the mouth like a damn hyena. He taught her well."

It's hump day—my favorite day of the week, thanks to

Mrs. Anderson's chicken and collards and the Kappas shimmying on the yard. It's also the only other day of the week Lucy has off, so she sits with Mama all day while I run around campus with Chelsea, pretending to be normal and working a late shift at the bookstore.

"Oh crap." Chelsea gasps, making my heart beat out of my chest. "No, she *didn't* just offer him a swig of her Big Red. This girl is lost."

There's a clump of chicken stuck in my esophagus when I narrow my eyes at Brandy's dainty hand holding her bottle in front of Ace's lips. It's like the summer I discovered Dough and fantasized about his mouth for an entire two months, but I never saw Dough's lips with a gloss of Hennessy spread across them—only Ace's. That reoccurring memory keeps me and my fingers up at night after I make sure Mama's in bed.

"She better not let him do that." Chelsea fans herself while dry heaving. "Ain't no telling where his lips been... just nasty. I mean, did you see that girl's inflated lips he went to prom with that year? It had the Twitter girlies in a whole tizzy. I showed Ms. Esther the picture, and she said they looked like an anu—"

"Girl!"

"What?" she squeals back, shrugging. "Too much?"

A sigh of relief comes out when Ace shakes his head at Brandy with a grimace.

He nudges the bottle away from his mouth as if he hadn't been slurping my backwash two nights before.

"Too damn much." I stuff a forkful of collards in my mouth. "Can we change the subject? You got this boy name in your mouth worse than Mama."

"Uh-uh, don't do me. It ain't my fault your mama and Marcus got you stuck with him for the rest of the semester just because your parents knew his parents back in the day. It is *just* a semester, right?"

"I don't know." I groan as he looks away from Brandy and up at me. "I don't have time for this. I *do not* have time for this."

"For what?"

I swipe my fingernail across the back of my neck, but it doesn't help because I'm not Ace.

"Uh... for all this salt Mrs. Anderson put on the greens."

"They taste fine to me." Chelsea shrugs, shoveling another forkful in her mouth.

I see him out of the corner of my eye, looking at the finger I used to swipe at my neck.

He smiles, and Brandy follows his line of vision. When she sees it's me he's looking at, she smiles too, and then she smirks. She's so nice-nasty and I hate that a part of her is even nice because I don't like her.

"Not them looking over here at us. Oh God, she's waving at you." Chelsea nudges me in my arm. "Wave back."

I wiggle my greasy fingers toward them. "She probably knows you been over here bumping your gums about her."

"That girl don't know me. You know I'm just a professional people watcher. Who knows... maybe they're meant to be. They might fool around and have a basketball team of light-skinned babies and by that time, we'll all have forgotten what he did. As the world turns..."

Brandy pushes up from the table while dropping her hand in his hair. She gives it one last scratch before strolling away while another annoying piece of chicken gets stuck in my throat.

"You have a sick imagination," I choke out.

"I have a realistic one. Boys like that are always forgiven eventually."

Just like I thought they were always regretful, but the smile he flashed my way in front of Brandy said otherwise.

"Why do you think that?"

"Because there's always a chick like Brandy hanging around ready to be his pretty redemption arc. She's safe for him—bright enough to make white folks believe it's okay for them to associate with him again, Eurocentric features on par for the Insta aesthetic, and easy to control in case he has another.... mishap. It's only been a couple years since it happened. It's still fresh on all the bird's brains. They'll be lusting over him on Twitter again in no time."

Everyone breezes in front and behind Ace like he wasn't a McDonald's All American, 2019's number one overall recruit, or Mama's new Zydeco partner. They don't even do a double-take at him in that corner alone, pulling his headphones over his head and shoveling a mouthful of collards in his mouth.

As soon as I get ready to poke a hole in Chelsea's theory, Bryson's lanky body blocks my perfect view of him.

"It would've been nice to know that you had to miss my practice yesterday," he says, plucking one of my braids while flopping in the empty seat across from me.

Chelsea smacks her lips. "It would've been nice of you to ask if you could sit with us."

"This ain't *Mean Girls*. Don't you have some praise dancing to practice, Virgin Mary?"

"Shouldn't you be icing those broken ankles, Juwanna Mann?"

"Anyway..." Bryson huffs, stealing a drumstick off my plate. "You could've text me."

"And said what? I'm leaving campus because Mama got

diarrhea and couldn't wipe her ass, so she called Marcus who *also* couldn't wipe her ass because he claims he has a weak stomach. So I had to catch an Uber to go do it because you had practice and Chelsea was at a meeting for the Baptist Student Ministry."

They both look at me with those stares I hate. They're not like Ace's that remind me that even at eighteen I can still learn how to play follow the leader all over again.

"My fault. I ain't know," he says, biting into the chicken.

"Sorry, Phat." Chelsea pats my hand. "My granny said they plan to add her to the sick and shut in list next Sunday and you know you can always stay at the house if you need a break. My room's empty since I'm staying on campus. Granny won't mind."

Then who would take care of Mama?

It's been five years and I'm still learning that people don't know what to say when I blurt out things I shouldn't.

"Yeah, thanks," I reply, rolling my eyes away from our table.

An earthy scent sneaks up my nose and I look up in time to catch Ace swaggering in front of our table, shoving his hat back on his head.

Bryson sucks his teeth like Lucy, but Ace is too busy pulling his headphones back over his ears to hear, or maybe he does and doesn't care. That blasé Californian attitude is in full effect today.

"I can't believe Coach gave me one of the librarians and let that dude have y'all." Bryson scoffs.

"Sounds about right," Chelsea replies. "Maybe you'll finally learn how to read without sounding out the words."

"Man, don't you have one of those holy conventions to go to, throwed off Mother Teresa?"

Their voices grow muffled while I follow the back of

Ace's shirt out of the cafe. Today I can't muster the energy to play referee between them because I'm too busy wondering how Ace would've responded to my embarrassing outburst.

"Anyway, *again...*" Bryson smacks, staring at me. "Y'all going to Splashtown or what? Quise say he chop it up with an Alpha in his journalism class that can get him pre-sales."

Chelsea rolls her neck. "Duh, it'll be the perfect opportunity to get myself in front of the eyes of my future sorrors. Front me the money and I'll pay you back."

"Fuck no, brokey. Better hit Marcus up."

"And will!"

"Too bad he probably got you blocked, stalker."

My eyes jolt back and forth between them. I try to hold on to their words and the last few hours I have on campus before they go back to being regular students and I go back to lie in bed with Mama.

"Phat, tell this troll Marcus only blocks me out of love."

I pull my lips between my teeth and glance over at Bryson.

"Phat!" she hisses. "Tell him."

His hazel eyes get big and he rolls them around. I blubber out a laugh while Chelsea crosses her arms.

"That secret language y'all have is giving very much second grade. Grow up!"

"Right after you." Bryson sweeps his hand across the table. "*Anyway*, Phat, you going, right?"

I shrug. "I wasn't planning on it."

All the tweets and flyers on campus made me want to plan on it, but I know better. Sacrificing Lucy's other day of the week she has off ain't worth it—not even to experience a real party for the first time in my young life that's feeling like an old life. That other day off is like my get out of jail free card and everybody knows that's a card you're supposed to hold on to.

"C'mon." He leans over the table and pokes his finger in my cheek. "I'll ask Ma if she'll sit with Mama that night."

My cheeks get warm and I pull back. "Maybe."

He sighs, smacking his lips. "Well, at least tell me you coming to practice later."

"Come to practice for what?" Chelsea cackles. "To see you twiddle your thumbs while Hollywood obliterates them ankles again."

"Get your lap dog, Phat."

I smile, shaking my head at the thought of missing out on another practice squirming against the bleachers, pretending to watch Bryson. "Nah. I close for Brandy today."

Anything is better than spending another hour clawing at the welts on my body while Ace dances around the court with the world in his hands.

CHAPTER SEVEN

Ace

"Damn. You an eighty-year-old deacon?"

I smile, rolling my fingers over the Chick-O-Sticks on the counter in the empty bookstore. "Teach the kid how to talk and she turn around and sneak diss. I thought we was cool after breaking bread? That's fucked up, brodie."

"My t-lady and brother taught me how to talk. Not you, *brodie*." Phat rolls her eyes while I lean over the counter, eyeing her little fingers pulling the Chick-O-Sticks from underneath mine.

They're decked out with the type of things girls obsess over—long ombré coffin shaped acrylics and rhinestones. She pops her gum and I like the sound of it just like I like the sound of her voice. The memory of her soft drawl from dinner led me from another practice and straight into the bookstore just to get a chance at hearing it again after Bryson gave up where she was when Marquise asked about her.

"My girl had to close at work tonight." He grinned.

So today me and Dough were the first ones out the locker room.

She chews harder on the gum and her fat cheeks jump up and down. "This it?"

"Yeah, unless you want something."

"I can buy my own shit."

I snort out a laugh, pulling my wallet out and digging my credit card from the folds. "It's more fun when I buy it though."

She stops, holding one stick in her hand and squinting at me. "Fun for you or for me?"

"For both of us."

That answer makes her smack her lips and snatch the card from my hand, but I know better. I've fucked enough women to know that smacking lips and snatching means I better stay my ass right here because she needs attention. She's angsty today—cursing at me when she knows better and snatching things out of my hands like we didn't have a *moment* the other night after dinner. She's a nut I have to crack and I don't mind it.

"Whatever," she replies.

"I'm just saying, if you need it, I got it. Us weak ass niggas be the most loyal."

"If you finally searching for an apology for what I said, you ain't getting one."

"I don't accept apologies, so I guess we the same type of people. How's Mom?"

Her eyes dart away as she swipes the card and hands it back to me. "Cool."

"Hm... cool like she ate a big ass breakfast this morning or cool like she threw it up?"

The plastic from one of the Chick-O-Sticks crumples under her fingers, and she stops moving to stare back at me. "Why you be eating candy all the time?"

"I like sweet stuff."

She scoffs, rolling her eyes. "Be for real."

"I am. You asked, and I answered."

"Yeah... but your answers be real slick like you talking about other stuff."

More little lady shit.

I chuckle, pulling the one she'd been holding from her fingers and tearing it open. "I don't be talking about nothing but the subject. Why you trying to control the vibe, *Lourdes*?"

"Why you such a control freak?"

"Because you said I could be." I break the stick in half and thrust a piece toward her. "Here. Tell me something good before niggas come up in here on some weird shit."

That makes her laugh like she knows I'm talking about Brandy and her tone deaf ways or Bryson and his constant tabs on her whereabouts.

Our fingers brush when she reaches out to take it and I think I hear Mom whispering to God, reassuring him I'll be careful with her.

She opens her lips and I swipe my hand underneath them to catch the wad of gum she spits out. Her nose wrinkles when it lands in my hand, but that doesn't stop her from popping the candy in her mouth.

"She threw up her breakfast this morning," she says between chews while leaning against the counter.

"Damn. What you cook this time?"

"Bacon, eggs, and she said she wanted grits, so I cooked 'em." She shrugs. "Oh, and I gave her an Ensure."

"The regular Ensure or the clear joint?"

"There's different ones?"

"Yeahhh, kid." I smile at the thoughtful expression on her round face.

My fingers tingle with the same want from the night in her driveway. They want to grip her nose and wiggle it, then run across her waist and squeeze it for making me work so hard just to get what I want. They're even trembling from being out of commission for so long.

She cocks her head to the side. "What it taste like?"

"Nasty as *fuck*."

She chokes out a laugh that makes her cheeks bunch up. "You really think she gon' drink it if it's nasty?"

I remember the lonely piece of Chick-O-Stick in my hand and pop it in my mouth to stop myself from leaning over the counter to pull her closer. The sweetness I told her I liked calms my trembling fingers just for that moment and I make them focus on the hot, sticky piece of gum she let me have.

"It's easier on her stomach than bacon, eggs, and grits," I reply between chews. "Clear Ensure and Zofran for nausea is like Jordan and Pippen—*hella* elite. Give her some toast with it. She'll like it because it won't make her feel like shit."

"You mean elite like Kobe and AW, but I get it."

"Oh, so that's the Ason Williams you like? Got it." I wink.

She rolls her eyes. "How you know all this stuff, anyway?"

I can tell her that Mom taught me more about the intricacies of a sick body than a doctor ever did and that things get worse before they get better.

I shrug. "Life."

But it's something CeCe has to tell her when she stops drowning her fears in liquor bottles.

"Hm..." She grabs for another stick on the counter, but I reach out and snatch it before she can. "Maybe I'll ask Marcus to take me to H-E-B to get some when he comes home and stops being a fuck boy. What's that other stuff you said?"

"Zofran?"

"Yeah, that." She eyes my fingers pulling open the plastic on another Chick-O-Stick. "H-E-B sell that too?"

I chuckle, pulling the stick out while glancing up at her. "Nah. That's a script."

Her mouth widens in a cute circle. "Oh."

She frowns like she's trying to take inventory of CeCe's pill planner from her memory while I take another bite of the candy.

"Zofran..." she mutters to herself, resting her chin in her hand on the counter.

I smile, chewing and watching her in all of her little lady glory with the weight of CeCe's poor health on her shoulders. It makes me lean on the counter too because I want a closer look at Phat...being Phat.

"Ace?"

Brandy's soft voice makes Phat jolt back from the counter, leaving me with her half of our Chick-O-Stick and her wad of gum stuck between my fingers.

I suck in a deep breath and paint on a smile before turning around. "Oh, what's up, Brandy?"

"Nothing, I was just passing by to check on Phat." She bounces on her heels and smiles too big. "I'm surprised you're still on campus. You usually jet after practice."

I nod, biting the corner of my lip and glancing at Phat, but she's already burying her head in another magazine I didn't see her snatch from the rack beside the counter.

I tear my eyes off her and narrow them at Brandy because her voice reminds me of LA. There's faux familiarity in it as if we talk every day when we only ever text about bullshit when I'm downing 1942 and in the mood for Phat. Even her face reminds me of LA. The lack of skepticism in her eyes when she beelined toward me in the back of the auditorium last week was too familiar and she smiles like all the women Mom told me I could fuck but couldn't bring home—the jersey chasers. They were the second girls Mom taught me about right after she taught me about perfect ones.

"Yeah, I had to stop and get my fix before I head to the crib."

"More candy?"

"Yeah." I swallow as she steps closer.

"Chick-O-Sticks today?"

"Yeah..."

"Nice! I love those too."

Phat huffs out a soft noise like she knows Brandy is a jersey chaser, too. The problem is that we don't know which kind she is—a wannabe WAG or a groupie. There's a difference. Wannabe WAGS want you stuck with them for a lifetime. Groupies only want you for a moment.

Brandy takes another step forward with an eagerness on her butterscotch face, like she finally had me cornered because I never texted her back.

"No text back and no follow back on Insta." She smirks. "I'm starting to think this thing me and you have is one-sided."

I swear I hear another soft noise come from the back of Phat's throat, but Brandy's eyes keep burning into my face as if she didn't hear it at all.

"Me and Insta don't get along."

There wasn't any social media app I got along with because the world wouldn't let it happen.

"I guess I should take back all those late night likes and comments on your two-year-old thirst traps then, huh?"

"I mean, if that's how you feel."

All of my clever one-liners got lost in the space between me and Phat, but jersey chasers don't care about that. Their sole existence revolves around coming up with the most clever way to get the jersey's attention. It's an art that I know too well.

"You still park in the garage over on Frost?" she asks.

"Nah... not today. I, uh, parked way out in Lot E."

"Oh, perfect. I'm headed out that way to the rec center. Want some company on your hike?"

I notice her teal sports bra and yoga pants for the first time. Even the dainty ring she has dangling from her belly-button doesn't make this *random* encounter exciting.

"Oh, nah. I know you have to check in on Pha—"

"She looks good to me. She's got her magazine and snacks... as usual."

"I—uh yeah. Just let Phat finish ring—"

"No need," Phat rasps from behind me.

When I whip around to get one last look at her fat cheeks, I catch her eyes rolling, but she straightens them up in time to plaster a smile like mine on her face.

"Here." She holds a plastic bag of my candy from her index finger. "Have fun."

I fold my lips under my teeth and bite down because it's the only way I know how to check myself these days.

I reach out and curl my fingers around the plastic, letting them sit there while we stare at each other with Brandy staring hard at us. "I'll chop it up with you later, kid."

MOM ALWAYS TOLD me she could see fear in a boy's eyes. It's how she'd pinpoint the troublemakers on my AAU teams. They were the ones that eventually stopped showing up to practice and later, when we got older, most of them stopped showing up in life.

"I'm pretty sure this the move Marshall used to bag Mama," Marcus says, sinking a three pointer with the flick of his wrist.

The ball goes through the netless hoop and bounces off the court.

"On God." I laugh, jogging toward it and swiping as it bounces past the double cup, gun, and TWIC card he left lying at the edge of the court.

I don't know what the rest of the team does with their host families but with mine, we ball—in CeCe's driveway when her and Phat are asleep, at the court in their neighborhood, and sometimes in the street of whatever random house Marcus is hanging at on the days he skips out on his job at the Port.

Thunder claps in the distance and sweat sticks to our bodies because a quick shower in Texas doesn't do shit to calm the humidity in the air.

I dribble up to him.

Fear dances along the edges of his irises. He smiles and I hear Phat's voice like I did when he first pulled up with her booming through his car's speakers.

"Mama said her fingers was numb again this morning," she rasped. *"Can you call Dr. Evanston's office for me?"*

I didn't think it was possible to miss a girl I'd never been inside of, but Mom must've told God I needed some act right for dipping on him, so he sent it as fat cheeks and an attitude. Now I'm missing a girl I never fucked.

"This probably the one AW used to get Angie." I cross Marcus up, but he doesn't stumble because he's too solid.

He howls, clapping his hands as I drive to the hoop and finish with a layup.

Playing basketball with Marcus is like playing ball back in Inglewood or Compton with dudes who were faster than Westbrook, shot better than LeBron, and refused to call the Staples Center by its new name. Dudes like that never looked at me any different no matter what someone had accused me of because I played AAU with their brothers, was brave enough to fuck some of their sisters and I wasn't a lame that needed to claim I was affiliated with any of them. I didn't need the clout or the protection because nobody ever had to ask me where I was from. So when the Pauley Pavilion banned me from their courts, they kept theirs open for me even though I wasn't their blood or loc. I was the *lil' homie*—and sometimes that felt better than being Pops' Junior.

I bounce the ball toward Marcus, and he grips it, pulling his jeans up at the waist.

It's been five years since his soles touched the smooth hardwood of an indoor court. He told me one night in his driveway between sips of lean and I can't tell if he's lying or just the product of a mythical goated dude named Marshall that died fulfilling his purpose in life.

Marcus dribbles toward me and I push my arms out, basking in the raindrops that touch my arms while I press him but he shakes me.

"This the one I used to bag *my* bitch," he yells, jabbing his shoulder into my chest and whipping around me.

He's so smooth I almost miss the ball whirling behind his back when I blink.

"She don't like it when I call her a bitch outside the bed though." He laughs, finishing with a layup. "So I gotta call her my gal unless I want her to fuck my head up with what the preacher talking 'bout at bible study this week and what my *other* bitch posting on IG."

I belt out a laugh that makes my stomach tight because I recognized the other voice chirping from his car after Phat's call. It was her little sidekick from practice, with a mouthful of metal and rosy cheeks: *"I want you to come to church with me this Sunday. It'll be good for us."*

He dribbles back to me with a sparkling smile.

"What about you, Kid?" He laughs, bouncing the ball back to me.

I catch it, curling my hands around its rubbery outside. "What about me?"

"Show me." He shrugs, squinting. "Show me the move that got you yours."

Mine?

She didn't even know she was mine.

I gulp down Phat's voice and try to nudge her out of my head, but like I said before, she's persistent. I dribble against the pavement, staring into Marcus' eyes.

He's not Bryson, so his arms shoot up and his chest pushes into my shoulder. "Oh, this it?"

He breathes against my face while my muscles remember all the movements the world tried to make them forget.

I push up to take the shot, but pull down as soon as he puts his arms up to block it.

My muscles don't need coaching on how to fake a dude out on the court. It's so second nature to them it's boring, but what isn't boring is Phat's eyes burning holes into my face. I need them. I need them *so* bad that when I step back and sink a three so nasty I can't control the words I blurt out.

"Yeah, this it." I nod with a serene smile. "She mine, but she too fucking scared to trust me."

I taste the metallic before I feel the impact. The heavy *thunck* from Marcus' knuckles ring through my ears as I slide against the concrete. I hear my teeth chattering against each other when another rumble of thunder claps in the distance.

"Man, what the fuck?" I yell.

Fuck a flight mode, my body goes straight into fight and I ball my fists at my sides.

Playing ball with Marcus is *just* like it is back home.

I push off the ground and barrel toward him, sticking my balled fist across his face. He doesn't let me get far. He rams his body into mine and pins my arms at my sides, huffing out loud breaths.

"What you pressing me for?" I hurl out, swallowing a glob of blood at the same time. "The fuck is wrong with you?"

"Babygirl..." he says, out of breath.

"*Huh?*"

"That's what Marshall called her—babygirl."

I close my eyes, shaking my head, but it doesn't matter. He already knows and the worst part is that I can't figure out how, but Mom was the same way. Sometimes she just knew shit.

"But she don't remember that. All she know is me, my voice, and the name I gave her."

"Phat..." I mutter.

"Yeah. *Fat girl.*" He smiles. "But my baby thinks she's

too grown and too cool for that, so we had to drop the F and keep it player."

I pull my lip into my mouth, sucking the blood from it while my stomach roils at the sound of him calling her *his* baby.

There's a layer of accusations between his words as if I already had my hands on her body, my mouth on hers, and my dick inside of her but all I did was feed her a bunch of words to think about when I left. I guess words can be just as damning as a touch.

Another loud rumble of thunder claps as a sheet of rain sneaks under the tin awning that covers the court. It washes away the blood leaking from my lip as he yanks me to my feet.

Our loud breathing combines with the smack he gives my back. "You hurt her feelings and I'll fuck you up. I don't care who son you is."

I fling my head up. "I'm Angie's son and you got me fucked up if you think she would even let you do that. Fuck you think this is? You keep leaving her at home by herself and hurting her feelings, I'll fuck you up. I don't care who son *you is*. We can squabble up, nigga."

Our chests pump in and out as we stare at each other with the rain pelting our bodies. I try to push away all the irrational thoughts I'm having about a girl that has all the traits of a pretend girl that Mom had me obsessing over.

Marcus belts out a loud roar of laughter.

He smacks me upside the head like Pops liked to do. "You dumbass cocky ass nigga. When AW called me from LA talking about your head was gone I knew he was just panicking. You still intact up there."

The muggy air sneaks down my throat at the thought of Pops dissecting my brain with somebody other than me, but

I can't blame him. If I ever saw my only son in handcuffs, I think I'd do the same.

"He called you?" I choke out.

"Yeah. He always call."

That bubble of muggy air explodes in my throat and I swallow it with the rest of the questions I want to ask but already know the answer to.

"He call every year on Marshall's birthday, but when he called me on a random ass Monday in September, I knew something wasn't right."

That random ass Monday in September always came back in bits and pieces of fuzzy blackness. No matter how hard I tried, I couldn't make out the faces of the LA County sheriffs deputies trying to get a glance at Ason Williams' son in cuffs—I just heard their star-struck voices and the strain in them each time they read my charges out loud.

Marcus doesn't close his eyes and shake his head. He keeps his eyes on mine and they drift down to the mural of LA tattooed on my stomach.

"So what'd he say when he called you?" I ask.

It's the first time I ever get the chance to ask how he talks about me to real people when I'm not around—not to lawyers, reporters, sports agents, or recruiters but to real ass people that had nothing to gain or lose.

"You don't need to worry about that. All you need to know is that I told him what he needed to do."

"You did?"

"Yeah. Told him to bring your ass back home for good. It took him two years to do it, but he finally listened to me. Shit, *fuck* LA." He holds his hand out and I grip it while he pulls me into one of those post-prison embraces.

"And I don't hurt her feelings on purpose," he mutters into my ear. "But I ain't as strong as you and her, a'ight? I—I can't watch Mama waste away in that house. So when the end comes I wanna see her just like Daddy did—cheesing with a head full of hair and his name on her lips from the stands in that gym I never got a chance to play in. You know, back when he was trying to just be somebody—back before that stupid heart attack took him out on that court."

CHAPTER EIGHT

Lourdes

There's a lot of shit they don't teach in school. They don't teach you how to pay bills, how to cook a decent meal, what to do if your mama can't keep breakfast in her stomach, or how to respond if that boy you hate and like keeps popping up at the wrong times.

I squint through the front door's peephole at Ace gripping his backpack. "What the fuck?"

He pounds on the door again and I want to throw up the bacon I ate this morning while Mama cursed Marcus out on his voicemail for not answering. Before *Divorce Court* came on, the weatherman said we were on the fourth day of a heat wave and the evidence drips from Ace's swollen bottom lip.

I glance down at Marcus' dingy high school jersey. I didn't have time to put on shorts and my legs are so hairy Chelsea can probably grip them for braids.

"I know you at the door, Phat," he says, making my stomach drop. "I heard you."

He turns his red neck as a car passes by and my eyes narrow at his head where Brandy kept touching it in the cafe. Chelsea's stupid analogies dance in my head, but I can't concentrate on them because his mouth starts moving.

"It's hella hot and you playing games."

Now, my eye burns because I'm too preoccupied with him to blink.

He smacks his lips. "Open your mouth, Lourdes. I'm not a mind reader."

I listen because that was his plan all along—to turn me into one of Pavlov's stupid drooling dogs like he did with Brandy. There's no more 'can you' and it's my fault, like he said. I'm not careful of what I agree to do for dudes that just... ask.

"Marcus ain't here."

"I know he not here. He called me."

"That nigga called *you* and not us?"

"Yeah." He shrugs. "I mean, I thought he had talked to ya'll. He said Mom had a doctor's appointment, and you got an appointment at the nail shop."

"And what's that have to do with you?"

I hold my breath for his eyes to roll like Marcus' do when I'm in the same funky mood as Mama. By now me and her are conjoined twins and I've stopped eating too.

He glances at his truck in the driveway parked next to Mama's Honda. It's the same fancy white Porsche with California plates he drove to our house when he came for dinner. When he turns back around, his lips tilt up and he leans in, smashing his ear to the door.

"What you doing?" I ask.

I'm supposed to frown but I can't just like Brandy can't keep her hands or eyes off of him, so my mouth gets stuck in this weird half-smile, half-frown.

"I'm waiting for you to tell me something good, kid."

He's talking the same shit he talked in the driveway when he was drunk and I'm his lone teammate on Planet Ace, so I got to think of something good—something that won't have him calling me *Lourdes*.

"That's what LeBron called you that time you hit that game winning buzzer beater against Villanova in the Sweet Sixteen," I babble out. "*The Kid.*"

It's another stupid thing I'm not supposed to say, but I'm used to my mouth betraying me when he's around.

"Then Dough named his last mixtape *The Kid*. It was the second mixtape in history to win a Grammy for best rap album even though it wasn't even an album. You were the only person he thanked during his acceptance speech. He didn't even thank the academy."

Now he knows more embarrassing things about me. One: I know about one of the most prolific nights of his basketball career because Marcus still doubles back to it on YouTube at least once a month. Two: I know every song on that mixtape better than I know my statistics formulas. Three: Boys I hate and like make me so nervous that I say things I should only think.

His ear lingers by the door, and he tucks his puffy bottom lip under his teeth.

Finally, he reaches up and taps his knuckles against the door. "Can you let a nigga in, *kid?*"

There's another wet spot in my panties, but I don't care because I'm too busy twisting the deadbolt and pushing against the screen door. When the sun hits his face, his eyes are soft like they were when I told him Mama won't eat.

"Nobody calls me that anymore." He smirks, glancing at my bushy, bottomless legs.

"Marcus still does."

He nods, toeing his Jordans off but keeping his back-pack dangling from his shoulder. "Marcus a solid dude."

"If he so solid why he won't answer for me and Mama when we call?"

Or help me get Mama out the bed? Or teach me how to cook for us since she can't even stand up long enough to boil water some days? Or come home like he supposed to?

"Ain't he your host nigga, anyway? Why you don't be with him? Why you keep coming around us?"

He chuckles and yanks his shirt up to wipe the sweat off his face. I swallow to quell the dryness in my throat from the sight of his inked up abs.

"I see the kid is angry today." He drops the t-shirt and smiles. "Anger's a good thing."

"Is this one of your good and bad metaphorical, analog-ical bullshit answers?"

"Nah." He turns and walks across the living room, toward the kitchen. "It's just words. That's all, Lourdes."

"Yeah... whatever." I follow behind him. "Don't come up in here being loud either."

The rest of my words get lodged in my throat. I can't tell him that Mama's wrenching stomach finally stopped and let her close her eyes—even if it's only two hours before she has to be at the clinic.

His socked feet glide across the kitchen floor toward the bottle of Paul Masson Marcus left next to the sink, and I remember the satisfaction that washed over his face after he took his first sip of Hennessy at dinner the other night.

"It ain't even eleven." I cross my arms, bounding up behind him. "Should you be drinking that?"

He grips the bottle, and I keep my distance while trailing him. He pulls open cabinets around the kitchen until he finds the red solo cups Marcus keeps hidden behind the paper towels in the pantry.

"I thought we agreed that you wouldn't cook her heavy shit," he mutters, opening the bottle and tipping it over an empty cup.

When he brings the drink to his lips, he glances around the kitchen at my desperate attempt to cook breakfast. The bacon was soggy with grease, Mama said the grits were too runny, and I forgot to grease the pan for the biscuits, so they're cemented to the baking sheet. This time, she hid her plate under her bed.

"Don't tell me what I should and shouldn't do." I scoff. "It's my mama—not yours. I can't wait for days while she twiddles her thumbs trying to figure out what she wants to eat or—or for Marcus to stop fucking around and bring me to H-E-B. I cooked what's in here."

I sound like Mama because me and her been conjoined for too long.

His lips curl around the rim of the cup and water pools in my mouth because I want to taste him again. My words were supposed to sting, but his eyes stay soft, like he understands that nothing I say has to do with him. His swollen lips climb into a sympathetic smile because I think he can read my mind sometimes.

"You know...I was mad as fuck that night LeBron called me The Kid," he says after taking another sip.

"What you was so mad about?" I garble out. "I don't think it's much you could've been mad about that night. People still talk about that shot."

His eyes sweep the kitchen floor, gliding across the tiles that separate us. My eyes do the same because I'm following his lead just like he wants—exactly like he planned. That one welt on the back of my neck prickles to the surface because it knows he's back.

"Life," he replies. "I was mad about life and how fucked up it is—how short the shit is, how unfair it is, how unprepared I was for it. It's a lot I could've been mad about that night, but nobody ever cared enough to ask."

I sigh.

"I remember looking at the score and asking myself how the fuck I'm supposed to be proud of *this*—how I'm supposed to be present in this moment when Mom can't even keep soup in her stomach."

For a second, I forget about my problems and think about Mama's words from that night in the kitchen—about Coach Williams and Angie being good people and how easy Mama made it sound to befriend a guy like Ace.

"Your mama stopped eating too? That's how you know all that stuff you be telling me about—the clear Ensure and Zofran?"

He nods and his eyes skirt away from mine. "Yeah... something like tha—"

"Phat!" Mama screams and I jump. "Phat!"

"Ma'am?"

"Who you let in the house?"

"It's me, Mom!" Ace answers, taking another swig from his cup.

"Boy... I thought I was gon' have to com—come out there with my pistol."

He laughs, but I can't because I hear the sluggishness in her words. I couldn't even ask for the rest of his story about her ghost of a friend who only exists in old pictures and in this boy who makes my body feel twenty different ways at once.

Mama chokes out a cough, and he takes another gulp to the head.

"I'll be in there to chop it up with you in a sec, Mom!" he yells while his cheek lifts. "Phat told me she was hungry so I'mma take care of that."

My eyes get big.

I don't know if his words are another one of those unknown but known sexual innuendos he likes to toss out in front of unsuspecting people that don't live on Planet Ace, but Mama's not stupid—at least she didn't use to be.

"Good... good—good..." Her words drift off and I picture her balding head sliding to the side of her pillow like it was when I left her to answer the door.

Today is one of those ugly days, so she's stuck. She's so stuck that Ace even has her on his planet where bad things are good, anger isn't a frowned upon response to life's bullshit, and he chooses the vibe so the house isn't angry anymore.

He snatches another solo cup from the pack he took from the cabinet and turns to the kitchen sink. My palms sweat when he swipes the water on and shoves the cup underneath it. When he brings it to his lips, my armpits tingle with sweat too.

"Hm... open." He pulls the solo cup from his lips and twists it to the side his lips covered.

Then he pushes it toward me.

My watering mouth opens and so does his. I wrap my lips around the rim of his cup and my eyes flutter until they're closed.

"Now who told you I can't drink and you can't be angry before eleven?" he whispers. "Hurry and swallow. I gotta hear the rationale behind this one."

I swallow, trying to hold in my smile.

One day I'll have to ask Chelsea if it's possible to know what someone's mouth tastes like without ever having your lips pressed against theirs.

"Uh... basic ass life norms tell us that." I choke on the water. "*Fuck...* that's cold."

His laughter echoes through the kitchen. "But does it taste good?"

Yes. It tastes like him.

I shrug with a grimace and it makes him laugh harder despite Mama being asleep a few feet away. "I don't know what the fuck basic life norms are, but I said you can be angry at ten 'o'clock this morning—so be angry. I told you, you were doing a good job."

"I can't be angry now that you telling me to."

"Why not?" He cocks his head to the side. "I thought I taught you how to play follow the leader the other night. I thought you was smart, kid?"

My stomach jumps from the giggles I let out between hiccups and his thumb grazes my bottom lip to swipe the wetness he's always imagining there.

"You a fucked up leader," I mutter around his thumb. "Your ideologies make no sense. Life on Planet Ace must be wild."

My face heats after I blurt out another thing he's not supposed to know about me—that I gave his brain a name.

His face relaxes into an expression I can't dissect with glowering eyes and flared nostrils. It's just like the one he gave me in front of Marcus when I forgot about his rules and tried to be the leader on Planet Ace.

His thumb falls from my lips. "You still hungry?"

I nod in a hazy-eyed daze as he pushes the cup back to my lips and his free hand crawls underneath my braids to that annoying welt.

Two warm fingers glide across it in slow strokes. "Go get dressed. Marcus got something to take care of, so he asked me to drop you and Mom off at your appointments."

I move before he can drop his hand and rush off to my bathroom. It's something about hearing "go" come out his mouth that sends my body surging. It's another way he's got me and Brandy conditioned.

Our house is so small that I can hear his and Mama's muffled voices from the shower when I cut the water off to shave my legs. I drag a razor against my shin while fighting to make out their words.

"What happened to your lip?" she asks.

"Took a elbow in a pickup game. Ain't nothing for you to fuss over."

"You still playing pickup games with random boys? Angie hated when you did that. Tell Phat to ice it for you." She sighs. "Did she eat?"

"Yeah... I told you I'd take care of it. Now it's the queen of the castle's turn."

"She ain't tell you I already ate?"

The razor slips across my skin.

"Shit," I hiss, reaching over the side of the tub and fumbling with the roll of toilet paper.

"You ain't got to lie to me, Mom."

They laugh together. I can't even roll my eyes because at least she's laughing with somebody today—even if it's not me.

"You know I had my friend send me some stuff from back home that'll have you eating all the fire shit you ain't had in a minute."

I snicker at the Los Angeles dripping out his mouth as I press the tissue into my skin. He must've taken another sip of that drink.

Mama gasps. "What you got, boy?"

"Shit, some Blueberry Dream, some Moondrop Grape, but you a special lady, Mom, so you deserve that OG Kush."

"Boyyyy. You gon' have me into it with Phat. I can't smoke no more."

"Nah, that's why you eat it."

They laugh even harder together and I smile at Ace's deep voice bouncing against our thin walls.

"But nah for real," he rumbles. "I brought you something for that stomach of yours. How that sound?"

"What is it?"

"Ensure—"

"Nah, nah." Mama gags. "Phat always trying to give me that chalky ass shit."

"Yeah, but you never had it like this. I got something special just for you."

"For real?" Mama gasps like he went to the factory and mixed up a special bottle of Ensure for her.

I choke on a giggle until I hear him rustling through a plastic bag.

"Yeah. I told you, you an OG Kush type of lady. I soaked them in clear Ensure just for you. All you need is one. It'll calm your stomach and by the time you done at the clinic you'll be ready to eat all the shit you never thought you'd want anymore. How that sound?"

"Mhmm." She hums. "You and Marcus one and the same, you know that, right? Coming in here sweet talking and bearing gifts. What you want?"

They laugh together again until Mama's low humming bounces off the walls. She only hums when she's eating something she has no business eating. Ace's deep laugh makes my lips climb higher until he blurts out a string of words that make Mama's humming stop.

"Can I spend time with Lourdes while you're at the clinic?"

Their voices stop and my foot gives out. I stumble over the side of the tub, gripping the edge of the sink and missing Mama's answer to his bold question. It doesn't sound like something a boy like him would even think to ask, but everyday I'm learning more about how wrong I am about boys like him.

A gentle knock on the door makes me pull myself upright.

I clear my throat. "Yeah?"

"You lost in there?" he asks.

"Nah... I—I'm coming."

"Yeah, I know you are. Come on. I'm waiting for you."

MAMA'S APPOINTMENTS at the infusion center last for four hours. So, that's four hours of being stuck with Ace and a body full of angry hives after we drop her off. She was so happy to ride in a Porsche she didn't even notice the cup in his hand on the drive to the Medical Center. Shit, her eyes were so heavy from Ace's concoction it wouldn't surprise me if she was already asleep at the clinic.

"You can go to jail for that," I mutter, glancing at the red solo cup in his left hand as he whips underneath the highway.

His buttery leather seats hug my back and I try hard to train my eyes *not* to stare at him, but it's an impossible thing to do—especially ever since he asked Mama that question.

"I ever tell you what the one and only rule is in the spaceships on Planet Ace?" he replies.

One of those half-smile half-frowns covers my lips.

Planet Ace.

That shit didn't freak him out.

I roll my eyes. "Nah. What's the rule?"

"Pilot." He flicks the turn signal on with the hand holding the solo cup and then gestures toward me with it. "Co-pilot."

His rules are just gibberish because I'm hungry again. The thirty-minute ride to drop Mama off worked my appetite up so much that I'm jonesing for his taste. I'm not brave enough to articulate to him that the way he describes my craving for him is even hive-inducing. *Hunger.* I don't think I've ever been hungry for a boy until now.

"Well... *pilot.* You going the wrong way. My nail shop sure ain't this way."

"Never question the pilot, *co-pilot.*" He snorts, dropping the solo cup in the cupholder between us and pulling a Dum-Dum from the other side of it. "I know where the fuck I'm going."

"You sure about that? That tattoo on your stomach says otherwise."

LA.

The quintessential hand-sign thrown up by a girl wearing acrylics and rings sits at the base of his stomach, covering his bellybutton. It was the only tattoo I had time to drool over before he dropped his t-shirt back at the house.

He unwraps the Dum-Dum and pops it in his mouth. "One thing Mom gon' always have is real estate in her hometown. I spent more than enough time here."

"That's how you know how to get around so good?"

He pulls the sucker from between his plump lips with a pop. "Yup."

There's more I want to ask, like what he did when his own Mama stopped eating and why she had stopped in the first place, but we're not on that level yet—at least I don't think we are. I'm still learning my way around him.

"Hm..." He dangles the stick in front of my mouth. "I hear your stomach growling all the way over here."

I open my mouth and he pushes it in as he eases to a stop at a red-light.

Now "open" is gone along with "can you?" Stupid Chelsea and Pavlov and his dumb dogs.

The Dum-Dum tastes like Paul Masson and him. He turns the volume to the radio up with a button on his steering-wheel and Dough's voice pours through the speakers, rapping about always being "a LA nigga at heart."

I figure this is what it feels like to ride down Sunset Boulevard in Los Angeles, but we're on Westheimer instead and it feels even better. The high rises and condos seem like places I can pop in and visit folks who don't know I exist. For once, I can say I belong among the Mercedes and Lexus in Ace's Porsche. I don't have that tugging at my ego reminding me of my outsider status like I do when me and Mama window-shop at the Galleria.

"Taste good?" He tugs the end of the stick on the Dum-Dum and pulls it out just enough for me to answer.

"It's a'ight."

Before I can fix my response, he snatches all of him and Paul Masson out of my mouth while pulling into the parking lot of a shopping center.

"Guess you not as hungry as I thought." The stick goes back into his mouth and he sucks it so hard I can hear the gushing of wetness draining into my panties as he backs into a parking spot.

He pushes the car in park. "C'mon."

"C'mon where?"

The only people in the parking lot are a group of white

ladies strolling in their Lululemon and gripping yoga mats under their arms.

"To get your nails done."

"Here?"

Uptown Nails and Spa looks like a retreat compared to MJ Nails where Marcus has a tab with Minh. A black awning covers its entrance and the letters on the door are so aesthetically pleasing I can't stop staring.

"Marcus didn't give me enough money to get my nails done here."

"Damn..." Ace laughs and pulls the solo cup out of the cup holder. "You must know how to do pedis."

"Hell no!"

"Shit, kid. How you gon' pay for the fill on them coffin-shaped nails then?" He pushes open the driver's side door.

I wrap my hand around the passenger door handle. "Hold up, Ac—"

He whips his head around with one long leg dangling outside the car. "I see I already have to make up a second rule for the spaceships on Planet Ace. Stop touching my goddamn door handles."

I fling my hand back and stare at him, sliding from behind the wheel. He slams his door closed and then gaits around to mine, yanking it open.

I stagger out behind him like I took another swig of that nasty alcohol he let me taste.

That momentary sense of belonging I felt in his Porsche disappears as the sun beats down on my faded leggings, flip-flops, and tank top. He swaggers ahead of me with the cup dangling from his fingers and the Dum-Dum stick in his mouth while I try to calculate what services I can afford in this uppity nail shop he's got me at.

"Bring your ass, Lourdes," he calls out over his shoulder. "It's hot."

I groan under my breath and hurry past the Lululemon housewives taking up space underneath the awning.

Inside, the cold gush of air soothes the burning hives on my exposed skin and I want to bury myself in Ace's side because he's the only familiar thing in the spotless entryway. I comb the walls looking for a price-list but it's nothing like Minh's shop where the prices were painted on the glass windows since before I was born.

A tiny Vietnamese girl shuffles to the front in Gucci sandals and there's a flicker of recognition in her eyes before she rushes toward Ace.

"Ace. You come back?"

He smiles down at her and that same ball of nerves from the day before in the cafe sneaks its way up my throat.

"What you in Houston for?" She throws her arms around his middle and the older white women stare at him from the pedicure chairs in the back of the salon.

I don't blame them. He's a sight—tall, caramel and carefree despite what people think about him.

"I live here now, Sunny," he replies, talking around the Dum-Dum.

"Live?" she gasps. "*Oh*, Angie would love that!"

Angie's name rings bells throughout the salon. The other employees shuffle from their stations at the sound of Sunny singing her name from the entrance. They all know Ace. They touch him like he's theirs and there's relief in his eyes.

Sunny notices me first. She tugs at Ace's t-shirt and he grips her around the shoulders, pulling her toward me.

"Who you bring for me?" she asks, smiling.

"A lil' piece of home," he mutters. "Take good care of her, Sun. Lourdes cheating on her regular girl today."

Sunny stares up at me with gigantic eyes like I'm not dressed in my best Walmart fashions and I don't know what home Ace is referring to. I *ain't* never been to Los Angeles.

"Pretty girl." She tugs at my hand and rubs her tiny fingers over Minh's work. "Hahn take care of your nails and I do pedicure for you."

ACE IS SO comfortable around campus and our house that I forget he has money sometimes. Not that upper middle class mini mansion out in The Woodlands money, but the type of money that affords him the ability to understand Sunny and Hanh's conversation in Vietnamese while they cater to my every need from my pedicure chair. He's so comfortable in Uptown Nails that he's popping the cork on a bottle while they giggle at his story about him and Angie missing their connecting flight from South Korea to Vietnam one summer. It ends with them running into Magic Johnson's wife Cookie in a Delta Airlines lounge while he's shit-faced drunk because Angie kept sneaking him glasses of champagne even though he was sixteen.

"You like Veuve, Lourdes?" Sunny asks, patting my leg.

"Excuse me?" I choke out, glancing at the white lady next to us.

She keeps staring at Ace, who's across the salon topping his solo cup off.

"Veuve. Champagne?"

"Uh... I never had it."

My answer makes them smile, and Sunny rolls back from the chair. "Ace, you fix Lourdes some too?"

He tips the bottle over two other champagne flutes.

"Nope," he says. "She a kid Sunny."

"Awww." She and Hahn giggle in unison until Ace brings them two flutes with the Veuve bottle dangling from his fingertips.

When they take sips, I'm glad they shut up because I don't have much longer on Planet Ace and they're hogging him with their Vietnamese inside jokes. He steals a rolling stool from in front of an empty pedicure station and rolls next to me.

I smell the Veuve bubbling from his cup as he pushes up the armrest that separates us. The champagne mixes with his earthy scent and acrylic.

"You always got a nail appointment when Mom goes to the doctor?" he asks.

"You always went to the nail shop with your mama?" I shoot back.

"Yeah..." He smiles with his lips, but not his eyes. "After I stopped playing ball, Mom moved back home, so I flew back and forth between her and Pops. We came to the nail shop every Thursday morning as soon as I got in from LA."

He makes it sound like he took a sabbatical from playing ball and not a forced leave and that married people lived in separate houses all the time.

I swallow a choke at the tiny pieces of his and Angie's history he keeps feeding me. "Was you a mama's boy?"

"Hell yeah. For an eternity."

The way his words sound make me lose the half-frown and now it's a full-blown grin. He sounds like he did when he was talking to Mama.

"What you smiling like that for?" He scoots closer and squints at Hahn, shaping the acrylic on my pointer finger.

"'Cause you sound like LA."

"And you sound like Houston." He chuckles. "Talking about, 'was you?' Country ass."

He's floating and I want him even closer.

I hold my breath at the sight of his little curls lined up around the perimeter of his head. There's another tattoo peeking from behind his ear in uppercase italics —*THE KID.*

"You ready to bust these pedis down for this expensive ass fill and pedicure you getting?"

My insides flutter and my mouth runs. "Jokes on you. Refill's forty, I got the basic ass pedi, and I got twenty bucks stuck in the bottom of my wristlet for Sunny and Hahn's tip. Marcus gave me *just* enough."

He's still leaning over my lap in a daze while Hahn swipes the brush down the length of another one of my nails. I hold my breath again for him to push up so I can see the tipsy smirk that's always there while he's sipping on *whatever* he's found to fix *whatever* he's running from.

When his face meets mine, the smirk isn't there though.

Instead, he pushes his lips forward like he's thinking hard about something. His eyes cast a trail from the roots of my knotless braids, to my lips, and over the tank top I've been squirming in since Sunny made me sit in the pedicure chair. It's different from the glowering flared nostril look. *This look* is nothing like the looks Bryson gives me.

"You forgot the rules to follow the leader already, Lourdes?" he asks.

His tone is the same as it was in Mama's driveway back when "can you" came before his favorite thing for me to do. It's a nice, warm cadence that doesn't match the words billowing out of his mouth and that look tells me he knows the answer to his question.

"No..." I reply with a swallow.

Afterward, my stomach folds as if I gave him the wrong answer, and I know it's what he intended when he taught me about following the leader on Planet Ace. The problem is that he's never told me what happens when I don't follow the leader.

He twists his lips to the side and shakes his head in a disappointed gaze that makes a fiery welt pop up between my legs. I have this stupid urge to hook my arms around his neck and explain myself, but I wouldn't even know what I'd be explaining.

He pushes himself from over my legs and picks up the bottle of Veuve by its neck again.

"I ever tell you how bad of a girl Lourdes is, Sunny?" He tips the champagne into the pedicure bowl. "She rolls her eyes at me, talks back, and tries to be a passenger seat driver in our car, but I still give her whatever she wants. I think I'm creating a lil' monster."

It splashes on top of my feet and legs and I can't believe he's wasting the rest of an expensive bottle of champagne —*yes*; I looked up its price.

Sunny and Hahn giggle while that same white lady from before rolls her eyes at us from beneath her readers. Sunny's fingers stroke the champagne fizz against my legs and she swipes a cylinder bucket from the cart sitting next to her. She takes out a piece of rose-shaped soap and tosses it in the water. It fizzes and makes the water feel like vibrating silk against my toes.

I shut my eyes.

I'm so preoccupied with Sunny, the bath bomb, and Ace's champagne bath that I don't feel his forearm land on my upper thigh until his scent wafts toward my nose.

"Answer my question," he mutters.

"What question?" I hiss as Sunny's fingers trail between my toes under the water.

"You always got a nail appointment when Mom goes to the doctor?"

"No... only when Marcus has the extra money. When he don't, I just sit at the house until she gets back."

"Why?"

My eyes jolt open to the back of his head.

He's watching Sunny give me the best pedicure I've ever gotten while questioning me about the unfair life shit he knows too much about. Maybe this happens when I don't follow the leader, or it could be what happens when he's tipsy and consumed with a place that reminds him of Angie.

The Kid is on Planet Ace and he's waiting for me to get back there to be with him.

I try to control my breathing as he cradles the solo cup in his hand and stares into the pedicure bowl, waiting for me to stop thinking about the small things in life—like the cost of a refill and pedicure.

"Because... it's—it's scary," I whisper. "So Marcus don't make me go and neither does she."

He doesn't say anything—not even when I touch the back of his head to see if his hair feels as soft as it looks like Brandy did. Instead, he leans into my fingers and lets me rub his curls with a curious stroke.

"It's okay to be scared," he replies. "I used to be scared, too."

"Of the clinic?"

"Nah... of what happens at the end of it all. You know, when God decides they had enough and all the pain stops." He pushes his head back into my fingers while I try to swallow his words, but they taste bitter.

I think I know why Angie stopped eating, but I can't say the word. It's a nasty word that we tiptoe around at home. Bryson blurted it once, and Marcus had to peel me off him afterward.

Ace nudges my hand off his head and twists his neck around to study Hahn's perfect coffin shape. I squirm while he picks up each finger one by one like he knows better than a professionally trained nail tech.

He slides his fingertips against mine. "Neuropathy."

"Huh?" I ask, crooking my head to the side and staring at his swollen lip Mama wanted me to ice.

"That's why Mom loses the feeling in her fingers sometimes."

"Who told you about that?"

"I heard you on the phone the other day when me and Marcus played ball." He sucks his bottom lip into his mouth while I study his face, because he's not like the other boys I liked.

That fat lip he's sporting tells me all I need to know.

I reach out and pluck another one of the little curls on his head, poking my finger through its swirly opening until he tosses his head back and downs the rest of the champagne.

Afterward, he shoves a hand between my closed legs and scrapes a finger down the new welt that's lying against my inner thigh. He stays glued there, watching Sunny and Hahn work while talking to them about their favorite topics —Hahn's upcoming wedding with her partner Valerie and Sunny's girl's trip to Miami. He's got the answers to their problems like whether Hahn should keep her crewcut for the ceremony and if Sunny's friend-group should stay at the SLS on South Beach or FONTAINEBLEAU. The best part is when he ropes me in as if I know what any of it means.

"SLS for sure. It's only right you hit up Hyde Beach," he says. "Right, Lourdes?"

I nod, staring at his fingers massaging my inner thigh. "Sure..."

"Ace like to party, Lourdes. He like to dance and have so many friends." Sunny giggles, wiggling her shoulders.

I don't know this Ace she's talking about, but I also can't focus on what she's saying because Ace's fingers inch further up my thigh while he stares at Kendrick Perkins yap on his phone. She left out the part about him also being a good multitasker.

"Nahhh..." He smiles, squeezing my meaty thigh.

His eyes don't leave his phone when he responds, but I see a flicker of sadness in them when he swipes to read a text message. The rough squeeze he gives my inner thigh tells me I need to put my eyes back on my phone.

At the end of our three-hour rendezvous, the bill is a whopping three-hundred dollars that Ace doesn't flinch at. He thumbs through his wallet like he did at the bookstore and pulls out that heavy black card he's always using. I search for Coach Williams' name on the face, but Ason Williams Jr. taunts me back for being nosey.

I hang beside him at the entrance, admiring Hahn's coffin shape that makes me regretful that I'd been getting subpar sets from Minh. The shape is sleek, and the acrylic is so thin, they look like my own. I'm already rehearsing my lines to run Marcus' pockets for the money to get to Uptown to visit Sunny and Hahn again.

Ace scribbles out a hundred-dollar tip like it's five bucks and slides the receipt back to Sunny.

"You come back for champagne and rose pedi next week, Lourdes?" she asks, grinning from behind the register.

"Yea—"

"Nah," Ace cuts in, making my eyes jump up to him.

He's too busy thumbing through his wallet to notice the panicked expression on my face. Maybe he's finally feeling the regret he should've felt after dinner the other night.

"We'll be busy in the next couple of weeks, but I'll let you know when to expect us, Sun."

A quiet sigh escapes my lips.

I don't even care that I don't know what he's talking about. I just know we'll be together again and he still doesn't have any regrets.

When we walk outside to the parking lot, my eyes won't stop grazing the back of his calves and the Jordans on his feet. The arrow on my like-o-meter doesn't exist anymore. It's malfunctioning and flying off the scale because my pussy is confused, like Mama says Chelsea's is: *"She need to go find a 'nice preacher's kid and stop all this Marcus nonsense. Her lil' pussy is hot and confused."*

I know that she means Marcus is too old for Chelsea. He's faster than she is, like Ace is for me, but Ace has this way of making me think I can catch up to him.

The sun beats down on my face. I'm full of hives, my panties are a mess, and my belly aches for one more taste of Ace before we pick up Mama.

As soon as he closes me inside and slides back behind the steering wheel, I snatch his cup from the cupholder and wrap my lips around the edge where I think his lips may have been last. The Veuve splashes against my tongue while he grips the back of my headrest, letting out a quiet laugh as he pulls out of the parking spot.

"Manis and pedis work up Lourdes' appetite and make

her think she can do shit without my permission." He smirks. "Now the kid's defiant. That's cool. I know how to fix that, too."

Those words are as good as *the look*. They both send my hives into overdrive and I think I fucked up that night I opened my mouth for him in our driveway.

CHAPTER NINE

Lourdes

Mama didn't lose all her hair at once.

We measured the time it took for her to go bald by chemotherapy infusions. On the morning of her first infusion I could still slick her hair into a bun, the night after her fourth one her edges went, and by the time her sixth one rolled around, the ziplock bag under her bathroom sink had an Afro in it.

Granny told us not to throw it in the trash because anybody could get ahold of it, so now it's just a big ole' lump of black staring at me every time I open her cabinet to look for a bonnet. She says she's going to burn it when she comes back to visit from Lake Charles, but Mama thinks if we keep it, it'll trick her hair follicles into working again. Now, it looks like midnight colored cotton and I don't know how much longer I can look at it.

"Get Naomi!" Mama yells from her bed.

I smile, pushing the plastic bag to the side and snatching Naomi from the back corner of the cabinet.

Naomi ain't nothing but a twenty dollar Shake-n-go I got from the hair store last month with Bryson, but Mama swore it was worthy of a name. Her strands are silky and I rake my fingers through them while putting on my best strut for Mama because she's stuck again today. It's a thing now.

Dr. Evanston told Marcus it was a "cognitive dysfunction due to the treatment of her diagnosis" when he called to complain about it, but none of us know what the fuck that even means. He wouldn't even tell us how she got that neuropathy Ace was talking about. He just prescribed more medicine we can't pronounce.

"Hey now!" Mama claps when I round the corner. "You... better... walk, girl!"

Her words struggle to come out between coughs while I ignore the cold bacon sitting on her nightstand. It's been there since this morning.

I giggle. "We gotta show Twitter this one."

"Okay! You better tell them Tweety birds that your Mama still got it."

I crawl into her unmade bed and plop it on her head as soon as she leans down. Even underneath her dim bedroom light, the strands shine. She flings her head back and a burn creeps up the back of my throat, but I ignore it and push my camera in her face.

"Pose for the camera..." I smash my finger against the phone while darting my eyes between the screen and her in real life.

It's a constant battle.

"Bet you didn't know I used to model, did you?" She tilts her head with a sly wink.

"Mama, being an extra in a Slim Thug video don't count as modeling."

She wheezes out a mixture of a cough and a laugh while

I do the one thing that keeps me from letting that burn take over and invade my mouth when I'm stuck in the house for days at a time: I tweet.

@babyphat04

Naomi Campbell who? Supermodel CeCe Hines reporting for duty.

@babyphat04

Ain't my mama fine?

"What they saying about me?" Mama asks, shaking her temporary hair like she has on a waist length lace.

I smile at the first wave of likes, then her favorites—the retweets. Most of them are people I never met and never will, but my burning throat don't care about technical things like that. All that matters is that their tweets don't trigger my moist tear ducts because even they know better than to say that ugly C word.

"They say you aging like fine wine, girl."

She shimmies her shoulders while I skim through their barrage of "Praying for you," and "You got this!" tweets.

Ten tweets later, the gentle wheezing from her chest makes me glance up from my phone because an impromptu photo shoot and going semi-viral for battling an endless disease tires her out most. It's not like back in the day where a blunt and a glass of wine put her to sleep after driving for MetroLift all day, toting Marcus around to his AAU games, and braiding my hair.

She lays back and catches my eyes before looking down at my fingers. "Marcus must got a nice tab over at Minh's, huh?"

"Huh?"

"Your new set." She nods at my new bedazzled nails. "That's some tough shit, girl."

Coffin-shaped, bubblegum pink, and rhinestones—lots

of them. Ace said they "looked hella good" when the sun hit them through his windshield.

"Oh... yeah." I shrug like I didn't already show Twitter the masterpiece on my hands because I hadn't left the house in days to show anybody else.

The only eyes they graced were hers and Ace's because I couldn't leave Mama at home to suffer with neuropathy alone and Marcus didn't notice anything but drank and weed most days. So, I missed an entire week of classes and forgot what the air tasted like outside because me and her are conjoined again.

"I think Ason liked 'em."

I snort. "What you talking about?"

"I saw y'all holding hands up in the car."

"You was high. You don't know what you saw. You slept the whole way home. It was so bad you ain't even eat your Frenchy's."

"I was *not* high. You know how I get after I leave the clinic."

That drive to our house was the quickest it'd ever been because Ace kept slipping his free hand under mine every time the car moved and Mama's eyes drifted closed. God was always doing sly shit like that—making the best times the shortest.

"Yeah you was. That boy wasn't holding my hand."

My body heats in all the embarrassing ways being inexperienced makes it while Mama gives me her best Miss Cleo look. She strokes her eyes against my face, hands and thighs.

"It's no reason to be shame about holding a man's hand for the first time."

"I held a dude's hand before."

"Bryson don't count. He still hold hands with Lucy when they make groceries."

"Mama, stop being messy!" I slap my hand across my face.

It's bad enough that Chelsea's had a more exciting love life than I have and she's a damn holy roller—she's kissed, stalked, fought, and her and Marcus fuck. Mother Lenola still thinks she's saving herself for marriage.

When I spread my fingers, Mama's still staring at me to confirm that at my big age, I held Ace's hand underneath the beaming afternoon sun from the passenger seat of his spaceship.

"It's okay to change your mind about people. You know that, right?" she asks.

"You blowing me with this whole 'me and Ace' thing. He's cool—that's it." I drop my hand from my face. "Why you not telling me what you tell Chelsea about Marcus' blockheaded tail?"

Ace and Marcus are the types of dudes she tells me and Chelsea to fuck with when we're mature and can handle grown-man problems—and according to the news, Ace has *plenty* of grown-man problems.

"Because Chelsea don't got a mama like yours or a mama like Ace had."

"She don't have a mama at all."

"No, but she's got Lenola, who's got a clean bill of health at sixty."

"Please, don't go there today." I blink away the burn in my tear ducts. "I held his hand—so what? You treat him like he's made of gold."

"Angie used to tell me he was." She shrugs. "You don't find many men like him. The kind that'll wipe they Mama's face with a smile after she throws up all the good food he tried to cook, or fly all the way from LA to Houston every week just to carry her from the bed to the wheelchair and then roll her into the nail shop so she can feel like a woman again even though that's the only time she leaves the house anymore."

Fuck, I hate being conjoined with Mama sometimes.

That ugly burning in my tear ducts overflows and wetness dots the inner corners of my eyes until Mama's puffy face gets blurry.

She gurgles out another cough and reaches for her ice water on her nightstand like she didn't fill in all the missing pieces of Ace and Angie's history he left out. The only thing that stops the hot tears from overflowing is loud jiggling at the front door.

"Open the door!" Marcus yells.

"I told you to stop leaving your fu—freaking key in the house!" I shout back, crawling out of Mama's bed with my thumbs on fire because I have too many vague tweets loaded into the chamber in my head, ready for me to fire out on my walk to the front door.

@babyphat04

You ever ask God why certain shit happens? Like, would changing shit in the past have any effect on the present?

@babyphat04

Like if they wouldn't have found that tumor that summer, would things be different or would they just have found it another summer and certain shit just happens no matter what?

@babyphat04

Or if I would've just kept my mouth shut, I wouldn't be obsessing over somebody I shouldn't obsess over, or maybe my obsession would've happened in another way even if I kept it shut?

@babyphat04

Anyways. It's complicated.

As soon as I curl my fingers around the lock on the front door, Chelsea's already in my inbox.

@Chelsea_Paige

First things first, kiss Mama CeCe for me. Okay, that's out of the way. Who are we obsessing over?

I roll my eyes while flinging the door open and finding Bryson standing behind it instead of Marcus.

He smiles and pushes a strawberry cool cup toward my chest. "The cool cup lady had strawberry today. I know that's your favorite."

Sometimes a test of loyalty is as simple as a cool cup and Bryson knows that because he's just like the *lil' perro* Ace described him as. He's always searching for different ways to make sure our loyalty stays intact, especially when he's trying so hard to be a boy that gives me hives.

Marcus pushes between both of us, sucking his teeth. "You better eat it, too. That was the last damn one."

I take the cool cup with a grin while Chelsea waits in my inbox, but waiting's never been easy for her, so when my phone vibrates I already know it's her.

I push the phone against my ear, peeling the lid off the cool cup as Bryson bounces on his toes like I'm going to kiss him for finding the most obscure flavor the cool cup lady has.

"Girl, what?"

"My bestie is obsessed with a boy and I find out *after* Twitter? I'm really questioning my position in your life."

When the sweet sensation of cold strawberry touches

my tongue, Bryson pushes his ear onto the other side of the phone. "She busy, Mother Teresa. Go read the Bible."

"Girl..." Chelsea sighs. "I'm slightly disappointed yet happy it's just lil' Like Mike you're obsessed with. I was almost worried it was *he who cannot keep his hands off Beckies*. I swear, every time I call Marcus, he's around. Let Brandy deal with that. Anyway, please tell me you saw the Pizza and Pearls event they're having on the yard tomorrow. Tell me you're coming."

She doesn't ask why I missed a week's worth of classes. She talks right over me and Mama's extended stay in the house while shooting a casual slug at Ace. Bryson uses the opportunity to smash his cheek against mine while the strawberry cool cup melts in my hand and they smother me with all of their freshman problems I can't relate to.

Ace

POPS SAYS every good ball player has a pre-game ritual.

LeBron James tossed chalk and Vince Carter did pull-ups from the basketball net but he says every *great* ball player has a pre-practice ritual—one that strokes the mind into a calm stream of thoughts to prepare them for the challenges that lie ahead on an empty court where there aren't any screaming fans but just the thoughts in their own head.

Phat is my new pre-practice ritual, but she doesn't know it.

@babyphat04 2d
New clawz on deck.

I smirk at the picture of her oiled up brown hands in the

passenger seat of my truck while the stinging heat from the outdoor court at Pops' strokes my back.

I study the picture, trying to pinpoint when I took my eyes off of her long enough that she had time to snap it, but after a week spent around her, I realize she's sly. She knows how to control her tongue around CeCe, twist Marcus around her finger, and she's convinced Twitter she's a full-fledged lady. There's different versions of her and I need to know every one of them.

@babyphat04 1d

What does it mean if a dude makes you hungry?

@babyphat04 1d

Because I ain't ate this whole week but when I think about him my stomach gets…weird.

Twitter is her playground. It's where version two of her plays.

Her tweets remind me that Bryson still doesn't know shit about being a man and he's handed me an open invitation to her mind through our teammates. Last night, LaQuan and Marquise wanted me to follow them back on Twitter just to say they had a blue check in their follows to "impress baddies." With one press of my thumb, I found Phat sitting in *Marquise's* follows because Bryson didn't know how to protect his "girl" from his thirsty teammates, just like he didn't know how to keep her mouth in check.

Now I have to be the bad guy because version two of her tricked me into logging back into my empty account where a million neglected followers waited. They all hoped I'd come back from the dead and say something profound, but all I wanted to do was play in Phat's playground and teach her something. So, I post a tweet for the first time in life—a subtweet.

@AceWilliamsJr

It means your body is telling you to eat the nigga. Duh, kid.

Then, I change my location in her favorite app to the one place me and her can exist without life's outside noise: Planet Ace. And after that, I follow her so she can find me and that lonely subtweet. I don't wait with a twisting stomach for her to respond because I know she won't right away. She has to think about it. Version one of her is still my little lady. That version doesn't even know how to flirt with me, or that the details of CeCe's declining health and her innermost thoughts don't belong on Twitter.

A patter of footsteps tap across the court.

"What got you smiling this early?" Pops asks, slurping his coffee.

"Cree sent something funny." I shrug and push up from the ground. "Nothing crucial."

"Could've fooled me. Thought your lonely tail might've made a friend."

Pops isn't like Mom. I can't tell him that Phat's natural scent makes my body restless, that Brandy wasn't home no matter how hard she tried to be, or that I didn't need a chaser with my drinks before bed anymore—I just needed Phat's thoughts.

I scoff. "You being a lil' dramatic."

"Not as melodramatic as you. You still holed up at Angie's?"

"Where else would I be?"

It was the only place in Houston besides Phat that felt good, even if I saw Mom's ghost in her favorite places sometimes. She stood behind the stove, watched the sunset from her balcony, and crawled onto the couch with me some nights. It was ours. It was the only sacred place we had that

Pops' absence hadn't tainted because he didn't visit it often enough to impact the energy inside it.

"Hmm... I don't know." He shrugs. "Maybe your own place, like most young men your age... or here with me."

"If you miss me at your crib, just say that, man."

He chuckles, but it's not a full-blown laugh. "How's your host family? LaQuan learned how to make tea cakes and Bryson told me he read *Between the World and Me* for the first time. I think I heard from everybody but you."

I smile, even though his words highlight the distance that's always been between us. "They're straight. Phat made us burnt hamburgers for dinner one night, and I ball with Marcus when he's not working."

He howls out a laugh at that and takes another sip of his coffee. He's never laughed that loud at anything I've said.

"How's CeCe? I haven't seen her since before Angie... you know."

There's hesitation in his tone. If I could, I'd tell him that CeCe's head is about as bald as his.

He keeps his eyes on my lips like he's waiting for me to slip up and tell him I don't know how much longer God will let her hold out here on Earth. Or that her house has all my favorite things that help me peel my eyes open in the morning—especially on struggling Saturdays like this when Mom fights me in my head because I'm tripping about her crisis-loving husband.

"She's good. Phat takes good care of her."

He nods and then steps closer to me.

His nostrils flare, and he sucks up the surrounding air with a frown. "You drove here?"

My eyes roll upward and I hold on to the "fuck" lurking in my mouth. "Yup."

"Oh yeah? How'd that work out for you?"

"It worked out perfect." I step away from him and bounce the ball against the pavement.

"You smell like a bottle of tequila."

I squat, waiting for the wind to carry Mom's voice, reminding me to flick my wrist. But the air is still and humid, so the only noise is the *swishing* net when I push the ball up and sink a shot.

"Look, I made it here, didn't I?"

"You made it on time to my backyard every day in LA for two years, but that doesn't mean a damn thing—anything could happen while you're out there driving like this. Angie let you run amuck—partying and hanging with God knows who. Now look where all that got you."

He's drifting back in time—talking like Mom is still here to get on his head for being so hard on me. I think it's a side effect of the crisis he's in.

He walks off toward the chairs he has lined up and down the court.

"I was hanging with your favorite baller, Javier, and the people he brought around when he wasn't on the court making you proud."

There was no one left from the people Javier brought around except Cree because once things changed, *they* changed, and I didn't blame them for it.

"Don't start this morning." He stops and whips his head toward me. "We both know I have a zero-tolerance policy for alcohol and drugs on this court. Your irresponsibility has nothing to do with Javier."

I walk toward the ball and swipe it before it bounces into the grass.

The chair's feet scrape against the pavement while he slurps his coffee. "Alcohol dehydrates the body and fucks up your motor skills. How the *fuck* you gon' read the defense and react accordingly if you still drunk from the night before?"

I dribble back onto the court, and the blazing sun stings my neck. He's already lined the chairs up while gripping his coffee mug. They're in the same positions he's been dragging them in since I was old enough to dribble.

"*And* it fucks up your judgement, but I think you already know that." He stomps a foot onto the chair, staring at me from half court with his mug at his lips. "A man's greatest enemy is himself, young man. When you gonna get that through your head?"

I run toward the chairs, but the Texas heat makes my limbs lose their agility. If I didn't know any better, I'd swear Mom had tied imaginary weights to them to fuck with me for fucking with her husband. She hated when I did that before Saturday morning practices.

"We didn't move here for regression. You have one life to live, and I made sure you'd be able to live it well."

After seventeen years, running drills with Pops isn't what it used to be. There's nothing left for him to teach me about basketball, so now he tries to teach me about life on Saturday mornings, but it's too late.

"I got a call from an old friend yesterday. Name's Mitch. He's an agent—retired now though," he says. "I met him golfing down in the Keys in the summer of '07. He says he knows a young agent that's hunting for some basketball talent. He's trying to expand the NBA arm of his agency and he's interested in you."

He shrugs, taking another sip of coffee. "His name is Blake Harvey."

The heat's swallowing my breath again so I can't ask why the fuck I would want to meet a dude named Blake, but Pops doesn't care because agents aren't lined up at his doorstep begging to court me anymore.

"I think you might be interested in what he has to say."

I charge toward the chair with the ball, whipping around it and sinking an easy floater while he keeps talking about Blake.

"He'll be at the gala next weekend."

I frown, tripping over my feet and puffing out a breath. "What gala?"

"The Shooting Stars Gala."

"You going back to LA for that?"

"No, it's coming here."

"But that's Mom's thing. She plans it."

All the tedious shit he never had time for were her *things*—galas, fundraisers, birthday parties, holidays, family vacations. She even helped dress me for prom. She's the only reason I know how to tie a tie.

"My staff took over."

"And you think they can do a better job than Mom?"

"That's not for you to worry about. You just make sure you bring your head because your talent can't sell you anymore. We're beyond that."

I scoff, rolling my eyes toward the sky. "Bring my head?"

"Yeah. I figured you could go about this meeting on your own. It'll teach you responsibility and professionalism." He slaps me across the neck. "You can't learn nothing if I'm there holding your hand all night."

Afterward, he strolls off toward his enclosed patio with his coffee mug and then turns his head. "Oh yeah, don't think I didn't find the new deed to Angie's spot when I boxed her stuff up to donate. I see you weaseled your way into another cushy condo. That's prime real estate you holed up in."

CHAPTER TEN

Lourdes

My body has this weird anticipation for Ace now that I'm a confirmed inhabitant of his planet.

I didn't even confirm my own damn inhabitance—*he* did after one of his followers jokingly asked if he'd been living on Planet Ace all this time that his Twitter sat empty. That surprised me just as much as it surprised them and to top it off, he followed me—basic *ass* me with my meager two-thousand followers. He didn't even have a real social media presence until me.

@AceWilliamsJr 2d
Yeah... just me and the kid. We just been chillin', playing follow the leader, and debating about basic life norms on Planet Ace. She loves it here.

The best and most annoying thing about being the only other soul on Planet Ace is that he can see every thought I decide to share in the one place I escape to when I'm stuck at home with Mama. It's a privilege and a curse because it's the only space where I can air out my new obsessive thoughts about him I can't say in person and then delete them before Bryson gets any ideas. Now I break out in a cold sticky sweat *and* hives when I know he's watching my timeline and thinking of his next tweet to disturb my body's equilibrium.

Last night, it got so slick because I tweeted something I shouldn't have after agonizing over it for hours. Mama thought I got a spontaneous infection at the kitchen table while I ate the McDonald's it took Marcus two hours to bring, but no, it was just me and Ace playing stupid Twitter games.

I tweet. He responds with a subtweet. I squirm and delete. Rinse. Repeat.

@babyphat04 1d

Earth is so ghetto. I would never have to eat cold McDonald's fries at home. Ugh.

@AceWilliamsJr 1d

Shit, come home then.

Two DMs, one phone call to Mama and twenty-four hours later, I'm standing at the end of my driveway waiting on Coach Williams' driver to pull up because Ace is still at practice and doesn't believe in Ubers.

Marshall's old Houston Rockets backpack dangles from my fingers because none of my purses are *in*. Mama sits behind me on the porch because she's not stuck today. She's just nosey and giddy that Ace called her to ask if I can spend time with him like an old ass man would: *"Mom, can Lourdes spend time with me tonight? I promise I'll take care of her."*

He's always promising Mama something—a laugh, a dance, and when me and her are conjoined, he promises himself.

"That's him?" she yells from her plastic chair on the porch as another black SUV drives down the street.

"Mama... that's a Chevy." I roll my eyes. "He said a Cadillac."

"Shit, they look the same."

"They don't look nothing alike—believe me."

"Well, it was the same colo—oh! That's him! That's him!"

My body jerks at her overreaction and I strain to see the driver behind the dark tint. All I know is that his name is Gus, and he's been toting Coach Williams and his family around since before I was born.

Apparently, nosiness can cure everything that's wrong with Mama because she damn near sprints to the end of the driveway.

Gravel crunches beneath the tires as Gus pulls in front of our leaning mailbox and parks. Mama strains her neck to see him as he pushes out of the driver's seat.

"Lourdes?" he asks, rounding the corner of the truck in a linen short set.

"Phat," I correct.

He smiles and nods. "Phat."

He looks between me and Mama while he thrusts his hand out for us to shake, but Mama don't shake hands.

She tosses her arms around his upper body in a tight hug. "I don't know a stranger, Gus."

His laugh sounds like it can shake the Earth. "You must be CeCe. Junior told me all about you."

"Junior?" I ask.

His voice sounds rich. His pronunciations are proper and poised, with a hint of a Jamaican accent, maybe.

He pulls out of Mama's grip and gives me a polite church hug.

"Yeah, Junior, but I'm sure yuh like fi call him Ace. He'll always be Junior to me though," he adds.

"Junior..." I nod, shrugging.

Mama slaps a hand on his chest. "Now, where you taking her to, Gus?"

"Mama," I hiss.

She flings her hand out at me, rolling her eyes.

"Straight to Junior's place. I promise. He's out of practice. He called and said he's home waiting for her."

"Alright now." The sun beats down on us while Mama brushes her eyes against his body.

"This is my last born, Gus. My baby."

"Junior did tell me."

"I hope he told you I'm a gun owner, too."

"Mama!"

Gus' smile doesn't fall.

He reaches out and wraps his fingers around her wrists. "He told me a heap of tings, but the most important ting he told me was that I must always convene with the queen of this castle before I put the likkle lady in my backseat."

That makes me smile, just like his phone call did.

The wrinkles on Mama's forehead soften. She pulls her wrists from his hands and pats them. The tiny "fine" she pushes out is her last stamp of approval.

I hurry toward the back door before she changes her mind and when the smell of leather hits me, so do the weird tingles in my stomach.

Gus climbs back inside behind the wheel. "Alright, likkle one, buckle up back there. I don't want any mishaps."

"Yes, sir," I mutter, pulling the seatbelt across my body as Mama waves at us through the tinted window.

It's quiet inside the truck except for the low hum of jazz

music. My body sways with the truck when he swerves to miss another pothole at my neighborhood's entrance.

He sucks his teeth. "Rassclaat roads."

I giggle to myself, holding onto the door until he glances at me in the rear-view mirror.

"You got a smile like Angie's."

That's how he breaks the ice between us.

"Oh, yeah? What kinda smile did she have?"

I saw it in pictures, but according to Mama, they didn't do it justice.

"You haffi see it in person. Meh cyah describe it. She had one uh dem once in a lifetime smiles."

His accent grows stronger and muddles the words, but that makes riding with him better.

"Are you gassin' me, Mr. Gus?"

His laughter rises above the jazz. "No, likkle lady. Me ah tell yuh why de bwoy see home inna yuh."

I laugh off his comment because I don't know what to make of it. It sounded like a mysterious Jamaican proverb.

"So yuh hangin' out wit Junior tonight?" He sighs. "Wha yuh tink bout that troublemaker, anyway?"

I don't have an answer for him because I think a lot about Ace—a lot that I couldn't say out loud.

"Yuh wan know a secret?" He hisses under his breath and swerves to miss another pothole.

"Uh..." I nod, leaning forward. "Sure."

"Meh bring him to his first day of basketball practice every season back in Chatsworth."

My insides flutter at the thought of a little Ace with the first day jitters.

"Where's Chatsworth?"

"Oooh..." he drums his fingers across the steering wheel. "A nice, quiet suburb deep in de San Fernando Valley."

"That's where Ace grew up?"

"Nah. Lottta famous people send their pickney to Pittman Academy—a private school. Celebrities don't live in Chatsworth though. Dem hire us poor layman fi drive dem pickney from Calabasas and Brentwood and fight up wit de traffic so dey kids can play ball wit AW's son and take Home Economics with Cedric the Entertainer's daughter. Issa place for them to be wit their own people." He sucks his teeth again, taking a turn. "Junior had plenty friends there and played alongside a heap uh youth dem. Plenty in the NBA now, but that bwoy can play circles around all uh dem still."

Even with all the past tense words Gus keeps blurting, I still can't picture Ace frowning—only him smiling and calling me "kid."

"You know, even when that bwoy got his car, him still ah make me bring him to his first practice. Says it's our tradition." Gus chuckles. "Ah meh even bring him to his first practice at UCLA. That's his daddy's alma-mater, yuh know?"

"Shoot... all real-deal basketball fans know that, Mr. Gus."

He laughs. "Hey, meh just wan'na know who de bwoy have in meh backseat."

"Basketball is a religion in my house."

The Williams *are* a religion in my house.

He laughs harder and then settles down as we glide onto the highway and traffic stops.

"Meh hate dis damn traffic," he mutters under his breath to himself until he finds my eyes again in the rearview mirror. "That's ah strange place dat, you know?"

"Where?"

"UCLA." He scratches his salt and pepper head. "Then

again, ah guess any place like that seem strange *and* exciting fi a black boy."

"What you mean?"

"Ah... nuttin ah chat me ah chat. Sometimes meh wish meh could go back in time and wave him back to the car after he buss out dat backdoor onto campus with dat smile he always smiling. Tell him to let me bring him back home to his mudda."

I see Ace's smile again. His stark white teeth and the pink hue of his lips that surround them.

"Anyway..." He sighs as traffic inches forward. "Junior told meh a lot while sitting in dat backseat travelin' to practice, but him words neva traveled outside these four doors."

"Oh yeah? Stuff like what?"

"Aha! Nice try! Meh cyah tell yuh dem ting dey." He taps the side of his head. "Dis ah ship of secrets. Anyone who ride in dat backseat 'ave their own treasure chest up here."

"Even me?" I smile.

"Even you, meh dear." Traffic clears and the car glides for another few miles before he hits the brakes again. "So, yuh ready to put your first valuable inside yuh chest?"

I glance out the window.

The city bustles around me. I hope I'm sitting in the same seat Ace sat in on his rides to his first days of practice. I close my eyes because I think I smell him underneath the leather and I think I've taken a sip of the Kool-Aid now.

"He's a legend," I utter. "That's what I think about him."

Gus howls out a hoot and claps his hands. "Respect! Respect!"

Legend feels safer than the other words he makes me want to yell to the world about him.

Gus turns the jazz back up, and I look at my phone, opening Twitter.

He exits off the highway as I scroll past Chelsea venting about Blythe's hoarder-like tendencies, Bryson's musings about the pre-sales he scored to Splashtown, and Ace.

I gulp.

"Yuh want de window down?" Gus asks, looking at me through the rear-view mirror with a grin.

"Yea—yeah."

He must've heard me dry-heaving over Ace's last subtweet.

@AceWilliamsJr 30m

Sent the car for The Kid. You know it's a special delivery 'cause we locked in.

Six hundred comments. One thousand retweets. Three-thousand likes.

The rest of the world is deciphering his subtweets using Dough's lyrics just like I am.

I fumble with the phone and put it to sleep as we glide through the busy streets of Upper Kirby. Gus makes a sharp turn and I'm gulping again at the sight those retweeters and commenters didn't have—their @AceWilliamsJr dressed down in fleece shorts, a vintage Lakers t-shirt, and more expensive ass sneakers that makes my crazy ass body swoon.

"Looks like yuh troublemaking Prince Charming awaits yuh," Gus mumbles with a chuckle as he pulls up to the curb.

"I don't think Prince Charming looks like that."

"Forgive meh." He laughs harder. "Your LA legend awaits yuh."

"That's more like it."

I lean forward, ignoring the wild thumping between my legs at the sight of Ace standing in front of a high-rise. The surrounding streets hum with folks walking their dogs, deep in conversation on outdoor patios at the surrounding restaurants or just heading to whatever's at their fingertips.

Ace tosses up his fingers at the truck and I lean forward over the middle console because my body doesn't care that I look like a fool—it missed his face. And my brain is on some other shit if it thinks it's going to overthink my ass into the backseat while he talks to Gus.

Gus rolls the window down before he pulls to a stop at the curb.

"Took you long enough," Ace says, poking his head through the driver's side window.

Gus sucks his teeth. "Cha meh take as long as traffic allowed...*bwoy.*"

I giggle. "I knew you was an OG."

Ace laughs along with me and reaches over Gus, gripping my nose between his index and middle finger and shaking it. His fingers smell like earth and weed.

"Here." He thrusts his other hand through the window toward Gus. "If you get caught by the Chief, you ain't get it from me."

My eyes grow at the joint dangling between his fingers.

"Yeah... yeah." Gus nods, snatching it. "Better not be no mid neither."

"Nigga." Ace cocks his lips to the side. "And you bet not been hitting them corners hard with my package in the backseat either."

"If so, yuh *good gyal* would've told by now."

I don't understand Gus' fast words until Ace's response bellows throughout the car.

"Oh, for sure. She know better. Just like she knows it ain't no substitute for daddy's spaceship. I thought you knew she was a Porsche girl?"

Now, my body is *real* hot because I'm finally home and I get to hear the slick shit he types on Twitter in real life.

He pulls out of the window and fans his hand toward himself. "C'mon, kid."

"Thanks, Gus!" I grin, climbing back into the backseat.

"No problem, Phat. Stay outta trouble."

I must look a foolish sight to Gus—giddy with hungry eyes. Meanwhile, Ace is so laid back I would've thought he was high if it weren't for his white eyeballs when he yanks the backdoor open.

I lean forward, but he doesn't let me past him. His eyes stroke my face in the same way it did back at Uptown Nails and I *think* I can read his mind today. He's telling me to settle down, but there's also something else going on up there.

"No more Twitter," he states in a matter-of-fact tone, as if we haven't been using it as a secret means of communication all week.

"Huh?"

"I said, 'no more Twitter,'" he repeats, reaching over me to snatch my backpack from the backseat.

It sounds like he's speaking a foreign language and my brain starts re-analyzing the subtweets I've already over-analyzed the entire week we've been playing. Because what the hell did I miss? I followed the rules—no naming and shaming, no face no case, tweeting and deleting—just straight subliminal vibes.

I stumble onto the sidewalk into his solid chest.

"Excuse me? I'm not understanding?"

He reaches around me, slamming Gus' door and tossing my backpack over his shoulder. "I'm not repeating myself again."

Gus hits the gas and eases away from the curb, leaving me in a fog of confusion.

Ace gives him a wave and then curls his arm around my stomach.

I scoff, stopping in the middle of the sidewalk. "Nigga, you can't tell me what to do."

I want to rescind my residency on Planet Ace, STAT, but Ace doesn't care.

He drops his arm and leaves me on the sidewalk, strolling to a side door connected to the building. I already want his calloused hands back on my stomach, but I'm supposed to be pissed off. That isn't how he's wired my brain though.

A white couple and their bulldog sidestep me as he stands at the door.

"Bring your ass inside." He rolls his eyes. "Got all these people in our business."

Damn him and that "our" shit. I hate and like that word just like I hate and like him, but I'm CeCe's child, so my feet stay planted on the sidewalk.

He leans back against the door with a lazy smile and slides my backpack off his shoulder.

"Your phone going off." He chuckles, pulling the bag apart and digging his hand inside. "This bet not be one of your lil' Twitter fans. Now I gotta tell them you in trouble and can't tweet because you're a chronic over-sharer."

It was probably Chelsea responding to my curious text from that morning about Bryson and what I should do if he tries to kiss me for the second time in our lives—*hypothetically,* of course.

When he pulls out my phone, I power walk across the sidewalk like he wants.

"Ace!" I hiss. "Gimme my phone."

I slam my body into his without thinking, and my hives come back in droves. They're so overwhelming that I forget why I'd been barreling toward him. He moves as quick as he does on the court and tangles his arms back around my stomach, pulling us inside.

"Calm down," he mutters into my ear. "Why I have to do all that to get you to come here?"

"Because..." I hold on to the rest of my shameful words.

"Because what?" He peels his arms from around me and glides towards an elevator at the end of the hallway we're standing in. "I guess you can tweet me and tell me next week if I let you log back on Twitter."

"You still on that?"

"Hell yeah," he calls from over his shoulder as the elevator dings. "Twitter ain't your diary."

There's a difference between getting in trouble by Ace than it is by Marcus. Marcus never banned me from any socials, took my phone for doing something I shouldn't and his chastising *never* made my nipples hard. Shit, nobody has ever done that.

Ace bunches my cellphone and backpack in his hands and walks into the elevator with me on his heels.

"I never said it was my diary." I cross my arms and try not to stare at the digital keypad he taps a key fob against.

I was so focused on Gus, Twitter, and everything about Ace that I didn't realize my innocent hypothetical situation I texted to Chelsea could come to reality at any moment because I was *here*, at his place. I've never been to a guy's place alone except Bryson's.

"But you overshare on there like it is."

"If you don't want the world to catch on to me and you shooting the shit with subtweets, then just say that."

He laughs as the elevator shoots up to the fifty-sixth floor. "You got our life all wrong."

"Here you go with this 'our' shit. Like *I* said, if you don't want people to know we cool or whatever." I flick my hands up. "Then I will gladly fall back."

The small of my back grows warm like I'm in an ambush. When the elevator dings again and I step forward, my t-shirt digs into the skin on my stomach as he yanks me back inside.

"Let me go, Ace—"

"You can keep cappin' to yourself if it makes you feel better. I don't care what people think about me or who I talk to." His palm slams against the elevator's keypad, forcing the doors closed. "You're the one that cares."

I do?

"Shit, it ain't like I blame you for caring. I'm not exactly Mr. Popular."

It's the first time he's ever hinted at the elephant standing between him and the world. I hear the regret in his voice, just like I heard it in Mama's while she studied pictures of her and Angie.

"Don't talk like that," I blurt.

He flashes a smile full of pity at me and stoops down to my ear. "Don't tweet our business like that."

I smell the alcohol on him now. It's an enticing tart scent because he makes everything alluring—especially grown-man shit.

He tugs harder on my t-shirt, pulling me back into him. "My problem is with you telling the world shit you should only tell me."

My gut doesn't sink like it should. I can't hear all the noise that he carried from Los Angeles to Houston—all the talk about what he did to *that girl*. I just hear him.

"'You ever ask God why certain shit happens? Like, would changing shit in the past have any effect on the present?'" He repeats my week old tweet verbatim.

He doesn't rehash the others I went back and deleted, but I know he knows them word for word too.

"There's nothing that can change what's happening in the present. Everything that happens in this fucked up life is out of our control, but you don't need to stress over that. Okay?" he says. "I'm *supposed* to tell you that. Not some fuck nigga on Twitter and not in a lame ass subtweet. So, you can take your L now or later—either way you gon' have to take it, because I'm tired of Twitter right now so we putting it on ice."

That urge from the nail-shop slams into me at full force.

I tug my t-shirt out of his hold.

I want to throw my arms around his neck and explain myself again, but I've learned some shit about Ace in these few weeks we've been living on the same planet. My excuses aren't what he wants right now and maybe, *just* maybe, that's what that girl from Los Angeles didn't get about him. It's a fucked up thing to think, but that's the type of hold I realize he has on girls like me—Pavlov girls. We're the ones who can still find beauty in a guy like him.

"I understand." I nod, crossing my arms over my midsection where his hands were. "It's just some things I can't talk to my friends about. I guess Twitter is the one place where I can get it off my chest."

His face softens. "Then get it off and give it to me, not the world."

"So you want my thoughts and now you want my problems?" I huff. "You're insane."

"Don't you know that's how things work on Planet Ace?

You created the place." He scoffs and his hand falls from the keypad. "I'm just living there."

The elevator doors open again.

"Here..." He pushes my cellphone toward me and I grasp it. "That nigga texting you."

"Wh—"

He grips my t-shirt again and curls it around his fingers, using it to twirl me around into the condo we've been arguing outside of—*his* condo.

"C'mon. You was supposed to be up here forty-five minutes ago. You know how much forty-five minutes costs us, kid?"

My mouth opens, but all I do is breathe in his scent that's in all the nooks and crannies of the place he calls home. It's the exact type of place me and Mama like to drool over. Thanks to HGTV, we know all the intricate terms— exposed brick, stainless steel appliances, an open floor plan and so much damn light God himself may as well have cast it through the windows.

"Damn," I utter.

Rap music thumps from speakers I can't see, and the space is so big that clacking heels echo throughout it.

"*Oh-kay*, thickums. You cute."

The owner of the click-clacking heels is tall, skinny, and possibly a Pavlov girl.

I screw my face up, just in case she is. "Thickums?"

"Yeah, you thick." She smirks.

She stops in front of us with a smile that's confusing. Her eyes are the color of ocean water with a tinge of red in their whites. They drag along my chest like Bryson's and I recognize her. She looks just like she did under Ace's arm in that prom picture Black Twitter went ballistic over. Too bad Chelsea isn't here to see that her lips are real.

"I sent you the right sizes?" Ace asks from behind me, kneading his knuckles into the small of my back.

The sweat disappeared, but my hives are still there and now I know what that weird feeling is in my stomach when I think about him. His knuckles stroke my back while I replay the words we exchanged. It's hard trying to keep up with him in his world, especially when he's giving me something no other boy has—butterflies.

"Tal vez, tal vez no." She shrugs. "I won't know until she gets from up under you, *Papi*."

Papi.

That's the word that confirms my suspicions. She's definitely a Pavlov girl—a leggy, Spanish-speaking one that's insinuating she's going to stay here with us.

"Hold up—hold up. What's going on?" I frown. "I thought I came to chill with you? Who is she and what the hell you needed to tell her what size I wear for?"

"Cree came to help us get ready," he replies. "We have somewhere to go tonight."

The sweat comes back, prickling my lower back.

"We do?"

"Yeah—a gala. You ever been to a gala, kid?"

CHAPTER ELEVEN

Lourdes

Cree knows more about my body than I do.

"According to Kibbe, you have a theatrical romantic body type. It's the sexiest—soft arms and legs."

I glance at my soft body in Ace's floor-length mirror, searching for the romance she's drooling over. My breasts are crying for a break from the push-up bra I shimmied into this morning trying to be cute, and I forgot to put the laundry in the dryer last night, so I have on period panties. It's a tacky combination for my first Netflix and Chill with a dude.

"Take your bra off too, babe," she calls from over her shoulder, rifling through a massive rolling wardrobe at the side of Ace's unmade bed.

She left the door to the bedroom cracked and his voice competes with the music while he talks on the phone.

"You want him?" Cree asks, making my heart jump.

"Huh?"

"You want Ace?" she smirks, lifting an arched brow. "To come help you."

She glides around his space in her strappy heels. Pretty girls like her are either real nice-nasty like Brandy or just plain nasty like the girls Marcus likes to fuck when him and Chelsea beef. I can't tell which side Cree falls on. I just know she's *definitely* a Pavlov girl.

"To come help me do what?"

"Help you get the bra off."

I throw a hand on my hip. "Look, me and him not doing nothing together, if that's what you tryna get out of me with these little questions and shi—"

"Chill..." She chuckles, walking back to me and holding a dark blue dress against my body.

"You probably should do that. You the one asking all these ridiculous ass questions."

She laughs harder, pulling back. "I just asked if you wanted him to come help you. I know how uncomfortable it can be to have a stranger see your body, so I—"

"So your solution is to suggest for him to come?"

"I don't swim in those waters, Lourdes."

"I told you, it's *Phat,* and swim in what waters?"

She snorts out a tiny laugh and swipes a tongue across her glossy bottom lip. "I like pussy. Ace is just the homie."

"Oh," I squeak.

My brain and face are never in sync, so my eyes get big at her suggestive comments about my body and my mouth is about to run before she stops it.

"You're good. I wouldn't disrespect Ace like that." Her eyelids dip as Ace pushes into the room with a thick-bottomed glass and a blunt that he hands to her.

I wait on him to gasp and run out like Bryson did once

when he stayed over and burst into my room by mistake, but Ace just strolls up to us.

I keep hearing all the shit he's talked since I been with him—putting Twitter on ice, fancy galas, and the way he called Planet Ace *mine*. All of it makes me cover my stomach and shift under his gaze.

Cree lights up and the nastiness I thought I saw in her eyes reveals itself for what it really is—concentration. She's trying to turn me into that romantic Kibbe shit she talked about.

A cloud of smoke billows through her nostrils as she nods her head to the bass thumping throughout the condo.

"Tu bebe es tímida." She nods at Ace.

"Sí, estoy trabajando en ellao," he replies in that swaggy Barcelonan-nanny taught accent I've replayed a hundred times in my head since that day at the bookstore.

I've probably came to it just as many times.

Cree curls her hand around mine, peeling it from my skin and running her finger across the ugly welts Ace always induces. "That looks dumb painful."

"They don't hurt that much," I mutter.

Ace slides onto the floor behind us with his legs cocked open and his back against the foot of the bed. "You sure about that?"

I feel like a skittish animal at the zoo. I curse all of God's light I admired because it's showing Ace all my imperfect parts—my soft stomach, thighs, ass, and those hives he's in charge of.

"She need another fit, Cree," he says, staring at my reflection in the mirror. "¿Cuánto por otra hora?"

"Depends..." Cree sighs, deep in thought. "What's the occasion?"

Our eyes meet in the mirror, and he picks the cup up, smiling over the rim. "Her first date."

"*Now* what are you talking about?" I roll my eyes. "Just because I never been to a gala before don't mean I never been on a date."

Offense is my automatic response to everything that makes me uncomfortable. I'm sweaty, itchy and now I think he's insinuating this gala is my first date. It *is,* but I can't admit it in front of Cree, no matter how much of a lesbian she claims to be.

"You still haven't looked at your phone, huh?"

"No, what're you talking about?"

"Bryson texted you, talking about he wants you and him to hit Splashtown together this weekend." He snorts. "I guess that means he wants to take you out on a date. I don't speak basic. So..."

"Ohhh," Cree sings, batting her long lashes. "Who's Bryson? What's Splashtown?"

"Un niño pequeño." Ace flings his hand out, pinching his index and thumb together. "Y una fiesta de fraternidad."

"¿La estás dejando ir?"

"Es tan curiosa como tímida. ¿No recuerdas tu primer año en la universidad?"

"Shit, no. It's a blur." Cree smirks. "Entonces, ¿qué va a hacer Papi mientras ella explora?"

"English." I roll my eyes with a gasp. "Please."

Cree smirks and takes another hit of the blunt before passing it to him. I wait for him to break another one of Coach Williams' zero-tolerance policies. Bryson finally gaining the courage to ask me out isn't at the forefront of my mind—Ace and this strange world he lives in is.

Cree's red-rimmed eyes stroke my face, and she smiles

bigger. "I was telling Ace that you must be a real good girl. He said you were and you're pretty too."

"Right." I snort. "Girl, I'm from Texas. I know when a bitch is talking shit in Spanish."

Cree and Ace howl out wild laughs. The humor doesn't hit me in the same way because I'm the only sober one as usual.

"I'll give ya'll a minute to sort this out. I have a call to make," she says, backing out of the bedroom and from the middle of another one of me and Ace's impending battles.

When she tugs the door closed, my hands go back over my middle while he breaks another one of Coach Williams' zero-tolerance policies. His pink lips cover the end of the blunt and I remember exactly why I hated his fine ass.

The wait for this one was worth it.

Ace

"CREE CAN'T DRESS you like that, you know?"

"Like what?" Phat asks, shifting her body under my gaze.

"With you being uncomfortable."

There's nothing about her that reminds me of LA. She's not like the girls there that know what it means when a man says, "I'm taking you somewhere." She even packed a cute overnight bag like we were going to have a sleepover because she doesn't have any expectations of me or any other man and I don't like it.

"Well, I'm half-naked in front of you and some chick you went to prom with back in high school who acts like...like..." she sputters, and I wait even though I know what she's getting at. "Like a girl you messed with, even though she claims she's a lesbian."

"I didn't know you cared about the girls I messed with."

"I don't." She frowns, like she's trying to convince herself and me.

The truth of it all is that she's unsure of me because she's still listening to the outside world and the things they say about me. Mom says it's what little ladies struggle with most—learning how to exist in a world that's always telling them how to think, dress, and act.

That realization makes me take the biggest toke of the blunt I can muster. When the cloud of smoke dissolves in front of my face, Phat's standing behind it—self-conscious, agitated, and hungry in a cheap ass bra and another pair of flowery panties I need to replace.

"Stop being weird and come here." I cock my head back. "Let me talk to you."

She huffs and crawls between my legs because I finally cracked her. When her back touches my chest for the first time, I get higher.

"How much will another forty-five minutes cost us?" she asks.

Us.

That makes my hands fall on her soft stomach and stroke the little red welts that are always there when they shouldn't be. "What you need forty-five more minutes for?"

"'Cause y'all blowin me."

I chuckle, letting my head fall to the side.

"Now tell me how much," she adds.

"Well... the kid's frustrated today. She had to get picked up by a strange man after taking care of Mom all day, sit in Houston traffic, got in trouble for telling Twitter our business, got asked out on her first date... and now... she's just tired from trying to control the vibe. Most important, though, *she's hungry.*"

I knead her stomach with my free hand while the blunt I shouldn't have burns in my other.

She lets out a tiny yawn and pulls her knees up to her chest. Having her so close while I'm lifted isn't good because I know we can't go back to how things were. I won't let us.

"By the time Cree finishes taking care of you, it'll be twenty-four hours since she landed in Houston. So hourly rates turn into daily rates. That's two-thousand dollars for a day spent fucking with us, kid."

She nods and closes her eyes as if the wasted two-thousand dollars is my punishment for pushing her limits and tricking her into being my brain for the night. This is version two of her—the one that gives me hell.

"And we have to tip her, too." I grip her braids this time to peek at the welt on her neck. "Can't forget that shit. She's a new business owner."

"How you end up being friends with her anyway?" she asks, pushing her head into my chest and forcing my hand away from her hair.

Cree's voice grows louder in the living room. We're holding her up from getting back to Javier, but she won't say it out loud to me. She never does. After everything that happened, she tiptoes between us, keeping us as separate as she can.

"I'm waiting..." she sings. "You took my entertainment away. The least you can do is tell me about your lil' prom date."

"Me and her brother Javier were cool first. We met at a basketball camp my Pops put on when we were younger. He ended up playing ball with me at UCLA."

Her body tenses, and she lets out a tiny hum.

"Me and him don't talk anymore, but I stayed cool with Cree after..."

"After what?"

"After... things changed."

I don't know how to describe that time in my life. I don't think Pops does either because the change happened so quick—in one night, to be exact.

"Hm... what about your other friends?" She ignores my vague words and picks at a piece of lint from the rug Mom picked out last summer.

"What other friends?"

"All the ones Sunny was talking about."

"They were never my friends."

She twists her neck, looking up at me with wrinkled eyebrows. "But you have at least one friend besides Cree, right?"

"Ain't no real friends in my life. It's always been a bunch of takers around—people that want, but don't give. So, it's just me and Cree."

"She's not a taker?"

"Nah... she just wanna see me live."

"And you mean to tell me you never *fucked* her?"

I smile, squeezing the pudge at the bottom of her stomach until she pushes my hand away.

"What you know about fucking?"

"Enough to know what two people look like after they did it."

A deep laugh shakes my chest. "*Your* ass better not be fucking."

That same sheepish expression she had back in the bookstore covers her face. "Shut up... just tell me."

"I *wanted* to fuck her."

To spite Javier. To even the score. To take something precious from him, like he did to me.

"Until I realized we liked the same type of females."

I still remember the car ride to prom where our lips almost touched until Cree big-faced me and threw up all the shit we drank out of the car window.

"I like girls, Ace," she said, wiping her face. *"I like girls, but Javi and Mama don't know that."*

They still didn't, so I hold on to her secret like she holds on to mine.

"Ha!" Phat laughs, closing her eyes. "I know what type of female that is."

I know what she's getting at and today isn't a day that I can ignore it because version two of her likes to push my limits.

"You don't know shit about what I like."

Nobody did. They only knew what the media told them. Never mind that I was a black bitch connoisseur. It didn't matter the country I was in, I'd find them with no trouble—even in white-washed countries like Sweden where they went crazy over my accent and the creative positions I could bend their brown bodies in. None of that matters when a leggy blonde cries foul though.

My hands roam back to her braids.

Her eyes pop open as if she's been waiting for this moment.

By now I've forgotten about the Maui Waui Cree brought me from back home.

Phat pushes away from me and twists her body around so she's on her knees in front of me with her breasts spilling out of her bra and her braids billowing over her bare arms.

There's a tinge of red in her eyes from the secondhand

smoke. I see the questions about LA swirling in them just like I saw fear in Marcus'.

"So what do you like, then?"

I pick up my glass. "You—just like this, behaving for me."

"You didn't answer my question," she whispers. "What kind of girls you like?"

My body sags as I mull over her multi-layered question she doesn't even realize is layered. "I like women."

"Okay, *women*." She rolls her eyes. "What kind of women do you like?"

"Perfect ones that know what it means to trust me."

"Trust?"

"Yup." I swallow another mouthful of the burning tequila. "That's it."

Her eyebrows furrow.

"So, all they have to do is trust you?" she asks as her eyes skirt away from mine. "And that's what you like?"

I nod, taking another swig of the tequila to the head.

I savor the bitter taste and the way it soothes those ugly ass memories I left in LA and rearranges them so they hurt less.

When I don't answer, her hands crawl onto my thighs and she leans forward. "So how you get them to trust you?"

I look at the blunt burning between my fingers while she tries to settle her curiosity about shit she shouldn't worry about.

"Why?"

"Because..."

Her nails scraping against my thigh gives me her answer. She wants confirmation that I'm building her up and teaching her to trust me like she thinks I did to the women in my past.

"You're confused," I reply, reaching out to grab the front clasp holding her breasts in her bra. "I don't have to get them to do anything, because it's already in them."

Her breasts fall out as Cree's voice sneaks underneath the bedroom door. They're nothing but a handful and look exactly how I imagined. Earthy colored nipples that excite my tastebuds. Areolas that wrap around them in perfect circles. Tiny bright streaks of stretch marks gliding down their tops that I can taste.

She rushes to cover them.

"Don't do that," I say, nudging her hand away.

She drops it and that makes the insides of my stomach fumble around. "Never do that."

Our eyes lock while I fight a losing battle with my brain.

"Why not?" She breathes out.

"Because I didn't tell you to."

"That's it?"

"I didn't know I needed to say anything else. You trying to control the vibe again..."

Her bottom lip trembles in a way that tells me she hears the warning in my words.

I reach out and curl a finger under the dangling strap on her shoulder, pushing it down. "Sit back. I wanna see you."

She pulls away from my thighs and sits against her heels. The soft flesh of her stomach dangles over the band of her panties while her bra hangs from her arms.

Her eyes dart from mine.

"You like your body?" I ask, laying the blunt across the top of the glass.

She shrugs. "Sometimes I like what I see and sometimes I don't. It depends on the day... or whatever. Why?"

I laugh. "What's the 'or whatever?'"

"Nothin," she mutters. "Forget it."

"Depends on the dude you like at the time and what the girls he's fucking look like?" I finish for her. "That's what you mean? That's why you keep asking me all these questions about the women I like?"

A sigh flies out of her lips.

Cree says I should get a PhD in women, but something like that would bore me. She never wants to admit that I've studied enough of them to surpass that—even more than her.

"This is the part where you answer me." I smile.

"Yea—h yeah." She rolls her eyes. "That's exactly what I meant."

"And the dude you like gives you those, right?" I point to the bulging red dot on her stomach.

She tries to scrape her nail against it, but I catch her hand before she can touch the skin.

"Don't do that."

"Is there an 'ever' that goes with that, too?"

"Nah...*this one* is just for now. I'm trying to see something."

Her sweat coats my hand. "See what?"

"All of you. Since I'm the dude that gives you those nasty hives." I swallow. "They're even on my favorite places —your neck, your stomach... right there in the middle of your left thigh."

She squirms.

"We missing one though." I squeeze her hand and drop it on her right breast. "I want one right here. Can I have that?"

The way her red skin rises beneath our fingers and prickles to the surface is like magic. A tiny gasp escapes her lips and one fights to escape mine because I've done some shit to women but never anything like *this*.

"That's perfect."

"What you mean, it's perfect?" she mutters, looking down at our intertwined hands. "They won't stop popping up."

"That's the perfect thing about them." I pull my hand from hers. "Now stop pouting and tell me something good."

Her eyes dart to the glass of tequila and then around my bedroom like she's taking me and my space in all over again. As soon as my back touches the foot of the bed, she chokes out the words, "I—I think I wanna taste you again."

All the pet names, praises, and filthy words I want to hurl her way get caught in the back of my throat because for the first time I realize how long it's been since I had a woman propped in front of me and begging. Even if Phat's begging is basic, it still makes my dick stiffer than I ever imagined it could get, so my brain stops and my dick takes over.

The music pulsing through the speakers gets louder and I know it's Cree nudging Phat. She's trying to bridge the gap between me and her so she can catch a red eye to Javier in Vegas.

My dick tells me it's now or never and I don't have time to get onto Phat for *thinking* around me before my middle and ring finger dive into the tequila.

"Open your mouth," I rasp.

And she does because it's been too many days since she had my taste in her mouth—five, according to her last subtweet before she came home.

@babphat04 1d

Finally going home after five long ass days. Sheesh.

I shove my fingers past her lips.

They're too big for her mouth and too calloused for her

tongue, but she's happy they're that way. I see it in her drooping shoulders as she sucks the tequila off them.

As soon as her eyes sag, there's a soft tap against the bedroom door that makes them spring open, but a gentle slap against the welt on her left thigh makes them fall again.

"Chill..." I mutter. "You been talking about home all week, so enjoy it."

"Ace..." Cree calls out. "Uncle Ason keeps calling."

She doesn't wait around for me to reply and as soon as her heels patter away from the door; I push my digits farther into Phat's mouth than I should. Her molars dig into the side of my fingers and her tonsils tickle the tips of them.

I swallow at the same time she chokes.

"Act right for Cree," I mutter while her eyes light up. "If you're a good girl, maybe I'll give Twitter back."

CHAPTER TWELVE

Lourdes

There's something wrong.

I don't think I'm supposed to like a boy's fingers in my mouth. I can hear Chelsea getting on my head just like she got on Brandy's, but the weight of Ace's fingers still sits on my tongue. She won't understand how good they tasted gliding down my throat or how the gruff voice he talks in makes me do crazy things.

"What the *fuck*..." I mutter, staring at my clothed reflection in the mirror I've been in front of all afternoon.

I look too good in this expensive ass piece of fabric Cree wrapped me in and I'm craving a boy's fingers. I want their texture, their smell and even their taste in the back of my throat again while he reminds me of the shit he taught me in my driveway.

There's an open valley down my chest where the gown's fabric splits. The tag on it says *Dior*. I don't know what to make of that or the double Cs on the clutch Ace tossed on the bed after he zipped me into my gown. I've never seen real Dior or Chanel in my life. It all even smells expensive.

"Lourdes!" he yells.

There's no urgency in his voice, but my body moves like there is. I'm still trying to get used to someone saying my real name so much—especially a boy that can say it in as many ways as he can. I'm worse off than I was before because now I'm stuck on this planet with him and I like it no matter how much shit Chelsea talks about what he might've done.

When I round the corner to the living room, he and Cree stand in the kitchen talking in hushed whispers. She tugs the tailored suit jacket he has on and I finally understand what rappers like Dough mean when they say they don't need a stylist. The only person Cree came to dress was me, because after twenty-one years of being rich, Ace can drape himself in a designer outfit with his eyes closed and look like sex and money rolled into one.

He smiles at me with bloodshot eyes. "Fix me something—"

"Nah. You're good for the night. Dior does a shit job of covering the smell of 1942." Cree pries the glass out of his hand. "Come here, Phat. Let me show you something before Gus gets here."

I walk up to them as she yanks his arm into her stomach.

She glances at me. "You ever put on cuff links before?"

Instead of blurting out the first smart-aleck response I can think of, I shake my head, heeding to Ace's warning.

Shiny little pins stick up from his sleeves and he's smiling at me like he was when he stuck his fingers in my mouth.

"Let me show you," she mutters. "It's easy."

She weaves the links in and out of his sleeve's cuffs real easy, like she said.

The air is thick between the two of them. Whatever they were whispering about before I came in the kitchen has them looking at each other like star-crossed lovers instead of the homies they keep claiming to be.

"You gon' send me the invoice or you want cash?" he asks, slurring his words just enough to make my palms moist.

"Cash."

"You gon' be back in time for Javier?"

"I don't know, Ace." She sighs. "It's not a big deal."

"It's his first game of the pre-season. That's a big deal."

"Okay... and there'll be others."

"But there'll never be another first pre-season game for him," he mutters, smacking his lips.

Pre-season game. First. Basketball Camp.

Now I know the Javier that's been lurking through tonight is the rookie from the most recent draft that everybody's been impressed with, except Marcus. He's something like a hometown hero for Los Angeles—born and bred to die on his home turf with his home team. He rode the bench in that game against Villanova where Ace shot that buzzer beater. People are always saying he's everything Ace was supposed to be, and his sister is here in Houston, fussing over a boy I hate and like.

Her eyes dart around.

There's something else wrong, and she knows it.

"Lourdes..." Ace says while his eyes dash from the glass he tried to hand me to a bottle on the granite countertop.

"Yeah?" I squeak.

"I can finish this." He twists his left arm where the

unopened cuff links dangle. "Go get Cree her money from my nightstand."

Their eyes shoot daggers at each other and damn if it don't seem like I'm in the middle of two lovers fighting. She drops his arm and stalks toward his bedroom, with me following behind her.

When she pushes inside, she stands back.

"Look..." I hold up my hands, surrendering to their weird friendship. "I don't know where it is."

Her face softens, and she chokes out a quiet giggle, shaking her head. "It's here..."

She walks over to the nightstand on the side of his bed and squats in front of it.

I stay by the door because I know how Marcus is about these types of things. I've been his sister for eighteen years and I ain't never taken it upon myself to dig through his wallet.

She tugs the drawer open. "Come see."

"Nah, just get what you need."

"Phat... it's not that serious."

A glass clanks in the kitchen, and she narrows her eyes at the bedroom door. Their silences, lingering stares, and secret arguing reminds me I'm not one of them no matter how many expensive gowns I put on.

"C'mon. Get away from the door."

I move next to her as Ace's phone rings from the kitchen.

"Anything he thinks is important is in here," she mutters while he talks.

"Uh-okay."

The drawer's full of loose papers, wads of cash, a passport, and a picture of Angie. She doesn't look like the Angie from the pictures Mama has stashed away in her bedroom closet. This Angie is frail, with a balding head and her lips against Ace's face. There's an ocean behind them.

Cree's fingers brush against their faces. She's touching everything but the money.

She slams the drawer closed and looks up at me. "Take care of my brother tonight."

He's brother now—not *papi* or *homie*. The word even sounds different coming out of her mouth.

"What you mean? He seems fine to me."

Besides being kind of drunk, kind of high, and a little unsteady.

"That's the biggest lie we tell ourselves about the people we care about," she replies. "He still thinks it's him against the world... and sometimes it is, but Uncle Ason can't see that."

A ball of nerves gets caught in my throat.

I nod with my mouth open. "You—you're not going to take the money?"

"Nah, I can't take money from a man like Ace. He already gives too much of himself to people that don't deserve him." She pops up from the floor. "If you'll excuse me, I have a flight he wants me to catch."

"BOY, you smell like dope, Savauge, and liqu—babygirl?"

That's how Coach Williams greets me after doing a double-take when Ace helps me climb into Gus' backseat.

I force out a smile.

The only people that have ever called me babygirl were Marcus and Mama because of Marshall. I know I smell like dope, Savauge, and liquor too, because Ace keeps finding my stomach and kneading it in his hands like he needs to touch me *right* there to function.

"I—I didn't know you were coming with us tonight," he stutters out while Ace climbs in behind me and slams us into the truck.

Coach Williams fumbles with his cellphone and grabs my limp wrist, tugging it up to look at my dress.

The possibility of coming face to face with him crossed my mind back at Ace's, but I didn't think it'd happen so soon. He sounds and looks a lot different up close. His bald head is shinier and his brown skin is deeper. There are moles around his eyes that I can't see when I watch him on TV.

He whistles, glancing at the clutch Ace carried for me while I struggled through his condo in the heels Cree shoved on my feet. Eventually she decided it was best I put on a pair of Jordans that she pulled from her suitcase before she left for the airport.

"Well, ain't you a sight for sore eyes, chocolate drop."

"Thanks." I shrink into Ace's side as he lets go of my hand.

He's talking to me like we know each other, but that's how it always was growing up. Mama's friends she ain't seen since she was pregnant with me, fussing over how much I grew up when they only ever seen me on her Facebook page, but there's a flicker in Coach Williams' eyes. It's like he *had* seen me as a baby and the nicknames he keeps dropping are names he's called me before.

He leans forward to look at Ace as Gus eases away from the curb and into the congested Friday night traffic. "I thought we talked about this, but it's only seven-thirty and it seems like you already got your mind made up about how tonight will go."

I gulp like he's talking to me and try to catch Gus' eyes in the rearview mirror like I did on the way to Ace's, but he's staring ahead like their words are background noise.

Ace swipes a finger across his nose and stares out the window.

I can't focus on what Coach Williams said because I'm too busy trying to remember the last time I heard Ace's voice. Somehow, it vanished on the way downstairs. I think I heard it last on the elevator ride down to Gus' idling truck.

"Perfect," he said, kneading my stomach as the elevator glided to the first floor. *"Live it up tonight, kid."*

I don't see how I can when his daddy's grilling him while the air in the truck stifles his voice. He even left his easygoing smile with Cree.

"Yeah... a'ight," he says.

There it is—his voice with all of Los Angeles embedded in the words.

"You gon' 'yeah, a'ight' yourself into an early grave one of these days." Coach Williams looks back at his phone. "Addiction is selfish. I ain't raise a selfish man."

Ace drops his head against the headrest and stares at the back of Gus' head.

He swipes his hand across his sagging eyes this time, and the open cuff links on his arm scrape against his cheek.

"Angie would hate this for you. Obsessing over news reports and expensive tequila didn't fix anything back then and it won't now."

Ace flings his head up with wild, red eyes. "Nigga, fu—"

"Your cuff links," I blurt, gripping his hot wrist. "I forgot to fix 'em before we left."

Hot, messy, bubbling family drama floats throughout the truck, but Gus just keeps driving.

I yank Ace's arm into my stomach and fumble over the

cuff links like Cree did in his kitchen. My heart drums against my chest. It's so quiet I think Gus can hear it beating because he turns up the radio to make sure the soft jazz drowns it out.

My eyes flutter up and slam into Ace's face as I finger the cufflink. I feel Coach Williams' hard stare and all the things I can imagine a daddy would say to a son that almost uttered those nasty words out loud. He keeps quiet though.

"Like this, right?" I mutter, pushing the small end of the link through the first hole in his shirt.

He nods, pulling his bottom lip under his teeth.

I try to be as gentle as Cree, even though something so tedious doesn't need gentleness. I pull his arm closer into my stomach, praying he feels the butterflies stroking my insides. It wouldn't shock me if he did because he's seen so much of me—much more than any boy ever had. The way he keeps staring at my fingers fumble over Dior cufflinks makes me want to show him the rest of me he didn't see because Cree was right. I had to take care of him tonight because Coach Williams can't see how fast he's crashing into Earth alone.

The jazz lowers to a soft hum.

"We're 'bout two minutes away from de Hilton Americas, Phat," Gus says, meeting my eyes in the rearview mirror with a smile. "Yuh nearly done?"

RICH PEOPLE PLAY MAKE BELIEVE a lot.

It's like when me and Chelsea used to play barbie dolls in my bedroom closet. We would dress them up in the best clothes Mama found for us at the Goodwill, set up the perfect scenes, and then put them in the wildest scenarios our brains could think of.

"You gotta smile, kid. Unless you wanna be on Getty Images looking weird," Ace whispers in my ear while we stand in front of the Ason Williams' Shooting Stars Gala step and repeat—that's what the white lady that helped me out of Gus' backseat called it—a step and repeat.

It ain't nothing but rich people taking a step, repeating a pose, and doing it again until somebody with an important job whisks them away.

"Please tell me what the fuck a Getty Images is?" I choke out with wide eyes.

He chuckles because rich people are so good at playing make believe that ugly words and potential fights don't exist when they interact with the outside world. All the bad shit that happened in the truck stayed there with Gus and he locked it away in one of his treasure chests.

"A big ass online database of any picture you can think of—even ones of me and you at Ason Williams' Shooting Stars Gala."

"I'm gonna throw up."

"No, you're gonna smile. The best perk about the world hating me is that nobody gives a fuck about me and my frowning lil' lady at my Pops' gala. Even if she is the first lil' lady I ever brought to one."

"I'm really gonna throw up."

"*No*, you gon' smile hella big for that camera over there." He points toward a camera with a blinding flash that knocks the vision out of my eyes for a second.

Those butterflies that had been fluttering in my stomach all night are going extra dumb because they know Ace looks perfect behind me with flushed caramel skin and a modelesque face that's like a magnet for every camera along this stupid step and repeat.

"I can't smile," I grit out.

"Yeah you can..."

"No—"

"What makes you happy?" he asks, talking, smiling, and gripping my middle all at the same time.

His eyes aren't bloodshot anymore because I found a bottle of Visine conveniently sitting at the bottom of my clutch. I doused his eyes with it after fixing his cufflinks before that white lady opened Gus' backdoor screeching about a step and repeat.

"Huh?" I choke out.

Somebody stole my Bubble Yum from my backpack and stuck it next to the eyedrops so I bit it in half and gave the other piece to him as soon as our shoes touched the red carpet. Now it's stale and his unsteady gait is steady again. The flashes from the cameras burn my pupils and I'm sure the makeup Cree piled onto my face will melt before we're even seated, but these screaming people don't care and neither does Ace.

"I asked 'what makes you happy?'" he repeats.

Now I'm too focused on looking weird and being so close to Ace that I feel parts of his body that I shouldn't, so my mouth tilts into one of those half-smile half-frowns.

"What does that have to do with me looking weird?"

"That's the trick to producing a genuine smile for good pictures. Talk to me about the shit that makes you happy." He pushes his lips closer into my ear. "At least that's what Mom used to make me do."

"Smile bigger, gorgeous!" a photographer yells. "Take another step this way, guys."

He waves his hand and shoos us to the side as Coach Williams smiles like an expert next to us.

"Bear claws from Shipley's... that squeaking noise tennis shoes make in the gym..." I babble back. "Mama's dancing... uh... Marcus' gold fronts an—and strawberry cool cups."

He roars out a deep laugh into my ear.

And him.

The boy that I hate and like at the same time makes me happy.

"Beautiful smile!" another photographer yells. "Scoot in closer to her, Ace!"

He digs his fingers into my hips and steps forward.

"Perfect," he whispers. "Mind over matter, kid."

I strain to glance up at him. He's flashing that same smile I see him wearing around campus. For the first time, I realize it doesn't reach his eyes though. It's just a pretty smile with no meaning.

"What makes you happy?" I blurt, trying to pull the taste of a Shipley's bear claw out the Bubble Yum so my mouth won't fold into another weird half-smile half-frown.

He sucks in a light breath and tugs me in closer by the hips, so it's impossible for me to move without taking him with me.

"All the perfect girls Mom used to tell me about existing in one lil' lady."

Rich people don't give you time to think about what they're saying. They just keep going. That same white lady that keeps yelling about the step and repeat waves us down the red carpet where more people hang around, thrusting out microphones to every person who walks by.

"C'mon," Ace mutters, pushing me forward and guiding us away from the flickering cameras.

I've never seen him battle with his body—not on the court, not with a basketball in his hands, not even when he's calling me "kid."

"Ace! D'you have a minute to talk with us?"

But this random reporter makes him pause.

He doesn't stumble or come to a full stop in front of the grinning, sweaty man, but I feel him take the tiniest tug of my hand like he wants to entertain the man's question.

"We're dying to know what's up your sleeve—"

"Greatness is up his sleeve, that's what," Coach Williams' booms from behind us.

When I turn my head around, Ace doesn't smile like he normally would. It doesn't even materialize when the reporter gets googly eyed over Coach Williams.

I don't even know what he would have told the man, because no one knows what's up his sleeve anymore. Ever since that girl did what she did to his reputation, basketball fans didn't find pleasure in sitting around wondering whether Ason Williams' son was gon' give boys hell in The Big Dance again or if he would do what everybody predicted and say, "fuck it," to go dominate in the league.

None of that happens anymore because, like Ace said, it was possible the world hated him and now there's something else wrong: I jumped headfirst into the Ace Kool-Aid and I can't even swim.

CHAPTER THIRTEEN

Ace

Blake Harvey is *thirsty*.

"What the fuck is tuna tartare?" Phat whispers, scooting her chair closer to mine at our table inside the ballroom.

"Exactly what it sounds like." He moves his chair next to hers. "It's literally fresh ahi tuna marinated with a blend of ginger, sesame oil—"

"I ain't gon' hold you. I don't even know what ahi tuna is. If it's not the kind StarKist makes, I couldn't tell you nothing about it."

He cocks his head back, pushing his eyebrows up.

Phat's being Phat and that makes me forget about the reporter's question from the red carpet. Now I'm too focused on her only ever eating StarKist tuna.

"Oh." He nods with a close-lipped smile. "Not a fan of Japanese cuisine?"

"I eat the sushi they sell at H-E-B sometimes." She shrugs, eyeing the tiny plate of tuna tartare in front of her.

"H-E-B?"

"Yeah. You know—the grocery store."

"Damn, they sell sushi at the grocery stores here in Texas?"

"Yeah... I like the spicy crab rolls."

"How could that even be appetiz—"

"A'ight, kid." I smile, yanking her chair as close to mine as it can get. "Put up or shut up."

I take a cracker from the plate and scoop up a hunk of tuna before biting into it. It melts against my tongue, but it doesn't taste like anything. Thirsty sports agents like Blake Harvey always make good shit bland—even if he is the only sports agent in the world still interested in me.

I shove the rest of my cracker toward Phat's lips because she's version one again—my little lady. She doesn't know what tuna tartare is, the addiction I have for reporter's voices, or that Blake Harvey isn't sitting next to her by chance.

"Ace..." she hisses. "Hakeem Olajuwon just walked by. I can't have him seeing me spit out tuna tartare."

"You won't spit it out," I garble out between chews. "You never spit out anything I feed you. You know better."

That makes her sink into my side and Blake watches how much I obsess over her obsessing over my taste no matter how I give it to her.

She opens her mouth without me asking—even if Hakeem Olajuwon might walk by and see how good she acts for me while I push the cracker inside her mouth. Her round nose scrunches and she chews slow enough for me to count each one. We swallow at the same time.

"How was it?" Blake asks.

I roll my eyes away from him, clearing my throat. Phat's eyes bounce from me and then to him as a waitress walks up with a glass of water I didn't ask for.

"It was good," she replies, nudging her elbow into my side like Mom used to when she thought I was acting standoffish.

"Better than H-E-B grocery store sushi and StarKist?"

"Hell yeah."

"More appetizing?"

"Yeah." She shrugs. "It was a'ight."

"So compliments to the chef are in order?" He smirks, picking up his flute of champagne. "He's from Atlanta. That's where that southern flare comes from. We'll never have tuna tartare like this in our lives."

"Oh, nah." She frowns, shaking her head. "Nothing against the chef or anything. Compliments to *The Kid* are in order. Everything always tastes better at home."

I laugh around the rim of my glass at the confusion on Blake's face.

He nods his head my way, acknowledging me for the first time since he slithered into the seat next to her.

"Drinking water tonight, I see. Water's a good choice."

"It's the best choice," I reply, draping an arm around the back of Phat's chair as the lights dim in the ballroom.

My head's not floating from that last shot of 1942 I guzzled before Gus pulled up because Visine, Bubble Yum, water, and outrageous ass expectations could steal the drunkest man's buzz.

"Oh." Phat gasps. "Is that Janet Jackson? Mama ain't gon' believe this shit."

Now I'm just buzzing from the sparkle in Phat's eyes because Janet's supposed to sing a couple of Mom's favorite songs as a favor to Pops.

"Do you think Lockwood was the best choice?"

Questions like that are always how thirsty sports agents get their fix. Back before that "random ass Monday in

September" Mom made them jump through impossible hoops to get to me, but now I'm wide open for them.

As soon as Janet whispers into the mic, Blake scavenges because everyone's focused on her—even Phat. Pops stands by the side of the stage watching our table even though he said he'd let me go about this alone.

"It was the only choice," I reply.

Nobody wanted me after what happened—not even a fucking junior college. If it were up to the NCAA, I'd never touch a basketball again, but they didn't understand how deep shit was. Pops said I was born with a basketball in my hands and Mom was always worried I'd die that way—the same way Pops said Marshall did.

"Is that facts or is that what AW hammered in your head?"

I swipe at my head as sweat pools against my lower back. "I don't know what you talking about, homie."

"I'm talking about LA, *homie*. I'm talking about AW's legacy those white folks tarnished."

His voice sounds like all the reporter's voices I obsess over. They know how to dress up ugly ass words for public consumption—tarnish and legacy. It's all just a fancy way to say I'm a failure.

"Or did *you* tarnish his legacy?"

I shift in my seat and glance at the back of Phat's braids that I twirled before they served our tuna tartare, and he pulled us off our planet.

"I mean, everyone knows this is his desperate attempt to keep your hand on a ball while the world moves on and the rest of your peers sign million dollar NBA contracts—you know, they say Javier got close to eleven mil, right? It's hard for any of us to say what's going on with you for sure though because AW's trained you up so well—to show instead of tell, not to speak even when we all know you have so much to say."

I swallow, searching for that last swig of 1942 I left on the counter back at home.

"I'm just saying—the world misses *The Kid*. Seems like they still call you that." He looks at Phat. "They miss the swag, the cockiness, and all the talk that a legend's son is finally living up to his father's legacy. A lot of 'em wondering if what happened ... even happened."

Those last few words pull Phat from Earth and back to our world. She shifts in her seat and pulls Mom's clutch toward her middle.

"Shit... did *it*?" he adds.

"I—"

"You sure asking a lot of questions for somebody that ain't even in they assigned seat," Phat replies, scrunching her nose as soon as Janet starts "All For You."

A swarm of flutters tickles the insides of my stomach and I slide my hand against that welt on the back of her neck.

Blake holds his hands up. "I'm not trying to step on anyone's toes."

"Well, you are."

"Okay, I hear you." He nods. "Look, Coach Williams knows me well—"

"Ace obviously don't."

Laughter spills out of his mouth, but Phat's lips don't budge.

"With all due respect, babygir—"

"I ain't your babygirl."

"Okay... *ma'am*. I'm talking business with our boy here."

"Nah, you're talking bullshit—not like a dude that's

supposed to stand on business and everybody knows the first rule of business is respect. You coming at folks sideways on some lame ass shit."

Her words fire out in short, rapid, spurts and her neck's hot beneath my fingers like she's always had to defend my name in heated battles against people who thought it was okay to play on my head—even people that claimed to know Pops so well. Now, she's version two.

She flips between the two so easily that I think I lose our rhythm until she swings her head to look at me with wild, wide eyes and I know she heard it all—tarnish and legacy. All the fancy ways a sports agent can confirm what I told her earlier—the world didn't want me anymore.

I grip her nose between my fingers and whisper, "Shhh..."

"But—"

"But watch Janet."

"Let me," I add, leaving the rest of my words to hang between us because Blake's staring at the way I make her settle down.

Her eyes dip and Blake's head bobs behind hers as he takes another chug of his champagne.

"Okay," she mutters.

"Record this song for Mom while I go chop it up with Blake." She doesn't smile until I do and that fucks my head up so bad that I almost grab her arm to take her with me.

JANET'S VOICE vibrates across the hotel and slithers underneath the doors of the ballroom while me and Blake stroll side by side outside of them.

"Smart move." He nods with a grin.

"What you getting at, man?"

He chuckles, bringing the champagne flute he took from the table to his lips as we stop in front of a pair of floor to ceiling windows. "Your *date*."

My palms get moist like Phat's lurking around to hear the word she'll equate with Bryson when she gets older because this was far from a date. This was everyday life shit that was expected of me as Ason Williams' son and would be expected of her if God let me keep her.

"What about her?"

"She's a black girl."

"And?"

"Did you watch the last draft, man?"

I swallow. "Kind of."

It played in the background while I was curled around a toilet back in my condo in LA. Adam Silver didn't even finish droning out Javier's last name before that 1942 came bubbling up my throat.

"Well, according to the 2022 draft, the future's... mixed." He laughs. "Black giants with ambiguous and lily white girls on their arms clapping it up from the audience as Adam Silver secures their new ambiguous families for generations to come."

I roll my eyes.

This is what my life is now. A constant loop of Twitter trigger words and hot topics.

"You're doing a great job. Superb." He curls his thumb and index finger together. "First the HBCU, now the black girl. You're so good at this shit that I'm convinced you two are actually a *thing*."

"A thing?" I scoff.

Like the world could handle me being in a thing with a girl after what some reporter told them I did with the last one. *That girl* wasn't even mine. She was just another fucking taker. She was like kryptonite to a black man—a blonde hair, blue-eyed devil. That's what Pops' lawyer, Quame, told me in his office when it was just me and him. *That girl* had more power than a boy who had the world.

"If you want to talk basketball, then talk it," I reply. "Leave Lourdes out of it. She don't understand any of this."

She was too young and sheltered to understand takers.

He nods his head, looking out toward the city.

Lights twinkle off the skyline and I wish I would've grabbed Phat's arm like I wanted so I could see her seeing this view for the first time.

"Yeah, you don't understand it either." He snorts. "Maybe your Pops does though. Maybe that's why he took the job at Lockwood and had you bring her here with you tonight. Maybe that's why he took my call? I mean, it's a great PR move for a boy without PR."

I shake my head. "You got this shit all wrong. What fucking PR? A publicist wouldn't touch me with a ten-foot pole right now."

Somehow that makes him laugh.

As if what happened is laughable. As if I'd use Phat to chase clout when her and her family were the only people that acknowledged the person I was before. As if Pops didn't have my life carefully planned and was damn near convulsing at the curveballs I kept throwing his way.

"Do I really have it all wrong?"

"Fuck you," I croak out. "I need a drink."

That really fucks him up and makes him topple over with the glass dangling from his fingers. "Damn, you had me going for a second there. Maybe you *don't* have PR. I guess that's why your Pops keeps you under his thumb. You're just as unpolished as the world thinks, but shit, you might as well say Harvey and Lee Sports specializes in you unpolished boys. Look what I did for Josiah Joseph."

"That was you?"

Everybody knows the story about Dough's cousin, but nobody knows the details. All we know is that the world changed—not him.

"That was me." Blake nods. "From gangbanger to Falcons poster boy. Not many can say they turned a gang into a movement, a street soldier into a civilian, a boy into a man."

I inhale the hotel's cold, dry air.

"Maybe next they'll say Harvey and Lee brought *The Kid* back from obscurity—from social pariah back to the Messiah of basketball. We'll bring the crown back to where it rightfully belongs. I can make your wildest dream come true."

"How the fuck do you know what my wildest dream is?"

"I think your Pops tells your story the best. What was that he told Sage Steele when you hit that buzzer beater? 'The kid was born with a basketball in his hand. It's no doubt he'll be larger than life. I made sure he'd be larger than I ever was. He's destined for the NBA.'"

My throat itches and I know it's nobody but Mom reminding me she tells my story the best. Even better than Pops.

"Fuck a basketball. You was born with the world in your hands," she said. *"That's worth more than any basketball could ever be."*

"I'm good on that right now."

"Come on, your Pops told me you wanted this conversation. Don't tell me *The Kid's* backing down from a challenge."

"Yeah, one that's not worth it."

"Man, didn't I just tell you I have droves of white kids claiming Thirty gang when they have no clue what that shit is? You're going to let your Pops down just like that? I can change the narrative for you."

"How you plan to do that?"

He shrugs and the lights bounce from the city's skyline to his eyes. "You of all people should know that I can't give away the game for free, but I'll do you and your Pops a solid and keep those pictures of you and babygirl from hitting Getty. I know a guy who knows a guy on their media team. Think of this as an advance because once one of those Instagram bloggers gets ahold of them, it's game over for you. There's nothing the world is more curious about than a dude they claim to hate. If you had a publicist, you'd know that."

He winks and I can see the horror on Phat's face if shit ever went down that way because she's fragile.

"An advance would insinuate we have a working relationship and we don't," I reply.

"*Yet.*"

"If this is how you conduct business, we'll never have one."

"Not too fast. I think you need me just as much as I need you. You have a legacy to protect. I could always let those beautiful step and repeat pictures get out and tomorrow babygirl can wake up with her face plastered on Instagram blogs. Think she'll stick around after that? Doesn't seem like she's planning a wedding anytime soon, like a normal jersey chaser." He reaches out and slaps my shoulder without looking at me. "I'm in town for a couple of weeks. Got the 911 gassed up for you to take it for a spin.

I'll let you get back to your date. I'm sure she's missing you, Kid."

PHAT WIGGLES her fingers underneath the moonlight. "Hakeem Olajuwon touched this hand. I ain't never washing it again."

"Dutty gyal." Gus chuckles, blowing a plume of smoke from the joint I gave him earlier in the day.

The warmth from the truck's hood burns my shirtless back as I stare up at the moon while their voices stroke my eardrums that Blake Harvey assaulted with his fucked up fancy words—Tarnish. Legacy.

My thoughts hadn't stopped since we left Pops at the Hilton and hit the Shipley's drive-thru for Phat's bear claws. Blake texted me as soon as she leaned over my lap to scream into the drive-thru speaker with my scent on her.

> 2128045609: I got those pictures taken care of for you. Your Pops was appreciative. You can repay me with that drive.

Now my brain keeps running in a constant loop of tarnished legacies, broken NBA dreams, and a perfect girl.

I look back at them.

"Pshh. Dirty shmirty." Phat waves a hand, bouncing next to me on the hood of the truck with her gown bunched at her waist. "Wait until I tell Marcus that I breathed the same air as The Dream. He gon' flip the fuck out."

"Lemme meh see dat hand," Gus says, turning around with the joint hanging between his lips.

"Look but don't touch."

He sucks his teeth.

She leans over me again with my welt teasing me from the back of her neck because she twisted her braids into a bun as soon as we pulled into her driveway. The humidity has her edges curled along her hairline and a layer of sweat covering her chest where her gown splits open.

He examines her little fingers as she bites into a bear claw with a grin. "Yuh hear dis girl and all dis rassclat noise 'bout a pissin' tail man, Junior?"

"I hear her," I rasp, swiping my tongue out because I think I can taste the sweat on her skin.

I hear the bold ass words she told Blake over dinner. I see the shy smile she gave anybody I introduced her to. I still feel her elbow in my side anytime she felt me drifting into myself because of all that talk about a tarnished legacy Blake brought up.

"Meh nuh see nothing different 'bout dis hand." Gus laughs, pushing away from the truck's hood and rounding it. "Look like de same likkle hand to me."

"Get that hate out your heart, pimp!" Phat screams between chews as he climbs back behind the wheel.

When the car door slams all their noise stops except for the little hums she lets out between chews. Her eyes scrape against my bare stomach as my dick twitches from the innocent sensuality she exuded throughout the night. Her stare reminds me I have one more thing to teach her before I send her back to Earth and let Bryson take her to the last party of the summer.

"Come show me that hand," I say, cocking my head back.

She thrusts it out and wiggles it in front of my face.

I blink hard. "I'm not Gus."

Or Bryson, or Blake, or any other man she might come across when I let her explore Earth.

She rolls her eyes with a sheepish smile. "Oh, you on Earth now? You been on Planet Ace since we pulled up."

"Yeah... been up there waiting on you to come home, but you too busy screaming about Hakeem Olajuwon and spending our money on nasty bear claws." I yank an arm from behind my head and pat the part of my stomach she keeps staring at—the part that says LA. "Bring your ass here and show me what you all geeked up about."

She chews the rest of the dough in her mouth in slow, grueling motions like she did with the tuna tartare. It takes a minute for her to drag her body close to mine—too long, but I let it slide.

A loud screech echoes through the night air from her knees rubbing against the truck's paint. When she swings her leg over my stomach, my hand clenches for the drink I've been wanting ever since Blake fucked my head up outside that ballroom. Her warm middle makes a gush of blood rush through my veins toward the head of my dick. It's so hot that I'm thankful for the scrap of lace Cree picked out for her to wear in the name of "no pantylines" because I can feel her lips against my stomach.

"Let me see that hand."

She pushes it forward in a slow motion until I snatch it and bring it close to my face.

"The Dream, huh?" I smirk.

She nods between chews but the rest of her body grows still. The rhinestones Sunny dotted onto her nails catch the moon's light and twinkle while I examine each finger, with Blake's assumptions and accusations floating in the back of my head.

"He ain't *The Kid*..." she mutters between chews. "But the nigga still goated."

A laugh bursts out my mouth. "Shit, he made the Rockets back-to-back NBA champs. *The Kid* never did no shit like that."

"Yet..."

"Didn't you hear what Blake Harvey said? I tarnished a legacy."

"Fuck that Carlton Banks ass nigga."

My stomach cramps so hard from laughing that I forget the bitter taste of those words coming out of my mouth for the first time. Times like this and words like those remind me that Phat's still a little lady.

"He never even looked you in the eyes when he was talking to you," she says. "Can't trust a man that can't look you in the eyes when he's talking about delicate things."

But then she'll say shit like that and remind me she's *my* little lady.

"Oh, so you care about who this 'weak ass nigga' can trust?"

She bites into her lip and glances at the space where our skin connects.

"I care about a lot of things," she mumbles.

"Like?"

"Nothing." She shakes her head. "Who was he anyway?"

I reach out and pinch a piece of the bear claw dangling from her hands. The little taste of her I sucked out of the Bubble Yum was long gone and I wanted more. I was just as hungry as she always was. I even wanted whatever was underneath that "nothing."

I push the dough into my mouth, trying to suck as much

of her as I can off of it. "A sports agent who says he can make my wildest dream come true."

"And that is?"

"Playing in the NBA."

"That's your wildest dream? To play in the NBA? He thinks you need help with that? *You* actually think you need help with that? Your daddy is fucking AW. You can speak different languages. You live in a penthouse with a view of the city. Yeah, some shit went down, but keep it a buck. That's really your wildest dream?"

"That's what he thinks my wildest dream is."

Really, it's Pops' dream and he's so good at twisting my brain around that sometimes I think it's mine too.

She huffs, shuffling against my stomach and sucking the tips of her fingers Hakeem Olajuwon hadn't touched. "If playing in the NBA isn't your wildest dream, then what is? What else could you possibly wan—"

"To hear my Mom's voice again," I blurt. "To ask how I'm supposed to survive this dumbass world without her? That's my wildest dream. I don't think he can resurrect the dead though. Do you?"

Her finger pops out of her mouth and her lips droop into a frown that I want to suck on because I'm saying too much shit.

"You know, she'd probably tell you it ain't always you against the world."

"Then who the fuck else I'm supposed to go against it with?"

She stares at me and her lips lift a little. She's looking at me like she sees Mom somewhere in my eyes and how hard life is when the world don't look at you with hope anymore.

"Your co-pilot." She drops her hand, shrugging. "Wasn't just one person on the dream team."

I thrust my head back and close my eyes. "You something else, kid."

"Nah, you are. Your mama wouldn't hate none of whatever it is you got going on up on Planet Ace. I give you permission to torture yourself with the what ifs sometimes." She rolls her eyes up. "As long as you give your co-pilot permission to tell you when you had enough. It helps."

"I thought I told you there's nothing that can change what happens in the present and to stop harping on it."

Waiting for her voice with my eyes closed has my other senses so heightened that I feel all of her—her hot pussy, the sticky wetness on her thighs, and the gentle thump of her hands falling on my chest.

"That's that shit your daddy put in your head," she whispers, scraping her nails down my skin. "But at home you can harp on whatever you want. I won't tell nobody that *The Kid* misses his mama sometimes. Shit, sometimes I be missing mine and she still here. My pilot is the only person who understands what I'm saying when I say that though."

Only kids with mothers like ours would ever get what she's saying.

I pull my eyes apart and find her staring at the tattoo of Mom over my left pec.

Mom's smile rests underneath her fingernails. It's bright like it was on the program CeCe wanted. The mega-church pastor Pops asked to preach at her funeral flashed it to the empty church. He told us to remember her as the Angie she was before the sickness got ahold of her, but he didn't know any better. Moms like ours were to be cherished as the ladies they were before and after.

"We both know Angie and CeCe ain't just have their friendship in common. It's deeper than that. I'm learning that all of this shit might be deeper than what I thought."

I hope that last line is for me. I'm desperate to tell her that shit *really* isn't what it seems and out of all the girls I've ever touched, she's the only one that would get it but Pops and Quame made sure I'd never have the chance to open my mouth about that night ever again.

I push up from the truck's hood while she stares at my chest.

I'm still hungry and I need more than the innocent little tastes I give her to settle that burning emptiness in her stomach because I'm bigger, with more experience and baggage than I hope she'll ever have.

I reach out and tap the back of her neck where the skin is always prickling to the surface. "Come here. Let me take care of these."

She doesn't move until I pull her into me. After we smash into each other, she twists her neck like she knows this is the only way to get rid of those burning hives she said didn't hurt so much. I know better though.

I smile at the way she pinches her eyes shut and grips my slick arms. For once I'm not beefing with Texas' weird ass humid air. I want it.

"Open your mouth," I whisper, pushing my face closer to the raised skin on her neck.

"For wha—ahh..."

That same *ahh* wants to come out of my mouth, but it gets trapped between my lips and her skin. I think it's in a good place because I have other shit to say—*important* shit.

"Because I'm hungry and I wanna hear you." I breathe out, letting my lips hover over her skin. "That's how you feed me."

I can't wait on her reply because I'm so hungry that even the little dots of sweat prickling her neck look good.

"O—okay," she stutters.

I swipe my tongue against the first dot and her nails dig into my arms while her middle curls into mine in a slow grind. My hands go numb at my sides because it's been so long that I don't remember how to touch places on her body I'm supposed to own.

I press my lips back onto her neck, talking against the skin. "Don't you wanna know how to feed me like I feed you?"

Tiny trickles of air blow out of her nose as she nods.

"Damn, kid." I chuckle. "You already fucking up. I said feed me."

I suck hard.

"Fuck...*Ason.*"

My name flies out of her mouth in a squeaky whine that makes my dick twitch as my hands grasp at the humid night air. Suddenly, it turns crisp and I smell the Pacific Ocean on her skin.

"You taste good—like the air on the PCH in summer."

I didn't mean to say it, but two years, too much pain, and a little lady have turned my words into ones I don't recognize.

She chokes on a laugh and a moan. "Where the fuck is that?"

It's where I'd make love to her in luxury villas and on white-sand beaches if I could. Shit, at least those words don't come out like the others did.

I clench her neck between my teeth and fix my welt with one last swipe and a suck because I'm greedy.

A hard *thunck* against the windshield makes her jump back and the feeling in my hands return. She peels her middle off mine and looks at the wet streak I force myself not to drag my fingers through.

Her eyes shoot from me to the windshield as Gus

pounds on the glass again. "Mi have a wife, yuh know? It's late."

I laugh, pulling my bottom lip between my teeth to taste the California summer one last time, but it's not the same.

"I didn't mean to do that," she says, widening her eyes.

"Okay." I curl my sensitive fingers into the palm of my hand.

I push up from the hood of the truck and swipe my fingers through the streak on my stomach anyway. It has all the traits of a woman who's never had a man push her body to produce something like it—hot, sticky, and soppy.

"Uh... I—I can get you a towel," she stutters, lifting her leg and flashing the dark spot in the middle of her blue panties.

She swipes at her neck, biting down into her lips while my fingers tingle and shout with the entire night at their tips, telling me to *just do it*. Shut her perfect ass up. Teach her that pleasure always comes with good shit like the streak on my stomach and sometimes it even comes with a little pain. Make her ass act right.

"Tell Gus to hold up a min—"

The sound of my open palm slapping against her lace covered ass sounds like water pounding the shore of El Matador. The rest of her sentence gets caught in her throat while my fingers sigh in relief at the tingling sensation they're left with after convincing me to do some shit I shouldn't have.

Her wet chest heaves up and down as she presses a hand to the hot spot I hit. Her lips get slack, like she wants to say something and if she has the nerve, my fingers had already convinced me to do it again.

"*Fuck* The Dream," I choke out. "Go wash that hand and check on Mom."

CHAPTER FOURTEEN

Ace

Mom told me one thing she loved and hated most about Pops was his drive.

"Uh huh." He nods, with his phone in the crook of his neck while motioning for me to come inside his office. "I will pour every dime from the Shooting Stars Gala into this basketball program. You don't have to worry 'bout that."

I drop my bag and fall into the chair in front of his desk. It's the only new thing in here. All the stuff the old head coach left behind sits in a corner in crumpled boxes waiting on Mr. Jackson and his custodial staff to toss it with the rest of the shit they left. He didn't even bother taking his championship trophy he won back when Marshall was living. I would've left it too. I don't think it's much I would've wanted to take from a place that could fire somebody just because a famous person offered themselves up like a sacrificial lamb.

"My primary concern is the facility we have for these kids. They're playing in an arena that was built in the eighties. Meanwhile, across the way, they got a million dollar state-of-the-art arena. We have to keep moving the goal post forward."

When Pops is deep in his midlife crises, the drive Mom hated and loved turns into *overdrive*.

He reaches out and snatches a pink stress ball off his desk.

It's the only thing here that represents her. There's no family pictures of us like it was back in his office in El Segundo. Back then, the players on his team used to joke he had shrines of me and Mom. He had a picture of me at every age with a basketball in my hand and a picture of Mom from every year they'd been together until she stopped taking pictures.

"I absolutely know how much a new arena costs, President Bolden. We're looking upwards of ten million for a team that hasn't won a title since I was in college."

I sigh, shifting around in the hard chair.

There's too much other shit I can do, like skip my biology class to put up shots with Marcus or check in on Phat's quiet timeline while taking 1942 to the head. It's all the shit my life revolves around these days.

"Listen, I know what I promised you when I made my proposal to come here, but what you failed to tell me was how much these boys have to sacrifice just to show up every day. We have no funds for scholarships, outdated equipment, and don't even get me started on that court. It's a joke. I proposed to work with the talent we had instead of bringing in boys from the outside and I'll stand on that. That was the whole point of bringing the Shooting Stars Gala back home. Look, I have something to take care of."

I scoff, scraping my fingers against the smooth leather chair.

"Let me get back to you on this."

He hangs up the phone and then takes a sip of his coffee before he can get out whatever shit's been eating at him since the gala. There's a lot that probably was—Blake Harvey, all those drinks I had, the blunt I smoked with Cree, and that moment in the truck.

He gulps. "That's Marshall's babygirl."

"Huh?"

"*Lourdes.*"

I almost sputter out the rest of that sentence Phat stopped in the truck because this new midlife crisis had him gone.

"Lourdes" didn't even sound like it was supposed to come out of his mouth. It sounded just as foreign as this office felt.

"Yeah, I know. You told me."

He nods while his eyes dart around my face like he's looking for evidence that I touched Phat in a dishonorable way, as if she wasn't the delicate little lady Mom told me she was that day I saw her struggling to flip a hamburger patty. He looks at me like Marcus did.

"Whatever it is you're trying to pursue, you shouldn't."

It's the exact opposite of what Blake Harvey thinks and out of everything Pops could've addressed, my new little innocent habit is what he's worried about.

I swallow her taste like I did this morning when LaQuan stomped into the locker room, talking about all the "hoes going to Splashtown" and Bryson climbed on the bench to shout him and his "girl" would be there.

Fuck.

I want to call her up and tell her I'd take her anywhere in the world, but I can't do it. Mom would have a fit if I took this experience away from her because all little ladies deserved a chance to experience parts of life without their men—even drunken college parties.

"I don't know what you talking about," I reply. "I'm not trying to pursue anything."

He pinches his eyes shut. "Now is not the time for that secretive bull you like to ride on. She doesn't know anything about life with you."

"Damn. I didn't know life with me was so hard."

"Now look, I ain't mean it that way, Junior."

"Oh, now I'm Junior." I laugh. "This is what you wanted me to leave class early for?"

Wrinkles pile between his eyebrows. I don't remember seeing them there before Mom left.

"I just knew you wanted to talk about Blake Harvey or —or the fact that they're saying Javier got an eleven million dollar rookie contract while I'm barely enrolled in college and riding the bench."

"I told you I'd let you go about this Blake stuff alone. You want to be an adult and do adult things—here's your chance. And you can't deny that Javi's an excellent player. Of course, he got that much."

"Right. You made sure he was an excellent player, huh?"

"Junior..."

"You probably floating right now. You got a whole team of your favorite thing."

"Junior, don't start this nonsense here. Don't act like I haven't given you the world—"

"You didn't. Mom did."

He slams a hand against his desk that would've made thirteen-year-old me flinch. "Yeah, and with who's damn money? Huh?"

But I'm older now and his interest in other kids doesn't

make me crawl into Mom's lap anymore. I stopped that shit when I saw the warmth in his eyes while he watched Javier dribble a ball around his mom, Josefina, and a pouting Cree at his camp back home. That warmth turned into admiration when Javier told the team Josefina cleaned houses for a living and sometimes he and Cree traveled all the way from Long Beach on the city bus just so Ason Williams could teach him basketball fundamentals he already knew.

"That's the thing. Everything is about money, opportunity and experience. You ever stop and think that maybe I don't want any of that? Huh?"

"Well then, what in the hell do you want? We've been doing this back-and-forth mess for years. I thought you were over this. You're jealous of kids with nothing but talent to get them by. Kids who don't even have a home to go to during holiday breaks. You get the most out of me—you get my damn legacy. That's worth more than any million dollar contract or pro bono coaching sessions I gave your friend."

I used to practice these conversations with Mom. It was the only way I could keep up with the facts and gain the courage to dispute the distorted versions of Pops' truth he likes to pound into my head.

"You're angry today, Junior. Angers a good thing," she'd say while I threw basketballs into the side of the house with a straight face after another missed dinner or celebration. *"Come tell me how you feel so we can tell him when he gets home."*

"Yeah." I laugh, nodding. "I'm jealous of someone who we both know will never be as good as me."

"Right and we both know why the world will refuse to acknowledge that, don't we? You ruined your reputation —not me."

It's just like the day after Mom left. Her body wasn't

even cold yet and that *LA Times* reporter had the nerve to call up Pops for a fucking statement: *"Mr. Williams, what do you and your family have to say about the LA County Sheriff's Department leak? There's reports the victim was afraid of proceeding with a criminal case due to the nature of her relationship with your son. Can you tell us who she was to him? Were they dating?"*

A fire ignites in my chest and I want my co-pilot to give me permission to harp on whatever the fuck I want. I want her skin in my mouth and her voice in my ear.

"You right." I grab my backpack. "Fuck this shit."

"I know you're angry, but don't use that language in here. I ain't Angie."

"Yeah, that's the problem. I'm *Junior* and you can't even tell when I'm angry or not. You too worried about the possibility of me being exactly what some *LA Times* reporter said I was."

Lourdes

"WHAT YOU MEAN you not going tonight?"

"You didn't see my tweet this morning?" Chelsea groans. "I thought I told you The Holy Convocation's today and Granny talking about she need help setting up."

I rake my fingers through my braids, staring at Lucy's text while Chelsea smacks on her gum over my phone's speaker.

Lucy: *Can't do it tonight mija. I picked up an overnight shift.*

"And that's going to last all night?"

"Look, you know how those things are. I also ain't

prayed all week and God ain't playing with me about it. I need every prayer I can get. Do you know Blythe been sneaking her funky, drum major boyfriend in while I'm sleeping at night?"

I blow out a breath and fall back against my bed. "Oh. For real?"

"And do *you* know Marcus blocked me on Insta again? Which I also tweeted about twenty-two hours ago and you have yet to acknowledge it!"

"I ain't see it."

"For somebody that sits on Twitter subbing Bry all day, you sure ain't see squat these past two days. Why the quiet timeline, bestie? What's up?"

Ace—he was up. He was up on Twitter telling the world my business in rap lyrics, subtweets, and questions, because somehow he knew I was still lurking on there. I didn't have time to deal with Chelsea and her church girl tweets.

@AceWilliamsJr 1d

Y'all remember your first date? Shit, mine was at the slauson super mall with Bri from Leimert Park. I ain't even get a kiss after I dropped a dub on door knockers and fake LV. Ha!

@AceWilliamsJr 1d

Niggas bet not be out here getting kisses off first dates if I didn't.

"You liked Bryson's tweet about Splashtown this morning and it's like I blinked and it was gone."

Because Ace didn't play about that shit.

@AceWilliamsJr 1d

What's that saying moms used to pull out when you didn't listen? Hard head makes a soft ass? That's how that go?

That's exactly how it went.

I brush a finger across the tender spot on my left cheek underneath my pajama shorts. It's been a week, and it still throbs when I sit down, and so does the valley between my legs. The skin on my ass is lighter, so it turned a nasty purple color yesterday and Ace told Twitter all about it like he was in the bathroom with me when I noticed it.

@AceWilliamsJr 1d

Purple's an elite color for sure. It's my favorite.

"Hello...?" Chelsea calls out. "Is this about Bryson's pipsqueak tail and the random texts you been sending me about boys pulling back? Is he trying to ghost you? Is this why you've been so quiet? Should I pull up to his musty dorm? I still can't believe you agreed to go on an actual date with him. Yikes."

I couldn't either, but it was a once in a lifetime thing just like Ason Williams' Shooting Stars Gala was. It was a way to peel myself off Mama's side for one night, even if it wasn't with the boy I wanted to go with. The boy *I* wanted was too busy giving me physical space I didn't ask for while dedicating his whole timeline to me. There hadn't been anymore spontaneous gala dates or pop-up visits. I still don't know how he figured out I agreed to go with Bryson.

"No! It's not about Bryson. Please do not pull up on him on your way to praise Jesus."

"Well, should I have Granny swing by and get you for the convocation?"

"*Hell* no."

She gasps. "Well, do you need prayer, girl? Is that what the Twitter silence is all about? You know I was just watching Sarah Jake's sermon about the power of silence this morning—"

"Chelsea! Please! I'm going to Splashtown *alone* with

Bryson because you flaked. My closet's empty, and Marcus forgot to take me to Target before he left for work this morning. Now Lucy talking about she picked up an extra shift tonight, so who the fuck gon' sit with Mama? I don't need prayer... I—I need..."

I fall back against my bed, staring up at the ceiling.

If I could click my heels three times and get transported back to the one place where I'm banned from thinking, I'd click them in a heartbeat. I *think* I need to bum a ride in Ace's luxury spaceship and dip off to the only place that felt right these days.

"Dang, girl. Okay... okay, maybe we can pray about all this later. Let's do this—how about I text Bryson and tell him you don't want to go—"

"No! Why the hell would you do that?"

"I don't know! I mean, it would easily solve all those problems you just listed. Just. Don't. Go."

"I can't *not* go."

And risk another weekend being locked away after Ace gave me a taste of freedom in the form of tuna tartare, Janet Jackson, shifty sports agents, and wet panties.

I close my eyes, swallowing my room's stale air that didn't taste like him.

"I mean, what difference would it make, Phat? I'm sure there'll be other partics."

"Yeah, for *you*! It would make a big difference, but I don't expect you to get it—"

The doorbell echoing through the house cuts into my words. It wasn't nothing but Jesus and that Holy Convocation she kept talking about that saved her from the evil words tip toeing on my tongue.

"Phat!" Mama hollers.

"I got it, Mama! Dang!" I push up, tripping over my

backpack that Ace slid onto my shoulder when he left me on the porch the night of the gala with star-crossed eyes and a throbbing ass.

"I gotta go, Chels."

I don't give her a chance to reply before I hang up and jog to the front door. I hold my breath for Lucy to be behind it, ranting in Spanish about how she gave up her shift for me, but when I fling it open, it's just a plump black lady in scrubs with a rolling backpack.

"Can I help you?" I frown.

She smiles. "Lourdes?"

"Phat."

"Sorry, *Phat*." She chuckles. "He said you'd say that."

"Who are you?" I peer behind her, looking for the "he" she's talking about.

It's nobody there but her and the heat though.

"I'm Jazmine. Junior sent me to help with CeCe for the night. He says you had somewhere to be." Her eyes trail my bleach stained sweats and tank top.

"Junior?"

"Yeah, well, Ace. Sorry, I know him as Jun—"

"I can't afford a provider, Miss."

"He *also* said you would say that. He told me to tell you tonight's on him."

My throbbing ass cheek thumps harder and that annoying wetness I can't get rid of gets worse. *Fuck... Ason.* The aftermath of the Shooting Stars Gala won't even let me call him Ace when I'm in a frenzy anymore. He's been Ason ever since he had my neck in his mouth and his hand on my ass for fangirling over a man that wasn't him.

I squeeze my phone against my moist palm with a sigh.

"Well." Jazmine laughs. "Can I come in?"

I step back and pull the door open wider, thanking God and this stupid boy that I hate and like.

"Phat! Who is it?" Mama hollers again.

Today we aren't conjoined twins—just normal ones. We argued over the streaks I left on the dishes and she ate a bowl of grits while we sang to "All For You" from the video Ace told me to record for her. She's not stuck today.

"Somebody who knows your bonus son." I smile.

The words feel as right as his mouth on my skin.

"Lord," she rasps. "What that boy up to now? Angie got her hands full."

Jazmine laughs without pointing out the obviousness of Angie being gone. My tongue is heavy because I want to have her call up Ace for me so I can curse him out, scream at him, and ask him why I don't feel bad for that girl back in Los Angeles anymore.

"Just lead the way and I'll take it from here," Jazmine says, pushing her stubby arm out.

I nod until she holds up a finger.

"Oh yeah. Junior said he left something in your backpack?" Her voice hikes up. "He didn't say wha—"

"She's down the hallway to the left."

I don't even do the polite thing and show her the way because I need to get to that backpack. I need to feel him, even if it's through whatever he left in it.

When I round the corner to my bedroom, Marshall's old backpack sits at the foot of my bed where I tripped over it. I scoop it up by the top handle and unzip it, pulling out the clothes I wore to Ace's condo and the dress I wore to the gala until I get to a piece of sleek fabric folded at the bottom.

I yank it out, hold it up, and then shove the bathing suit to my nose.

I try to inhale any piece of himself he might've snuck in

that bag, but it makes my stomach twist harder. Whoever said absence made the heart grow fonder didn't take girls like me into account. We're the confused ones who don't even know our bodies well enough to understand how to make them stop humming for grown men we think we can catch up to. We don't want absence. We want presence.

I drop the bathing suit and fumble with my phone, because I can feel him wherever he is. It's a gift and a curse of being a Pavlov girl.

@babyphat04

Fuck that girl. How you let her on our planet and she ain't know that the first rule is that you get whatever you want? I created a monster. Not you.

I refresh and refresh with big eyes and burning fingertips like he wants until I see it.

@AceWilliamsJr

'Cause she was just visiting. You know all lifelong residents belong to me. Log off before I take this stupid bird app away for good.

I already feel the throbbing between my legs from his warning. It's another thing I don't think I'm supposed to like —a man that spends too much time obsessing over everything I do.

"DAMN," Bryson chokes out behind our screen door in swim trunks and a tank. "Marcus got a raise at work?"

"Mind your business." I smile, shuffling from foot to foot in my two-piece and sarong.

There was even a matching scarf folded at the bottom of my backpack. I tied it around my braids like I saw Dough's girlfriend do with hers in another magazine spread that revolved around her style. Mama hooted and hollered afterward talking about it was the "finishing touch" to the best *Tarjay* outfit she'd ever seen while Jazmine took her blood pressure. Never mind the Dior logo printed all over the swimsuit.

Red creeps up Bryson's cheeks and he flings the screen door open, but I step forward.

"What you doing? I wanna see Mama before we go," he says.

"She sleeping."

"But I hear he—"

"That's the TV. Marcus' friend back there sitting with her."

He smacks his lips. "Man, why you playing? Let me see Mama."

"Bryson..." I push my palm against his chest. "For real. I just got her to relax. I don't want her getting all hyped back up."

Another boy that always seemed to beat him to the punch in his own territory had already hyped her up. The noises he overheard were her and Ace talking on Jazmine's phone. I heard them from my bathroom while shimmying into another expensive piece of fabric he decided we should own because on Planet Ace we're obsessed with possessive pronouns, Dior, and secrets. He and Mama hadn't shut up since Mama asked him what he had planned for the night.

"Shit, fix me a drink and watch the Rams whoop up on the Cardinals. How that sound, Mom?"

Lonely—Mama said it sounded like a lonely night for a boy as bright as he was.

I curl my hand in Bryson's tank. "Please..."

I can't think of any reason Bryson needs to interrupt

him and Mama's boring conversation about the Rams and the Cardinals.

He shrugs. "Fine. I'll talk to her when we get back."

I tug him inside and close the door. "Yeah, do that. Let me go get my bag. I'll be back."

I catch him swiping a hand across his springy curls while glancing at my ass before I walk back to my room to grab the only thing Ace hadn't upgraded—Marshall's dingy Houston Rockets backpack.

His voice makes my stomach tight when I pass Mama's room.

"Lourdes left yet?" he asks as I swipe the backpack off the floor beside my bedroom door.

"Sound like Bryson here now. You wanna holler at her before she go?"

"Nah. Maybe if she not having too much fun, she'll check in on me."

My stomach gets tighter when I pull the door closed and head towards Mama's room.

I'm homesick. That's the only explanation I have for the distance I feel between me and him. There are still some things I don't know how to say to him out loud without him coaching me to do it, and this feeling is one of them.

I linger outside the door, trying to spend one last second obsessing over him like he does with me.

"A'ight," he says, brushing against the phone's receiver. "I just got to my friend's. I'll call and check in on you in a few, lady."

My hand hangs from the doorknob while I listen hard for another girl in the background, because Brandy's the only *friend* I can think of since Cree caught that flight back to Los Angeles. Maybe he's doing shit grown folks do while me and Bryson go suck up the sweat and twerk music at the last party of the summer.

Mama squeals out a raspy laugh. "Boy, I ain't Phat. Ain't no need to check in on me like I'm a baby. I know she got you lost tonight."

"Damn." He grunts. "Why she do me like that, Mom?"

"Because you got her spoiled—just like your daddy had Angie. Ason used to stay on your grandma's phone asking 'bout that girl."

There's the faintest sound of a feminine voice in the background, but my homesickness could've been making me imagine it.

"Hmph." He scoffs. "Maybe I do."

I raise my hand to push on the door.

"Tell me what you want me to tell her. I'll be the bad guy tonight."

Mama's last words and the little giggling voice on his end make me stop. I *didn't* imagine that.

"Tell her... tell her no drinking," he stutters out. "An— and make sure her phone is charged and... oh... and to bring her backpack—"

"Okay, okay. You taking this harder than me now."

"Oh, it's like that?"

Jazmine and Mama laugh while I take a deep swallow.

His anxiety over me and this *moment* makes my breakfast sneak up my throat because he sounds more like a man that won't ever get to experience another college party and less like the carefree senior he's supposed to be. There's also that giggling feminine voice that makes me want to choke on it.

"Yes! Go have fun with your friend. I got the baby."

My breakfast inches further up, and I gulp it back down as soon as I push the door open. Jazmine grabs her phone back from Mama like Ace hadn't been on there, demanding I don't do shit with a girl giggling in his arms.

"Come sit before you go." Mama pats the bed next to her. "I'm gonna give you the same talk I used to give Marcus back when he was in school."

I have to force my body to sit next to hers because it's stiff with too many feelings shooting through it.

"You being for real?" I ask. "Or you just making up stuff?"

"Now hold up, dammit. You know your mama is as real as they come."

If she was, she wouldn't have been taking orders from a twenty-one-year-old that never fathered a child.

She squeezes my wrist. "Absolutely no drinking tonight."

My nostrils flare.

"Don't get in the car with people you don't know or people that's been drinking. Bring your backpack and make sure your phone is charged in case I need to get in touch with you."

Or Ace needed a way to obsess over me more while she slept the night away.

She reaches out and squeezes my cheeks. "But most importantly, have fun. Life ain't long enough to *not* have fun. Don't you ever forget that."

CHAPTER FIFTEEN

Lourdes

"Hold up... hold up! All my freshman ladies make some motherfuckin' noise!"

That's all Splashtown is—noise. Screaming, laughing, hot ass noise in a pool on the Southwest side that ain't big enough to hold everybody here.

"You already know what it is, DJ G5, on the ones and twos! We lifted in here! It's hot as a bitch but not hotter than the last fucking party of the summer! Ya feel me?" DJ G5 talks so fast my eyes cross.

Bryson tugs me through swarms of sweaty bodies as the sun beats down on my skin. I keep stretching my neck to look for Chelsea like she'd ditch the Holy Convocation to look like a fish out of water with me, but I know it's just wishful thinking. Nobody comes between her and God—not even Splashtown.

Bryson twists his neck. "Quise say they over there in the corner. C'mon."

I nod, clutching my phone in my hand because he convinced me to leave Marshall's backpack at the house.

"You not twelve." He laughed. *"Please, leave that."*

So I left it next to the front door, even though Ace insisted I bring it like the control freak he was.

We bypass braids, weaves, wigs, Afros, two-piece swimsuits, one-piece swimsuits, *no* swimsuits. Some girls know Bryson and they stop to remind him they do while fluffing his hair and tugging at the chain around his neck.

I push up on my toes as another one prances off with her friends after flagging him down.

"Who's that?" I ask, pressing my lips close to his ear.

"She's in my psychology class."

I look around for any familiar faces from my classes, but it's hard to find them when I only see them twice a week. Sometimes I don't see them at all. I don't see any of my co-workers from the bookstore—not even Brandy. I stretch my neck, looking for her blonde springy curls one last time. It's just more wishful thinking.

My shoulders droop until Bryson yanks me up a step and pulls me toward a corner where there're no weaves, wigs, or braids—just a bunch of boys.

I yank his hand.

"What?" He turns around. "What's wrong?"

"Ain't no girls over there."

He rolls his eyes and swings an arm around my neck. "Chill. It's the team. They know you with me."

His croaking voice doesn't convince my wild nerves to settle like Ace's does. It makes my pounding heart speed up while I tug at the sarong around my waist.

"I never seen you dressed like this." He smiles, pushing his lips to my ear like I did his.

All of his moves mirrored mine since we left the house.

On the drive here, he didn't touch my arm until I touched his by accident when I took the aux cord from him. He didn't grip my hand until I reached out for his when I saw the line of people stretching outside the building. I forgot how much of a scary boy he was. I even forgot how different his Honda was than Ace's spaceship, even though I've ridden in it a thousand times. Planet Ace had a weird way of wiping my memory of the tiny unimportant shit other boys do on Earth.

"Uh... thanks?" My mouth turns down.

He laughs, pulling me in closer. "It's a compliment. You look... good."

"I do?"

"Yeah...you don't see all these dudes staring at you."

"No."

Having a boy stare at me while under Bryson's arm isn't the same as having a man stare at me while under Ace's at a gala. Ace would've curled his arm around my stomach and introduced me as "Lourdes" to any man that was dumb enough to think he wasn't with me, but Bryson doesn't.

"Y'all know Phat, right?" he yelps, dragging me into that corner with all the boys he plays ball with.

I know some of their names from practice. A couple of them even follow me on Twitter. I recognize the rest of them by the positions they play. Marquise almost snaps his neck in two when he tries to peek behind me, but I tied my sarong so tight I'll probably have to cut it off when I get home.

LaQuan nods, gripping a bottle of Hennessy by its lip. "We know Miss Attitude."

"*Miss Attitude?*" I scrunch up my face.

They laugh hard and I follow their eyes to my titties I

couldn't cover up. I scoot behind Bryson, but he pulls me back beside him.

"Yeah. You went ham on Hollywood." Marquise smirks.

"Don't *nobody* go ham on Hollywood." LaQuan chimes in, squeezing his solid body between Marquise and us.

"Y'all so scary." Bryson rolls his eyes, yanking me closer.

"Nah, you the scary one! He almost had your ass crying at practice. Don't act like we forgot!"

"Fuck y'all! He ain't have me about to do shit but knock his ass out."

They all howl out deep laughs at the ridiculousness blaring out of Bryson's mouth like I ain't been fighting his battles since we were six.

"Man, go 'head with that. Hollywood don't even be on that type of time." LaQuan flings his hand out, pursing his lips.

"What he gon' do? We all know who he like to fuck up and it sure as hell ain't niggas."

It's the type of low blow somebody throws out in a nasty argument with a person they never want to talk to again, but Bryson said the insult so easily, like he practiced it when Ace wasn't around.

Nobody answers while I bite my tongue. I didn't forget that girly giggle from Ace's phone call with Mama, just like I didn't forget that bruise on my ass, so I bite harder to make sure I don't give Bryson the same treatment I gave Blake Harvey. It's a weird space to be in but it's the confusion boys I hate and like cause.

LaQuan shakes his head. "You trippin'. Don't bark if he not here."

Exactly, but still fuck Ace. Maybe Mama was right. Maybe I am spoiled. Maybe it's why I don't know who to hate more—him, Brandy, or that silent girl in Los Angeles

I'm always battling with because we're all his little Pavlov girls.

"Yeah, whatever." Bryson shrugs. "What y'all drinking?"

I cross my arms. "Lucy let you drink now?"

"Who the fuck is Lucy?" Marquise asks, laughing.

"No damn body." Bryson narrows his eyes at me and I lower mine. "Gimme some Henny."

Marquise shrugs and tilts the bottle over his lips, water-falling it into his mouth.

My tongue curls behind my lips because I can't forget the way it burned when I tasted it from Ace's cup and the way he makes everything taste better—even nasty ass Hennessy and obsessive instructions to Mama. It's more confusion for me to obsess over.

They let out hoots when another boy comes behind Marquise with a bottle of something I don't know the name of. They push it my way, but I shake my head even if it is a "fuck Ace" night and my mouth is watering for him. It's pathetic.

"C'mon!" Bryson shouts in my ear. "You gon' let me drink alone?"

"Yup." I smile, bouncing my shoulders when DJ G5 switches songs. "This ain't kindergarten, boy. We don't have to do everything together. You got to grow up one day."

He smiles like he did when I used to sneak over to his house to help Lucy make the masa for tamales. I almost feel bad for being stuck on a different planet with another boy until DJ G5 says *fuck all that*.

"Man... please tell me my nigga *Hollywood* is in the building, or—or like that boy Dough say 'The motherfuckin' *Kid*.' I need to know the story behind this joint right here. I gotta take y'all back to *Cali-Cali* for a minute and if y'all see

Hollywood on campus, tell that boy DJ G5 said welcome home to the H! Shit, you innocent in my book!"

I grin.

The Williams must be a religion in his house, too.

There are some feelings I can't name—like the way the air tastes when I finally breathe it in after being stuck in the house for a long time or the tingling in my throat from rapping the words to one of my favorite songs about a boy I hate and like. That air I haven't tasted in a while is sweet with Ace's flavor fluttering in it as I shout out the words to a song I know by heart. It sounds different in a place full of other people that know it too. It sounds the best in Ace's spaceship though.

The music cuts out and we're left shouting about how Dough "been through some shit that'll make the coldest nigga's heart bleed" but he "came back like *the kid* in the sweet sixteen."

"He the lil' nigga that laced me up, taught me to find home in my bitch now we *glocked* up, *rocked* up, all up on yachts and *stuff*, eatin' lobster that Ason Williams' private chef plate *up*."

"Damn!" LaQuan shouts. "I told that nigga to come! I told him!"

I smile at his dimpled cheeks and my stomach flips with another feeling I can't name—the one where life is sometimes as simple as overhearing the DJ shout-out your loner of a teammate after the world turned on him one summer.

"Bro, I got that on my story!" Marquise bounces on his toes. "Everybody rapped that shit! Everybody!"

A hard hand grips my waist and I look up, catching Bryson's heavy eyes on me.

"You still obsessed with Dough?" he shouts, rolling his eyes.

I shrug, biting into my bottom lip and fighting off the butterflies swarming in my stomach.

The beat changes to a classic and another bottle I can't name lands back at my lips. It teases me with the possibility of Ace's taste swimming inside it. He was right about what he told me in our driveway. Getting a taste of what was in his cup that night didn't make me want it ever again. Instead, it made me want *him* even when he did things I didn't like.

Bryson circles his hand around my waist while I stare into the clear liquid. "Come on, drink that shit!"

So I do.

I open my mouth and wait for him to pour. When it splashes against my tongue, I hold in a choke while I wait on Ace's flavor, but he never told me it was so hard to find it on Earth.

That warmth he told me about in my driveway covers my entire body this time. It wraps me in its arms like Mama used to do when she was still herself and I'm still that light-weight that does stuff without Ace's permission, so my body moves to the beat. Bryson's hand sneaks around my waist as the music gets raunchier and I try to remember how Ace feels under my bare legs.

DJ G5 starts another song that reminds me of the type of boy Ace is. He's the type that can produce little ugly reminders on my body that I'm one of those lifelong residents he was referring to, and he can make any rapper sound smoother just from dropping his name in a verse. They all swore they were "ballin harder than Ason Williams' son," but none of them really were.

"Oh, shit!" DJ G5 shouts. "We going up in the corner up top—throwing ass and taking shots! It's definitely a Texas *lituation*!"

I swipe Bryson's hand from crawling under my sarong as the music strokes my legs and I swallow another burning mouthful of clear liquid somebody dangles above my lips. Ace *has* to be floating in this one.

"Ugh." I grimace as Marquise laughs.

"Not a Casa type of girl?" he yells.

"Hell no!"

I'm an Ason Williams Jr. type of girl and he didn't explain that no matter how many little shots I swallow to chase his taste in a building full of strangers, I'd never find it.

THAT WARMTH that scooped me into its arms is like magic.

It fixes whatever I think is wrong, like all the loud noise that Splashtown produces. It quiets everybody's hollering into a nice, comforting hum and I wonder why I even hated all the noise. It turns Bryson's teammates into swarms of buzzing bees that act like I got honey stuck to my skin because they keep brushing against it, even though Bryson told them there wasn't enough for them. It even made him look different. He wasn't lil' Bryson that got his braces off the summer before tenth grade and that same warmth made him brave—*too* brave.

"Hold on," I mumble, pulling his hand away from my sarong again. "I need to pee."

Bryson smacks his lips and leans his body over mine. "Hold it."

"No! I been holding it."

He rolls his eyes and I try to ignore the throbbing full-ness between my legs as another bottle makes its way around our corner. Blurry faces and numb feet keep my head spinning and my ass rolling into Bryson's center.

I'm not the only girl in our corner anymore because DJ G5 named it the "vibers section." Those same weaves, braids, and wigs from earlier weaseled their way in to vibe with a team they don't look twice at on campus.

"The *Hollywood* effect." LaQuan grins, slapping Bryson in the chest.

"Yeah, whatever." Bryson rolls his eyes. "Half these females be the main ones talking slick about him."

His face stretches into five different blurred versions of itself. The enticing mirage the liquor created drains while my bladder throbs and he gets more agitated at Ace's ghost hanging in our section.

I push away from him again.

"I told you to hold it," he says, gripping my arm and pulling me back into him.

"I can't! Let me go."

"I'm not walking you down there. If we leave, somebody might take our spot and I'm not waiting outside no fuckin' girl's bathroom, anyway."

"I don't need you to walk me." I snatch my arm away. "I'm grown. I can walk my damn self down there."

"Well, be grown then. Go walk yourself."

How did my bladder turn into an argument? I guess liquor makes us fuss about everyday things that wouldn't matter if we were sober. I've added it to my list of all the strange magical things it does.

I push out of our corner and a girl eases into my spot in front of him as soon as I step down into the pancake of bodies below us. I float between them, elbowing away strange hands and ignoring girls' stares until the girls' bathroom sign sticks out against my blurry vision.

"Finally," I huff, pushing inside.

It's as loud inside as it is in the party.

I stumble into a line of gossiping girls. Their voices and the liquor remind me of Chelsea's made-up stories about the random people we see around campus.

I fall into the gritty wall, shifting my weight from one foot to the other, fighting against another wave of homesickness while another Dough song blasts through the speakers.

This time all the things I tried to fight my homesickness with falls by the wayside—the giggling girl, Bryson, my first party alone. Now, I'm just tired of the warmth and chaos liquor causes. It's no wonder Ace didn't want me having it.

When it's finally my turn in line, I stagger into the open stall. Toilet paper and pee line the rim of the toilet. I don't have anywhere to sit to make my circling head stop.

DJ G5 scratches the record again. "Y'all still ain't seen Hollywood in this bitch? Somebody hit that nigga up and tell him we on one in here just for him!"

"Ugh." I groan, following DJ G5's instructions and going straight to Twitter.

@babyphat04

I want hom.

@babyphat04

I want go hom

@babyphat04

I want to go

My fingers slip as I slide down the side of the stall with all the letters from my phone's keyboard dancing across the screen.

"I...want...to..." I gurgle up the liquor that still doesn't taste like Ace.

It has Bryson's and everybody else's bitter taste and I

can't believe I forgot how to spell "home" when Ace reminds me how all the time.

"C'mon," I sing, refreshing his timeline. "C'mon... Ason. I need yo—"

The phone vibrates between my fingers. An unsaved number covers his timeline with all of our insiders because he's not scary like me. He never tweets and deletes.

I swipe up. "Not fuckin' right now. I can't remember how to spell. Ace is gon' flip the fuck out that I can't spell hom—"

The vibrating stops and starts again as soon as I try to sound out the letters.

"Fuck," I hiss, pounding my thumb against the green button. "Stop calling m—"

"Where the fuck you at?" Ace rumbles through the speaker.

His anxiety about this moment lives in his voice. He sounds confused and more stressed than me.

This is one of those times I'm supposed to toss my arms around his shoulders and explain myself. I should squeeze a tear out too because there's something in his voice that tells me he might be a sucker for my "fat baby" tears, like Marcus calls them.

"I—I'm in the bathroom." I whine. "I had to pee and I—I wanna come home."

"Where's Bryson?"

I hope he's so far away that the crowd swallows him. I hope I can scrape his smell from my nose. I hope Ace doesn't feel where he touched the bruise on my ass. I hope—

"Where's your backpack? I thought I tol—I thought Mom told you to keep your backpack with you?"

"He—he told me to leave it."

"Who?"

The fog in my brain makes his voice so loud that my ears ring.

"Bryson. He said I'm not twel—"

"Don't leave that bathroom."

"But I—"

"Ace?" Brandy asks in the background. "Is everything good?"

I didn't imagine it this time. That's where her blonde springy curls had been all night.

"Do you understand me? I said don't leave that bathroom. I'm coming."

"Brandy?" I gasp out. "That's who the fuck you had giggling in the background while you talked to my mama, nigga?"

"Hey, stop it. You drunk. I hear it—"

"Sh—she's at your place?"

"Hell nah. Are you crazy? Why the fuck would I bring her into our space? You got drunk and lost your mind?"

Our.

There he goes with that "our" shit.

I choke on a hiccup before gurgling out, "Fuck you and fuck her."

Ace

"EASY," Brandy hisses, holding onto her seatbelt. "You're going to get a ticket."

"Then I'll just pay the fucking ticket." I slam my hand against the steering wheel, gritting my teeth at the car inching under the red light in front of us.

"Are you sure everything's good? I heard you on the phone outside the truck at the gas sta—"

The GPS cuts into her words and I thank God for the four-minute warning it gives my nerves. I have four minutes to swallow the chaos 1942 always provides, and four minutes to convince myself that racing to a random address on the Southwest side with Brandy in my passenger seat *isn't* an overreaction.

I scrape my fingers across my head.

It's not an overreaction. Phat's drunk. Her tweets and her voice told on her.

"Ace," Brandy sings, gripping my forearm. "Talk to me."

I shrug her hand off. "I'm good."

That's how she ended up here. She came singing in my ear, asking what my plans were for the night, like she knew I needed a place to waste time while Phat played on Earth without me. As soon as I pounded my fist on her apartment door, I knew I needed to go back home. I couldn't talk to any woman that didn't live on my planet, breathe my air, or understand that I always got what I wanted—even my addictions. Now she's stuck in my passenger seat because jersey chasers were always the easiest way to waste time until they weren't.

I ease off the gas as I come up on the street with all the telltale signs there's a party happening—a full parking lot, loud bass, and even louder people spilling outside the entrance.

"Splashtown?" Brandy frowns, turning toward me. "I thought we were going to Whataburger?"

"Yeah... we are. I—I just need to check on somebody real quick."

"The person you were yelling at on the phone?"

"Ye—nah. Look, just chill right here. I'll be back."

I pull into the first empty parking spot and hop out before Brandy can ask more, like why I'm trampling through muddy ass grass in Jordans and agonizing over Phat's text that pops up on my phone.

> Phat Girl: I'm good Aso. I'm stayin here. Go
> wit Brandy and I'll leave you tf alone

Phat Girl.

That's how she's saved in my phone because it's how she's saved in Marcus'. He didn't hesitate to send her number this morning on his way to work without me having to ask for it, all because I mentioned it's where she'd be. Splashtown had all the men in her life in a tizzy—even him.

When I get closer to the building, my body can't fill with anxiety at the thought of stepping foot into a party after so long. My eyes don't even drift to the bare asses giggling and trotting past me with suggestive stares.

As soon as I make it to the entrance, the buff security guard grins, shaking his head.

"Oh, you shonuff Hollywood." He laughs, pushing his hand out to dap me up. "The party been jumping. You fashionably late? This must be what y'all do in LA."

I glance at my muddy Jordans and fleece shorts. "I came to pick somebody up."

That's what I concluded after Phat's rambling text. Splashtown was going on ice with Twitter.

"Somebody?" He laughs, gripping my hand in his. "I know that look."

My red eyes? Flaring nostrils? My eyebrows bunching together?

"Gon' 'head, man. Get her up outta here and keep it player. I don't want you in the news again. You know how these females be."

"Yeah, a'ight." I smack my lips. "Where's the girls' bathroom?"

"Over there on the left."

He waves his hand and looks away as another group approaches him. I shake my head and ease through a bunch of girls blocking the way inside. They eye me up and down.

I can't remember walking into a party alone back in LA but in Houston I'm an expert at existing this way—with the stares, the nudging of the homegirls, and the crooked smiles from dudes that had the same beliefs as that security guard.

The dirt caked restroom sign hangs to the left like he said. I push inside where girls wait in a noisy line for the next open stall.

"Damn..." one of them smiles up at me. "What girl you in here looking for?"

"Me, *duh*." Her friend giggles. "I'm a basketball type bitch or whatever. My ex-nigga played for U of H and I liked for him to take the pussy sometimes, too."

"Girl! Shut up!" They laugh together while my neck burns.

I squeeze past them, skipping the line and staring at the closed stalls with noises coming out of them I can't un-hear.

I tap my knuckle against the first door.

"Lourdes..." I call out over the music, pulling my phone from my pocket. "Where you at?"

I press her name and listen for a ringtone, a vibration, or her mouth while I keep dragging my knuckles against the stalls, ignoring the chipped paint scraping against my skin. The call rolls to voicemail.

"Okay, fuck it." I huff, bending down and searching for the black leather slides I picked out and her brown toes Sunny painted bubblegum pink. "You always wanna play games."

"I wish my man would come looking for me up in the women's restroom," another girl sighs from in front of the mirror. "It's giving obsessed."

"Girl, no! It's giving Sagittarius teas. My ex was a Sag. He had a big dick. I love this for her, whoever she is. *Period,*" the girl next to her chirps as soon as I catch Phat's round toes curling inside her sandals.

I stop and tap on the door. "Open up."

"No. Leave me the fuck alone."

"*Oop,*" one girl drying her hands squeaks.

"Man, stop playing with me and open the fuck—"

The girly chatting in the background stops. I feel them staring at the back of my head while I stare at bubblegum pink toes.

I blow out a breath. "Open the door, Lourdes."

The lock clinks and the hinges squeak as she pushes it open.

I squeeze through the crack, prepping myself for what a college party can do to my little lady who still thinks she's Marcus' fat girl. Pops was right about one thing. Addictions are selfish.

She glares at me from in front of a tissue clogged toilet while the conversation shifts from Sagittarius with big dicks to "which bitch this *Hollywood* nigga fucking on the low."

"I thought I told you I was leaving you the fuck alone," she croaks out with red eyes. "Go be with that girl."

"Brandy?"

"You know who the fuck I'm talking about."

Alcohol is funny. It's arrogant. It's dizzying. One time somebody told me it's like taking shots of dopamine to the head.

"How much did you drink tonight?"

She shrugs and looks at her twisted sarong.

The humid air has her baby hair curling along her fat cheeks under her scarf and I hate that I don't know how any of the shit on her body ended up the way it did.

"I asked you how much you drank."

"Go to hell. You drink all fuck—"

"Watch your mouth." I breathe out. "Do you hear me?"

Her chest pumps out in quick motions, and mine does too. "Why? What you gon' do if I don't? Hit me? *Make me* give you what you want like you did that girl?"

I swipe my tongue out to wet my dry lips while I stare at her wearing everything I obsessed over for this moment— the one where she'd go out and do the things a girl her age should do without me. It's all the shit I already did and couldn't do anymore because of those last few words she hissed out.

I take a step forward and she stays planted.

"That's what you think I did to her?" I ask.

I can't even say her name anymore. It's lodged somewhere deep in my throat where I tried to bury it with all the shit I keep torturing myself with.

"No," she squeaks, lifting her chin and squinting at me. "That's the problem with me and you."

"What is?"

"Her."

It's just like that day in my bedroom where LA hid between our words. Now the girl whose name I can't even utter is back. That's the shit they don't tell men like me about afterward—how the girl never leaves our subconscious. She's *always* there. I can't even drown her in alcohol, no matter how much I try.

"I—I remember reading the way she looked for the first time back when that report leaked online," she whispers with a slur. "White, blonde, blue eyes."

She swallows and her throat bobs. "My heart ain't know which way to beat—with her or with you."

I reach out and curl my fingers in her sarong because they're screaming at me again.

"I hate that girl." She stabs a finger into my chest. "I hate her so fucking much and I hate your ass too beca— because I should believe that girl. Right? I should believe what she said you did."

"Lourdes," I mutter, yanking her to me.

"I saw it on Twitter. I read about the horrible shit you did." Her eyes widen. "But then... I saw you at—at practice, dribbling that ball like you was born with that shit in your hands and smiling like it was impossible that you could ever do something so ugly to anybody."

"C'mon," I whisper, pulling the scarf off her head and clawing my fingers through her braids. "You drunk, kid."

She pushes her chest so far into mine that I think I can feel her indecisive heart beating. Her arms knock my hand from her hair as she thrusts them around my neck and my loud ass fingers are almost at their breaking point because they want me to reward her for being so damn perfect.

I smell sunscreen and the tart scent of whatever alcohol she let other dudes feed her while she dangles from my neck. Her eyes are wet, like she has to convince the world that I was never a bad person—maybe just a misunderstood one.

"I *am* drunk," she murmurs. "And I'll do it again. Is that how she made you do what you did? She did all the shit you didn't like for her to do over and over again? Do you hear what you're doing to my head? I'm blaming her. I'm not supposed to—to do that."

Tears line the rims of her eyes because alcohol is irrational too. It's almost as irrational as my loud ass fingers because they've heard enough. Their nerves drum against the muscles, warming them up.

Toilets flush next to us and the girls keep rotating in and out of the stalls as if I never ran in on them. Their loud voices overpower ours, and the DJ screams in the mic.

"Hey!" Phat hisses, slapping her fingers against my cheek. "I said I'll do—"

"Close your mouth," I mutter, twisting her braids between my fingers.

Sometimes my fingers are just like alcohol—arrogant, dizzying, and irrational. They don't know any other way to exist. So, when Phat's braids whirl between them, they feel at ease.

The skin on her forehead tightens as I yank her braids back and stare at her lips like I did that hive I had to cure. They're full, wet, and dying to show me how far we are past the point of no return and, most importantly, they *close.*

I press my nose against hers and drag it until her soft breaths turn into hard ones. "Those the thoughts you have when I fuck around and let you control the vibe?"

She nods her head.

"Now you see what happens when I let you leave home?"

My mouth hovers over hers and our lips scrape.

"Tell me you'll come back home," I breathe into her mouth. "Tell me you'll come back home and act right."

"But Ason..." she gasps out, closing her mouth again.

It's not Hollywood, Cali, Ace, or *The Kid*—it's *my* name that she took and made hers on the hood of Pops' truck that night.

"No...no." I shake my head. "I don't think you understand. I'm not negotiating with you, baby."

Her eyes flutter like she's satisfied even though our

tongues haven't touched. I can't front and call her "kid" right now—not when she's gasping out my name like I'm inside of her. So baby it is.

"*That's* the problem with me and you." I flick my tongue against her bottom lip. "I let you get away with too much...like you think I'm actually here to go back and forth with you about this shit."

She opens her mouth and claws her fingers against my head.

It doesn't matter that I have her hair tangled in my hand or that I never gave her the satisfaction of letting LA creep its way between us—she still wants me.

"I'm not goi—going back and forth with you. I'll stay off Twitter. I won't drink—"

"You telling me everything I don't want to hear right now."

The *real* problem with us is that Phat's a lot like alcohol and my problematic fingers. She's a double shot of dopamine and she makes me do shit I shouldn't.

The rumbling stall door blends in with the music playing and the girls' loud mouths as I push her against it. I can't hear them comparing me to a big dick Sag or calling me *Hollywood* with disgusted curiosity because sometime between the DJ's last transition, the double shot of Phat I took to the head has me hoisting her legs around my waist and pressing her back against the door. I don't even remember how our tongues got tangled together, but they collided as soon as she pressed her lips against mine.

"I'll act right." She groans around my tongue. "I'll—I'll come back home and act right for you."

Her tone is exactly what home should taste like—sweet and satisfying. She doesn't know how to kiss, but that makes it better. All she wants is to taste all of me and CeCe was right, just like Pops was. Addiction is so selfish that I can't help but spoil her.

"I can't believe I let him bring you here," I mutter as her lips latch onto my bottom one. "Why I let him do that, baby?"

There it was again—*baby*.

She sucks hard like she wants to leave proof that she turns me into a bitch when we're home and even simple things like her being a shitty kisser makes my dick push against my briefs.

"Hm? I should've made you stay with Mom, huh?"

She nods like any of the shit I'm saying is rational or healthy, but nothing about me is either of those things, and I think she knows that because she's my little lady. She doesn't know to stay away from men like me.

"Tell me I was hella stupid for this shit." I wrap my fingers around her cheeks, pulling her lips from my bottom one. "Tell me I'm dumb for letting other niggas see how good you look in Dior."

She smiles and squeezes her legs around my waist like we haven't been beefing for the past hour because the last party of the summer tested us.

"You *hella* stupid." She sighs, closing her eyes and hiccupping a breath full of alcohol.

"And you're fucking drunk." I mutter, scraping my nails against the bruise on her ass. "Fuck."

CHAPTER SIXTEEN

Ace

The stall door's lock clinks again and when it swings open, I realize a walk of shame in a girls' bathroom means something different now. Back in LA, me and Javier used to keep a running tally of our embarrassing stumbles out of girls' bathroom stalls. I had the lead before shit happened.

"You a'ight, girl?" a different girl asks Phat as I pull her toward the entrance.

The line for an open toilet is a lot shorter and the primping girls from the mirror left. It's just me, Phat, and five girls narrowing their eyes at me.

Phat wrinkles her eyebrows. "Ye—yeah... I'm good."

She looks between me and the girl like she doesn't know if she should thank her for her nosy concern or tell her that just five minutes before we stumbled out of the stall; she was sucking on my bottom lip.

The girl looks us up and down.

"C'mon, let's go." I pull her hand and drop it because I

know what life is like outside that stall and that drunk rant she went on tells me she doesn't.

The rest of the population doesn't live on Planet Ace like Phat. Most of them don't question anything that's fed to them—not even about a kid like me.

"We going home?" she asks, tilting her head.

"Yeah. I'm taking *you* home to Mom."

"No...no." She tugs my shirt while I try to step forward.

Their eyes are like ten pairs of lasers zeroing in on my mouth when Phat slurs her words.

"Yeah...c'mon." I stare back at the one who asked Phat if she was a'ight. "Brandy's in the car waiting for us."

I need to leave a name, a breadcrumb, an alibi —*anything*. It's the aftermath of the carnage from LA.

"You brought her here with you?" Phat asks.

"Yeah. What else was I supposed to do? Leave her on the side of the road?"

"Why the fuck would you do that?"

The girls whisper.

So, it's like ten pairs of accusatory eyes wanting to know if Brandy is "a white girl" and if I'm brave enough to "touch a bitch" while they're watching. Phat's too drunk to understand though.

"Aye..." I breathe out, darting my eyes between her and them. "Let's go."

"No—"

"I said *let's go*."

There's a chorus of "ohhhs" when I push out of the bathroom with Phat on my heels. When we pass the security guard, he smirks at her twisted sarong and scarf dangling from my fingers.

"Have a good night, *Hollywood*." He chuckles. "Stay outta trouble."

"Yeah... whatever, nigga." I toss my hand back, swiping Phat's to pull her into the muddy field I waded through to get to the entrance.

"Get on my back." I crouch, yanking her arm.

"I don't wan—"

"Okay. You want me to buy you nine-hundred dollar sandals again?" I grit out. "Fuck it. I'll buy them. Bring your ass on."

"Cree let you pay nine-hundred dollars for sandals?"

"Yup. Nine-hundred dollar shoes for you to fuck up, a thousand dollar swimsuit that didn't even get wet and a six-hundred dollar scarf for you to play around with. What else you want to argue about tonight?"

I frown, pushing my foot into the soft grass. I swat away the humidity, mosquitoes, and annoying satisfaction of Bryson never having the privilege of picking out anything to go on her body. It wasn't shit but that sneaky 1942 creeping back into my tastebuds to mingle with Phat's kisses she gave me that she won't remember tomorrow.

"Nothing," she mumbles, clawing her fingernails into my shirt and lifting her leg. "We already argued 'bout everything."

"Thought you wasn't getting on?"

"I—I can't keep my feet on the ground."

"I'mma kill that nigga," I mutter, squatting.

"You can't just be killing niggas... unless it's on the court. I always su—support you killing niggas on the court. You do that shit effortlessly." She twists her legs around my waist and curls her arms around my neck like a lazy koala while blurting out the shit she probably always keeps in her head.

I hoist her up while taking wide steps to the back of the field.

"Ason?" she gurgles out.

"What?"

"I'm sorry."

"What you sorry for?"

"For this—for real. I should've gone to—to the Holy Convocation with Chels. I think you would've been okay with me going there."

"Wasn't nobody bringing you to no damn holy convention." I smile, stumbling down paths of cars while pulling her closer into me.

She groans into my neck, rubbing her nose against my hot skin.

"I was just homesick," she mumbles.

That right there really makes me want to give the finger to Splashtown and Bryson, but I yank her legs closer around my waist.

"What you know about being homesick?"

"I know liquor definitely don't taste the same as it do when I drink it from your cup and you were right—I never want that shit again."

I bounce her up and down, passing up foggy car windows and arguing couples. "You drank after somebody other than me? That's nasty."

"Not on purpose," she garbles out, sucking in a breath against my hot skin. "I regret that shit."

"I bet."

"I don't understand why you got *so* much beef with me all the time—'no Twitter,' 'act right,' 'don't give Mom that,' 'you trying to control the vibe, Lourdes, 'no drinking,'" she huffs in a deep voice.

I smile wider. "Yeah, whatever."

"I'm the one that's always in trouble."

"Because you don't listen."

"Listen?" She hiccups. "That shit shouldn't matter when I always give you whatever you want. I gave you my first date, my first real kiss..."

"You don't know what you talking about—you just talking 'cause you drunk. You won't remember none of this tomorrow."

"No. I get it now. Splashtown is *not* an appropriate first date—Ason Williams' Shooting Stars Gala is."

"That wasn't a date."

"It wasn't?"

"No...it was just everyday life shit."

"Oh, now you in your feelings? I only broke one tiny rule, but it's—it's because you weren't here. Fuck, I just wanted yo—"

"Lourdes?" I call out, glimpsing at Brandy's wild blonde curls in my front passenger seat.

"Yeah?"

"Shut up."

"O—kay," she gurgles out, pushing her lips against my neck with a loud sigh.

It's been a long time since I had to control two girls in the same space. As misogynistic as it sounds, Mom was the one who taught me how to do something so backwards because in our world, jersey chasers and perfect girls had to co-exist at some point. Phat's drunk and she's mine, so she's the most malleable and the wildest. Mom said control always started with the girl that belonged to me.

"Baby?" I call out again, bouncing her up while crossing over another hunk of mud.

"Uh, huh?"

Honesty comes next, even if Phat will only remember incoherent chunks of my voice tomorrow like I wanted.

"Can you listen to me real quick?"

"Uh, huh. I'm listening."

"Brandy is in our front seat right now—not because I wanted to make you mad or hurt your feelings." I talk slowly, being careful to think about each word before I say it, because that's just as important as being honest. "She's there because I'm a man and sometimes men do stupid shi—"

"Dumb *ass* shit."

"Don't interrupt me."

Another hiccup gurgles from the back of her throat as she nods into my neck.

"Sometimes men do stupid shit when we can't control certain things or situations, and tonight I did a stupid thing."

The only way I know she's listening is by the tight squeeze she gives my neck.

"I been drinking and you have too, so if anything happens between you and her in that truck, I'm going to be the one in trouble—never you or her. I'll never let anything happen to either of y'all despite what you think about each other. Do you hear me?"

Her legs squeeze my waist this time and now I have to direct because direction is the second rule of control.

"I want you to get in the backseat and act right for me until I can get her back to her apartment. The less trouble you give me, the easier it'll be for me to get rid of her and the quicker we can go home."

Her body gets still.

Maybe she can see Brandy taking selfies in my front seat from our spot between two cars.

I hope not.

"Tell me how you feel right now," I demand. "Tell me what you need from me."

Support is always last. It's like the cherry on top of an

emotional rollercoaster of a conversation like this. Sometimes it was how I ended up in bed with both girls at the end of the night, but this wasn't that type of situation. This one is delicate. My little lady is having her first grown up night.

"Lourdes?"

A tiny mewl comes from the back of her throat and the warmth from her middle burns through my shirt when she thrusts her hips into my back.

"Open your mouth," I add. "I can't read your mind."

Crickets chirp in the distance while the music from the building thumps between our bodies.

"Will I always wanna fuck you after you do stupid man-things that hurt my feelings?" she blurts.

A swarm of butterflies burst out of the cages in my stomach as if this drunken *hella* toxic conversation is the definition of romance, and I almost choke on them.

"Nah, that's the liquor talking." I swallow the butterflies. "You'll wanna kill me *first* and then fuck me after I make it better and I promise I'll always make it better."

I breathe through the fluttering in my stomach. "Let me put you in the car so I can make it better. A'ight?"

"'Kay..." she squeaks out against my neck one last time before I take the last few steps to my truck.

"Phat?" Brandy gasps when I yank the backdoor open and drop her inside. "You okay?"

I see the subtle eye roll Phat gives her underneath the interior light and I hold in a laugh, slamming them inside together.

When I pull open the driver's side door, Brandy's leaning over the console with her head poking in the back-seat, babbling about how dope it is that the rumors are true about Pops giving us host families. She's already come to her own conclusion about me rushing across the city for my "host sister." Neither of us correct her.

"Cute swimsuit." She grins, bobbing her head toward Phat. "Where'd you get it?"

"My nigga."

I blow out a quiet laugh, pulling my bottom lip into my mouth to suck her off of it.

"I didn't know you were dating somebody."

"I'm not. Can you lea—"

"Lourdes," I call out, backing out of the field and easing back onto the road that led us there. "Put your seatbelt on."

She smacks her lips, and I hold in my urge to reach in the backseat for her. I flick my turn signal to merge into the line of cars leaving out and lean back in my seat.

Brandy pulls her head from the back and flashes a shy grin toward me, but it's not like Phat's little half smile-half frown.

"Hey, I gotta get her home. You mind if I cut our night short?" I ask, lifting my lips into a calm smile.

"Oh." She frowns. "I mean, I was really hungry."

"Don't trip. I still got you. Uber Eats on me?"

"I guess. I really wanted to hang out though. You sure you can't swing by after you drop her off to her mom?"

Another one of those soft sounds eases from the back of Phat's throat.

"Nah." I shake my head, pulling my phone from my pocket and unlocking it. "I have to wake up early to check on somebody."

I dangle it in the backseat toward Phat. "Chop it up with Phat. She'll order you whatever you want. It should be at your door when we get to your place."

Letting go is the worst part of control. Mom always said the aftermath of letting go would tell how well I controlled a situation. Six years and hundreds of unpredictable girls later, I still get tense before the first interaction.

Brandy rolls her eyes at me and turns into the backseat. "Can you order me a chicken strip basket?"

They stare at each other.

I eye my wildcard in the rearview mirror, pouting and pressing buttons on my phone.

"Mhmm. What else you want?" she asks, pursing her lips to the side.

"A Dr. Pepper with light ice. Oh." Brandy snaps her fingers. "And onion rings. You getting something?"

I guess Mom always knew best.

I smile, turning up the volume on the radio.

After an easy Uber Eats order, an attempted goodnight hug from Brandy that Phat thwarted with a pretend nauseous stomach, and a drunken Shipley's visit, we end up back on the Northside.

The living room television casts a soft light across the living room as I push open the front door and stumble inside with Phat tangled around my waist.

"Go shower and get in bed," I whisper, scooping her backpack off the floor.

Whatever she drank has her hands sneaking under my shirt and her eyes heavy. "D'you get my bear claws out the car?"

"Mhmm." I peel her hand off my skin and push my nose into her braids. "Go get ready for bed."

I can't lose myself like I did in that bathroom stall because she won't be drunk forever. Eventually she'll sober up and realize what was said, done, and why I was always trying to keep her off of Earth.

She hooks her arms around my waist as I push forward

with us together. "Go to bed. I need to let Jazmine go and check on Mom."

"I can do that. "

"Not while you drunk, you not. You know better."

Another mewl claws from the back of her throat and I think I want her soft and drunk like this forever until she turns around, stabbing her finger into my chest.

"Don't you *ever* let that girl in our front seat again. Girls like her will end dudes like you."

I grab her finger, curling mine around it while smiling. "Been there and done that. Go to bed."

Another jersey chaser had already ended me, but I know Phat can't handle that story.

Lourdes

A LOUD, screeching buzzer pounds into my eardrums and Jalen Rose talks to me in my dreams.

"Last night the Lakers took on the Suns in another preseason matchup in Vegas. This preseason has definitely been a struggle for the purple and gold without Ason Williams. Rookie Javier Quinones had a solid night—eighteen points, six rebounds, two assists. I don't know how the regular season will look for them, Jacoby. I think the Lakers organization is still struggling from the loss of AW."

"Absolutely and let's also be mindful of the tremendously hard year he's had with the death of his wife Angie and the controversy surrounding his son—"

I bite on my tongue and push against my mattress, but my body won't move. It's stuck. I can't even yell at Jacoby for having the nerve to talk about Ace, and I swear some-body took a sledgehammer to my temples.

"Be still. You can't do push-ups with a hangover, kid."

My arms collapse and I realize my mattress isn't under me. Ace is.

I fall face first into his bare chest, gurgling out a groan.

"A hangover?"

"Mhmm." He hums, tapping against his phone's screen.

There's a block in my brain from last night. I hear DJ G5's screeching; I feel myself peeling Bryson's hand off of my ass; I see Brandy's blonde curls and I taste Ace's smell deep in my throat. But the rest is black.

Jalen Rose screams at me this time like he's disap-pointed that I got drunk for the first time.

"Damn, can you not? Too loud."

There's a trail of slobber on Ace's skin and hangovers are so tough that they overpower the other feelings I should have, like embarrassment and confusion, because I couldn't even remember how I ended up on top of him.

I swat a hand on my head, but there's nothing there except my frizzy braids. I glance down and catch a whiff of Ace's scent because I'm in his Gallery Dept. t-shirt instead of Marcus' old jersey.

I strain my neck to get a glimpse of Marcus' shadow lurking under my bedroom door, but there's nothing. The AC kicks on and the hum from the unit outside my bedroom window is like a punch to my throbbing temples.

"This got to be what death feels like," I mutter, swiping a hand across the slobber on his chest.

"It ain't."

"Is this how you feel after you drink?"

"Not anymore." He reaches over to my nightstand,

picking up two pills and a glass of water while I hold on to his biceps. "Here."

"You not thirsty?"

"Nope, and you not slick." He pushes the cup against my lips. "Open your mouth."

Taking a sip from a cup that his lips hadn't touched first is as bad as the sledgehammer to my head and my frost bitten toes. The water is warm and bland.

He stares at me through heavy eyes like he wants to make sure I'm swallowing every single drop. When he decides I had enough, he yanks it back and pushes the pills toward my lips.

I open my mouth wide enough for him to stick them on my tongue and then I wait while he stares at me like he's trying to decide something. It's a Pavlov moment because I know I should close my mouth, but I'm left there like an idiot with Tylenol on my tongue and Ace squinting at me.

"Hm." He pushes the glass back toward my mouth.

After I swallow the pills, I open my mouth right back up. "Di—did something happen last night?"

He blinks so slow that it makes my gurgling stomach twist. "Yeah. You went to Splashtown."

"And?"

"And Bryson let you drink and let you wander off by yourself."

I turn my neck, looking for my phone, but it's across the room on top of the backpack I swore I left by the front door.

"Yeah, you left that at home, and no, he didn't text or call. I checked."

"Oh."

There's something he isn't saying and I think it might be worse than the fact Bryson didn't take care of me like he should've—as if anything could've been worse than that.

"Did something else happen?" I mutter.

"Yeah...you kissed me."

"I—I kissed you?"

"Mhmm...in a nasty ass bathroom stall because you had me driving across the city to pick your ass up."

"Oh, fuck." I bury my face in my hands and wait on the regret to come out of his mouth for real this time, but I hear the pounding thunks from the headache rocking my skull instead.

This is as bad as the *other* trail of wetness I left on him after a night of Janet and tuna tartare.

"I didn't mean to do that."

Now I sound like the regretful one. I can't even remember how good he tasted.

"Do what? Worry me to fucking death or kiss me? Be specific."

I pull my face out of my hands. "Sorry."

His cheek lifts and the smile he gives me afterward is lazy but comforting. Neither makes me stop holding my breath until his deep voice rumbles from underneath me.

"Not even gon' lie, that shit was hella mid. You can't kiss for shit, baby."

Baby comes out slow and my stomach jumps like he just told me some real player shit—not that I'm a terrible kisser. That block in my brain clears and I almost hear him calling me that at another time and in another place.

Baby.

I inhale his smell from his shirt and my mouth lifts into one of those half-smile half frowns. "Forget you. I was drunk."

We laugh together in quiet huffs and a sharp pain shoots through my head.

He drops his phone beside us with a thump. "Yeah... you were real drunk."

Afterward, his fingers jump to my braids. They push into my scalp in soft circular motions and I hear in his words that I did more. It's in the "baby" he mumbled and in the satisfaction of his admission that I was a terrible kisser.

"What else did I do last night?" I whisper.

Pushing the words out is torture and waiting for his answer is even harder.

"You told me you hated Cheyenne."

"Cheyenne?" I frown. "Who's that?"

He swallows, tilting his head. "The girl who made somebody like Blake Harvey believe that my wildest dream is to play in the NBA."

Attaching a name to a scandal is another feeling I can't pinpoint. I just know that it's not satisfaction because I hear the weight of her accusation in Ace's voice. For the first time, I wonder how it feels to carry that weight on his shoulders.

"Is it true? You hate her for real?"

My mouth hangs open again.

Mama wasn't lying when she told me how blunt alcohol makes folks.

I nod, but I wish I could shout that shit into a mic with thousands of people watching, like DJ G5. This moment isn't how I always imagined it in my head. It's messy.

"I—I... shouldn't hate the girl," I stutter out. "It's just now that I know *all* of you I—I can't see how you could ever do something like that to somebody."

All the seconds, minutes, hours and days spent tiptoeing around this girl and now I know her name. It's not as opulent as I expected, but that's what happens when I let my imagination fill in the grey areas of reality. She's not "that white girl" anymore. She's *Cheyenne*.

He pushes his forehead against mine, twisting my braids between his fingers while I wait on him to tell me he's innocent and promise me that Cheyenne is a liar. Instead, he croaks out something even worse.

"I'm sorry."

It isn't, "I didn't do it" or "I did it, but it was a mistake." It's not even a hint, but my mind doesn't care about rational shit when I'm existing on Planet Ace.

"What you so sorry for?"

"That I can't take you to a basic ass frat party, carry your drunk ass to the girls' bathroom and make out with you there without her ghost haunting you."

It's all about me and not her and I don't know what to do but to open my mouth for him in all the ways he taught me.

"*Ason...*" I whine.

He smiles, pushing his mouth against mine.

On Planet Ace, there's no such thing as drunken kisses, confessions, or Los Angeles girls. It's just us.

His hand falls from my braids to my cheeks. He cups and squeezes them while I rock against his stomach. His touch and the friction from my rocking are better than any shuffling I can do with my legs to get rid of his hives.

"Now, tell me something good. Make me forget about her," he says against my lips. "Tell me why you shouldn't get in trouble for last night."

It's too hard to do that because his tongue pushes its way inside my mouth when I'm supposed to be doing what he says, but he doesn't care.

"Because I'm home, acting right for you," I murmur against it, smiling.

It's the one thing that made it from behind that block in my brain from last night.

When I rock back again, my hand brushes against *it*. That's the only way I know how to describe the first dick I ever felt in real life. *It*. When my hand slides against the tented fabric of his shorts, he pushes it.

"Nuh uh." He wraps his tongue around mine, sucking my hellish Splashtown hangover off it. "You can't have my dick if you don't even know how to kiss me."

A comeback gurgles up my throat and bursts out in a moan that makes his other hand crawl up his t-shirt I'm wearing. He grips my ass so hard that his nails dig into the skin and scrape across the bruise he left there.

The way he talks to me in these types of moments is something else I like that I shouldn't—just like his fingers in my mouth.

He pulls his tongue off mine and looks at me. "You hear me?"

I nod, chasing his mouth, but he doesn't let me get far before he smooshes my cheeks between his hand again. "And you can't have me unless you want a flawed, fucked up person. That's what you want?"

That last sentence doesn't come out in a smooth shit-talking tone. He gasps it out in a rasp and I never been so desperate to have a flawed fucked up person, so I nod.

"No." He pecks my lips between two slow shakes of his head. "You not supposed to agree to that."

Tasting him with sober tastebuds is what he must've been talking about when he said I tasted like summertime on the PCH because he tastes like the first real day of fall in Texas—when the weather is crisp and that nasty suffocating stickiness isn't floating in the air.

"Yeah I am," I breathe out.

His fingers creep along my ass and then fall to my thighs in a place where no other fingers have been except my own. There's something about existing together on our own planet that makes me fearless, so my legs open wider to make room for him.

"Who taught you to open your legs like that?" he mumbles, dragging his lips to my throat.

"You."

He laughs, opening his mouth against my skin. "I taught you how to open your mouth—not your legs. Why you can't ever act right for me?"

He nudges my legs open wider between each word, like he's doing ordinary shit. The block on my brain from last night turns into a fog of lust, and I don't worry about his rough knuckles scraping my skin while he rolls my panties down.

He smiles again.

"Is baby still wearing childish ass flowery Victoria's Secret PINK panties?" He chuckles, making my cheeks warm. "Lay back so I can see you."

When the cold gust from the vent above my bed touches my bare vagina, that lusty fog lifts from my brain in an "oh shit" type of way.

Before my hands decide to stop tripping and reach out to cover what nobody's looked at but me, Mama, and God, I'm already free-falling against my shaggy comforter.

"Nuh uh." He shakes his head, biting into his bottom lip. "You know better."

This must be one of those things with an "ever" that he told me about back at his condo, so my hands fall at my sides. My heart beats in a slow, panicking rhythm because I don't know where Marcus is or if Mama's having a good day and can push herself out of bed.

He studies my fuzz covered middle with my PINK panties balled in his hands.

"So... what's the deal, kid?" he breathes out.

"W—what?"

"You said you want a flawed, fucked up person."

"I... I do."

"Why you talking like I ain't already dumb for you? Like I ain't race across the city with another chick in my front seat to get to you last night. Like Marcus ain't press me over you. Like you don't already have me? Why you even want a man like me?"

The words follow his head as he dips between my legs.

I think there's only so much imagining somebody can do before they conclude that the scenarios that live in their imaginations ain't shit compared to how they feel in real life. Real life is *so* much better.

Ace's soft lips against the most sensitive part of my body is like a satisfying ending to a good ass story. They peck and pull the skin while I squirm against his face and when his tongue twirls between the lips, my back thrashes deep into the bed.

"Fu—ohh," I gasp out something between a moan and a curse while he kisses me in soft, teasing motions.

I reach out to find his head, scraping my fingers across his scalp and the sides of his face. That makes his head bob and his tongue thrust harder, like he wants the world to see the evidence of what he's doing to me. I hear him slurping the wetness that's always there when he's around.

"Lourdes?" He hums out.

"Yeah—yeah, As—?"

"Can I have you, baby?"

The question comes out like the other ones he's so good at asking and I don't think he's talking about fucking. Boys like him aren't supposed to ask questions like *that*. At least that's what I learned on Earth.

Another cold gust tickles my skin as I peel my eyes open and look up at him hovering over me with red scratches across his temples and a glossy coat of my wetness on his lips. Sun rays sneak between the blinds and bounce off his sad brown eyes.

It's the first time I ever seen them this way.

I push up on my arms, waiting for him to crack a smile and tell me I'm "hella sensitive" for thinking he's for real, but all he does is drag his fingers across my thighs.

"I told you, you get whatever you want," I whisper.

"No, you told Twitter that. I want you to look me in my face and tell me that shit."

My eyes scrape across all the parts of him that make my frilly panties wet—his pink lips that never complain about the shitty card somebody dealt him one summer and his eyes with that sadness in them like he's had nothing worth keeping.

"I'll give you whatever you want, Ason."

The words come out crystal clear without any doubt in them.

He sighs, crawling on top of me. Our faces smash together and his lips cover mine.

"Open your legs wider." He breathes into my mouth, marching his fingers down my stomach and between my legs.

They pat my lips and then push down, rubbing in slow, hard circles that make my hips chase their movements. He pulls his mouth from mine and plants it on my forehead.

"Open wider for me."

When he slides his fingers to my entrance, my body locks.

"Don't be like that. Relax for me."

For him.

I wish somebody would've explained that lust and all its whimsical endorphins make me want to do anything for him, like take his long finger without fussing about how much it's stretching me out in ways I've never been.

"That's right, baby."

He cheers me on like he's watching me play ball or solving the greatest mystery, but all I'm doing is taking his digit with my eyes closed and his lips against my ear.

He works it in circles, easing the tension from my walls and my shoulders.

"You wanna know something?" He kisses my lobe, crooking his finger.

I nod, choking on a moan.

"When I asked if I could have you, I meant like on some forever type shit."

"Me too." I gasp as he pushes his finger further than my little one has ever gone.

It's a snug fit, and he reminds me by cursing under his breath. In bed he's like Dr. Jekyll and Mr. Hyde. The unpredictability keeps me clawing at his hair.

"Prove it," he says, pulling my nipple into his mouth. "Show me forever."

Forever goes good with the flick of his thumb against my clit. It makes me suck in deep *long* breaths while he laughs.

I gasp. "How the fuck I do that?"

He curls his tongue around my nipple. "I don't know. You the one agreeing and shit."

"Aso—ahh." It was his thumb again.

"I want forever," he sings. "I'm wait—"

"Put another one in." I thrust my hips up and spread my legs wider, like he keeps coaching me to do.

"There you go, baby."

His words are gentle, nurturing and calm and remind me why I'm so obsessed with him.

"You still can't have my dick though." He laughs, nudging another finger inside me, and sliding down my body.

Having any part of him inside me makes me think of irrational shit like how his dick might feel plunging inside of me. *That's* the forever I want.

"But..." I gurgle out.

"I think your eyes are bigger than your stomach." He smiles from between my legs. "You better start listening to me."

I don't have a chance to dissect another one of his sexual innuendos before his tongue thrashes against my clit and his fingers stroke in and out of me in smooth, twisting motions. The sudden build up of warmth between my legs makes my nerves tingle with satisfied sighs. Words fall out of my mouth that I don't know the meaning of. In between them, I call Ace a jumble of something that makes him push his heavy tongue against me harder and my legs clamp around his head. I'm cumming, but I can't mold the words in my mouth to tell the world, so Ace helps me along the wild, rolling waves of pleasure.

"Shhh...you want everybody to hear what you call me? That's for my ears only," he hisses, nudging his other fingers in my mouth. "Open up and give me my pussy, baby. You can't take it away—not yet. You said I could have you forever, remember?"

I can't even appreciate his outright nastiness for the first time because I'm too busy suckling on his fingers and rocking my hips against his face to soothe the aftermath of the trip he took my body on.

I squeeze my eyes together and wait for the post-orgasm shame to wash over my body from the words we exchanged and the places he saw that no other boy has.

He pulls his fingers from my mouth. "Lourdes?"

"Ye—yeah?"

"Tell me how you feel."

Somehow there's a difference between that and, "are you okay?"

I tap my tongue against the roof of my mouth and squirm as he pulls his fingers out of me. I miss them already.

"I feel drunk again."

When I peel my eyes open, he's kneeling between my legs with his fingers in his mouth and his abs contracting with the heavy breaths he's pushing out. He's breathing like he's the one that came.

He pulls his fingers out. "As long as you drunk off of me. I'll take that."

My phone chimes from across the room, but we don't tear our eyes from each other's.

"Go get it," he grunts, slapping my thigh.

I twist and push from underneath him, gloating at the heaviness of his hand dragging against my ass and the back of my legs when I climb off the bed.

When I turn the phone over, it's the text he was waiting on.

Bry: You good?

That's it. He didn't race from his dorm to beat on the front door and make sure I was home. He didn't even call.

"That's him?" Ace asks.

I nod, staring at the disappointing check in. After

twelve years of friendship and hundreds of strawberry cool cups, I thought we were better than that.

I glance around my desk for the first time that morning.

An empty Shipley's bag hangs off the edge. My swimsuit and sarong sit in a folded lump, and Ace's mud-caked Jordans are shoved under the desk. It's easy to connect the dots of the aftermath of Splashtown.

My bed creaks.

"You good?" Ace reads from over my shoulder, chuckling. "Tell him—you know what—nevermind."

He reaches over me, swiping the Shipley's bag and balling it up. "He always so careless with you?"

"I—I—no."

The cursor in the message box blinks while it waits for me to figure out what to type, but I can't think of anything because the boy I hate and like isn't smiling anymore. There's a smatter of red along his caramel cheeks.

"That's hard to believe."

"I don't think he did it on purpose."

That was that strawberry cool cup loyalty talking.

"Man, fuck that shit. *He* picked you up from this house in perfect condition and that's how he should've brought you back to m—"

I hold my breath for him to belt out the rest, but he stops himself.

"Next time, bring that backpack with you. If you think it's so childish, I'll buy you a purse to take." He dumps the Shipley's bag into the trashcan next to my desk. "You should ask him how he talks about you in a room full of men and then tell me if you still think he didn't do it on purpose."

He mutters the last words under his breath, but I hear them loud and clear. There's more that he knows and he won't tell me, just like he won't tell me more about Los Angeles or Cheyenne.

He breathes over my shoulder while I reach out and pull the front zipper of the backpack open. I was too excited about Dior swimsuits and Splashdown that I never even touched it. There's a credit card stuck to the front of my Bubble Yum that's tucked deep into the pocket.

"What's this?"

"You should always have your own when you going out with a boy," he replies, shaking his head.

"I don't have my own when I go out with you."

"Because I'm not a boy. That's the *real* problem with me and you. You keep thinking I am."

My fingers slide across his embossed name on the credit card while the cursor waits for me to ask Bryson the questions he wants answers to.

The phone chimes again.

Bry: ??

A hard tug on my braids pulls my eyes away from that teasing cursor.

"Last night, Mom told me she wanted grits for breakfast again. Fuck him and take care of her."

"Grits?" I croak out.

Never mind the drama waiting on my phone—Mama wanted grits for breakfast. That's the only thing that matters to a man that's constantly living on his own planet.

"Yeah. The grind don't stop just because you fucked up and *got* fucked up. I made hella pots of grits after getting lit." His fingers land at the center of my ass in one of those "don't do it again" slaps that sting so good. "Go take care of your business. Underage drinking is a no-no. I don't care how bad you missing me."

He scoffs. "You must not want Twitter back that bad."

As soon as his words come out, *his* phone dings like everybody on Earth woke up and realized how good of a time we were having at home.

CHAPTER SEVENTEEN

Ace

"Babygirl must've had you busy this morning." Blake chuckles, staring at Marcus' baggy blue Polo that Phat handed me before I left her house.

She wouldn't peel herself out of my t-shirt and I wouldn't make her—not even when I got his text in her bedroom.

> 2128045609: How about that ride you owe me? I got the 911 gassed up just for you. Meet me at the Post Oak.

It was the shittiest way to crash back onto Earth after floating on Planet Ace all morning with her legs wrapped around my head, but takers didn't care that I watched my little lady have her first orgasm from oral while floating in the clouds at home. Takers never cared. They were just as shiesty as they were thirsty. So, I kept him waiting while I sipped on Hennessy, kissed on Phat while she cooked grits, and held CeCe's spoon at breakfast because she said her hands weren't working. I don't think her eyes were either because she didn't even notice I had on Marcus' shirt or that I slept in Phat's bed.

"She must've had you *real* busy." He looks up at the scratches along my temples, dangling the keys to his 911 in my face. "Had me waiting all morning."

The parking garage shakes as cars zoom in and out. I let the keys hang from his fingers.

"Yeah, I figured you didn't have anything pertinent to discuss."

"Now, now." He holds up his hands, smiling and pushing the keys into my chest. "Don't be like that. I just want the same thing your Pops wants for you."

He turns and spreads his arms out. The Audemars Piguet on his wrist twinkles in the dark garage.

"I read in *Time* magazine that you're a Porsche man. I mean, it didn't come out of your mouth but out your Pops'. He said you bought your first one at fifteen." He whistles. "*Fifteen.* You even had a license then?"

I swallow, staring at the pitch black 911. "Nah, but I got a fat ass check under the table from Nike for hooping in a rare pair of elevens in my first high school game."

"Ha! I'm sure it ain't stop you from taking it for a spin and fucking off some of that fat ass check you got just from hooping in a pair of sneakers nobody can even afford. Don't seem like anybody stops *The Kid* from doing what he wants." He shrugs. "Well, *almost* anybody."

His voice echoes throughout the garage while I try to ignore the taste of Cheyenne's name on my lips. Saying it after two years is exactly how I thought it would be—bitter.

"Come on. Get in." He taps the driver's door. "Take me around your city. It's yours now, right?"

He doesn't wait for me to agree before he walks over and gets into the passenger seat.

I look over my shoulder, waiting for Phat to come out of the shadows with her little mouth twisted, telling me how much she hates corny ass Carlton Banks niggas like Blake, but I put her to bed after she cooked breakfast. My little lady didn't know how to survive hangovers and I didn't know how to survive random ambushes by agents.

I walk forward, yanking the door open and Blake is such a sneaky taker that the interior is set up just right with Dough blasting, candy in the console, and 1942 on the floor next to his leg.

I stoop down, sliding behind the wheel.

"Can't have you riding around just any kind of way." He swipes the bottle off the floor and unscrews it. "What you think?"

"I see you coming correct this time."

When I push the keys in the ignition and the car revs to life, it's almost like I'm *that Kid* again.

"I had to. Your girl called me out." He laughs as I pull out of the parking spot. "You know my dad would say she's a spitfire."

"Yeah... she something like that." I grab the solo cup from his hand and take a sip that feels too good.

"Tell me about her. What all she know?"

"She knows to be a good girl for me, to mind her brother, and to take care of her mom. That's all *you* need to know."

"Come on..." he blubbers out. "Don't give me that evasive ass answer. I'm not a gossip blogger, dawg. I wanna know more about this lil' fling you got going on. It's gotta be real, right? She's still around."

He glances at the Dum-Dums, picking one up and rolling it between his fingers.

"Ain't no fling going on. Didn't I tell you to leave her out—"

"Look, man, I'm just giving you the preview before the main show."

"Huh?" I stop at a red light, whipping my head over to him.

"The 1942 already got you hypnotized? I got another advance for you, brother—better than the Getty one."

Only a sports agent could dress up manipulation and make it as enticing as a reporter could. I always wondered if their bad habits developed over time like mine or if they were just born fucked up.

"So, what's this one about?"

"Twitter."

"What about Twitter?"

He shifts in his seat and pushes his hand into his pocket, pulling his cellphone out. A horn blares from behind us as he holds it in front of me like he did the keys. There's a Word document on the screen—a long one — but that's not the important part. The headline is.

"'Is *The Kid* back on the rebound after his flagrant foul in Malibu?'" he reads, sliding his finger under each word. "Clever headline, fucked up subject."

The horn blares again and I slam my foot on the gas, zooming off.

"Easy. Babygirl would kill me if you get pulled over with that cup in your hand. We not working with LAPD here."

"What is that?"

"It's an article."

"*Nigga*... I know that. Where'd you get it and what does

it say?"

"Well, I can't tell you where I got it, but I *can* tell you what it says." He glances at his phone while I down another mouthful of tequila.

"Slow down. I ain't even started yet."

"Read that shit," I grit out.

"Maybe you should buckle up first. This may be a long ride."

The narrow-eyed stare I give him makes him hold his hands up in surrender and he reads.

"'After a lifetime of social media silence, basketball aficionados that hang out in the Twittersphere woke up to a pleasant surprise six weeks ago—the return of *The Kid* better known as Ason 'Ace' Williams Jr. The mysterious baller is known for his notoriously mum media presence and most recently—controversy. However, us diehard, basketball-heads know that in the land before egregious accusations, *The Kid* was something like a silent icon known for his rare captionless drippy Instagram flicks and hubris on the court. So why the sudden reemergence after so long? I think I found the answer, and it has nothing to do with basketball.'"

There's a deep burning in my throat when I glance over at Blake's smug expression while he reads the mouthful of addicting corniness some reporter typed up.

"In late August, *The Kid's* sleepy timeline suddenly woke up with a strange change of location—Planet Ace? Afterward, a tweet appeared, and I immediately picked up the phone to call my colleague, Dave Burns. Together we cross-referenced the tweet with rap lyrics, did a deep-dive into *The Kid's* pre-controversy interests, but alas we ended back where we started—with a tweet that had no context until Dave pointed out that *The Kid's* following count had changed. It's number jumped from five to an uncharacteristic eight."

"Hm." I scoff.

"Should I keep going?" Blake asks.

I stare ahead at the dancing lights on Westheimer while I speed underneath them. The reds mix with the greens and yellows.

"Don't act like you don't already know what my answer is. That's your job, ain't it? To know all the fucked up things about me?"

"I guess that's a yes." He laughs, looking back at his phone. "'Suddenly, that tweet with no context wasn't so mysterious once we ventured to the timelines of the three new accounts on his following list—two of his new teammates and a freshman girl at Lockwood State who goes by the handle @babyphat04. To the average Twitter user, it may appear the former five star recruit has been talking to himself in cheeky riddles and spouting Dough lyrics now and then over the past six weeks, but us Twitter sleuths think otherwise...'"

He stops and presses the side of the phone, but I need to hear all the ways those reporters bumrushed their way into me and Phat's world. It was invasive and too reminiscent of my past life where everything about me was newsworthy—even my prom date.

I drop the empty cup in the cup holder, gnawing on my bottom lip and pulling into a shopping center parking lot.

"I'll ask you one more time, Kid. What all does she know about you?"

His question takes the excitement and heart pumping adrenaline out of pushing a 911. Now, it's the same as driving a Honda.

"Everything."

"Don't lie to me. I did you two solids for free."

"Yeah, that I didn't fucking ask for."

"Come on, you'll thank me *and* repay me for this later when I rehab your image. Now tell me..." He tears the plastic from the Dum-Dum. "Does she know how pervasive sugar cravings are for an alcoholic trying to kick their habit?"

He turns to me, biting into the sucker, and humming to himself.

"Or is that something AW still ignoring? I mean, shit, I can't blame the man. He's already one scandal in the hole. I don't think he can afford another one with you being all PR-less and what not. What would the headline for this one be? I'm not as clever as that *Times* writer, but shit, I know it's a word out there that rhymes with alcoholic." He bunches his eyebrows together while chewing.

I swallow an even more bitter taste than Cheyenne.

"You don't know what you're talking about."

"I read the leaked sheriff's report, my guy. Not the part they released to the public with Cheyenne's description and the vague details of what she says you did...but *all of it*. And at the end of it, all those rumors rumbling in the sports world about your little habit didn't sound so much like rumors anymore." He glances at my empty cup.

"I'm telling you, you don't know what the fuck you talking about."

If he did, he'd understand why. How else was I supposed to slow down Doctor Lee's words when they came pummeling out of his mouth in riddles filled with medical jargon? Only a shot of 1942 could help me decipher what metastatic meant and what it had to do with Mom.

"At least tell me this—does she know what happened the night y'all celebrated Angie's birthday on that yacht in

Malibu? Did you explain if Cheyenne happened before or after you told Dough all the inspiring shit a nineteen-year-old kid could tell a grown man? Did you tell her if your Pops paid Cheyenne and her family off like everyone believes and then had her sign an NDA just in case she came knocking back at your door asking for more to help soothe her wounds? Or does none of this encompass the *everything* you're talking about?"

"This what you wanted?" I ask. "To get all the answers to the questions those fuck ass reporters been asking for the past two years? You wanna use my answers to blackmail me even more?"

"No, no, no. You have this all wrong. I'm trying to show you the way—lead you to greener pastures. There are two very apparent things you want in this lifetime and that's playing in the NBA like your Pops and to be the man you were before. Let's face it..." He holds up his phone. "This will no doubt come with its own mess. You think they crucified you before? Well, wait until this hits the blogs without me cleaning it up for public consumption. The redemption is always harder than the condemnation but if you fuck with a guy like me, I can make redemption as easy as dribbling that ball you love so much. Or I can sweep this right under the rug where it belongs, so it doesn't see the light of day because you and I both know she's not ready for it. She's unpolished, inexperienced, and young. I can talk to her though—show her how good life can be when you're always ten steps ahead of the rest of the world. Because, let's be honest, what do you think she would do if she woke up with the world at her front door without warning, asking why she's entertaining an accused rapist? Babygirl ain't ready for that. Life with you ain't no walk in the park, brother."

PART 2

THE FIRST DAYS OF FALL

CHAPTER EIGHTEEN

Lourdes

Chelsea found the location to the interest meeting for the sorority she's obsessed with and I can't pretend to care because I keep tasting Ace's tongue. I want to tell her it tastes like the sweet stuff he likes and the bitter liquor he drinks, but I can't. I can't even tell her what happened at Splashtown every time she stops babbling to break through my thoughts and remind me I went to my first party with a boy and not her.

Getting blackout wasted is a mind-fuck. I don't know why anyone would purposely do something so confusing to themselves. Parts of that night come back to me in inconsistent chunks. The worst parts are the moments I can't understand, like Bryson's faceless teammates tugging at my swimsuit and his hot breath in my ear. They make me analyze and re-analyze Ace's words from the day after: *"You should ask him how he talks about you in a room full of men."*

"Are you sure you don't want to come with me?" Chelsea blurts, taking a breath and shoving her sunglasses up.

Blades of grass poke my palms while I stare out from her blanket onto the yard. "You know I can't stay late Tuesday."

"Okay, hear me out. I mapped the whole afternoon out."

"Chels—"

"Just listen! Okay, so boom, stats ends at three-thirty. We jet from campus to your house to check on Mama CeCe, change clothes, jet back to campus, and hurry to the Bates building."

"That sounds irritating."

"It sounds perfect!" she squeals, curling her fingers in a circle in front of my face. "We impress the girlies, get noticed, and we'll be litty in no time."

I pull my knees into my chest, shoving down the sunglasses I borrowed from her dresser before we hiked across campus to people-watch and gossip on the yard. Really, it's just Chelsea gossiping while I watch for Ace. Even the thought of him strolling past me makes my thighs tingle in the places his fingers pressed into. It's even worse than those hives he used to give me. I don't know shit about addiction, but I think I'm in the throes of one.

"I don't wanna be litty." I frown.

"Ugh, is this about the money again? I told you, just tell Marcus the business office said you owe a balan—"

"Hollywood!"

My thighs start tingling again while my eyes dart around behind the glasses' dark lenses. Chelsea keeps chirping like a little high-pitched minion and I don't know why I expect Ace to look any different after what happened between us, but he doesn't. He looks as good as he did before he swaggered off our front porch in Marcus' Polo talking about he had somewhere to go. He looks as perfect as he's always telling me I look and I'm just as bad as Brandy, so I'm drooling over his crispy lineup.

"It's a perfect idea," Chelsea finishes.

I nod even though I didn't hear half of what she said. All I hear is the roaring laughter from the team as they push their phones into Ace's face.

"They're so loud. Probably watching that video." She smacks her lips. "Why you ain't tell me our school went viral for like two seconds on Twitter over the weekend?"

It hurts, but I tear my eyes away from Ace's bright smile. "What you talking about?"

"Hello—*Splashtown*. Little Miss 'I'm going to my first party but can't tell my bestie all the tea.'"

"Girl." I roll my eyes. "Weren't you at a holy convention?"

"Yes, but I can praise the Lord and stay abreast of the happenings of my peers. Ain't nothing wrong with that."

"Bet Mother Lenola wouldn't agree with that."

"Her and Esther cluck like two hens. They can't talk—"

"Okay, reel it back in. What went viral?"

"Everybody rapping to "One of One" on one of those basketball dude's TikToks. It spread from there, to Insta and to Twitter. There was a whole debate about it on Twitter. Some girl from the SGA called everyone that had the nerve to support Ace or that song misogynistic rape apologists. Then someone called her a *word that rhymes with moon* for sticking up for a white girl who's lying for clout. Then it turned into a black versus white thing and at the end of it all, I heard Ace is messing around with somebody on campus who definitely ain't Brandy."

My throat closes.

"Wha—what you mean?"

"Girl what do *I* mean? Which part are you even asking about? Shoot, weren't you there because you keep acting like you weren't?"

"I—yeah. I was there."

"Okay, well, if you're not going to give me details about what happened with you, at least spill the tea on somebody else. Was he there with a girl?"

She sounds like a babbling minion again and I'm dying for a breeze to sweep across the yard to calm my hot skin.

My eyes dash back up to the basketball team's huddle in front of the cafe. Ace isn't smiling anymore. He pushes Marquise's phone away with a nudge and bumps forearms with him like he has somewhere important to be, but I know better. Even viral moments aren't the same for him because of her—because of *Cheyenne*.

"Nah, Chels. I didn't see him with a girl." I swallow. "He wasn't even at the party."

"Damn. Twitter tea proves to be stale once again. Well, how was it overall at least? Great, not so great? Horrible? You been dead silent since Saturday."

I push my thighs close together and twist the lower half of my body to stop the tingling. "How was what?"

"Keep up, Phat. Splashtown."

Oh, *that*. It was nothing like the parties me and Ace have. It wasn't explosive, like his face between my legs, and Casamigos tasted nothing like his tongue. Splashtown didn't ask me for forever or slide its fingers inside me like it was lost and searching for home.

"It was lame," I reply, swiping my tongue across my lips. "You didn't miss nothing."

She exhales. "Phew! I just knew you and lil' Calvin Cambridge had fun without me."

Even her dig at Bryson doesn't make me laugh. Somehow Splashtown was like a turning point for my mind and body. They were consumed with Ace and I didn't *think* I liked Bryson anymore. I knew I didn't.

"Phat?" Bryson's curly mop blocks the beaming sun as he walks up to us.

"Speak of the devil," Chelsea grumbles. "You're gonna live a long time, Tiny Tim."

"Man, not today, a'ight?"

She snickers and looks off.

"You can't answer my texts and calls, Phat?" he asks. "I even DM'd you."

I shrug.

All I hear is Ace's deep "fuck him" in the back of my head and his irrational thoughts of what could've happened to me while I wandered off into a sea of drunk strangers.

"*Somebody could've taken advantage of you,*" he said, pushing a solo cup to his lips in the kitchen the next morning.

After it came out, he buried his face into my neck like it wasn't supposed to.

"Oh, so we just shrugging now? That's how it is?" Bryson asks.

"You wasn't so concerned about me when you let me go off by myself Saturday. I don't remember a lot, but I remember that."

Chelsea gasps, pushing up on her knees. "You left my bestie for dead at that party?"

"Please, mind your business." He pushes his hand out toward her.

"No! Anything could've happened to her."

"You wasn't even there!"

"Negro, I ain't have to be there to know that's not something you effing do."

Chelsea's alternative curse words and irrational thoughts that sound like Ace's makes me push up from the blanket.

I shouldn't have done that because now I'm face to face with Bryson. His red cheeks don't even make me soft anymore.

"I didn't call because LaQuan told me he saw you leaving out with Ace."

Chelsea lets out another ragged gasp.

"He said you came out the girls' bathroom with him," he adds.

"It's even worse than I thought." Chelsea pants. "Lourdes, di—did he do something to you? Bryson, I could ki—"

"Kill me? Kill me for what? *She* left with that nigga."

His excuses are as bad as Chelsea's roundabout accusations. Now I'm so warm that a trickle of sweat glides down my back.

"I was drunk," I mumble.

"Oh my God. You didn't tell me you got drunk!" Chelsea pushes up from the ground. "Is that why you been out of it today? Do we need to go to health services? If you were drunk, that means you can't remember if he did something. Come on."

"Wha—no." I swing my head between her and Bryson.

His face changes too, like he's realizing the seriousness of what could've happened.

"I'm serious, Lourdes. Why'd you say he wasn't there?"

We've been best friends for ten years and I've never seen her as serious as she is now. It's in her wide brown eyes.

Bryson reaches out, tugging at my t-shirt. "Did he touch you?"

I scoff. "Are you serious right now? Are you changing your tune because of Chelsea?"

"I'm dead serious. You need to tell us if he did something to you."

"Or how about *you* tell me if your teammates did something to me since we're so concerned about who touched who?" I pull my t-shirt out of his grip. "As a matter of fact, maybe there's something you need to tell me because they sure had their hands all over me without me asking for them. I don't remember a lot, but I *do* remember that. I guess y'all were hoping I didn't. I guess that's the reason for all the alcohol you kept pouring down my throat."

There's a mixture of expressions his face twists into—shock, confusion, and then his eyebrows crawl together. "Are you trying to accuse me of something?"

"Did you tell them something about me, Bryson?" I ask, fighting off the prickly sensation of their sweaty fingertips crawling across my waist.

He doesn't have to say it. I feel the truth in the air's stillness between us. I can imagine all the words he said to them he won't say to me.

"Don't make something out of nothing and don't flip the script. You got drunk and left with dude. Own your shit, Lourdes."

"Get back." Chelsea pushes her arm out toward him. "You ain't say she was drunk. He could've did anything to her."

"He didn't! They're the ones that were touching me. I—I was drunk and scared because I was alone, so I texted Ace because I knew he was going to be out with Brandy."

I gulp down the rest like how those unintelligible tweets he made me log in and delete after breakfast Sunday morning were for him, how *I* was for him, and how dead ass serious I took the promises I made to him even if I wasn't brave enough to tell anyone else about them.

"They were over on the Southwest side, so he scooped me up."

Bryson nods, biting into his lip while Chelsea takes my hand.

She still doesn't trust my reassuring lies. Never mind that the real vultures had already tainted my curiosity about college parties. She should've been thanking Ace and his control-freak ways, but I forgot how weird shit was on Earth.

"You could've called anybody, Lourdes. Me, Lucy, Marcus." She bobs her head. "Why the *heck* you didn't call Marcus to come get you? I would've rather you called anybody but that boy. If Marcus finds out you let him pick you up, he'll—"

"He'll what?" I snatch my hand.

"He'll go ballistic!"

"Would he really?" I push my eyebrows up.

"Of course he would! He would've came and picked you up. You know tha—"

"Yeah, *would've*—like in the past. I don't think you get that shit isn't like it used to be."

Only one person did.

Neither of them understand how five years could change a situation, a family, a person. Marcus couldn't even make it through our front door most days. I don't think Dr. Evanston's fancy medical terms could explain how Mama's diagnosis made her only son switch up or how college warped my friend's brains into selfish cesspools.

I snatch my hand out of Chelsea's and grab my back-pack from the blanket. "I'm gonna be late for class. I'll talk to y'all later."

Ace

"THE FIRST GAME is a couple weeks away and y'all still playing like a high school JV team." Pops crosses his arms in the center of the court. "Partying, drinking, and more party-ing. Half of y'all couldn't even get here on time today because you were still hungover from Saturday night. I ain't got no sympathy for you."

LaQuan groans next to me on the bench even though it's been two days since Splashtown. The team doesn't know how to deal with Pops when his drawl takes over. They don't know that a double shot of whatever fucked them up over the weekend is the only way to practice through a hangover either.

"When Southern come blow you out on your own turf, I don't want to hear a damn thing." He swipes his bald head. "What the hell is a Surftown, anyway?"

Marquise coughs. "Uh, it's Splashtown sir—"

"Boy, I don't care! The point is all those folks y'all were up there parlaying with at a water park don't have to be on this court with you. They're there for a good time, not a long time. That's it."

I heard this speech before too. He pounded it in my head after me and Javier's first weekend away at UCLA. The point was that I'd never make it to the NBA by getting fucked up every weekend. I guess he was right.

"They're not working to turn this team's reputation

around—*you* are! Y'all are working to turn this campus around. You think folks wanna donate their hard earned money for a bunch of knuckleheads who can't even show up and show out when asked because they're too busy snap-shotting and Instagramming themselves turning up over the weekend?"

"It's Snapchat..." Marquise groans under his breath.

Pops glares at him, twirling his finger around. "Snapchat ain't gon' get you a new gym. I'll tell you that much. Go wash up!"

Their groans and grumbles blend as they push up and fall over each other.

We walk into the locker room with Pops' hot words hanging between us. The door doesn't even close all the way before their eyes plow into me like we didn't just get our asses served to us.

I guess they're still big eyed about a two second viral moment that doesn't matter anymore. That type of shit came and went and when it went, controversy always followed. I heard the whispers as soon as I sat next to Brandy in biology, but she didn't care. Jersey chasers only cared about the nuanced details of their prowl, like if I'd be starting in the first game of the season.

"I'll be there." She grinned. *"Even if you blew me off this weekend to play DD. I know how important first games are for you athletes. My ex had so many annoying pre-game rituals."*

LaQuan coughs and nudges me from behind. "So how was your weekend, Hollywood?"

I shrug, walking to my locker and flinging it open. "Straight. I stayed in."

"Bet you did," Bryson mumbles under his breath.

I pull my head out of my locker and look over at him, but he has his head down, yanking the laces on his shoes. "You say something?"

"He said 'bet you did,'" Marquise says, staring at both of us, smirking.

LaQuan flings his towel out while the rest of the team laughs. "You messier than a female."

"I'm just assisting with facilitating a discussion, man."

"Coach should've never taught your ass what 'facilitate' means." LaQuan howls.

There's something cooking, and the pecking order is at work again.

I pull my slides out of my locker while keeping my eyes on Bryson, but he still won't look at me. I want to look him in his face though. I want to see if there's any regret in his eyes because of how he did Phat Saturday night. I'm still not over it and I don't want her to be over it either.

"You good, homie?" I ask him.

"Yeah, I'm good." He kicks off his sneakers. "You good?"

Marquise snickers. "Translation—Bryson is tight because you left Splashtown with his gal. So he's far from good, my boy."

Bryson smacks his lips and flings his head up, squinting at him. "Okay, you can stop *facilitating* now."

I don't feel the stomach-dropping doom that I should because one of them caught me and Phat leaving. Instead, I'm hot. My tongue burns in the places Phat touched it and my lips are on fire, but I can't tell them that the plotting and planning they've been doing on her will never come to fruition. She couldn't handle it, just like she couldn't handle that article Blake dangled in my face.

I snort. "His *gal*? Phat ain't never had no boyfriend."

That statement wakes Bryson up and has everybody staring at us.

No man ever had his face between her legs, his fingers inside her or her commitment—only me. Maybe she kissed a boy or two before, but that was it and I'd already forced myself to accept that I didn't get to her lips first. Mom couldn't negotiate with God about *everything.*

"How the fuck you know anything about what she had?" Bryson asks.

Marquise flings his arms up. "Maybe she told him. Maybe you getting played."

"Played?" Bryson snaps his neck back.

"Or y'all could just shut the fuck up about some business that ain't yours," I blurt.

Bryson huffs. "Fuck you mean? She *is* my business."

"Oh, for real? You always spread your business around so easily for other men to stick their nose in it?"

He pushes up from the bench with his untied laces dangling from his shoes. "Didn't I tell you that you don't know shit about me and her? Y'all know he likes to listen to our conversations when he has them headphones on?"

"As I should. Niggas get to college and become master storytellers. It gives me my laugh for the day." I chuckle, collapsing onto the bench he pushed up from. "Since we sharing information about each other so freely—y'all know Bryson a capper? Or maybe he's just slow. Brodie been in a one-sided relationship all semester."

I twist around to study their faces and swipe my tongue across my lips to chase the one taste I need besides Phat after another Blake Harvey ambush. That glass I left on the island at home was waiting for them to cover its rim, but I was too busy arguing with a boy, all because my little lady wanted to be grown for a night.

The team folds their lips under their teeth, hold in laughs, and shift under my gaze while I look at every single one of them.

"Major capper," Devon, one of the shooting guards, snickers.

"A capper?" Bryson sputters. "The last thing you should be worried about is me lying because if you touched Phat, I'll—"

There's something about my control freak ways that makes me light on my toes.

I push up from the bench and walk up on him because images of Phat half-naked, wandering around a party full of strangers keeps replaying in my head. "You'll do what?"

LaQuan's beady eyes grow when I push Bryson back against his locker.

It's quiet now. There's no more sniggling—just heavy breathing coming from Bryson's flared nostrils.

"Y'all give me and Bryson a minute to chop it up." I push him closer into the locker.

Marquise sucks his teeth. "Damn, Cali, I ain't even got in the shower—"

"Nigga, walk your ass to your dorm and shower. We can't even set a screen but y'all worried about pussy that ain't yours and will *never* be yours."

"Alright, alright, alright, damn." His words come out fast. "Season just started and freshmans already got my man out his body. Fuck, bro."

Fuck being out my body. I'm not there yet. Instead, I'm trapped inside of it and I see red. It creeps along Bryson's cheeks in a slow crawl while the rest of the team packs their bags in silence.

"Hey..." LaQuan grips my shoulder. "Take it easy, bro."

It's been so long since I existed in a locker room I forgot

how often the pecking order needs reinforcement for lame freshmans like Bryson. They need constant training and his bold ass behavior reminds me how lax I'd been because the pecking order operates a lot like jersey chasers. Neither cared how much smut was on my reputation. According to both, I still exist at the top.

When LaQuan's slides scrape across the floor and the door slams, I grip Bryson's collar.

"What you gon' do? Beat my ass?" he sputters out. "You think that'll make me take my foot off your neck? I ain't starstruck like these other niggas."

His chest heaves in and out. "I know what kind of person you are and I don't care how many times your daddy denies it. I know he's trying to set you up to give you that lil' redemption story you been wanting."

I listen for the moment that he realizes this shit isn't even about basketball, but I know it won't come.

"You got everybody on your side, but I ain't impressed by money and fancy cars. I'm not a dick riding motherfuc—"

"You a lot dumber than I thought."

"Nah, you *are*. Fling your privilege around—beat my ass. I'd be happy for you to do it. Maybe we'll finally get rid of you for good. Nobody wants you here, you know that, right? I'm just the only one bold enough to say it to your face."

I laugh, nodding. "Bold and stupid. I keep forgetting how small your brain is. I guess that's why you need Lourdes around to hold your hand every fucking day."

"Keep her name out your mouth—"

"Or what?" I step forward, crushing our bodies together.

I keep my eyes on his, but he can't return the favor

because he's just a bold, stupid, selfish boy that Phat's confused about.

"Or *what*?" I ask again.

"Or—or—or…" he stutters out. "I'll tell Marcus you—"

That shit makes an even louder laugh fly from my gut while he looks at everything but me.

"Tell him what?" I ask, smiling. "Tell him how you brag about fucking his sister to niggas when he's not playing big brother to you? Tell him how she's been *your girl* since the semester started? Tell him how you let her drink at a party and left her to fend for herself while you chased pussy the rest of the night?"

He blinks up at the ceiling because he still can't look me in my eyes. He can't even deny what I'm saying because we both know it's true.

"How about you tell him this—tell him I'll do them niggas just like I told him I'd do him if they even breathe Lourdes' way again. Tell him I'll be *so glad* when she stops thinking she's grown and being curious about dumbass parties and little boys that don't know enough about life to keep her safe. Tell him I'm still holding shit down at the crib while he steady running, so Lourdes made it back home safe, but she's still in trouble for drinking, Mom didn't hide her breakfast in the trash Sunday morning but the neuropathy got so bad in her fingers I had to feed her. Because I'm not scared of him—you are. This shit don't have nothing to do with basketball. It's bigger than that."

I could curse him out for the foul shit he's done to Phat since I met him, put him on his knees and make him call her and apologize while I watch, but that was impulsive and impulse is shit little ladies don't need—especially mine. Mine needs stability. Mom said it was a must, but she didn't have time to tell me how to control my impulses while keeping shit stable. There's a lot she didn't have time for but Bryson wouldn't know it because he thinks like Pops and not like me and Mom, so as soon as he opens his mouth with a rebuttal my impulsive ass does exactly what Phat doesn't need.

A loud crack echoes through the locker room.

I can't even feel my knuckles crash against his eye because impulse numbs it all.

He heaves in and out and pushes against me and he's talking, but I can't hear anything. Impulse gets rid of that too.

Somebody curls their hand around my shoulder and tries to yank me back from him.

"Ace, bro. Let go," LaQuan hisses, peeling my fingers from Bryson's collar. "He leaking all over the floor."

The red I saw sits in droplets along the concrete floor while Bryson groans out and slides down the lockers.

LaQuan squeezes his burly body between us, but I'm not done.

"Apologize," I grit out, pushing into LaQuan's back.

"Apologize?" Bryson sputters out around a glob of blood. "I'd never apologize to you—"

"To Lourdes."

"Fuck you! Get outta my face."

Sometimes Mom said impulse gave me superhuman strength. It's what helps me grip LaQuan around his neck and yank him behind us.

"Ace!" he yells while I squat to make Bryson look me in my face one last time.

All the shit he's too naïve to know about swirls on it. Impulse. Stability. Perfect little ladies. They even make impulsive ass words fly out of my mouth without me thinking.

"I'm not Coach Williams. I'm not here to give you motivational speeches and tell you how proud I am that you wiped your ass this morning. I'll knock your ass out every time you walk in this bitch if she don't tell me you apologized.... and she'll tell me when I ask her—believe that. Your *gal* will do anything I ask her to do."

CHAPTER NINETEEN

Lourdes

It's been a week since Splashtown and I've realized that sometimes a test of loyalty *isn't* as simple as a strawberry cool cup.

"Come on," Bryson begs from behind our screen door, crunching the plastic cup in his hand. "You still mad at me?"

This morning between *Divorce Court* and *Maury* reruns, the weatherman said it's the first day of fall in Texas and Ace is tripping the fuck out on my phone because Mama threw up a Mexican pizza from Taco Bell. I don't have time for Bryson and melting strawberry cool cups, so I curl my fingers tight around the door handle every time he tries to pull it.

I don't even ask about the black eye he's sporting. I saw the ugly purple bruise along Ace's knuckles when he cornered me in the kitchen after shooting ball with Marcus the other day.

"I think we should put parties on ice with Twitter until

we learn how to control ourselves," he said, dragging his wet face against mine. *"They make us act out of character."*

I didn't have to be Einstein to connect the dots.

Marcus drags his feet behind me, smacking his lips. "Stop messing with that boy and let him in. Lucy already blacked his eye for getting drunk last week. He look pitiful."

"Yeah... pitiful and annoying." I drop my hand from the handle while my phone vibrates from the entryway table.

Bryson pushes his way inside as soon as I swipe it up to look at it.

One of One

That's how I saved Ace in my phone because that's how I saw him saved in Marcus' one day. It's the last song on Dough's mixtape, the one I hear them shooting around to the most, and it made our school viral for two whole seconds according to Chelsea. Now I think I get the lyrics.

> One of One: Why you let her eat that?

> Me: 'Cause that's what she wanted after her infusion. Just like I want you to leave me alone.

> One of One: I see you capped out early this morning. Feeding my mom that nasty ass shit. I don't know how bone broth turned into Taco Bell. Imma get your ass.

> One of One: Call me

"So you can't speak?" Bryson asks, creeping up behind me.

I roll my eyes and brush past him. "Nope."

> One of One: Oh, you really want me to leave you alone? Bffr.

He's sipping because his texts aren't like those subtweets I fell for—they're worse.

> One of One: You don't wanna come home to a nigga no more? a'ight bet.

There's a sink full of dirty dishes, Mama's nauseous and Ace is drinking on a Saturday morning when he should've been headed to Coach Williams' house like he told me he planned last night because he never stops shooting that ball. Not even on the team's off days, but today is different.

I fumble with my phone, pressing it into my ear as I pass Marcus and Bryson in the living room. I head straight into the kitchen toward the sink.

"If you not calling me to come pick you up, I'm hanging up," Ace garbles into the phone.

"What you been drinking?"

"What you been spending all our money on this week? I'm looking at the credit card statement now—Uber Eats, H-E-B, H-E-B, Walgreens, more Uber Eats. Shit, I might as well buy stock in Uber and H-E-B."

I giggle, knocking the knob forward to the sink.

"Victoria's Secret? More flowery PINK panties for me to keep?"

"It's about to get cold. I needed a jacket."

"It's Texas. It never gets cold. I'll take you to Aspen in March and let you taste the snow. Get you a Canada Goose instead."

That heavy card he swiped at Uptown Nails and in the bookstore isn't stuck at the bottom of my backpack anymore. It's sitting in my wristlet even though my first date with

Bryson was long gone. I didn't use it until Ace called me one night when I was starving and Marcus was missing in action, asking why it wasn't being used like the control-freak he is: *"How the fuck you sitting there hungry? You got a credit card in your wallet with a honeybun for a limit. Use that shit."*

Seeing his name pressed into the front of it every time I take it out to use it is another irrational thing that makes me high and want to follow him wherever he goes—even to the end of Planet Ace.

"I don't know shit about Aspen in March."

"You better not. That's for me to teach you—nobody else."

"Ain't you supposed to be paying the credit card bill—not harassing me about men that I'll never come across?"

"You damn right you never will. I won't let you." I smile against the phone. "I know one thing—you gon' have us living in a cardboard box 'cause you wanna buy jackets to wear in eighty degree weather and make Mom live off Uber Eats because I don't make you cook like I should."

"Take the card back then."

"No. It's an essential. That's not something I take away. Twitter's not essential, drinking when you not twenty-one isn't essential, Bryson *for sure* ain't essential." He sucks his teeth.

I let out another quiet giggle at the slur in his words. "You can't shoot threes when you drunk."

I brush my hand against a plate while I listen to his soft breaths over the phone.

"I'm not drunk."

"Then what are you?"

"I'm celebrating."

"Celebrating what?" I ask, wrinkling my nose.

"The quicker you get Mom better and clean up the house, the quicker you'll find out. How you wanna get home?" He talks fast in excited spurts that make me lightheaded.

When I don't answer, he grunts out another drunken hum. "I asked how you want to get to me, baby? I'm letting you be grown again. Don't fuck it up."

Baby.

My stomach and ass get warm. It's that anticipation again. It's a wild way for my body to behave and I don't think I'll ever get used to him referring to me as something so intimate. I don't know how we got here, but we are. It makes my stomach tingle with butterflies again.

"Gus..." I sigh. "Can Gus come get me?"

He chuckles. "Why you want Gus?"

"'Cause I been acting right this week." I shake my neck like he's there to see it. "I deserve to be chauffeured across town."

It wasn't like my other options were doable—an Uber would have him tripping out more because he couldn't control who was behind the wheel and he wasn't fit to drive his truck at the moment. Gus is the only realistic option, but I can't let him think that. It's a part of my addiction. I'm at the point where I know my substance inside and out and a part of knowing Ace is knowing how to control his control-freak ways.

"You been a'ight," he mutters. "Let me see what I can do. You just get Mom taken care of."

I smile while trying to plan all the excuses I can feed Marcus to get out of the house.

It's not Lucy's other day off so I have to keep my get out of jail free card tucked next to Ace's black card in my wallet. Ace is way up on Planet Ace where I'm "baby" and nobody else can take care of "baby" or "Mom" like he can, so he's tripping. I can't have him call Jazmine while he's tripping because I'll fuck up the little slack he's giving me to be "grown." His grown is different from Mama and Marcus'—it's not cursing, drinking, or going out to parties: *"It's just figuring out everyday life shit without me sometimes because I want to feel confident that you can take care of home if I ever have to step away."*

That's the explanation he muttered to me on the phone after the credit card fiasco.

"You hear me, baby?" he asks.

"Yeah, Ason. I hear you."

"I'll send you Gus' number." He hangs up and the phone slides down the crook of my neck.

I scrub faster and rinse the last plate off so good Mama won't have anything to say about streaks.

When I push out of the kitchen and into the living room, Bryson and Marcus are staring at *SportsCenter* from our leather sectional's sinking cushions with their mouths open.

I march in front of the TV, crossing my arms. They groan at the same time.

"You think you can sit with Mama for a lil' while? I need to go somewhere."

Marcus pulls his lips from my strawberry cool cup. "Where you going?"

I look over at Bryson. "Can you give us a minute?"

"You want me to leave?" He frowns.

"Yeah..."

He swings his head toward Marcus like we're ten again and Marcus can make me play nice when I'm mad, but those days are gone.

"Not leave-leave," Marcus mumbles, sucking on a chunk of ice. "Let me see what babygirl got going on."

Bryson sighs, pushing up from the couch.

Our eyes circle each other's in a weird dance because this is the longest we've ever beefed besides that time he smashed his lips against mine under our basketball goal the summer before eighth grade.

"I'll meet you outside." Marcus tosses his chin up to the front door. "We'll work on defense again."

I roll my eyes away from his as he walks to the front door with slumped shoulders.

When it slams shut, I push out a deep breath. "So, can you?"

"What y'all mad at each other for?" He wags his finger between me and the front door.

"Ain't nobody mad at that boy."

"You never turn down a strawberry cool cup."

"Well, today I did. Is there a problem with that?"

"Yeah...it means you mad."

I squeeze my eyes closed, blowing out another breath. "I came to ask you for a favor, not to talk about me and Bryson."

He eyes me up and down while the rest of the cool cup melts in his hand. "Did Lucy give him that black eye, or was it you?"

"*No*, Marcus. I don't even care enough about him to use the little energy I have to punch him. He's not even worth that."

"Damn. The dude ain't even worthy of a punch? That's fucked up."

"No, what's messed up is what he di—you know what, never mind. Can you sit with Mama for a few or not?"

It's another thing Ace hammered into my head that day

in the kitchen while he brushed his wet lips against mine: *"Be a good girl for me this week. Be nice to Bryson because he's still learning how to use his words and don't fuck Marcus' head up with shit that I have under control."*

All of it has my burning body in overdrive because I *need* him. Sneaky kitchen kisses between pickup games wasn't enough.

"How long is a few?"

"Can you do it or not?"

"Hold up. Drop the attitude. You the one asking me for a favor."

I cross my arms while he looks at me like he's searching for evidence of the trail of kisses Ace left down my body. He's doing all the things Marshall never got a chance to do.

He bites into his lip while the cool cup melts in his hand. "Yeah, I'll sit with her for a few."

I wait for the who, what, when, and where speech to come like it would've back in the day, but I'm being too hopeful.

"A'ight, cool." I drop my hands at my sides. "Call if you need something, I guess?"

"Mhmm." He hums, cocking his head to the side. "Get out the way."

I smack my lips and walk off.

"Fat girl?" he calls out behind me.

"Yeah?"

"Tell that nigga to take it easy today." He slurps another chunk of ice in his mouth. "I know a few brave dudes that fell before."

His words make me choke on my tongue until Bryson bursts through the front door, gasping to catch his breath. "C'mon, Mar!"

GUS TALKS in grunts on Saturday mornings.

He doesn't ask why he had to pick me up a block away from my house and he doesn't get Mama's permission before I get in his backseat like he promised her. He just grunts a "hello," a "buckle up," and curses about the *rassclat* potholes in the streets.

The ride to Upper Kirby is so quiet I hear the little creaks and thumps the truck makes along the highway. There's not even jazz playing to drown out the noise from traffic.

I count the grey hairs on his head to pass the time. I think there's forty-two of them. The last one sneaks out of my eyesight when he whips down Kirby, so I don't know if there's forty-two or forty-three grey hairs.

"Here we are, meh dear," he grunts, pulling to a rough stop in front of Ace's building.

"Thank—"

I don't get the rest out before he turns around in the driver's seat and dangles a key fob in my face.

"Here." He sucks his teeth. "Junior says stop leaving it in here. He says dat's how tings get lost."

"Uh... that's not my key, Gus."

"Tell him dat. Meh just relaying his message as requested."

I frown, curling my hand around the fob and taking it.

"Yuh know how tuh use it?"

"Yeah." I nod, gripping my backpack and pushing the back door open before he can.

He hops out of the front seat while I stare at the high-rise shooting into the sky.

It's not like the first day I came here and Ace stood on

the curb waiting. The bustling traffic and people walking the sidewalks don't entice me like they did that day, because I'm too focused on getting up to the fifty-sixth floor by myself. Being grown is lonely.

Gus stands beside the back door. "Phat?"

"Yeah?"

He swipes his hand, motioning for me to get out. "Hold de fob against de box by de door. It'll unlock it."

He smiles for the first time since I met him idling in front of a random house in my neighborhood. It's not a real one though. His eyes aren't sparkling enough for it to be real.

"Okay," I croak out, climbing out of the truck with my childish backpack in tow and a stomach full of excited butterflies anticipating Ace to round them up, but my mind isn't in sync with my body. Those fluttering butterflies don't understand something isn't right. Gus didn't have any stories to tell me about Ace on the ride here and I still didn't get what Marcus meant back in the living room at home.

"Meh take off once I know yuh inside." He nudges me toward the building and I stumble forward, glancing back at his fake smile. I hold the fob up to the silver box and the door clinks just like he said it would.

I look back again, and he's already closing himself back into the truck, so I slip inside the building.

When I make it up to Ace's, it's quiet inside. Cree's not stomping around in heels and Dough isn't blasting. There's the quietest thump from Janet playing. His curtains dust against the hardwood floors because the balcony door is open wide enough for gusts of wind to sneak in.

The first days of fall in Texas never actually feel like fall, but this one does. It feels like Ace's lips against mine. When I see the back of his head resting against a chaise on his balcony, the tightness that's lurking in my shoulders from the trip upstairs disappears. I forget about the quiet ride with Gus and drop my backpack and the fob in the entryway.

The wind keeps sweeping his scent inside, so I follow it all the way to the french doors until I find him. His long arms rest against the back of the chaise and there's a glass curled in his hand. Suddenly, I remember how much I love the first days of fall in Texas.

"That's you, kid?" he rumbles, making my stomach jump.

"Yeah..."

He takes a long sip from the glass and my body tries to calm itself from the hot anticipation of finding my way back to him.

"You take care of the house?" he asks.

I nod until I remember he can't see me. "Ye—yeah. I cleaned up."

"And Mom? Who there with her?"

"Marcus. He said he'll sit with her for a minute."

He lets out a faint chuckle.

"Gus take care of you?"

"Yeah, Ason. He did. He wasn't driving crazy."

"Good..."

"Ason?"

"Yeah?"

"Why'd you want me to have that key?"

"I ain't never heard of somebody that got a home, but no key to it. You don't want a key to me?"

It's a tricky ass question in true Ace fashion.

"No—yes. I—I want a key to you," I stutter out.

"That's what I figured. Now come here." He waves his

hand that's clutching the glass. "I guess I can let you be grown sometimes."

I smile.

It's not one of those weird half-smile half-frowns. Those don't exist anymore. The only ones I know now are the kind that hurt good and make me question my sanity. I smile *big* until I round the corner of the chaise and catch the setting sun glaring against his wet face and bloodshot eyes.

"Ason?" I choke out.

It's the first time I realize that men I hate and like give me something worse than hives. They give me deep, heart-pounding, gasping for air, fucked up panic attacks because I'm stupid enough to think I can fix everything that's wrong with them.

He doesn't even reach out to swipe the tears from his face, so they keep falling in fat, angry streaks. All I hear is Marcus telling me to tell him to take it easy today and Gus sucking his teeth while shoving his key toward me. They all know what's wrong but me.

"Why you over there?" he mumbles. "Come let me have you."

It's another question that's not a question anymore, but I don't care. I walk over to the chaise and throw my legs over his lap so I can obsess over the tears rolling down his cheeks. My sandals slide down my feet while I swipe my hand across his face, but they're moving too fast.

"You said I could torture myself sometimes," he says. "Remember?"

I nod, glancing at the empty liquor bottle on the ground next to his foot. "I remember."

His buzzing phone doesn't even make the tears stop. When I pull my eyes away from the liquor bottle, I see Coach Williams' name covering the screen.

Pops.

That's all it says. There's not an emoji or a picture to go along with it, and I hate that. When he hangs up, the ten other missed calls from him and Cree sitting on the screen tell me what kind of day it is on Planet Ace.

"What you got going on, Kid?" I ask, flipping the phone over and wrapping his face in my hands like he did to mine the morning after Splashtown.

"Shit..." he rasps out. "Been waiting for you to come home all day."

"What you need me for?"

He looks past me, swallowing with a loud gulp. "I can't celebrate alone."

There's that talk about a celebration again and I can't digest the word while his face is slick with tears that don't look like joyful ones.

"What we celebrating?"

It's a scary thing to ask when his brown eyes are so hollow, but it's Ace—the man I hate and like, the man I swear I knew in a past life, the man that gave me hives and cured them. Shit, nothing is ever as scary as it seems on his planet.

"Mom's birthday," he replies, looking back at me. "I'm a mama's boy, remember?"

A desperate groan gets caught in my throat and it *is* as scary as it seemed.

I reach out to catch the new tears that fall with his admission, but I'm too slow. They roll over my fingers and leave me with no choice but to do another scary thing.

I press my lips against his warm cheek and catch them with my lips. "I remember. For an eternity, right?"

He nods, nudging my face from his. "It's my first one without her."

The aggressive texts, Marcus' vague statement, and Gus' glum mood make sense now.

"That's why you wanted me home so bad?"

His tongue darts from between his lips. "Don't get shit confused. I always want you home but to—today I *needed* you home."

As if I didn't halfway wash a sink full of dishes and run a block to Gus' truck—as if my body didn't know he needed it too.

I don't know how to mourn first birthdays because I was too little to remember Marshall's. I just know how to live with the birthdays that come after. The house gets real still, and it's the only time of the year Marcus can't step foot out the front door. Nothing's left of Marshall at our house because Mama got rid of it all except some pictures she made Marcus put in the attic. She even gave his ashes to his mama, but his birthday is the only time of the year we all can exist together without fussing.

I smash my lips against his cheek again.

A salty tear trickles into my mouth, gliding against my tongue and it makes me want to throw that question he wanted me to forget back into the Universe. I want God to tell me why certain shit happens. Why would he take a lady like Angie away when Ace needed her to help him understand that it's not just him against this shitty world?

"Lourdes?" he asks, picking up his vibrating phone and pushing it into my chest.

"Ye—yeah?"

"Why won't his selfish ass get that the only person I want is right here?"

"Don't say that." I slide my hand down his cheek, chasing more never ending tears. "It's his first one without her too."

"Nah...it's not."

"What you mean?"

He nudges my hand away and scoops his arms around my ass, pulling me closer. When I'm right where he wants with my head on his chest and his lips against my ear, he starts. The words trickle out with a painful strain.

"When I'm a father to my son, I pray that I'll never give the world more than I give him. I pray that I never leave my wife to teach my son about the ugly ass ways of the world because I'm too busy teaching him he can't stop shooting a ball until his arms cramp. I pray that I never distort my wife's idea of what a perfect birthday is for her and I pray that when it's time to lay her to rest that I'm not selfish enough to keep the rest of the world from mourning her death because I didn't spend enough time with her when she was alive."

I sigh against him, trying to imagine him as a father and husband. It's easy to do, but hard for me to understand the stupid man-shit Coach Williams did to Angie.

"How many did he miss?"

"Enough." He grips me harder. "Enough for me to believe he doesn't deserve to feel as shitty as I do today. He should treat this birthday like he did the other ones."

The tiny gusts of wind brush against my arms and settle between us while I try to think of the right things to say even though Mama says that's the worst thing to do because people do it to her all the time.

"It's kinda like ripping off a bandaid," I blurt, trying to inhale each sniffle he sneaks out. "Right now it's that little corner piece you keep picking at. It hurts so bad because you feel each hair that it yanks off your skin so you push it little by little. It stings, but you want it off so you keep torturing yourself until finally it's the end, and it's hanging off that last piece of hair. So you say 'fuck it,' and yank it off but at the end of all that, the cut not even healed because you was too impatient but it's okay because you giving it air —letting it soak up the sun and heal without hiding. I'll help you peel that little corner piece off today. No more torturing yourself alone."

I don't know what's supposed to come after I bare my ugly thoughts like Mama said I should. Should we kiss now? Should he tell me thank you?

He chokes out quiet gasps of air.

I think I made it worse.

Tears well up along the inner corners of my eyes until I hear his raspy voice.

"When do we get to the 'fuck it' part?"

"I don't know, but we not in a rush so don't worry about that right now. We do it little by little, remember?"

He nods, sucking up another breath until his phone vibrates again.

He swipes it from the couch, and I feel where he's going.

"Don't!" I catch his arm midair, peeling the phone from his fingers. "Don't do that."

Even throughout our tussle, Coach Williams won't let up—hanging up and calling right back.

"Well, handle it then." He lets me take it and then pushes his empty glass toward me. "Handle that and come back so I can have you."

I fumble with the glass and the phone while pushing up from his lap.

I guess this is what comes after I bare my ugly thoughts. None of it is as easy as Mama made it seem.

I don't answer the phone until I step inside and pull the doors behind me.

"Junior..." Coach Williams croaks out as soon as I answer. "Don't do nothing stupid today."

The phone dangles from my hand while I look around Ace's condo without that blur of anticipation covering my eyes. I see everything that I couldn't when I first got here. Balloons, a cake box, and a bundle of shopping bags on the island, but what's next to it is worse.

"I know it's you that took Angie's key from the console in my truck. I'm downstairs. Open up right now." He huffs into the phone. "Junior! Talk to m—"

"Coach Williams?" I mutter, staring at another half-empty liquor bottle next to the shopping bags.

"Babygirl? Tha—that's you?"

"Yeah, it's me."

"You up there with Junior?"

"I am." I nod, walking into the kitchen. "I—I'm here."

We're both stuttering all over the place while I shove the faucet on and stick Ace's glass under it.

Janet's still whispering in the background, waiting for Angie to come back to squeal and dance to her singing like Mama does.

"Lourdes, let me take you back home to CeCe."

Hearing him say both of our names is weird. They come out like he'd been dreading the day he would have to say them—especially Mama's.

"Why?"

"Because I need to talk to Junior about some things you won't understand. I want to get you back home safe. CeCe would kill me if I let something happen to you and I promised Marshall..."

"You promised Marshall what?"

"Let's not talk about that right now. Just come on down and I'll take care of Junior."

The cold water douses my hand and I yank the glass from under the faucet. I shove it off to take a slurp. All his talk about "Junior" and "safety" has my mouth dry. He keeps talking about Ace like he's not his son and like I couldn't take care of him.

"Lourdes!" Ace yells from outside, giving my legs that urge they always get when he's calling for me. "Bring those bags when you come back!"

His voice shakes as I stare at the intimidating shopping bags. They're big, black, and have our favorite designer pressed into the paper: Dior.

"Lourdes..." Coach Williams' voice drops. "Junior isn't well enough to be pursuing this thing with you. I want to take you home—"

I yank the phone from my face and end the call. I can't hear anymore. He sounds like the reporters, the random people on campus, like Blake Harvey, like Bryson, like Chelsea, like my brain before I saw Ace's smile that day at practice. He doesn't sound like home.

I snatch the shopping bags off the table and walk back to the patio, where Ace is still staring out into the city.

"You ready?" he asks.

"Ready for what?"

"To open your gifts."

"But it's not my birthday, it's your mama's."

He pats his thighs, and I follow the sounds, gripping the glass and bags. "Come here. Let me talk to you."

More butterflies flutter in my stomach as I stumble over to him and climb back into his lap.

I don't bring up Coach Williams and neither does he, but my mouth gets dry again because now I know why they can't see eye to eye on such an important day and I want to know what he promised Marshall.

He pries the glass from my fingers, taking a sip.

When he pulls it back, he smiles. "Water?"

"Yeah...your co-pilot says 'enough.'" My fingers crawl through his low curls while he laughs with a wet face that just won't stay dry.

It doesn't matter how many times I swipe my fingers and lips across it. The tears keep falling while I keep waiting for the boy Coach Williams described on the phone to pop out.

"Now why you buying me gifts on your mama's birthday?" I mutter. "We supposed to celebrate her today."

"We are." He pries the shopping bag's strings from my fingers and pulls me into his chest. "You know, before there was Planet Ace, there was a place called Angie's World. In Angie's World, birthdays are days for giving—not to yourself, but to the people who give so much and never get anything back."

My body sinks into his and I realize there's nothing better than sitting on a penthouse balcony overlooking the city while listening to Ace talk about his mama like she's still here.

"Oh, yeah?" I whisper. "How that work?"

"On her thirty-ninth birthday, she sent Gus and his wife back home to Negril. On her fortieth birthday, she invested in her favorite nail tech and helped open Uptown Nails..."

I twist in his arms, swiping at another wild tear on his cheek. "And what about the next one?"

"Her forty-first?" He smiles, clawing his fingers through my braids. "She threw her only son a party on a mega-yacht in one of his favorite places. Even if he didn't think he deserved it."

"Why would you think you didn't deserve it?"

"Because I couldn't control it." He swallows. "By then,

her cancer was so bad that none of my elite combos worked anymore. So, the doctors put a feeding tube in her stomach."

Cancer.

There's that word I hate.

I try to force it out of my head, but I forgot Ace can read my mind sometimes.

Maybe he can see how my fist connected to Bryson's cheek on our porch on the Tuesday Dr. Evanston told us Mama had a tumor in her colon. I still hear the way it rolled out of his mouth when the rest of us weren't brave enough to mutter it.

"What ya'll mean Mama got cancer?" he asked, frowning.

"It's okay." Ace pushes his lips to my temple. "I hate that word too, but it's safe between me and you. You know your pilot is the only one that gets how ugly that word is."

A hot, wet tear trickles down my face.

I reach for it, but his lips beat me. He's not scary like I am, so he doesn't hesitate to swipe his tongue through it and press his lips against my face afterward to soothe the skin it burned.

"C'mon..." he mutters. "Let me see what Angie got you this year."

He laughs and I gurgle out a mix between a laugh and a sob because I never wanted to love on a lady whose presence I didn't remember *so* bad. I never wanted to keep a self-proclaimed "flawed, fucked up person" *so* bad.

I move too slow, so he nudges my hand away and pulls apart the biggest bag.

"Cree always telling me that the best way to fight my candy addiction is to indulge in a lil' retail therapy. I need to stop listening to her before I have us in that cardboard box for real." He laughs, pulling out a purse. "I know you committed to the Rockets, but I don't play for that team *or* the NBA. So I had to get you something else."

He pulls out a purse.

It's THE purse from that *Essence* magazine. The one Dough's girlfriend had slinging from her shoulder, but she has all the swag to carry it and I don't because I've been holding on to Marshall's tattered dreams since I was twelve.

My mouth turns dry.

"Yet," I choke out. "You don't play in the NBA yet."

He laughs, lifting my arm and sliding the bag's strap on it. "I forgot you think you Cari Champion. Nobody wants me on their team, kid. Not even the Rockets."

It feels like the night of the gala again.

"I still want you to carry the backpack, but I saw this and thought about my lil' lady. Carry it on your next date, that way niggas know if they act up..." He pulls open the leather flap, pulling out a card like the one in my wristlet, but this one has my name stamped at the bottom. "You got your own shit."

Our fingers glide across my name together until he reaches out and squeezes my chin at the bottom.

"You got one more. Pull it out."

I stick my hand back in the shopping bag and pull out a folder with Jazmine's card stapled to the front.

"'Comfort Care Private Providers,'" I read to myself, dragging my eyes over the glossy folder.

"If you ever need to breathe... or if you ever feel like it's too much—Jazmine's ready. She took the best care of Mom when I couldn't," he mutters, tugging one of my braids dangling in my face.

"Ason... I—I can't afford this."

"Stop it." He shakes his head. "It's on me... it's always on me, baby. Don't you ever forget that."

I fold my lips under my teeth, staring at my new shiny unlimited get out of jail free card that didn't have any conditions attached to it.

I never knew it was possible to feel my heart beat in another place besides my chest. Right now it's in my throat because Ace is silly enough to believe that another man can make me as crazy as he does. He makes me *so* crazy that my beating throat is about to blurt out something else no one would ever care to know about me but him.

"That backpack was Marshall's." I swallow. "He wanted to play for the Rockets when he left Lockwood. Marcus always told me that's what Marshall admired about your daddy the most—the fact that he actually made it and became the guy he dreamed of being. Thank you for not thinking that backpack is childish because it's the only thing of his that Mama forgot to throw out on his first birthday in Heaven. I didn't know Marshall, but I know he would've loved the way you love on her."

CHAPTER TWENTY

Ace

I need a bigger dose of Phat before she leaves me.

"Your mama liked chocolate?" she asks, licking the chocolate mousse from my spoon at the island in my kitchen.

"Nah, she didn't even like cake."

The giant chocolate mousse cake sits between us with a generic "Happy Birthday, Angie," scribbled across it. When I opened my mouth to tell the cashier at the bakery to add Mom's age, my words bubbled up my throat so, "Happy Birthday, Angie" was what the girl kept while I threw up a fifth of 1942 in the parking lot.

Talking about Mom today should be hard, but Phat makes it easy with innocent questions about her like she's trying to paint her own memories of Mom in her head. She wants to know the important shit—Mom's "teams," her favorite color, and if I thought her and CeCe ever beefed about that time Pops crossed Marshall over at the Fondé.

"Hm..." Phat thrusts the spoon back to me. "So why you get chocolate then?"

I shrug, swiping my tongue against it like she wants because she's not brave enough to tell me to kiss her so she can taste me. "I like chocolate."

She snickers, hunching her shoulders up and licking the spoon where I did. "*The Kid* really likes chocolate. Interesting."

She wiggles her eyebrows and I *really* need a bigger dose of her after a day of drunk texts and fucking crying.

"Already sneak dissing and you only been home for a few hours." I shake my head, smiling. "Don't tell me you're naïve enough to believe everything people say on the internet."

"I saw the prom picture with the rest of Twitter." She shrugs, cutting around Mom's name on the cake. "Remind me to freeze that part before we go to bed."

All of it makes the aftermath of my crying less embarrassing—her digs, the careful way she preserves Mom in any way she can, the familiar way she says "bed" as if she knows I'm not letting her leave tonight so Marcus will have to face his fear.

"I know Cree told you she's a lesbian and she ain't even white—she's Mexican."

"If she's a lesbian, then why she went to prom with you?" She rolls her eyes, twirling the spoon around.

"Don't be ignorant." I snicker, leaving out all the sordid details between me, Javier, and Cree. "Friends can go to prom together."

Her mouth gets wide and her cheeks push up like I'm spilling the juicy gossip she's been waiting on. "Don't tell me *The Kid* got curved on prom night."

I shrug, letting her come up with her own conclusions

and fill in the missing pieces of Cree's coming out story that I'll never tell.

"Eres un chismoso."

"Here we go." She pulls her head back, rolling her eyes. "How many damn languages did Angie make you learn?"

"Enough. How I'm supposed to conquer Earth for us if I'm monolingual?"

"Monolingual? If you're low-key a nerd, I won't judge."

"You wish I was a nerdy ass nigga. I'm sure it would've made it easier for you to hate me like you wanted to."

She shrieks out a loud laugh that fills the condo and makes me lightheaded. "Just answer my question. How many?"

"Enough of 'em to get us by if you decide you want to globe trot after you leave your soft ass husband and come back home when we get old. I can take you on a gondola in Italy or to the Mekong Delta in Vietnam..."

"Or you can take me to taste the air on the Pacific Coast Highway in the summer." She leans forward, smirking. "I looked it up."

I smile and look into her eyes, trying to inhale that night on Pops' truck. "Wherever you wanna go."

She hums, sticking the spoon back in her mouth. "So, did you and Cree end up on the PCH prom night? Is that where you *allegedly* got curved?"

"We back on this?"

"We never was off it. Answer the question."

I widen my eyes and bunch my shoulders up. "As soon as we pulled up to prom, she admitted that she only agreed to go with me because she had a crush on Willow Smith. She knew her songs word for word, but Willow skipped prom to go to a bonfire in Malibu that year."

"You went to high school with Will Smith's daughter?"

She howls. "You know what? Don't even answer that. Of course you did. You rich folks are something else. So after the curve, did you end up fucking another chick or what?"

"You too curious about fucking, kid."

She wiggles her eyebrows with another smirk. "Well, if you didn't fuck Cree, you must've fucked Brandy. She's definitely your type."

I let the silence linger between us until the little smirk falls from her face.

"I only like chocolate cake. I only fuck chocolate bitches. No, I didn't fuck Cree because she wanted to be Mrs. Willow Smith and I *for sure* ain't fuck Brandy—you was tripping with that one. Are you satisfied now?"

The way her cheeks jump up tells me she isn't, so I crook my finger and beckon her chubby face over the cake.

"You believe too much Twitter gossip," I mutter, wiping a smear of chocolate off her chin. "See why I took it away?"

Just the mention of Twitter, makes my stomach twist. It's a harsh reminder of those reporters lurking in our space, reading our insiders, and tainting a place she thought was safe. That article was an ironic way to have my point proven —Twitter shouldn't have been her diary, but it also shouldn't have been a free for all for thirsty reporters either. Now her playground will never be the same.

"You took it away because I let you be a control freak when I'm bored sometimes." Her chin bounces against my fingers. "I can log back on whenever I want—"

The rest of it gets caught between our lips because I'm tired of playing games. If it were up to her, we'd dance around Mom's cake all night arguing about girls who didn't matter.

I find her tongue and wrap my lips around it.

"You know better than that," I mumble between sucks.

"Just like deep down you know what kind of girls I fuck. Stop playing with me with your non-kissing ass."

I taste the chocolate mousse and feel the vibrations of a deep, guttural moan clawing up her throat. I like the way she tries her hardest to chase my tongue and mimic my movements. The spoon clanks against the island as I slurp her bottom lip into my mouth. When I pull back, it bounces from between my teeth, so I go after it again, pecking it over and over.

"I'm tired of playing twenty-one questions," I mutter between pecks. "Tell me something good. Tell me how much you missed me."

A loud gasp escapes her mouth, tickling my nose. "I—I think I wanna—"

"Nuh uh, we not doing that shit tonight. Tell me what you want—*for real.*"

"You," she hiccups out, pulling her lip from between my teeth and brushing her eyes against my torso. "I want you."

"You already got me."

She shakes her head. "I-I want you to *you know.*"

My eyebrow raises and that familiar tingle takes over my fingers because she's being both versions of herself. One can't even articulate the words and two can't help herself anymore after I had my fingers deep inside her. I need to tame both.

"Nah, I don't. You want me to what?"

I really don't want it to come out of her mouth, but I know it will anyway and it'll make that jonesing for a bigger hit of her worse. It's my fault for making her so curious in the first place. All the signs were there—all the questions about Cree, other girls, her drunken joke about wanting to fuck me after I hurt her feelings, the way her body curved into mine the morning after Splashtown.

"I wanna have sex."

My lip tilts up, and I let go of her face.

I swipe my finger through the chocolate icing while my dick gets stiff in my briefs. "Why you wanna do that, baby?"

"Why not? You already had your fingers there."

"There's a big difference between a finger and a dick."

"It was two, not one, but anyway..."

I laugh while sticking my finger in my mouth and sucking the icing off it. "If you think two fingers is equivalent to my dick, then I'm disappointed in you."

She pulls her bottom lip between her teeth and shrinks into herself.

Her expression reminds me of how I got sucked into her in the first place—mahogany skin that I wanted to taste, childish shit like thinking sex is a simple task she can mark off her "things to do" list, and round lips that call me *Ason* now.

"You being too grown today." I sigh, poking my finger back in the chocolate. "Did I give you too much freedom?"

She squirms around on the barstool, rolling her eyes, and it makes my dick even harder. "I ain't one of those girls that thinks my virginity is some important thing to hold on to until my perfect Prince Charming comes to stick his perfect dick inside me."

"*See*...you being too grown."

She smacks her lips. "No, I'm not."

"It's nothing wrong with being a virgin. It's precious."

"Damn, you sound like Chelsea's granny, Mother Lenola."

"Mother Lenola is a smart lady. Keep playing with me and I'll have your ass at that next holy convention with Chelsea. You'll be a virgin until you're married."

"Ason!"

"Baby!" I mimic her whine with a deep laugh. "Okay... okay, let me hear the rationale behind this one and I'll think about it."

"The only rationale that you need to know is that virginity is a social construct I don't agree with. I'm fine with my flawed, fucked up dick that's attached to a dude that'll never be Prince Charming because he's too busy being a legend." She pushes away from the island after reminding me she's *my* little lady, no matter what happens. "We both know how short life is. I ain't waiting around until you think you're worthy enough to fuck me."

Damn, Mom was right. Little ladies are little ladies until they just aren't anymore and it's nothing I can do to change that.

She glides around my kitchen, digging through cabinets until she finds the cling wrap she's looking for. My dick is at full attention now. There's no more room for it to grow.

She lays the cling wrap over Mom's name and presses the sides of the cake like she's taking care of something delicate. "Mama never let us cut the name off. We'll freeze it."

I push my tongue against the roof of my mouth and swallow the rest of her and the chocolate.

"Okay," I croak out.

"I'll get the cake next time," she replies, shuffling to the freezer with Mom in her hands. "They forgot to put how old she was turning."

That right there is the reason I can't stop myself from taking more of her when I shouldn't. Shit like that makes me want to call up Blake and tell him, "fuck it, let the world know" but I know better.

"Hurry up before Marcus start blowing me up." She frowns, power-walking to my bedroom.

There's another wet spot in the back of her leggings but

this time there aren't any flowery pink panties for me to tease her about and I think I know what that two-hundred dollar charge from Victoria's Secret was on our credit card statement.

I curl my fingers around the bottom of my shirt and yank it over my head because one thing Blake didn't realize in his whole analyzation of my fucked up brain was how pervasive my cravings for Phat were. They supersede any Dum-Dum and Chick-O-Stick cravings because she tastes better than Don Julio, Clase Azul, and Patrón.

"Ason!" she yells, making my ass slide off the barstool.

I grab the remote to the sound system and walk toward the room behind her. As soon as I pass through the doorway and see her sitting in the middle of my unmade bed, I grab the remote from my dresser and turn Janet off.

"You cutting off the music?" she whispers, pulling her legs underneath her.

"Yeah, I wanna hear you when we make love, not Janet."

She laughs while plucking at a loose thread poking from my comforter, and her eyes dart away from mine. "Ma— make love?"

My stomach is at my fucking ankles because I'm selfish, just like Pops. All my brain keeps telling me is to take a bigger dose of her even if it's a dangerous thing to do because version one of my little lady is curious, and I always give my little lady what she wants.

"I know you don't actually think we fucking." I swallow. "You trying to control the vibe again like I didn't explain this to you already. Why you can't ever act right for me?"

Her stomach jumps and mine follows because we both know the type of things those words wake up—dilated pupils, bruised asses, and sloppy first kisses.

I drop the remote back on my dresser and walk toward the bed. She pulls her legs from underneath her and spreads them open like she did that morning after Splashtown because she's so damn perfect.

"You don't wanna make love to me?" I mutter, gripping her thighs and pulling her into my bare stomach. "Guess you really don't want to come home to a nigga no more."

It's just mind games and word play I would dole out to experienced women because I'm still full of 1942 even after her attempts to flush it out of my system with water, cake, and childish games. Even if I wasn't full of it, we'd still be in the same situation because I've been fucking up ever since that night in her driveway.

"Shut up," she mumbles, pressing her lips to my stomach and dropping wet, sticky chocolate kisses along LA. "Stop playing with me."

There's something worse happening in her head and God, I know Mom promised you I'd be careful with her, but my baby is hardheaded.

She pushes back and pulls her tank top over her head like she's an experienced woman, but I feel her trembling legs against mine. I have her head fucked up with credit cards, kissing, and the endless attention she deserves. It's so bad that hives prickle her soft skin again.

When she reaches for the waistband of her leggings, I reach out to yank her hand back. "Stop..."

"Nuh uh." She shakes her head. "I—I can take it. I trust you."

She says those last few words as clearly as when she told me I could have whatever I wanted and that's the problem.

I squat in front of her. "Listen... I know you have all these intelligent, *hella* progressive thoughts about your virginity bu—but are you sure you want to do this? With me?"

The questions I'm blurting out are supposed to cure the guilt eating at my liquored up conscious.

"Look at your stomach," I mutter, dragging my fingers across the new welts.

"So. Take care of 'em like you did the other ones." She smacks her hand on top of mine. "They're yours. They're yo —your fault, so take care of them."

I try to remember how we went from metaphorical expressions to make it easier for her to ask for me to her outright demanding my dick, but then I remember all the shit the last days of summer took us through. It's no wonder we're here. She wasn't careful of what she did for unworthy men like me that just... asked.

"Okay," I choke out. "I'll do that."

Her chest jumps up and down with adrenaline filled gasps while I hook my fingers through her leggings' waist-band. When I pull them down to her ankles, I swallow the rolling waves in my stomach because I already know how this will go.

Having sex for the first time isn't the glamorous shit all the sex-positive girls she follows on Twitter gloat about. It's painful, bloody, and when I peel her new lacy thong down her legs, I remember how horrible of a time it's going to be for her because she could barely take those two fingers she keeps obsessing over.

"Can you spread your legs again for me?"

"Uh, huh." She gasps, kicking the rest of the fabric on the floor and spreading her legs so far apart that I see the glistening wet dots hanging onto the curly hairs of her pussy.

It's mine, and she knows it because I see the careful

planning that went into this moment—the shaved bikini line, the request for me to add another finger to prep herself for when she got the courage to tell me to take it, the new panties. It's *definitely* mine.

"I think we need to talk," I mutter, blowing against the hood of her clit that pokes out.

Her back thrashes against the bed. "Ason, don't fucking start—"

"Watch your mouth." I sigh, pressing my tongue against it and slurping it into my mouth with the rest of the shit she wanted to say.

It's crazy that both of us think we can have a civilized conversation with my pussy propped in front of me like this. The loud, painful squeal she lets out while I suck makes this battle in my head a lot less fucked up.

"Aso—"

"Tell me something good—right now," I garble out, swiping my tongue along the delicate folds and chasing her wetness. "Make me feel less fucked up for always giving you whatever you want, even shit I shouldn't. Tell me I'm wrong for packing my shit and moving into your ass. Tell me I'm wrong for finding home in you, baby."

"I can't." She gasps. "I fucking can't, Ason. I just want you inside of me. Jus-just let me have that."

Her words are desperate. I can hear how long she's been wanting this and wanting me, but there's something else I need to teach her about life with me on this planet she created.

I yank my lips away with a smack. "Why should I do that?"

She rakes her nails across the side of my face, whimpering out a pathetic groan while my skin burns. "Because I'm not careful of wh—what I do for you when you just ask.

Because our good is whatever we choose. Because I know it's going to hurt like a bitch, but I'll take anything you give me because I hate and like you so fucking much. Because even at the end of all this, when you end up in the league where you're supposed to be, with a girl on your arm that's nothing like me, I'll still let you come home whenever you want. I'll *always* let you come home to me."

I ALWAYS THOUGHT the setting sun against the Pacific Ocean while my favorite rapper performed in the background was perfection. I was silly enough to believe climbing over the side of a yacht with a glass in my hand and falling feet first into the ocean on one of the best days of my life was *hella* perfect, but now I know I was wrong.

"Why is my baby always trying to be grown?" I croak out, twisting Phat's braids around my hand while she fights to get the condom over my hard dick.

"Shut up," she rasps. "I *am* grown."

Her voice is hoarse from screeching out how sure she is that she's mine and I know what perfection is for real now. It's being naked on our knees in the center of my bed with a pile of magnums dumped next to us because she's hard-headed, just like I told God.

"Move. Let me show you." I knock her hand away and pull the stretched condom off the head of my dick. "First of all, don't you use another man's condoms. Always have your own."

She rolls her eyes like we're bickering about Mom or the other mundane shit she hates.

"Ason..." she groans, leaning back while I catch the foil packet between my teeth and rip it open.

"Don't 'Ason' me," I mutter, pulling the condom out. "Gimme your hand and don't use your teeth like I'm doing. Always be careful when you're opening it."

She thrusts her hand out. I snatch it, prying her fingers apart and pinching them around the condom's tip. I push it toward my dick and smile at the way her eyes squint because she's so serious about this.

"Squeeze the tip," I mumble, cupping her round chin in my hand and nodding when she does. "That's for the cum."

"This is supposed to be sexy. I feel like I'm back in junior high, reading some corny ass article in a *Cosmo* magazine me and Chelsea snuck out of Walmart."

My stomach cramps as I bellow out a loud laugh and swat her hand away. "This *is* sexy. I'm taking care of you and your body like I'm supposed to. Any man that can't take care of you don't deserve any pussy. Now lay back before I change my mind."

When her head hits my pillows and she looks up at me with a wide grin I'm done for. My dick doesn't care how corny teaching her about her body and condoms is, it won't let up, and neither will the wetness between her legs.

She's not hiding behind her hands anymore, lying about the hives I give her, or being ashamed of the strange things I do to her body. Now, it's like she's proud of that shit.

She curls her arms around my shoulders, and I lose my breath for a second.

"Put it in and talk to me," she murmurs, pushing her lips against my ear. "You said we needed to talk. So talk."

There's a glint in her eyes and a relaxed smile on her face. I don't wait for another nudge from her before I nestle my dick at her entrance.

"A—Ason," she stutters with a choke when I push the head in.

Her eyelids flutter closed, covering that exciting glint, and the first tear escapes.

"See what happens when you don't listen to me," I whisper, kissing the tear away and easing another inch of myself inside of her. "Now I gotta be the bad guy. Why I'm always the bad guy?"

"Be—because be—cause," she gasps, taking another inch. "I can't ever act right for you."

"*Never.*"

"Now talk."

"Nuh uh. I need to focus on you right now."

"Stop thinking and talk," she hisses.

I try to herd my wild thoughts together and line them up so I can make sense of them for her. I want to make sure I don't say anything that'll scare her away and ruin this perfect day that will be seared into my memory, but she feels so good that my wild thoughts go scrambling and run right out of my mouth anyway.

"There're some days I can't fully remember," I blurt.

"What you mean?" She winces.

Fuck.

She tries to respond again but nothing comes out except another tear because I'm halfway inside of her and she feels exactly like the sun off the Pacific Coast, even with a cape on my dick.

I suck in a deep breath.

It helps me pace myself so I won't dive into her like I wanted to do off that yacht I told her about.

"Like days where there's black spots in my memory. Days where I can't remember the beginning or end because I made sure I couldn't. Days where I strayed so far away from home that I felt hella strange when I finally made it back."

I feel the moment Phat leaves her life as a little lady behind, even though she doesn't believe in that type of shit. I feel the exact moment her soul stretches just enough to make room for me. Those feelings make me rotate my hips to write my name on the walls of my forever home while she screams out in gibberish and pain.

"Mind over matter, baby." I gather her lips between mine. "Today is a day I promise I'll remember forever, just like all the other days me and you spent together. I feel hella good because I didn't jump over the side of that boat like I wanted to do at that party I didn't deserve. Today is a perfect day for me and you."

"That's a fuckin' long way down, Kid," Dough told me while I stared into the clear blue water. *"What you searching for down there anyway?"*

"Home, brodie," I replied. *"I woke up this morning on some dumb shit because God always be talking to me the loudest when I'm off 1942. He say I gotta find a new home because he taking mine back. I can't argue with him about shit like that, you know?"*

"You sure you wanna make that jump?"

I did.

I planned it while Mom slept in my cabin and Pops called with his fifth ETA of the day. When me and Javier snuck off to smoke a joint with the deckhand, I asked him how deep the water was where we were anchored, and how rough the currents were because Mom would've wanted my body afterward. I didn't want to make shit hard for her, but God had me fucked up if he thought he was taking her and I wouldn't go, too.

I pinch my eyes shut, sucking in the breeze that always comes when I have a part of Phat in me.

I feel the *exact* moment when she realizes she can't go

back to being a little lady. All of it hurts, but she doesn't care. Instead of complaining, she locks her legs around my waist and tangles her feet behind my back.

She chokes out little grunts that sound nothing like moans and I can't pull my lips off of hers because I want to feel everything she feels. The pain, confusion, and pleasure. Her breath glides down my throat while I try to breathe for the both of us.

"How you feel?" I mutter into her mouth.

Her tongue twists out of my tongue's grip. "Like I want you forever. Like I'd follow you anywhere you go. Like I'd kill you if you ever think about jumping off of anything again. Keep talking and show me forever."

Our mouths and tongues swirl together again in a panic and it feels just like I knew it would. Just like Dough told me it'd feel when I found her.

"You ain't gon' find home down there, twin. Believe that," he said, pushing his head over the ledge next to mine.

His cuban link chain slapped against the side of the boat while we both stared into the water.

"You'll find it in the person you least expect, at a time where you at your lowest but don't know it yet. You'll feel it when you hear her voice first though. Maybe it'll make your heart beat in the lamest way or your stomach queasy because she smells so familiar. But your Mom gon' be right there inside of her, telling God, 'that's her.' She's it for you. You can't beef with God forever, because at the end of it all, you'll find your forever home again. We all do." His caramel arm swiped around my neck and in the distance, Cree's voice mixed with her feet pounding the boat's deck.

"There you are! Thank God you found him!"

I shouldn't, but I push as far into Phat as I can go. Her groans turn into tiny, labored pants that make *me* pant, while her fingernails claw into my back. All of my pumping and swirling motions are for nothing because she's so inexperienced that just the realization of me being inside of her is what excites her most. It's in her panting that's turned into little amateur moans and the way she copies my movements as if she's doing something.

I laugh into her mouth. "What you moaning for?"

"'Ca—cause I feel you."

I pull back, staring at her wrinkled eyebrows and wet face. "You can't feel shit but friction and rubber, kid."

We laugh together while I peck the places on her I never have the time to touch, like the tips of her cheeks and the shell of her ear. My hand sneaks between our bodies and I strum my thumb over her moist clit.

"As—Ason..." She moans for real this time with wet eyes.

"What you crying for? I'm here."

Her swirls turn into pumps against my dick and thumb.

"I want you."

"You got me."

"No, I *want* you." She gasps, pumping faster. "I—I want you to tell me something good like—like last time."

I wheeze out another laugh while the buildup of an orgasm trickles through her limbs.

"What you want me to tell you, baby?" I ask, thrusting faster.

"Tell me what you told me last time."

It takes a second before I get what she's getting at and when I do; I think my dick does the impossible and gets harder.

"What? That it's my pussy and nobody else's?"

She nods with her eyes pinched together while I try to

match my thumb's strumming with the deep strokes I'm delivering.

"*Oh*," I sing. "Now you wanna act right for me?"

She nods again and her mouth falls open. "You the only nigga I know how to act right for."

There's that drawl I'm obsessed with. It makes my head spin and all the tricks to help me keep my pace are useless because Phat won't let me. I fall back over her and scoop her lips back into my mouth, trying to swallow that drawl and those words.

I breathe out. "Because you know better. Just like you know that even at the end of all this, when you're where you're supposed to be with some man that's nothing like me, it'll still be my pussy. Right?"

"Yes!"

That one syllable echoes throughout the room and bounces off the walls, and it's no disrespect to Janet, but that "yes" sounds better than anything she ever sang in my house. That "yes" and Phat's pussy sound and feel exactly like *home.*

CHAPTER TWENTY-ONE

Lourdes

A pounding *thump* makes my eyes spring open.

"Ugh." I groan, rolling over into a cocoon of blankets. "Fuck."

For a minute, I forget where I am until I smell Ace deep in his comforter. All the light from the floor to ceiling windows in his bedroom shines over my naked body.

"Mhm." I moan, smacking my tongue against the roof of my mouth.

I can taste him and smell him and I want him. I guess this happens after making love. I never asked anyone what the difference was between it and sex, but I think I know now.

I have aches in places I didn't know existed and a tingling sensation on my ass because a slap there is how Ace said "good morning." Afterward, I heard him muttering to himself about me. It wasn't anything important—just something I imagined he tortured himself with when I left him alone.

"*Lourdes,*" he mumbled against my stomach. "*Who gave you that name anyway, baby?*"

The soft thrusting of his toothbrush against his teeth and the quiet muttering from the anchors on *SportsCenter* is how he told me was starting his day. The only way I knew he left was when I heard his voice.

"*Order breakfast when you get up,*" he rumbled between brushes while running his hand across my ass. "*Card's on the island in the kitchen.*"

My brain is full of fuzz. Virginity is still that useless social construct I always believed it to be, but now I get what Ace meant with all of his contemplating over a flimsy piece of skin in my vagina. The change is subtle and more mental, but I feel it. I feel him. I taste his words. I even feel like I was on that yacht he told me about between strokes—that same yacht he almost jumped off of.

The memory of his words makes my body jolt from the bed. I can't tell if they were real or if I made them up in my head, so I climb out of bed to make sense of it, but I stumble over our clothes in a daze.

I pick his shirt up, pulling it over my head and following the loud noises echoing throughout the condo. Loud bangs replace the thumps and I forget the words I was supposed to make sense of when I round the corner to the living room and see him through the french doors.

I walk over and push them open.

The muscles in his arms bulge while he pushes a dumbbell toward the morning sky from a yoga mat.

Sweat rests along his body while I try to hold my breath because he's a different Ace than he is on campus. This Ace looks like that NBA player he was supposed to be by now.

He rests the dumbbell on his chest and pushes out a loud breath. "No breakfast?"

"No," I squeak out.

He snickers. "Come here. You too grown to kiss me good morning?"

"You mean *tell* you good morning?"

"Nah. I know what I said." He pats his stomach. "Come let me have you for a minute."

"It's concerning how much you like tasting my morning breath."

His abs contract while he sputters out a laugh. "I like tasting your pussy too, but you ain't complaining about that. Now I need to have both because you playing games early this morning. Bring your ass here."

I thought I was ready for the day he stopped dropping sexual innuendos, but my moist inner thighs tell me otherwise.

I patter across the balcony and squat on his stomach. His natural scent wafts up my nose and those butterflies he created start fluttering in wild spasms. There's a wet spot underneath me again, but I don't care this time because I made love to a man I hate and like for the first time. That wet spot is the least of my worries because I need to feel him again. *Now.*

He sits the dumbbell beside us and pushes up on his forearms. "Open your mou—"

I thrust my lips on his and savor the grunt he belts out. Our tongues collide and I try to copy the ways his glides around my mouth when I let him have me. My hips grind into his stomach like it's second nature, and he smiles.

"Mom better stop letting you listen to Janet. You not about to be fucking anytime and any place."

I squeak out a laugh, pulling my tongue away from his. "Shut up. You don't even believe in fucking."

"Nah, I believe in fucking *for sure*. I just don't believe in fucking you. We don't do that, and we never will."

His fingers crawl up his shirt that I'm wearing and my hips start those second nature moves again. I can't believe none of those *Cosmo* magazines me and Chelsea snuck out of Walmart prepared me for the aching throb between my legs when Ace wasn't inside of me.

"Come in," I mutter.

"You tryna control the vibe." His hand goes up the back of the shirt. "That's how you get in trouble."

I smack my lips while trying to rock away the throbbing.

"I'm not finished with my workout."

"Cut it short."

"I never cheat myself and you shouldn't either."

I roll my eyes, thrusting my face into his neck.

"Ain't even brush your teeth or wash your face and you want me inside you. That's not good. Are you pouting?"

His words sound good, and they probably taste even better. It doesn't take long for my rocking to wake him up.

"Answer me," he mutters, pulling me closer.

I nod, swiping my lips against his neck with each one.

"What you pouting for?"

"Because..."

"Because *what*?"

I'm still new at this, at him, and at sex, so sexy words don't fall out of my mouth like they should.

"I can't read your mind. What you pouting for?"

"Because I—I want you again," I stutter out.

I sound like I did last night when I asked him for it the first time in the kitchen—young and inexperienced.

After a moment, he sighs. "Take it then."

My eyes grow. "People can see us."

"Nah, we too high up and even if they did..." He smiles. "Fuck them."

This is the side of him I saw in that first practice—the one that had him running suicides with a smile.

"Can you put it in for me?" he asks, pumping his hips up and grabbing the sides of his shorts.

He rolls them down between us. I lift just enough to see his dick and I'm as fascinated by it as I was last night.

It's so captivating that it makes me believe that if I taste it, just like it is, I'll start understanding all of Ace and the confusing words he breathed into my mouth while inside of me. I can't believe he ever wanted to jump off the ledge of anything without me. That wasn't how life worked on Planet Ace. I'd follow him to the end—always.

I grip the base of his dick like I've done it a thousand times before, and it makes him laugh. When I place it where I *think* it should go, I sink down and now I understand how cravings form. Those *Cosmo* magazines also forgot to mention how making love drapes a cloak of irresponsibility over your brain. Skin against skin makes that forever we're always talking about seem real, and I'm ready to try to make love to him again.

This time is all body *and* mental. I feel every throb of his dick and every vein that's etched on it. It's a snug fit that makes my eyes roll into the back of my head. *This* time is the real deal. It's what those girls on Twitter are always chirping about when they admit the embarrassing things they've done just to get back to *this* feeling.

"Fuck..." Ace murmurs, shoving his hands onto my legs and easing the rest of himself into me. "You feel us?"

"Uh, huh," I squeak out, choking on a moan that's fighting its way up my throat. "I—I can't move."

His Adam's apple bounces in a harsh jump underneath

the morning sun, and a stinging slap against my ass makes *this* even better. Now I feel all of him—his dick jumping in rough twitches against my walls, its warmth, my wetness.

"Pick your legs up for me."

I nod, dragging my legs against the yoga mat and pulling them up. When I plant my feet on it and look at his strained face, I know this is the real forever he was talking about. I can see the words in his eyes before they come out of his mouth, so I try to hold my breath to get ready for them.

"Don't you *ever* have your ass down on Earth trusting a man like you trust me."

There's no corny follow up question like, "do you understand?" or "am I clear?" Instead, he blurts out, "Is this what happens when you let me be a control freak?"

I groan out a "yeah," that turns into a moan while I try to comprehend the good words he's feeding my inexperienced brain.

"Can't trust another man to take care of my pussy like I take care of it, right?"

I shake my head this time because I'm afraid another moan will belt out into the morning air for all the city to hear. Another slap echoes through it instead because Ace doesn't care. All he cares about is leaving another purple bruise on my ass because I can't ever just act right.

"Open your mouth and answer me."

I open it and a bunch of gibberish pours out with promises of forever and him buried deep in the unintelligible sentences.

"Yeah... that's what I thought," he grunts. "Now, go 'head."

My eyes fight against the gushing sound of our bodies colliding, the birds chirping in the distance, and the cars gliding on the streets below us.

Every time I try to peel my eyes apart, I see Ace through the slits, resting back on his forearms watching me go 'head.

He reaches out and traces his fingers along my inner thigh.

"Is this what mornings sound like with you?"

I think he's talking about the sounds bursting through my ears until his fingers pinch my stomach and I hear my voice blending in with the birds' chirping.

"As—da—" I whine, pushing my body down more even though I don't think there's more of him left for me to take.

I reach past his hand and I *almost* make it to my throbbing clit he strummed the night before, but I should've known better.

"Don't do that," he mutters, knocking my fingers away. "I'm trying to see something."

I can't do shit but nod and savor all the words he's told me while we played together on Planet Ace. Now I know they were calculated, and it makes the throbbing inside me that much better, so I move in up and down motions like I think I'm supposed to.

"Stop jumping up and down on my dick," he rumbles. "That's not how you do that."

"It ain't?" I groan to myself, smacking my lips.

Another *thwack* against my ass lets me know it wasn't an internal groan and my brain can't keep up with what's pouring out my mouth.

"Are you talking back to me, Lourdes?"

I shake my head so hard, my braids slap against my cheeks and he laughs.

"*'Nigga, you can't tell me what to do.'*" He mimics my voice from a time that seems so long ago. "I can do whatever I want with you. I was telling your ass what to do back before you even knew I was. Now, let me show you something before you think you supposed to just jump on my dick for the rest of forever."

His tone is more gruff and cocky than it was last night, but I want it that way. Chelsea would say he had me trained well and I would agree with her with no fuss.

He leans back more and looks at me—like *really* looks at me, wearing his t-shirt with sleep crusted around my eyes and my edges fluttering against the fall breeze.

He reaches out, tugging up the bottom of the shirt and tucking it into its front collar while pulling our bodies back against the french doors. As soon as his back touches the glass, he slams his mouth into mine.

"Good morning," he mumbles, sucking on my tongue. "To my perfect baby, who thinks she's grown with morning breath and frizzy ass braids. They never told me just how defiant your ass would be."

I don't know who "they" are or how this part fits into his dick riding lesson, but it feels right and he feels harder inside me.

His lips glide along my tongue. They move so slow that I feel my hips rocking, telling him not to leave me yet.

"Act right," he hisses, hanging on to the tip of my tongue. "I'm not ready for that yet."

Sitting on his lap with something so precious throbbing inside me is like torture until he pulls his lips off my tongue and plants them against my neck. They leave a trail of wet hot spots down my chest until he slurps one of my nipples into his mouth.

I fight against my hips until he stops and grabs ahold of my hair to keep my head steady while he looks at my face. The sun's rays dance across his lips that I used to stare at. He pulls his bottom one under his teeth like he's on the court, and I want to know everything he's thinking.

"Use your hips and take your time." He smacks his lips against my cheek. "Show me what feels good to you, not what you think I like."

What feels good is *deep* slow grinding against his dick while his head falls back against the french doors and he watches me with a smile. It doesn't take long for me to lose my breath and for my legs to tighten, but he tells me "it's okay" in a quiet murmur. He says I'll "get better with time" while tugging my feet from the mat and pulling my knees beside his body.

Afterward, he reaches out to swipe a thumb against one of my eyes. "How I'm homesick while I'm inside you? Why you so pretty and perfect for me, baby? Hm?"

He belts out question after question that I don't have answers to, and even if I did, he wouldn't understand me because the only words I know how to say while he's living inside me are whatever version of his name feels right. At least until he blurts out one last thing.

"What I'm gonna do when you leave me?"

I don't know what's worse—his words, being too tired and consumed with pleasure that my body's shutting down, or knowing that we can't live connected like this forever.

His fingers dig into my hips and he guides me up and down because I need more practice. His legs fall behind me and he buries another inch of himself inside me I didn't think was possible.

"Fuck... Ason," I cry out. "I—I feel you for real this time."

He rocks his hips into mine in a slow grind that's better than the ones I gave him. "Shhh. I know. Let me get it out for you."

He picks me up, sliding me along the length of his dick until I'm right at the tip, dripping and crying, because I don't think I'll ever feel this close to euphoria again.

His dick lingers at my entrance.

Now I know what girls mean when they talk about their wildly irresponsible sexcapades, but I also don't believe there are other men out there that make love like Ace.

"Ason..." I beg, trying to push down.

I can't even believe my voice is mine while he holds me above his dick, teasing me like I'm not going insane. "I—I promise I'll act right. I won't leave you. I'll never leave you. I—"

"Shhh." He swipes his tongue against my lips and drags me closer. "You thinking too much about shit you don't need to worry about right now. Let me finish telling my pussy good morning."

I'll have to find another girl that's made love to a man she hates and likes and ask her if it's normal to cum on command for them. I don't even need to strum my thumb against my clit in elaborate motions like I do when I'm alone. All I need is Ace's dick inside me, his mouth on mine, and his voice.

"There you go, baby. Ride that shit out."

I feel like I'm on that beach I used to imagine myself on when I heard him talk.

"Open your mouth for me."

The ocean water brushes against my toes and there's a calm breeze tickling my skin while he pushes his fingers into my mouth to soothe the shock. I suckle on them, obsessing over their familiar dips, grooves and callouses. His other hand scrapes along my ass between slaps while he groans, and I remember what happens at the end of irresponsible love-making.

I open my mouth, choking, but I'm too slow because

he's already yanking us apart and pulling his fingers out so fast that I don't have time to savor one last taste.

"Fuck, fuck, fuck." My eyes grow at the smooth way he pumps his dick between us without losing control of me. "You see what you have me doing? Talking about you gonna 'act right.' Yeah fucking right."

A hot splash of moisture lands on my stomach and I laugh. "That was supposed to go in the tip of the condom, right?"

"YOUR HIPS SPREADING?"

Mama isn't stuck today. In fact, she's so much like herself that she's leaning against the island in the kitchen while I wash dishes.

My eyes get big while I stare into the glass underneath the water. "Last time I checked, I was still the same size. I didn't have any trouble when I put on my jeans this morning."

"Hmmm..."

When Mama "hmmms" she's not thinking and I want to fuck Ace up for making her "hmmm" in the first place, even though I would never do that. I don't want to fight him. I just want to fuck him all the time like he said I couldn't do. That's the type of shit irresponsible love-making does, but when I ask him about it, he tells me I'm crazy.

"What?" I ask, shrugging. "Maybe that new medicine they have you taking got your eyesight fuzzy."

"Don't no new medicine have my eyes fuzzy."

I hold in my giggle. "It got you eating other stuff besides grits."

"Yeah, for now."

"Don't talk like that. I haven't seen you eat that much since the beginning of summer."

"And I never seen you call a doctor's office before. Is my Phat growing up?"

I choke out a giggle because I can't tell her that I think making love makes me feel invincible too, so I called up Dr. Evanston's office and made a fuss about her non-existent appetite. After the office staff got in a tizzy, I asked his nurse about that prescription Ace told me about—*Zofran*.

I shrug. "One of us has to grow up and we both know it's not Marcus."

She laughs in a way I haven't heard in a few days. I look over my shoulder and find her bent over the counter, with her shoulders jumping up and down.

The last time she laughed like that was when Ace dropped me off after a morning of lovemaking on his balcony and sharing bear claws in a Shipley's parking lot. He barreled through our front door and took off to Mama's bedroom like a bat out of hell, because he said he missed her.

I turn back to the glass, smiling at the thought of his lips being wrapped around it.

Mama hums while shuffling to the refrigerator. The melody of "Anytime, Any Place" makes a shiver crawl up my spine and I hear Ace's laugh.

"So, what you and Ason had going on the other night?"

The glass slips from my fingers under the water. "What you talking about?"

I squeeze the dishrag like I plan to squeeze Marcus' head if he told Mama my business.

"You know I ain't never been the sharpest tool in the shed, but I don't think you spent the night with Chelsea like Marcus said nor do I believe Ace picked you up from her dorm the other morning, but what do I know? I'm just an old sick girl that's coming out of a two-day funk."

I shift from foot to foot like she can tell my virginal ass isn't virginal anymore. "That's definitely where I was and Ace *definitely* picked me up after talking beacoup crap because of how early it was."

"Like all that crap he talked when he told me you weren't drunk after that party last weekend?"

"Mama..."

"Lourdes..."

She lets out another "hmmm" and shuffles across the kitchen.

I can't turn around to look at her because I feel like I'm twelve again trying to explain to her I woke up with blood in my panties.

"Did you use a condom?" she asks.

"Mama!"

"What? Ain't nobody shocked 'bout this but you."

"I—I don't know what you talking about," I stutter, ignoring the tingling on my thighs where his fingers were.

"Don't get amnesia now. I figured he'd be calling for you anyway."

"And how you figure that?"

"The first birthday is always the hardest. Glad I slept through it."

There's a lot in that one statement she unloads in the middle of our kitchen. I feel it in my chest, especially after the secrets Ace whispered into my ear the night we made love. I still hadn't pieced it all together though.

I turn around, swiping my hands down the length of my jeans. "He cried."

"That's what real men do," she replies, pulling a chair

back from the dining table and easing into it. "I'd be worried if he didn't."

I lean against the counter, staring at my pink toes.

The image of his wet red face is stuck in my brain and there's another grainy one of him climbing over the ledge of a boat. I wish it was clearer.

"His daddy called while I was there."

"So you *was* with him, you lil' liar."

She skirts around my mention of Coach Williams like he wanted to do to our names that day on the phone. It's like they were both dancing around each other even though they had so much in common and so many people they loved standing between them.

I smack my lips. "Mama..."

She laughs. "What? I got cancer, but I'm not stupid."

"Don't say that."

"Say what?"

"Tha—that word."

It doesn't sound as okay as it does when Ace says it. When it comes out of Mama's mouth, I can only see *the end* and, just like Ace, it makes me wonder what happens afterward.

"Oh, girl." She rolls her eyes, picking a piece of lint off her housedress. "I can say 'cancer' if I want to. You don't have to live it. *I* do."

"If you would've told me that a month ago, I would've agreed," I mutter. "But I never seen a grown man cry so bad behind his Mama."

"Oh, he's a grown man now?" She raises her eyebrow and my eyes dart away from her.

"I never said he wasn't."

"Don't stand up there and tell stories now."

"Mama, don't start."

"So, what he buy you?"

"How you know he got me something?"

"For the hundredth time, I know my friend and I know what kind of man she raised. Angie was a go big or go home type of girl in life and in death. Her birthday was her jam."

"He got me a purse," I mumble.

"A purse?" Mama whistles. "What kind?"

"You being too nosy now, but it was a nice one."

I leave out the credit card and the Comfort Care Private Providers welcome packet because I still hadn't digested it and I couldn't do it without Mama inserting her biased opinion because of her love for Angie. Swiping his card was different, but having one with my name embossed on the front and his funds attached to it makes me light-headed. And giving her up to Jazmine isn't as easy as it sounds.

"Nice like that bathing suit he got you for the party?"

I roll my eyes, fighting my smile. "Thought it was the cutest *Tarjay* swimsuit you ever saw? I'm not the only lil' liar around here."

"Keep on rolling them and they might get stuck like that."

"Yeah, whatever. She ever got you any extravagant gifts on one of her birthdays?"

"Who? Angie?"

I nod.

Mama smirks. "Yeah, she did."

"Well... what she get you?"

Her eyes dance around the kitchen with that glint Gus was missing the other day, and then she smiles—big.

"The fall Ace turned three, she enrolled him in school in LA for the first time—a private school the other ball play-er's wives recommended that cost my damn salary just for a semester. She documented that whole semester to me over the phone."

Her shoulders bounce as she lets out another raspy laugh that makes me smile because even when he's not here, Ace still lights up our house.

"He got his first crush there—a little Spanish girl that belonged to one of the local politicians. God, Angie had a fit. Me and Marshall laughed because the boy was only three, but Angie wasn't having it. Well, during that same semester, me and Marshall found out we was having you. You wasn't nothing but a lil' seed in my belly, but Ason and Marsh were already calling you 'babygirl' even though we ain't know if you was a girl or a boy yet. They just *knew*."

I choke on the air between us while Mama's eyes light up. It's different from the glint. This light is as rare as her laugh. We seldom get both, but like I said, she isn't stuck today and now I know why Coach Williams can belt out babygirl as easy as they said Marshall could.

"I remember Angie calling me up the morning of her birthday, right when Marsh was getting up to go shoot at the gym on campus. It was about four in the morning. She sounded so light and clear-headed, like she'd been up for hours." Mama smiles, looking up. "I could barely get a 'girl' out before she screams 'Lourdes!'"

She waves her hands around, hacking out a tiny cough between movements. "She says, 'that's babygirl's name! *Lourdes*.'"

My heart pumps like I'm there with Mama, listening to Angie scream out a name I never understood.

"Where she get it from? How'd she find that name?"

Mama gets real still and stares at me with her lips inching up.

Her eyes cast a lazy trail from my head to my toes while

I grasp the counter to keep myself from falling further into her story.

"Well...it was the little girl's name—the one Ace had a crush on. Angie *loved* that name, but not the idea of him loving some strange girl whose heart she didn't know. She always told me you'd be the only Lourdes that belonged to him—not some damn girl in LA. It didn't matter if he was there or if you were in Houston. She always told me that y'all would find each other some way—through basketball, sickness and death. She'd make sure of it because she knew *my* heart and she knew what kind of little girl I'd raise." She lets out a deep sigh. "I told you she was a good woman. It didn't matter how much money she had, how busy she was, or how far apart our worlds were—she was always my good girlfriend. God knew what he was doing with me and her, and Angie knew what she was doing with you and Ason. She was always ten steps ahead of everybody else."

You know that deep sense of relief that comes when you finally get something right after getting it wrong for so long? Light shoulders? An instant feeling of gratification? Deep, easy breaths?

"*Lourdes,*" Ace mumbled against my stomach. "*Who gave you that name anyway, baby?*"

I hold on to his voice from that day with more annoying fluttering butterflies that just won't stop.

Mama slaps her thighs with another grin before getting up from the chair. "I love you and Ason, but I'm too young to be a granny and ya'll aren't ready to be anybody's parents. Tell him to use a goddamn condom."

CHAPTER TWENTY-TWO

Ace

When a man says he can't describe what pussy feels like, it's true. It's an impossible thing to do, but I'll try.

Phat's pussy feels like the first morning in a while that I didn't wake up without a shot of 1942 to warm my muscles. She feels like the first time Gus drove me to basketball practice and told me about my personal treasure chest in his head. She feels like Mom's laughter. Shit, she even makes me feel *soft,* so I want to speak first when I see Pops standing on the side of the court before practice.

After fifty missed calls over the course of a week, he looks at me like I'm a ghost floating across the court—like I'm dead right along with Mom.

"Afternoon, *Coach,*" I say, gliding toward him.

"Williams."

His voice is emotionless and I'm a sucker for that shit so I offer myself up because thirteen-year-old me still exists in my head sometimes.

"I can work with Sanchez on defense," I reply.

His eyes get big and then sink back into slits so quick that I wouldn't have noticed the change if I didn't know him.

"Alright... alright." He nods with his squinted eyes on my lips.

There's a lot of unspoken shit floating between us on this court, but that's how it's always been—especially when I go against his controlling beliefs because little did Phat know, Ason Williams Sr. was the original control freak. I guess it's one of the few worldly things that didn't revolve around basketball that he taught me.

He sweeps his hand toward the court and I jog there, waiting on Bryson to realize what's happening while he dribbles around by himself.

The rest of the team hangs around doing their own drills because defense is still Bryson's weak spot no matter how many times Marcus blows me off to practice it with him and Pops lectures him about it. Pops won't let him focus on anything but *it* until he's able to defend in his sleep because defense is in the AW starter pack for perfect players. It's why I knew it so well.

"Sanchez!" Pops yells. "Get with Williams!"

He looks up at Pops with his healing eye.

Now it's a light shade of purple and his iris isn't a deep red that makes Marquise cringe every time he walks in the locker room.

He struts across the court with his chin up like Phat forgave him even though I know she didn't. She told me so when my face was between her legs after another sneaky link up between pickup games with Marcus at their house. I didn't even have to ask about him by name because another good feeling that pussy produces is enmeshment.

"Tell me how you feel," I groaned out at her.

Bryson dribbles the ball in a lazy cadence while bumping elbows with LaQuan on his way to me.

Everybody on the team knows what happened back in the locker room without LaQuan even opening his mouth to tell it and there was nothing left to say because it was that tried-and-true pecking order at work again. What's done is done.

When he dribbles up to me, I don't see fear in his eyes—just the disappointment from Phat's non-response to another one of his texts I saw on her phone. Her answer to my request came out between deep labored breaths while I rocked her through an orgasm in their kitchen pantry.

"I'm still angry. The—the whole team thinks I'm a hoe because of him," she stuttered out, raking her nails across my face. *"You said I co—could be angry, remember?"*

His eyes crawl over the scratches across my temples like Blake's did while Pops claps his hands in the distance. "Let's go, Sanchez!"

I snort, waving my hand, beckoning him to me.

"Yeah." I mimic Pops' loud clapping. "Let's go, Sanchez."

Good pussy can make a man feel a million different ways at once, but it can also magnify those feelings—especially when a man's sober for the first time in a long time. I can even see with clear eyes today.

Bryson's not the same Bryson from the first practice. A lot of shit's happened since then—freshman growing pains, the last party of the summer, and a last reminder of his place in our locker room. He's still that lame freshman with a big mouth, but the last party of the summer made him brave enough to bark more, and now he has a chip on his shoulder.

He bounces the ball slowly, staring at those scratches

again like he's trying to decide if they're from Phat's pretty coffin shaped nails that I pay for now or some other girl.

"You good, homie?" I ask.

"I ain't your fucking homie."

I laugh and clap, because again, good pussy magnifies the wild feelings it creates—especially the sober ones. But the funny thing about good pussy is how crazy it makes men —even men that's never been in it because somehow we just know when a girl has it. It's in our nature. It's how Bryson knows the scratches along my forehead are Phat's and the only way he knows how good her pussy is when he's never even had it.

He shoves the ball into my chest. "Go 'head, *pussy.*"

"Oh, big brother Marcus teaching you well?" I grip the ball and square up.

"Yeah and after me and him finish balling, Phat teaches me some better shit." He winks his healing eye, throwing his arms up.

Marcus must've finally broken him down and hammered the most important part of defense into his head that Pops couldn't teach him. It was mental.

The shit he's saying isn't true, but one thing about sobriety is that it fucks with my head worse than when I'm home. His words are just words, but they feel real in my sober head.

I jab step and wait for his reaction, but he doesn't drop off like he's supposed to.

"Good job, Sanchez!" Pops yells. "Hold steady!"

It's kind of like that bandaid analogy Phat used.

The best way to get into an opponent's head is little by little.

We fall back into our stances from before. I jab step

again and hold the ball. He follows. We dance around each other while he keeps talking.

"You know I was just over there, right?" He pushes up against my shoulder with his arms spread. "On her porch, in her house, in her face."

"Oh, yeah?"

"Yeah."

"I'm glad you made it in the house this week, homie. I know how crazy Mom gets about letting strangers in."

I bring the ball down and cross left, driving off his shoulder and going straight to the hoop.

"Watch that right side, Sanchez!" Pops yells.

As soon as I'm back in Bryson's face, his mouth runs again.

"You a weak ass nigga. You was bragging about holding her down but she ever tell you how long we been friends?"

Today, he finally gets that it was never about basketball and always about Phat. I just hate it's on a day where I can feel all my senses.

"For twelve years."

I feel the desperation in his tone. I hear his hot breath. I smell the epiphany he had over the weekend. I taste the good shit between me and Phat I can toss in his face.

"You know how many fights we had?" he asks. "She always forgives me, eventually. You should ask her how she felt about you before you moved here. She ain't into rapists, my nigga."

I square up and dribble again with him in my ear.

He snickers. "I was here before you and I'll be here after you. She'll do anything for me."

Those words aren't like the ones he spat at me in the locker room.

He belted that shit out like somebody told him all my

trigger words and he went and practiced it in the mirror for the day I had to face him with nothing in my system.

I don't care about the hoop anymore. I charge him and throw my shoulder into his chest so hard he stumbles back. His feet tangle together, and he falls, sliding across the slick court with a nasty squeak that makes everybody pause.

"Hey! Hey! That's enough! Williams!" Pops shouts.

I crouch, holding my arm for him to take while Pops hollers in the background like we're squabbling for real.

Bryson stares at my arm like it's a speck of dirt until I force my hand into his and yank him up from the court.

I see the tension in Pops' shoulders out of the corner of my eye when I pull him in. He looks like he's holding his breath.

I press my mouth near Bryson's ear. "I hope you talk this good when you finally go apologize to my baby for ruining her rep she cares so much about."

He pushes out of my grip while I stare up at Pops, smiling.

I slap his back. "Good defense, Sanchez."

Blake Harvey: Tick Tock. My reporter has a deadline to meet. How about me, you, and babygirl have a nightcap? Let me talk with her—with your permission, of course.
Maybe I can get her on board. Rockets v. Lakers. Tip off @ 7. Let's talk business.

I THINK the thing Pops hates most about me is how much my addictions control me. It doesn't matter if my life is existing on deadlines and threats of exposure—I still make time for all of them.

I shove my phone into my short's pocket and stare at Phat behind the register in the back of the bookstore.

I'm still covered with sweat and replaying Bryson's words in my head when I stagger inside, grip a handful of Dum-Dums and dump them in the middle of the magazine she has her head buried in.

"Uh, excuse yo—"

She swallows the rest when she flings her head up and finds me staring at her with red eyes, flared nostrils, and bunched eyebrows.

"You got me?" I ask, nodding toward the candy.

She nods with the same little smile she has when I'm inside her and pushes her hand into her back pocket. When she pulls out the credit card with her name embossed on the front, my heart starts pitter pattering in my chest like I guzzled a shot of caffeine.

She twists the credit card machine toward her while popping her gum and sticking the card inside with a grin. "But I'm always in trouble for spending money on H-E-B and Uber Eats. I'm surprised you don't got a mouthful of cavities."

I can't hold back anymore, so I wrap my hand around her cheeks while she's running her mouth.

She tugs her face out of my grip, snatching the card out when the machine dings. "What you got going on? Your smile missing."

All I hear is Bryson spitting out the shit he probably feeds her every time I come up in their conversations. I should be relieved because I know she can't handle the article living in the files on Blake's phone. She can't handle me or us existing on Earth together where I'm not her legend because I'm just a dude who fucked up no matter what she thinks or who she hated.

"Take a break." I thumb her bottom lip and drop my hand.

"I just clocked in."

"Who here?"

Her eyebrow shoots up as soon as Brandy pushes from the back storage room.

"I had a feeling you'd be by soon," she says, grinning at me with her blonde curls poking in every direction. "You still owe me for Splashtown weekend, remember? Let's make it happen before the first game."

When she notices the wild look on my face, her eyes dart between me and Phat, but Phat already has her head back between the pages of that magazine.

"Cool... can you cover for Lourdes for a minute?"

The air whips beside me as Phat flings her head up.

Brandy's face falls along with my stomach, but she doesn't understand how hunger works. Only Phat does.

"Uh, okay? I guess." She tilts her head. "Did something happen?"

I frown. "Yeah... I need to talk to my—"

"I won't be long, girl." Phat chuckles, crumpling the suckers in her hand.

She turns around, picks up Marshall's backpack, drops it, and then picks it up again like she doesn't know if she should stay or go.

Brandy's eyes narrow when she comes from behind the counter, yanking my arm. We stumble out onto the yard and she lets go as soon as the first group of people pass us.

That nasty sinking feeling from practice comes back and I don't need 1942 to do irresponsible shit. I just need her in whatever way I can get her.

"Come to my truck." I walk off. "I wanna talk to you."

She follows behind me, blowing out a breath. We don't

talk on the way to Lot E. Our arms brush against each other and now and then I hear her take a deep breath I want to swallow because I don't know how to explain that Blake Harvey has us living on deadlines and under his control and I don't know how to stop it.

When she sees my truck sitting in the back row, she glides toward the passenger door, flinging it open when I hit the key fob to unlock it. Even seeing her familiarity with my vehicle makes my dick hard and has me soaring to the driver's side door.

As soon as I climb behind the wheel, she messes with shit—opening the vents, dropping the suckers in my cup holder, and swiping the visor down to play with her hair in the mirror.

"Okay, you interrupted my shift and now we're all alone on Planet Ace," she sings, brushing at her edges. "Who did you something?"

Everybody—Blake, Bryson, Pops, Brandy, the world. Everybody who just wouldn't let us be.

The cold air from the vents blow against my hot face while I stare at her in all of her post-virginal glow. She flings the visor back up and turns to me.

"What you mad about?" she asks, sounding like Mom.

Mad?

Me and that word hadn't mixed since Mom was still drinking wine on her balcony with her feet kicked up and here was version two of my little lady telling me that somehow she knew all about it.

I push out of the truck because everybody has me *fucked* up. They have me so bent that I can't feel the sting when my skin gets caught between the back passenger door handle and the car. I yank it and get in.

When I close the door behind me, Phat whips her head

around with her eyebrows pinched together.

"What you doin—"

Her legs scrape against the middle console and her teeth chatter against each other when I pull her into the backseat with me.

"What's wrong?" she gasps landing on my lap. "Why you so mad? Was it your dad—"

"I'm not mad."

"If you're not mad, I need to go back to work. I thought something was wrong."

Pops don't even know when I'm fucking mad but somehow this girl that I'm *so* obsessed with thinks she knows. She can't even tell another man that she's taken, but she thinks she knows when I'm mad.

Mom would tell me it was my ego that had me tripping. I hear her clapping and laughing in the back of my head when our lips collide and telling me that *all* former little ladies thought they knew everything just because they weren't little anymore.

I yank at the string dangling in the back of her smock and rip through the knot because it's just another thing in the way of me getting back to the one place I need to be. I pull it over her head, taking her t-shirt with it. All her breaths and complaints run together while I stare at her breasts spilling out of her bra.

"I'm being for real. Your lil' girlfriend is nosey as hell. If I'm not back in five minutes, she gon' tell our manager, Kelvin, I left and then I'll get written up. I'm already halfway employed."

Womp. Womp. Womp.

Why didn't Mom tell me that little lady's complaints sounded like nails on a fucking chalkboard when I wasn't floating from 1942? I don't even have any clever comebacks.

"Ason?"

I swallow at her cheeks jumping up and the way she's straddling my lap. She even has the audacity to throw her arms around my neck like everything is cool, like I wasn't pressing dudes over her, like I'm not going fucking insane with a bunch of feelings and nothing to numb them with, like I wasn't experiencing a day I would remember from beginning to end for the first time in so long.

"Baby..." she mutters, tilting her head. "See, you ain't even arguing with me right now. Man, what you so mad about?"

"Baby?" I frown, pushing my nose against hers.

Of all the things my brain wants to push out, that's all it can produce because she had the nerve to call me *that*. I ain't been that since I came out the womb.

"That's what I said..." She closes her eyes when I nuzzle my nose against hers. "*Baby*."

"I ain't your baby."

Her eyes spring open and I know this isn't some shit I can take away from her. It's an essential in her eyes.

"You ain't grown," I mutter, taking her bottom lip between my teeth. "Why you always wanna be so grown? You supposed to stay *my* baby forever. Why you don't want that?"

A low whimper crawls from the back of her throat, making my body surge forward.

I guess the one good thing about going without 1942 is being able to feel every part of home, like the lacy fabric of Phat's bra digging into my angry fingers, her pert nipple gliding across my tongue and her fingernails digging into my neck while she gasps for air. All of it blends together in a nice sensation that makes me think I took that shot of 1942 after all.

"Hey..." she squeals as I yank the rest of her dangling bra down her stomach. "That's new. I bought it for you and you ain't even look at it."

"I'll buy you another one," I mutter, pulling her into my chest and reaching for her backpack in the front seat.

"What you looking for?"

"Condoms."

She buries her head in my neck, laughing, while I unzip it and rifle past packs of bubblegum and notebooks.

"I don't think I'm experienced enough to be carrying around condoms for spontaneous, angry after-practice love-making."

After a long, hard blink, I let out a snort, pulling my hand out of her backpack. I collapse into the backseat, bringing her with me. It's a mistake because she's revved up and brave today, so she pulls my hand on top of the button on her jeans.

"But I want you to figure this shit out," she says. "Because I wanna experience spontaneous, angry after-practice love-making for the first time."

That's all it takes for me to yank at the button and unfasten it. We work together, peeling the jeans off her legs, rolling my shorts down, and I can't believe she let me talk her into my world so easily. I can't believe she trusts me *this much,* but then again, it was what I wanted all along and like she said—I always got what I wanted.

I twist her body around in my lap and pull another pair of new lacy panties to the side, plunging inside of her. She takes me with her legs spread over my thighs like she's had me a thousand times before. I bury my face in her neck while she pushes out high-pitched groans until she belts out the new word she associates with me now.

"*Baby*..." she groans, thrusting her arms onto my head

and thrashing against my dick like we didn't talk about this shit already. "Wha—what you so upset about? I feel it."

Upset, mad, angry. Those words don't exist in my vocabulary because they don't change anything. Instead of telling her so, I wrap one hand around her braids and grip her breast with my other.

"What I tell you about jumping up and down on my dick like that?" I grunt into her neck.

"Not to do it." She breathes out.

"Then stop."

She sinks back on me and relaxes into a slow grind that doesn't settle my brain.

I turned her into a talker after only three rounds of making love. Instead of choking on my name, she's belting out complete sentences and questions that I don't have the answers to.

Shit, I'm not even stable enough to figure out how to make love to her responsibly. I'm being that impulsive ass man I swear she doesn't need so I savor this moment—us with no barrier between us again, her smell, the wholeness I feel from her body on top of mine, and us dancing together with that article lurking in the shadows because I don't know how to protect her from it.

We grind together in an easy rhythm. She wraps her hand around mine, belting out a moan that makes me try to dive further inside her even though there's nowhere left to go.

"Tell me you won't leave me," I grit out, pinching my eyes shut.

"I—I won't."

"No matter what?"

"Yes! No matter what!"

"Don't fuckin' lie to me."

"I'm not!"

"Fuck..." I gasp, trying my hardest to make more space inside of her for me to take up. "Prove it then. Show me forever."

She thrusts her head back and shoves her mouth on mine, like I wasn't trying to bend her in half to satisfy an impossible need. When she opens her mouth, all of her words fall into mine.

"I will. J—just tell me what's wrong, baby," she mutters, letting me catch every word. "If I did something, tell me how to fix it."

I don't know how to form words she can digest without choking on them. We're vibing on two different frequencies because her pilot can't get his shit together.

"You different today." She cups my cheek, swirling her tongue against mine. "I can tell you ain't been drinking. I can feel and see all of you."

That shit right there makes me stop to wrap both arms around her waist just so I can sit in this moment. She stops too.

"Let me fix it." She breathes hard. "I wanna fix whatever it is."

God, I know. I know. I'm supposed to be careful with her, but my baby isn't just hardheaded. She's curious too.

I swallow hard. "Can you get on your knees for me?"

She nods and eases off of me.

My eyes are so heavy that I can't do shit but watch her adjust the passenger seat and climb onto the floor between slow blinks.

When she's there, on her knees, staring up at me, my mouth goes dry.

"Ain't nothing for you to fix." I reach down and brush

my knuckles down her cheek. "You didn't do anything but be your perfect self. Do you understand?"

She nods again, leaning into my hand.

"I—I'm the problem. Okay? Only me."

I'm flawed, fucked up and addicted to things that won't do anything but destroy me.

I'm so fucked up that all I can hear is Bryson's voice bragging about how my baby did the unthinkable for him that one day in the locker room. He's so green that he thinks he owns her by default, but that's not how life works—not on Earth and especially not on Planet Ace. Now I hear Blake trying to convince her that life with me was worth it, even if it wasn't a walk in the park.

"Open your mouth like I taught you," I whisper.

Bryson wouldn't even know what to do with her like this —on the floor, with her mouth open, staring up and waiting on my next thought, breath, and move so she can follow. He doesn't know shit about having so much control over something so precious and I guess that's the only way I can cope with all these upset, mad, and angry feelings Phat says I'm experiencing on a day where I'll remember everything.

She exhales when I guide my dick into her mouth and pass her teeth.

She doesn't know what to do with it, so it sits there until she remembers the times I pushed my fingers down her throat to make room for this moment. There's no elaborate tongue tricks, deep throating, or hand-twisting, but I don't need that from her. She suckles on it like she's soothing herself instead of me while I rake my fingers across her face.

"Are you showing me forever, baby?" I smile.

She pinches her eyes shut. "Mhmm..."

The soft vibrations from her humming climbs up my

body and I want to talk again like we did when I fell into her for the first time.

I exhale, relishing in the warmth from her mouth. "You being a good girl for real today? Or are you running game because you know my head gone?"

She hums out an incoherent response with her eyes still closed.

"Look at me when I'm talking to you."

She nods, swallowing another inch of my dick and then prying her eyes apart.

Our eyes lock.

Hers are heavy like she downed that glass I left by the kitchen sink this morning, but I know she's just drunk off of me again.

I brush my knuckles underneath her eyes while Bryson's voice bounces around my head and takes up space between her grunts: *"I was here before you and I'll be here after you. She'll do anything for me."*

My hips thrust up without my brain guiding them. They're slow strokes that give her a chance to taste every part of herself she left on me while grinding in my lap. Tears well along the edges of her eyes while I push as deep as she lets me until she lets out a ragged choke and braces herself against my thighs.

I swipe the tears away. "Shhh. Mind over matter, remember?"

It's a reminder for myself too, because she was right all along. I haven't drank today, so how the fuck can I stop when she can feel all of me now?

"Take it," I grunt out. "Take it for me."

Her throat relaxes.

I grip her braids and pull out of her mouth just enough to get what I want because I made her crazy enough to give me *anything* I want. She even wants to absorb all of these feelings that I swear I haven't felt in so long.

I massage the base of her throat. "You'd do anything for me, huh?"

She gives me more enthusiastic nodding that reminds me of how wild Bryson's imagination has to be and how obsessed I have to be with Phat for me to beef with another dude so much in my head.

"I know." I coo, pressing my fingers into her tiny Adam's apple and making it harder for her to hold steady while holding on to all of me. "Since you'd do anything for me, I should make you take your ass back in that store and tell Brandy how much money I spend on you. I should make you tell her how you wanted a break just so you could come and fix shit for me. I should do that, huh, baby? Make you tell her you always getting your way because I got you so damn spoiled."

Satisfaction coats her face after my angry words fall out like she didn't have all the power to fuck up Brandy and her jersey chasing ways.

"You won't do none of that though." I shake my head, pushing further into her mouth to induce another choke. "You talk all this good shit when we home, but down on Earth, you won't even tell a nigga that I can't breathe without you. Why you won't tell him that *I'm* the only one that's ever been inside you? Why you won't tell him I'm the beginning and end for you? Hm? Why you won't tell him how good I feel?"

She's the beginning, *middle*, and end for me, but I've already told her enough simp shit to last a lifetime.

"Spontaneous, angry after-practice love-making? You really think your ass grown." I laugh, stabbing the soft insides of her round cheek and then patting it with my fingers. "You ain't grown until you learn how to open your mouth and check a chick for insinuating that you ruined some non-existent shit between me and her. Fuck her. I don't even want her and you *know* that, but you keep letting her between us."

Fuck.

I don't know how I can survive more days like this, where the muted feelings I usually shake off have me by the balls right along with Phat's little fingers. She doesn't even care that I'm losing control of myself and us.

"Maybe I should check you?" I frown. "Make you put that job on ice with Twitter because you won't open your mouth."

She cries out an agonizing moan like my fucked up solution is perfect because I made her this way.

I dig deeper into her mouth, swallowing the rest of what I want to ask, like if she'd open it when the world found out about us, or if she'll trust me enough to follow me to the end for real.

I hold my breath for her grimace, but nothing happens— not even a choke. My hand nuzzles against her throat while my dick sputters in wild spasms while she *fixes* shit like she promised. Meanwhile, those feelings she saw within me spill out along with my seed.

"Your heart know which way to beat now?" I choke out, milking myself into her mouth.

She nods, whimpering, swallowing and taking all of me.

"Good. Now you can go back inside and tell Brandy that you have to leave early. We gotta go take care of something tonight." I swipe my hand across her wet face, picking up her spit along the way. "You ever seen your team play from a private suite, baby?"

CHAPTER TWENTY-THREE

Lourdes

Cree came back.

She breezed through Ace's condo long enough to leave an NBA game-worthy outfit on his bed for me. This look is a curated casual get-up. There's a graphic shirt with a throwback picture of The Dream pressed onto the front and Jordans to match Ace's because he likes corny shit like that. She texted me with updates while I sat in Sunny's pedicure chair and Ace chirped on the phone beside me coordinating a last-minute babysitting gig with Jazmine for Mama because my get out of jail free card doesn't hold weight anymore.

> 5622543654: Hola hermana, I left your clothes on Ace's bed with matching ones to make him smile tonight. Wear your Saddle bag and take good care of him.

Four hours and five errands later and we're speeding through downtown to the Toyota Center because spontaneous angry after practice love-making makes me skip to the end of Planet Ace—even if Brandy looked at me like I had lost my mind after I told her I had to leave early with Ace's taste on my breath.

"You just got here?" She frowned. *"Where did Ace go?"*

"Yeah, but I—I have a family emergency," I replied while Ace's truck idled in the parking lot behind the building. *"Just tell Kelvin I'll make up the hours."*

It was kind of the truth. There *was* an emergency. It was written in Ace's dark gaze when he strolled up to the counter with clear eyes for the first time since I met him. I'd somehow transformed into Angie Williams' lil' wannabe daughter-in-law because of the secret Mama told me in our kitchen and I couldn't leave him alone with clear eyes for the first time. Angie wouldn't let me.

Dough beats through the speakers in his truck while I stare up at the city lights bouncing off the skyscrapers.

"Is this more everyday life shit?" I ask, glancing at him from the passenger seat.

His cheeks sink as he slides a Dum-Dum from between his lips while pulling into a parking garage attached to the arena.

"Yup." He shrugs, pulling behind a Bentley. "More everyday life shit, kid."

I'm too scared to ask what a real date with him is like and if the girls from his past experienced opulent everyday life shit with Ason Williams Jr. My brain screams, "duh," but my fumbling gut says otherwise.

The car glides up the floors of the parking garage as he pushes his sucker in front of my mouth. "Why? You don't wanna do everyday life shit with me?"

I *do.*

I want to make love on penthouse balconies, play dress

up and get whisked away to elegant galas, taste shit I only hear about on television, go to an NBA game on a random ass weekday, make spontaneous angry after-practice love, and most of all I just wanted to do that shit with him.

I open my mouth, letting him push the sucker between my lips.

"Taste good like you, huh, baby?" he mumbles, gripping my cheeks while pulling into a parking spot.

It tasted nothing like me and everything like him.

"Nuh uh. We don't have time for me to take care of that. Stop twisting over there," he adds.

It takes a minute before I realize I'm squirming in his passenger seat because life on Planet Ace really *is* wild.

I grin around the sucker, slurping his taste off and biting into it while he puts the truck in park. He pushes out and rounds it while I crunch on the last piece.

As soon as he pulls my door open, he takes me by the hand and tugs me out. We walk side by side toward the building and I'm so wrapped up in him I reach for the door handle.

"What I tell you about that?" he rumbles from behind me.

My hand slides off like it did each time he slapped it off a handle back at the gala. I grow warm as he yokes me into him.

He tugs the door open. "Act right for me tonight."

I didn't plan on it.

Walking into The Toyota Center is like hopping on a time machine and heading back to a time when Angie was still living, Coach Williams ran the league from The Staples Center, and Ace was *The Kid* without a salacious reputation. It's full of basketball lovers like me and Marcus.

"AWII—*my nigga!*" a staff member bumps fists with Ace as he pulls me under his arm. "Welcome home, dawg."

"'Preciate it, brodie." Ace smiles, darting his eyes away and pulling me toward an elevator.

We take an isolated route where there's only staff idling around and shuffling important looking people past us. Each time we come across somebody new, I'm reminded why I'm so obsessed with Ace.

"How you doing tonight, Charese?" he asks the elevator attendant after glancing at her name tag when we walk inside.

She can't talk because she's too busy blushing and smashing her fingers against the button to take us up to the three-hundred level suites.

She eyes Ace's arm around my waist, but he's too busy fussing over my nails to notice her. She reminds me of myself back before I knew about life on Planet Ace. She has my complexion, my build, and my curiosity about a boy that's nothing like I imagined him to be.

"New clawz on deck." He laughs, pushing his lips against the tips of them and kissing each one Sunny took her time shaping while he talked on the phone.

"It ain't the same." I roll my eyes. "I need to show Twitter."

"Fuck Twitter. They didn't watch you choose between Passionately Plum and Purple Power for thirty minutes. *I* did that."

The girl giggles, and he whips his head over to her, smiling. "You see what I have to deal with? Spoiled ass."

He winks at her, and I see the familiar twinkle in his eyes. It's what was missing when I thought I knew everything about him and Brandy that day in the bookstore. Chelsea spent all that time bumping her gums about

Brandy being his pretty little redemption arc when it was girls like me who were his weakness all along.

The night is young and feels good, so I let my chin fall onto his chest while the elevator shoots us up into suite-land.

"First of all, it took two minutes for you to watch me pick a color and then you went outside to talk on the phone some more." I frown. "Don't cap."

"A'ight, we'll go back tomorrow and I'll leave my phone in the car."

"No. I'm not bothering Sunny again." I whine until he covers my lips with his.

Charese's eyes widen as soon as mine droop and I forget about life outside the Toyota Center, where I'm too afraid to do shit like this.

He grips me harder around the waist and my stomach drops as the elevator bobs and comes to a stop on level three-hundred. Our tongues brush right as the elevator dings and the doors slide open.

He pulls away, yanking me out. "We'll chop it up with you later, Charese. I'll send my girl to give you the score at halftime."

That shit makes my insides fumble and I think it makes Charese's too, because her cheeks lift like he called her *his* girl. I think it's the excitement of him being wilder than our minds could ever imagine because he's existing back on Earth like he did before folks ran him up to Planet Ace and left him there for me to find.

Our pointer fingers tangle together in a loop as we stroll toward another wide-eyed attendant.

"Why we watching the game from a suite again?"

"Suites are for business and courtside is for appearances," he rumbles in my ear while the attendant escorts us to our new home for the next three hours.

"You're here to do business?"

It's too late for me to get an answer because suite thirty is a few steps away.

The attendant pushes the door open and my fumbling gut comes back when I see Blake Harvey standing at a bar nestled on the left side of the suite in an expensive tracksuit.

"So, this is the business?" I choke out.

"Phat, you made it." He lifts his arms, waving us toward him.

I gulp at the sight of the shiny bottles of alcohol and white men hanging around while the lights dim in the arena.

There's a glow around Blake that makes my palms sweat and I remember why I hated his treacherous Carlton Banks ass.

I look up at Ace, but he's already distracted with a fire in his eyes that I want to put out because this is the part of our everyday life shit I hate. It's not spontaneous angry love-making—it's spontaneous bullshit.

"Come over here." Blake smiles, eyeing my Cree approved athleisure get-up. "Matching ones. How Insta-gram-worthy of you two."

I try to digest all of it—the open-air suite, the glass of liquor waiting for Ace sitting next to Blake's elbow, and his interest in me *again*. None of it will go down and Marcus' little anecdotes continue to reign supreme because Blake still isn't standing on business. I see it in his eyes. They're empty.

Ace dips his hand underneath my graphic shirt and we step forward together, but walking towards Blake is like stumbling into a lion's den even if I have Ace as a shield.

Blake grabs the glass of liquor and hands it to Ace with a smile when we approach him. "Can I?"

The rest of his question is missing, but it doesn't stop Ace from pushing his lips against my ear.

"Go chop it up with him for a minute. If you ever feel like you need to come home, I'll be right over here," he whispers, soothing my hot ear with a kiss. "I'm not going anywhere."

This everyday life shit is so confusing. All I know is that I have no business talking *business* in a suite with a man like Blake.

Blake takes my limp hand. "Who you going for tonight?"

"The home team," I mutter as he pulls me away from Ace and toward the seats at the edge of the suite.

"I guess the t-shirt should've clued me in, huh? No love for LA?"

"Nope."

"Cold blooded."

"Nah, just unbiased. They ain't been the same since AW left."

"I concur." He motions toward an empty seat. "They've lost their luster, and they might never get their best man."

We both sit down as I mull over his words. "You mean Ace?"

"Yeah...you know everybody was banking on him eventually playing for his Pops—even their rivals."

"Guess so."

He's blabbering all the words that Ace is always running from.

I look at the court, seeing Ace's face enmeshed with the other faces in purple and gold uniforms. Instead, he'll be wearing a maroon one next week, playing on a court with boys that have half his talent, and no cloud of disappointment over their heads.

"You know, I think we both want the same thing for our boy," Blake says, talking over the announcer's deep voice.

I glance back at Ace taking another shot of liquor to the head.

"We do?"

"Absolutely, Lourdes. I can call you that, right?"

"No. You can call me Phat."

"Okay. Phat it is. How you feel about our boy playing among the big dogs?"

"Our boy" sounds as fake as the other lame shit he's said since we walked in. It's another thing Marcus would've pointed out. If a nigga had to call you *his boy*, you most definitely wasn't his boy at all. I thought Ace knew that.

He leans over the bar, smiling at the bartender while she slides him another drink and for the first time in my life the squeaking sneakers against a basketball court make me nauseous.

I turn back to Blake. "He *is* the big dog."

He laughs, pulling me in by the shoulder. "I ever tell you how much I like you?"

"No, and I wasn't holding my breath to hear it."

"I told Kid you were a spitfire."

"You did?"

"Yup. It's a compliment."

The announcer cuts between our words. "That's two in the paint for *Quinones*."

I shrug from under his arm and glance back at Ace. He's sipping from another full cup and talking to a white man who keeps clutching his shoulder like he's making sure it's really *The Kid* getting drunk in a suite with him.

"What else you told him about me?"

"Aht, aht. That's between myself and my future client."

When I whip my head back toward Blake, he's staring onto the court with that annoying glow on his face.

"That's what all this about? You still trying to court him?"

"What you know about courting clients?" He grins.

"I know enough about it to know you still ain't standing on business. You can't court a man who don't wanna be courted."

He takes a sip from his glass and chuckles. "Contrary to what you think, I'm actually courting you, my dear."

My ears ring as the buzzer sounds, signaling the end of the first quarter. The Rockets are in the lead, Ace is almost tipsy when he started the day sober, and now I know I wasn't mistaken—Blake Harvey is too interested in me.

I gulp, tugging my bag into my middle. "What you need to do that for? I'm not a basketball player."

"Not at all. But *my* basketball player has a lot of vices and right now you're his favorite. You know what a vice—"

"I'm young, not stupid, and ain't nothing immoral about me."

"You're right. There *isn't* anything immoral about you, but there is something immoral about his obsession with you. He can't put one foot in front of the other without your reassurance."

"What does that have to do with you?"

"Oh, it's got a lot to do with me. When I take a client on, I'm not just taking them, I'm taking their families and their problems, too. Sadly, in *The Kid's* case, he's a lot like a lone wolf. There's not a gang of hanger-ons trying to ride his coattails or a bunch of broke family members that want his money. So it's just you, him and all those problems he's so good at hiding."

"He's got his daddy too." I frown, shifting in my seat at his insinuation of Ace and his problems.

Blake scoffs. "I think you've been around them long enough to know how ridiculous that sounds. Do you see his Pops in this suite?"

"What the fuck do you even know?"

"I thought you knew? My job is to know *everything*."

"Oh, it is?"

"Yeah... this thing is kind of like a cycle, you know?"

"Enlighten me."

"I stay in the know to make *and* keep you happy, which keeps Ace happy, and in return, he makes me happy—like one big happy family."

Now it's my turn to scoff. "A'ight, *Barney*. I'm good on the PBS after school special shit."

"I'm just saying, Phat, I see the way he looks at you and the way you look at him, but I'm skeptical of you sometimes."

"Skeptical?" I pull my head back, frowning. "Says a crooked ass sports agent."

My insult makes a loud laugh roar out of him. "You talk all that rah-rah shit about him and his talents, but life with a kid like him isn't sunny."

His pompous accent melts into a northern twang and I hear the grittiness he tries so hard to bury to intimidate people like me. His words sound too similar to Coach Williams'.

"You don't think I know that?"

"You know it but you haven't *actually* lived it, babygirl. He has you on another planet, and that's the problem. Let me show you something." He leans in close to me, nudging his shoulder into mine. "You see that section down there?"

He wiggles his finger to the area along the court he's

been eyeing since he sat next to me. He doesn't wait for me to reply before he runs his mouth again.

"That's where the players' families, wives, girlfriends, and side chicks sit. If Ace has it his way, you'll be plopped right in the melee for him to blow you kisses while he warms up or whatever the fuck he likes to do before games."

I squint at the cluster of people until I zero in on a mass of curls and high-yellow skin that looks too familiar. The more he talks, the more I concentrate on trying to make out the features of the girl, but we're too far up.

"If you were living all that rah-rah shit you like to talk about, you'd have no problem being down there."

I swallow a mouthful of words at the thought of a camera being shoved in my face just for being Ace's. "I—I don't."

He whips his head around and stares at me right as the jumbotron flashes an image of the girl and a leggy blonde sitting next to her. "So you're telling me, you'd have no problem sitting courtside, just a few feet away from your boyfriend's victim?"

Victim.

The word comes out in broken syllables as Cree nudges the girl so they can cheese at the jumbotron together. I want to throw up that strawberry Dum-Dum this time because Blake is the treacherous fucked up Carlton Banks I said he was.

"Damn... oh, you ain't know?" He flings his finger from me to the jumbotron and then looks over his shoulder to make sure Ace is deep in another sponsored bottle of tequila. "You see, the curly headed one is—"

"Cree."

He chuckles. "Shit, maybe Ace wasn't lying. Maybe he

told you a lil' something. He ain't tell you the juicy part though, right?"

"What the fuc—"

"Hey, don't curse at me. You should take all of what I'm about to give to you for free because these things are important, Lourdes. I *never* work for free."

I can't even curse him out for calling me Lourdes. I'm too focused on the girl next to Cree—the *victim* with dirty blonde hair, porcelain skin, and a deep dimple that sinks into her cheek every time Cree says something to her.

"Once upon a time in LaLa Land..." Blake chuckles around the rim of his glass. "Javier Quinones and *The Kid* were good friends—so good that Javier and his sister Cree spent endless amounts of time with the Williams family. You know AW loves a great charity case. He likes to swoop in and take them under his wing, give them his knowledge—"

"His time..." I croak out, remembering the tortured look in Ace's eyes on Angie's birthday.

Blake grins and nods like we're having a tea session, but there's a nasty bitter taste in my mouth from that strawberry Dum-Dum.

"He gives them his time, resources, and his attention—much more than he gives our boy. I think by now you can grasp that Javier isn't just a standout player by happenstance."

My eyes brush Javier's lanky frame as he goes in for a smooth layup that only Ason Williams can teach. Cheyenne claps with her back straight as a board and a fling of her hair.

I open my mouth to breathe because Ace isn't sober enough to save me if I go flailing down the rows of seats below us. He's fucked up, just like Blake wants.

"It took some time for me to connect the dots of this saga and remind myself that *The Kid* is human—flawed but human. I mean, we all make fucked up mistakes. I don't know if they're all as serious as raping a good friend's girlfriend on your Mom's birthday on a superyacht during a drunk tirade because alcohol is another one of your vices but hey, a mistake is a mistake. Am I right? Now, she gets to sit pretty along the courtside with her future sister-in-law while the world tries to decide whether they should still like you for your talents or hate you for the rest of your life for doing something so detestable to the most protected species in America—a fucking white girl. Word is, Javier's supposed to propose any day now to solidify his new family-man image to go with that eleven million dollar rookie contract the Lakers threw at him thanks to Ace's *daddy*."

This is it. This is the worst part about my obsession with men I hate and like. It's those deep, heart pounding, stomach twisting, dry heaving panic attacks that no one told me about.

"Shit, if *The Kid* would've done something like that to a girl like you, all would've been forgiven and he would've been balling in the league right now. Kinda' fucked up, huh?"

I choke out a dry heave that makes Blake's eyes grow.

"Are you okay—"

I jump up and push past him, climbing the steps back into the suite two at a time, but even while drunk, Ace still has an imaginary rope tied to me. His droopy eyes land on my face while my body tries to decide if it should run home or back to that parking garage.

"What's wrong?" he asks, reaching for my arm.

It slips between his fingers as I search for a way out of this everyday life shit he has me involved in. I need to tell

Mama that my relationship with a grown man was short-lived. I need to go back to boys without vices and closets full of dirty blonde skeletons.

All it takes is for the announcer to belt out one last monotonous nod to the visiting team's standout, Javier Quinones, for my body to make its final decision.

I take off outside the suite and back to Charese in her elevator. Her cheeks drop as soon as she sees me power walking toward the doors with Ace on my heels.

I glide inside and slam my shaking hand against the button to close the doors before she can.

"You a'ight, girl?" she asks, frowning.

I check my wild reflection in the elevator's doors and plaster a smile on my face. "Yeah... yeah. I left something in the car. He just tripping because he don't like me wandering around by myself."

Her eyebrows crinkle while she nods, and I don't take in any of the words we say as the elevator shoots down to the floor that leads out into the parking garage.

We exchange goodbyes and I stumble past the staff members whose faces were a blur while I was under Ace's arm. I dig my phone out of my purse while pushing outside into the empty garage, but I don't get far before I hear him behind me.

"Lourdes!" His voice echoes and I pick up my pace. "Come here!"

It's that rope again. It has my feet contemplating how smart it is for us to stumble back home, because Ace hates when we don't listen to him.

"Baby..." he slurs, making my head whip around. "Tell me what's going on. Do I need to go talk to that ni—"

"No!" I squeeze my eyes shut and then fling them back open.

He's only a foot away, holding an empty glass in his hand, and my feet keep inching toward him when they shouldn't. His smile is missing again and his red eyes tug me closer to him while I try to shake the thought of him and his *victim* out of my head.

"B—baby..."

Hearing about the accusations when we're miles and galaxies apart on two different planets is different from hearing them after I've lived on Planet Ace for two months. Now I know all about Cheyenne. Shit, I know more than I ever wanted to know about a girl I was sure I hated until I realized she's more than just a headline or a tweet. She's real.

"Why you ain't tell me?" I choke out.

"Tell you what?"

"Tha—that she was here. Th—that she's friends with Cree. That you knew-her *knew-her*. That she was Javier's girl. That she was there on that boat on your mama's birthday! That it happened *that* night! Tha—that you were drunk when it happened."

The glass slips from his hand and shatters against the ground. It's the perfect representation of the obliteration of the shield surrounding Planet Ace. Our home is in jeopardy, and I don't understand why he made it that way.

He shakes his head, stepping forward and reaching out to me. "How the fuck was I supposed to tell you all that? Huh?"

"I don't know! But I would've preferred to hear it from you than some man who looks at you like a walking dollar sign." I glance at his trembling fingers grasping for my shirt.

"He wasn't supposed to tell you any of that. He was just supposed to talk to you about—about..."

"So you planned for this? For him to bombard me with

this shit so I can reassure you that he isn't some shiesty man and you can feel better about agreeing to work with him? That's the business you had to handle up in that suite! You let him do the dirty work for you instead of telling me the whole story yourself!"

"Hell no! I—I'm just trying to protect you." He tugs at my shirt. "You don't understand it all."

"Protect me from what? Huh?"

All I can picture is Cheyenne's deep dimple, his hands on her, and all the drinks he took to the head. He backs me into a car while I try to cut that imaginary rope between us, but it's too late and I think I see the truth in his eyes.

"Tell me what happened," I whisper, gripping his arms. "Tell me what happened with you and her that night on that boat. Don't dance around the shit. Tell me the fucking truth, Ason."

He swallows hard and I smell the alcohol on his breath while he tries to string his explanation together. I finally see all those vices Blake talked about.

"What if I told you I couldn't remember everything that happened that day?" he asks, yanking me into his body. "What if I told you it was one of those days with spots of black every fucking time I try to wrack my brain and go back to make sure it *didn't* happen? I don't remember shit but Dough pulling me from the side of the boat, telling me the same shit my Mom would tell me—all the shit about me finding you. I don't remember the partying, the drugs, or her. What if I told you I didn't even have her taste in my mouth the next day and the only bruise I had came from Dough's fingers pressing into my neck because he told me he'd never let me drown even if we only met that day? The only thing I remember is waking up on an empty yacht the next day with Pops standing over me. If I had told you all this shit, would you have still stayed home? What happened to our good being whatever we choose?"

He chokes on "home" and it's just as painful for him as it is for me because my heart tells me that the man I hate and like would never do such a disgusting thing, but what will the world think about me? I'm the girl that still can't believe that he did something so terrible—even through his sketchy explanation. I feel it in his touch, I hear it in his voice and I see it on his face everyday he pops up at the right and wrong times, but Blake's right to be skeptical of me.

"I'm going home—to my *real* home, Ason. I'll drive us there if I have to."

PART 3

THE END OF IT ALL

CHAPTER TWENTY-FOUR

Lourdes

"I'm really rethinking my position as your bestie," Chelsea rattles in my ear.

I wheeze out a deep yawn while slapping at the space next to me in bed, but it's empty. The emptiness reminds me of the lingering mess that's left between me and Ace—all the vices and family secrets fueled by alcohol that no one ever bothered to warn me about. Not even Cree.

I pinch my eyes shut, fighting against the remnants of his taste from the promises he kept breathing into my mouth while we waited on my Uber in that parking garage. He don't even believe in Ubers, but he still put me in one.

"I'm your real home. I don't care what nobody says or what happens," he said, curling his tongue around mine. *"I promise I won't get lost on Earth and I hope you promise me the same, baby."*

I didn't realize how grim and final his words sounded—not when I relieved Jazmine, kissed Mama goodnight, or shrugged Marcus off when he came in high. I was just going through the motions, but now, with Chelsea breathing in my ear about Splashtown again, I feel the aftermath.

"Man..." I smack my lips. "I told you nothing happened to me that night of the party, Chels. Hang it up. I'm good."

The line gets quiet and I curl my legs into my stomach, trying to inhale the last whiff of Ace that's left in his Gallery Dept. shirt I can't give back.

I wait for her comeback, and her raspy giggle, but nothing happens. She doesn't even threaten to tell Mother Lenola on me.

"I think you need to log back on Twitter."

"I'm on a break."

"Yeah, now I think I know why."

Serious Chelsea is such a rare occurrence, but I've gotten her twice in one semester. She's so serious this time that I don't even recognize her voice. It's stale.

"What's wrong? Don't tell me you been on there arguing with Beyoncé STANS again about her history of blasphemous music. I'm not reporting profiles this early—"

"Lourdes..."

My real name? Damn. This really *is* serious Chelsea.

I push up from the bed, rubbing the crust from my eyes. "Chelsea... what's going on?"

"I don't know. You tell me. I just found out from the internet there's nothing going on with you and Bry. There never was, was it? Sheesh, Phat, you even went to a gala with him and you didn't even bother to tell me?"

"H—him?"

"Yeah, with *Ace*."

The phone slips from my fingers, and I fumble to catch it.

Opening Twitter again is like landing back on Earth headfirst. It's been so long since I played on the app that the colors and words overwhelm my eyes. They cross at all the notifications waiting on me.

@Jessskeepthefaith

@babyphat04 ain't no way you heard what @AceWilliamsJr did and said let me hop in the group chat.

@Dinero88

Y'all can't tell me @AceWilliamsJr not using @babyphat04 for clout. Just two years ago he was fucking straight kardashians. Sistas, please love yourselves and stop letting these lost brothers use you for media makeovers.

@MarcieMounds

Black women, can we please stop normalizing being black men's saviors? We're supposed to be soft life queens. @phattykoo Drop the rapist.

Fuck deep, heart-pounding, gasping for breath, fucked up panic attacks. I'm having a hand trembling, stomach bubbling, dizzying, dry mouth reaction to the world finding out about Planet Ace's existence.

"Lourdes?" Chelsea rasps while *One of One* covers my phone's screen.

I swallow the cotton in my mouth.

The texts come next. Ding after ding from Bryson, old friends I hadn't heard from since Mama got sick, and lastly, Ace.

I swipe down on his.

> One of One: Get off of twitter

> One of One: Now

He doesn't understand that I can't though. There's a type of torturous soul stabbing satisfaction that comes with settling my curiosity as I read tweet after tweet with Chelsea breathing in the background.

"Lourdes, are you okay?" she whispers.

I don't have time to think about how okay I don't feel. On a random ass Saturday morning, the world broke into my home and I never felt so exposed in my life.

"How?" I choke out, scrolling past pictures of Ace's lips against my ear at the Shooting Stars Gala. "Who did this?"

And why'd they do it? He told me the world wouldn't care. They hated him.

@Soufcentralbaddie

Y'all's insecurity and colorism is showing real bad. I've never seen so many miserable people projecting so hard on this app. You're gorgeous @babyphat04! Secure the bag and the fine ass man, sis. the kid's real fans know what type of time he be on. That girl at UCLA is a known bopper. Real LA bitches know what's up.

He calls this time.

"Lourdes?" Chelsea says louder, while I stare at his name. "Why didn't you say anything? I—I would've—"

"Did what? Call me a drooling dog like Brandy? Shit, a rape apologist like the rest of Twitter?"

"No! I'd never do that."

"They're calling him a rapist, Chelsea. A *rapist*."

"Well... that's what he did," she whispers.

For a minute, I forget I'm not talking to somebody who lives on Planet Ace. According to her and the rest of Earth, Cheyenne's word is the only one that matters. They don't care that Ace is a person too—that he's Angie's son and the type of man that gave me anything I asked for, even when I couldn't give him the one thing he wanted most.

The weight of last night and right now is too much to hold. The trembling in my arms won't go away. It keeps drifting to my fingers that refuse to accept Ace's phone calls and respond to his texts.

All I hear is Blake laying out the missing parts of Ace's puzzling life for me. He filled in each piece that Ace would never give me and now that I had them; I don't blame Ace for keeping them a secret, because of how jagged they were. They were so jagged and his words were so unsure that my brain was fighting my heart for the first time in my life.

"If I knew you were dating him, I would've supported you."

"Dating?" I gasp out.

"Well... that's what the article said."

"*Article?* What article?"

"The one on TMZ, but I saw it on Insta and—and somebody on Twitter says it came from the *LA Times*."

I fling my blanket off my legs and sprint toward the bathroom.

That vomit that kept easing its way up my esophagus sits right at the base of my throat when I charge toward the toilet, knocking the door closed behind me.

"Phat!" Mama hollers from her bed. "Stop slamming my damn doors!"

I curl my arms around the toilet's cold porcelain sides.

"Are you throwing up? Shit, Lourdes. I—I mean shoot. I'm coming over there."

"No!"

Pink froth pours out of my mouth between violent chokes. Soreness rolls through my stomach while my body tries to evict anything that's left in it, but all I had yesterday was a strawberry Dum-Dum... and Ace.

"Breathe." Chelsea pants, gagging along with me. "Just breathe. We can fix this before Monday."

"Monday?" I wail out, coughing.

"You're coming to campus, right?"

I forgot that time still exists on Earth. There, my life doesn't revolve around opulent galas, on-demand bear claws or obsessing over Ace's next touch. On Earth, time moves at a blinding pace. Mama's still sick. Marcus can't cope. And I'm that nobody that everybody knows now because of a man they taught me to hate.

I gasp out another choke. "I can't go back there."

"You can't dropout over this. You wanted to enroll with me and Bryson so bad. You begged your Mama for this. You can't leave over some boy. There's a million other dudes out there and you're going to let one force you into hiding because of something *he* did."

"He's not just some boy and you don't even know if he did it!"

It's scary the way the words build in my throat and push out without help—even after learning about those jagged unsure pieces.

"So you *are* dating him? Jesus, Lourdes, you're confusing me!"

"I—I don't know! You the one confusing me! You said you'd support me and now—now you're saying something else!"

The phone slides from my fingers and crashes onto the floor. One last violent spasm rocks my stomach before I push away and patter towards Mama's room.

Her eyes open when I push the door forward.

"What's wrong?" She pushes up on her elbows with trembling arms. "I heard you in the bathroom. I hope you ain't eat that chili at the game last night. You know I can't get up to help you clean up no throw—"

"I'm not going back to campus," I blurt with a hiccup.

Her eyebrows curl. "Why not? What's wrong?"

"Why didn't you tell me?"

"Tell you what, babygirl?"

"How fucking easy it is for a man to rip my heart out and hold it hostage like this? How I'm supposed to get it back after dealing with him and his grown-man problems?"

She doesn't respond to the jumble of words I vomited in her doorway. Instead, she pats the space next to her and I climb onto her bed. When she rakes her fingers through my braids, I hold my breath for her to give me the answers I'm searching for.

I want her to give me the blueprint for navigating life with a man I can never seem to catch up to, no matter how hard I try. I want her to fix it even though she didn't even do anything wrong. She didn't get so drunk on a yacht that she couldn't defend herself to the world. She didn't harbor secrets that confused me.

"Do you trust him to fix whatever's wrong?" she asks.

I close my eyes. It's a simple question for my heart, but a complicated one for my brain.

"I—I don't know," I stutter.

"Well...the only way to get your heart back is to trust him to meet you halfway and give him the chance to give it to you," she whispers. "If he took care of it while he had it, let him keep it. If not, you gotta take it back."

Ace

LITTLE LADIES ARE TRICKY CREATURES.

Apparently, making love doesn't suddenly make them full-fledged ladies like I was dumb enough to think and they don't keep standing the first time they're tested—they fold.

"The world is a scary place for a lady that don't know herself yet, but you'll be patient when the perfect one come along." Mom laughed, curling her toes around the rails of the iron surrounding her balcony. *"Do your job as a man and lay the right foundation and she'll find herself and realize that all she needs to do is trust you. Believe me, as a former little lady, I'm an expert at this shit."*

I watch those same rails from Gus' backseat until he pulls away from the stop sign outside my building and turns onto the next street.

"Since when meh haffi drive yuh tuh de first game of de season?" he rumbles from behind the steering wheel.

"Ask Pops. He's the one that sent you—not me."

"Probably 'cause he smell that stinking tequila on yuh all the way from campus." He laughs, sucking his teeth. "What poison yuh pick today?"

I swallow, leaning into the door and the warmth from that poison Gus is talking about. "Nothing too crazy. Something that still let me see straight enough to call Mom."

The tequila made me lose count of the number of times I did it. Pressing her name and obsessing over the gnawing anticipation of what might happen had turned into an obsession overnight.

"And how dat ah go fi yuh?"

"It didn't."

"Meh thought yuh knew dem nah use phones up in de sky by now?"

"Right, my dumbass woke up thinking Mom was gon' answer my FaceTime call and explain how to hide from all those takers she was always trying to protect me from or to tell me how to handle this dream girl she was always telling me I'd marry before I die."

My knuckles still ached from Blake's face landing

against it somehow, and Phat *still* wasn't answering my calls. I had no choice but to try Mom. She always answered when I strayed away from home and was trying to get back.

He laughs hard, slapping the steering wheel. "How's de likkle lady? I miss her in my backseat."

"Hiding."

"From you or the world?"

"Does it matter?"

"Don't catch nuh attitude wit me 'cause she have yuh balls inna her likkle hands."

"My fault, Gus."

He sucks his teeth again. "Meh nuh cancel my *LA Times* subscription yet and meh know yuh nah do it neither. Cool write-up dem ah give you two—me nah like de tacky headline though."

"Ha!" I blubber out a guffaw. "That cool write-up got her hiding."

That, my smutty ass past, and the pictures Blake had been bribing a Getty staff photographer to hold on their cloud until my time was up. It wasn't like he gave me long. It only took a month for him to let loose on the havoc *I* wrecked in just two months and at the end of it all, I still wasn't anywhere closer to Pops' NBA dream. After that night at the Toyota Center, Blake had probably tarnished my rep even more to any agent that would listen because he didn't understand how precious perfect little ladies were.

"Meh figure so," Gus replies. "Poor baby. She'll come around."

Poor baby is right.

My baby is curious, defiant, and worst of all—afraid. All of this shit had her regressing to the immature freshman I knew she was back when I first met her. All the trust I built between us went crumbling after one fucking night.

"But wha yuh expect? She's nah built like yuh." He glances at me in the rearview mirror.

"That's supposed to be a compliment?"

It's a funny thing to say because a nigga like me was made up of fucking putty—at least my brain was. It was so malleable from all the shit I was always chasing to make it solid like reporter's voices and expensive tequila.

"Nah no compliment, an observation dat." He hisses after rolling over a pothole. "Many men been in yuh position. They bask in glory when they up, but few could withstand the fall. You, meh friend, have withstood not one but two falls."

"You fucking right I have."

He chuckles while merging onto the highway.

"Hell, maybe even tree if yuh count this whole *LA Times* debacle. Dem bastard reporters know how to irritate old wounds, eh?"

Boy, did they, and the funny thing about falls is how time consuming they are. You have to take the healing second by second, minute by minute, hour by hour or my favorite—peeling that corner of the bandaid little by little.

This fall ain't no different. It's been three days and twelve bandaids since I had my mouth on Phat's. I should really fucking stop counting just like I should stop reading that article, but my soft ass brain didn't have an off switch for things like that.

"I guess this is what happens when I go about things on my own to learn responsibility?" I snort. "Pops told me he'd been doing me a disservice and then says 'fuck it' and leaves me to fend for myself against a crooked ass sports agent all because of some pipe dream he's holding onto."

"Yuh ah give meh more loot to add to yuh chest?"

"Maybe..."

There wasn't a lot left to add. Gus had it all in that chest —the backseat fights between me and Pops after he settled the dust with Cheyenne and her family, Mom's crying fits every time a new reporter decided people hadn't already heard enough about what happened to Cheyenne, and me. It took a year for the shock to wear off and when it did, I couldn't keep anything down except that stinking tequila Gus always hated.

"Your fadda is human, Junior."

"A *selfish* human."

"Aren't we all?"

"I don't know what it is about me that makes the world want to fuck me over." I sigh, glancing at my phone, where more unanswered texts from Cree stare back.

> Cree: Can you at least hit me back so I know you and Phat are good?

> Cree: I told Javi I needed to stay back. I can talk to her if you need me to.

> Cree: Can I call her?

It's just like before. She's stuck somewhere between the truth and a grey area under Javier's watchful eye. Two years later and she's still struggling with her loyalty to both of us.

"Listen... de world fucks us *all* ovah, but what can we do 'bout it?"

I flip my phone over and try to answer his impossible ass question, but nothing comes out because life is that bitch I can't fuck and ghost no matter how many times I try to. She just keeps coming back through other people.

"Meh and Angie ah have dis conversation plenty times

driving 'round LA," he adds. "Especially toward de end before she came back to Houston fi good."

I breathe in, trying to suck in her metallic scent from the leather, but it's not there anymore. Pops made sure it would never come back after she left him to come home. He was the one that made me detail the fucking truck to get her smell out of every piece of fabric as soon as Gus got back from dropping her off at the airport.

"Did she ever find her answer?" I ask.

He chuckles, whipping through lanes of traffic and taking the exit to campus. "Nah, Junior, she nah find it."

"So that's it? Nobody knows, huh? Not even her?"

"She ah tell me she wasn't looking fi an answa because she know yuh find it just like yuh find home again. It all takes time. Most important ting fi understand is dat not everyting in life is happening *to* you. It's just happening—death, disappointment, scandals, crooked sports agents. Dese tings would happen wit or witout yuh. De test is how yuh handle that happening, because all we can control is ourselves."

He turns down one of the back streets leading to campus and pulls into the same staff lot he parked in on my first day of practice. "Now, meh question to you is, do yuh fold wit yuh likkle lady or do yuh keep being solid until she ah learns how fi be a lady without your hand holding? Meh know some good men dat folded, but meh know some great men dat's built fi dem things."

After he parks the car, I try to mold my brain into something solid enough to withstand another day on a campus where people will pick at my old wound with their soul crushing stares and sharp whispers. It'll be even worse than before because I'm the alien that took one of their own even though they didn't cherish her when they had her. Niggas that didn't understand how curious she was about love and life or how afraid she was of experiencing the endings of both were suddenly outraged that she'd given *me* the time of day. They didn't even know how beautiful she was with my name on her lips and how easy it was to talk to God again when I looked in her eyes.

They didn't know what it felt like to find home again after being lost for so long.

CHAPTER TWENTY-FIVE

Ace

"Sanchez, what the *fuck* are you doing?" Pops yells. "Get your goddamn head in the game!"

Bryson turns to him from the court and tosses his arms up with his face screwed.

"Boy, you better fix your damn face!"

It's the first game of the season and we're still playing like a high school JV team and Pops says it's my fault. I can't keep my dick in my pants. I can't respect his boundaries and his friendships. I can't lead a team even though I've led hundreds. I can't stay off of gossip blogs. I'm impulsive and unstable and he should've sent me to that therapist like Mom said.

"*Will you ever roll over one day and say 'geez, my Pops gave me a life most folks dream of. The least I can do is make him proud?'*" He asked from behind his desk before the game. "*Or do you just wanna eternally fuck me over for the rest of our time here on Earth together? They said Blake needs stitches. You better be glad he didn't call the goddamn cops on you and all we got is another fucking write-up on TMZ. I thank God Marshall ain't here to see this all play out with his babygirl. What the fuck were you thinking?"*

"You good?" LaQuan asks from the chair beside mine on the sideline.

Thanks to his failing grade in english and my smutty rep, we're riding the bench together.

I shake my head, holding onto the vomit in my throat. "I'm good."

"Your head saying one thing, but your mouth saying something else. I know it ain't my business but... but how your gal holding up?"

It's quiet enough in the gym that I can hear the wavering in his stuttering. People would rather see fifty dudes cross in a probate on the yard rather than watch Southern blow us out on our own turf just like Pops said would happen. Marshall was probably shaking his head from up in the sky at the mess I made—another losing team in his gym and some nigga he didn't know calling his daughter *mine*.

"She not." I swallow. "She not holding up at all."

The funny thing about men is that we don't have to announce to each other who's ours. The moment he saw Phat leaving Splashtown with her hand tangled in mine, it was stamped.

"I don't think I'd be holding up if I was her either. Niggas be real bold behind a screen."

"Yeah, I know all about that."

"Bet you do. I saw those tweets about you—even way back when shit first went down with that white girl. It's like the whole basketball world stopped. I don't know if I could've got up and came to some fuck ass game with the whole world in my business again." The referee's whistle weaves through his words and he shakes his head at Bryson's second turnover. "Useless ass freshman."

"I never miss a game—no matter what. That shit ain't in my blood."

If I missed, I would've let all of Black and feminist Twitter win with their finger pointing, harassing, and accusations. Mom told me to never let them see me sweat, so I didn't, and I wish Phat wouldn't either.

"I don't think shawty would let you miss a game. I heard her getting on Bry's head from the stands. I know you don't want smoke with her. She take ball *real* serious."

I laugh, and it feels good. "Nah, you got it twisted, homie. She don't want smoke with *me*. Baby think she know better than me but I keep her ass in check."

He laughs hard until Boris, the assistant coach, cuts his eyes at us.

"Yeah..." He nods, looking down. "I figured you'd be on nigga's heads after what happened at Splashtown. My brother used to always tell me if I fucked with a man's home, I best be ready to throw down, and for what it's worth, I never touched her that night."

Both of our eyes brush Bryson on the court, guarding with his arms slack.

His healing black eye wasn't just for him. It was for every dude on the team—for the ones that thought they had a chance because of Bryson's fan fiction about her, the ones whose fingers brushed against her at the party, and the ones that had her on their radar just because they knew I had her.

LaQuan snorts. "I'm sure you know he ain't taking this whole thing well."

I frown, shaking my head, thinking about Gus' pep-talk before he dropped me off and Bryson's reminder of how long he'd been in Phat's life. By the time I made it to the gym, the team was in their uniforms and on the court, so I didn't have time to absorb his new feelings after the *LA Times* messy exposé.

"I wouldn't either if I was holding onto something so precious for so long. He still a useless freshman but y'all boys take it easy on him—let him breathe," I reply.

"You doing the same?"

"I'm trying—trying to be less impulsive, more stable, less fucked up. Trying to control myself and not the world. I guess it takes time though."

"I hear that, fam."

I choke on a hiccup full of 1942. "Fam?"

"Yeah, *fam*. You the one that told me that every nigga need a family. My brother say I can't keep letting you ride dolo out here."

"You got to be kidding me! Another foul?" Pops screams, forcing us to tear our eyes off each other.

He squats, staring at our team on the court in distress. The ref shrugs while blowing his whistle.

"Sanchez!" Pops shouts, waving his hand. "Go sit down!"

The hiccup full of tequila comes back up while Pops shakes Bryson by the shoulders.

Bryson has the worst case of performance anxiety I ever seen, and anxiety doesn't have a place on Pops' team because he hates losing in basketball and in life. He spent millions of dollars on holistic treatments when Mom's chemo didn't work and fought Shaq in the locker room during halftime because his head wasn't in the game during their fourth championship run. He'll do anything to win.

He turns to the bench. "Williams! Get over here!"

He'll even have my drunk ass sub into our first game of the season.

LaQuan pushes his hand toward mine, waiting for me to grab it. "Go get this dub for us real quick. That hangover gon' be worth it, Kid."

Kid.

He's not the rest of the team, but he's somebody that matters—somebody that's not pressing me over my impulsive ways but taking me for the mess that I am.

I lock fingers with him, gurgling up that hiccup I kept holding on to. "I got you, brodie."

My shoulder bumps Bryson's on his lonely trek to my seat next to LaQuan. He looks empty. His eyes brush against the stands and I know who he's looking for.

I reach out, nudging his shoulder. "Pick your head up."

He glances up at me, squinting his eyes, and then collapsing in the chair.

When I get to Pops, he's swiping his sweaty head like he's in that game with Shaq again and I try to hold on to Gus' reassurance that he's human even if I can't see it myself.

"I'm putting you in," he says, looking out onto the court at Southern's huddle. "Just do your best."

My best?

I play my best when I chug a head full of all the shit Pops swears will send me to an early grave—all the expensive tequila, reporter's voices, and the stress from wishing that Mom would just fucking come back and Pops knows that.

When I check into the game, I know today is another day that will be full of black holes I jump into, chasing after Phat, Mom, and all the life shit that she left behind for me to figure out on my own.

Tomorrow when I wake up curled around the edge of the toilet, I won't remember Pops throwing his phone at me with the *LA Times* article loaded on the screen, the tinge of red on Bryson's cheeks when he glided toward the bench, and all my calls Mom ignored from up in the sky.

Lourdes

"TALK about an explosive first game for Lockwood State. After a shaky first quarter against Southern, the Lions found their footing with former Bruin, Ace Williams. I mean, this *kid* dominated during this matchup. Thirty-five points, ten rebounds, and fifteen assists," Scott Van Pelt's voice booms from the living room. "Lest we forget, former Laker Ason Williams Sr. is the Lion's new head coach. He's dominated plenty games in his heyday on and off the court, and most importantly, he's Ace's dad. Way to make Pops proud, kid! Now, let's work on staying outta trouble."

In a perfect world, playing good basketball would cure cancer and stop gossip, but every time I unlock my phone, I'm reminded in the most obnoxious way that I don't live in a perfect world anymore. All good basketball does is put a sloppy bandaid on gossip-fueled scandals and it's another thing involving Ace that I'm bombarded with.

I curl closer to my pillow in bed, scrolling past all the new intrusive tweets that litter my timeline ever since Armageddon happened on Planet Ace.

@RitaVonTease
Our man did his thing last night @babyphat04
@Jason_Jones2
You seen this @babyphat04? Not this dude randomly

knocking out sports agents and raping girls. How much you gon' take?

@GimmeMoore23

I feel sorry for @babyphat04. Anybody check on her?

Chelsea did—nonstop. Instead of making up stories about people on campus, she makes them up about Ace. They're wildly inaccurate and over the top. She was convinced that the showdown between him and Blake was about me being "a black girl" after TMZ plastered the grainy pictures of their scuffle in the Toyota Center parking garage to the world. She was already trying to "mentally prepare me" for when Ace decides to "go back to his Becky loving ways." This morning, she almost convinced Marcus that he needed to commit me because I stopped answering her calls. It's the only reason he didn't leave me alone with Mama.

Then there was Cree. She wouldn't go back to Los Angeles and she wouldn't stay out of my phone like she wasn't in on keeping secrets from me, too. I was "hermana," "Phat," and then "Lourdes" the more desperate she was to convince me I should go back home to a man who supposedly did something so foul to her *other* sister.

> Cree: Can you please answer my calls Lourdes? I'm still in Houston. I can't leave with you and him like this. My spirit won't let me.

Technically, she could and I didn't know why a person playing on both sides of a scandalous coin cared so much. If Mama wasn't stuck today, she'd tell me my gut was trying to say there was more to Ace's story with its unstable jagged pieces, but how much more could I stomach without throwing it up? My heart is confused on which way to beat again, especially when its owner keeps tugging at it and stroking it from our balcony back at home.

"Look, baby. You see Planet Ace right there?" Ace asks, zooming into the night sky from the chaise on his balcony.

I told myself I wouldn't open the video messages last night, but my mind is fried from trying to adjust to life back on Earth. So, I keep opening them after closing Twitter. Over and over again.

Stars dot the sky like tiny specks of glitter while I stare at the late night video from my cocoon in bed.

"If I buy a real spaceship for us, will you come home?" He wiggles his pinky finger in front of the camera while I spread my own fingers across the screen to get a better look at it. "I pinky promise I'll let you be the pilot sometimes and I'll even get The Dream to hit your line."

There's a tequila bottle next to his leg in the second video he sends.

"Did you delete Twitter like I asked?"

I shake my head into my pillow like he can see me.

"You know, one of the only good things about being on Earth is that people's attention spans are *hella* short there. Next week people will forget about us, about me, and about any fucked up man-things I did to hurt your feelings when something more interesting happens, but you gotta follow the leader on this one, kid. Let me make it better. I told you I'd always do that."

I swallow the chalky taste in my mouth.

"But what about the rest?" I rasp out.

Like the fact that Cheyenne wasn't just "that white girl from Los Angeles." She was his friend's. Or the fact that he drinks so much that there are days he's lived with black holes in them, so he couldn't even remember a day that changed his life—a day where he strayed so far from home that he almost didn't make it back.

All the stuff Coach Williams accused him of torturing himself with had overtaken his life and I couldn't ignore it anymore—not the drinking or secrets, but I still didn't hate him for any of it. I was just sorry he had to live that way. I finally put some of those jagged pieces of his story together and so far, the picture it's forming is uglier than I thought and I *still* didn't have all the pieces.

A soft tap on my door makes me sink underneath my blanket and swipe out of the video.

"Fat girl?" Marcus whispers.

His slides scrape against the floor, and the door thumps as it closes. "I don't think Mama want them bacon and biscuits I cooked. She threw it up... and she's real hot."

"That's because it was too heavy."

The blanket muffles my words, so he murmurs out a "huh" and the scraping gets closer.

I open the side of the blanket and poke my lips out. "The food was too heavy. Give her a half of pill from the bottle on her nightstand, a clear Ensure, and take that cover off her."

I wait for him to say something, but all I hear is Scott Van Pelt's voice sneaking under the door.

"Okay. Bry came by again earlier. He left you another strawberry cool cup in the freezer."

"Okay..."

"Fat girl?"

"Yeah?"

"You good?"

"Yeah. I'm good."

He knows about that article, and he knows *I* know he knows about it. Even Granny knows about it. I heard her telling Mama over the phone that she heard "the radio" talking about me and Ace yesterday morning and asking if it was true. Mama doesn't lie to Granny, so she told her it was. Now I'm dodging Granny's calls too.

I wait for his slides to scrape against the floor again and for him to push out of my room, but nothing happens, so I fling the blanket off my head to help him find his way out.

"You can leave no—"

The rest of my sentence gets swallowed by his bushy eyebrows crawling together and the cold black gun in his hands.

"What the hell, Marcus?"

"Did he hurt your feelings?"

"Who?" I frown, pushing up from my bed. "What you talking about?"

"Ace..."

"Huh?" I swallow more chalk while pushing the blanket off my legs.

"You heard me."

"I—I thought ya'll were cool?"

"I'm asking about *you* and him."

I look at Ace's shirt I dug from the bottom of my laundry basket and try to put everything that happened into words.

I've been waiting for this since Angie's birthday. It didn't matter how much Marcus wanted Ace to take it easy that day or how much basketball they played together—he was still a man I hated and liked and all those men had to be dealt with eventually.

"I—he—I don't know."

"What you mean you don't know? You been locked in this room ever since that shit hit the news. You need to tell me if he hurt you."

"It's not that simple, a'ight?" I shake my head, looking up at him.

He folds his lips under his teeth. "I'm trying to make sense of all this shit—of your face being all over IG every time I open it, of—of my niggas asking me if that's your man now, the pictures of him knocking ole' boy out after the game the other night. What the fuck is going on and why he not over here making shit right if that's your man?"

He shakes his head like the thought of me having a man is some outrageous thing—like I would live with Mama for the rest of my life.

"Oh, now you wanna know what's going on with me?" I blurt. "Where you been the last five years? Huh?"

"Don't. Don't do this shit with me right now. I just wanna know what's happening and you would too if you woke up to my name being in everybody's mouth."

"What's happening?" I scoff.

I didn't even know how to simplify what was happening while he existed somewhere else. It was a mouthful that I couldn't articulate without falling into a crying, blubbering mess because my non-virginal freshman ass had really encountered a man and he took me through some shit Mama couldn't even prepare me for.

"I'm raw. I like somebody that the world hates and I feel *raw*." I gasp out. "Like somebody just stripped all my clothes off and left me outside for everybody to see. It's like every time I get covered back up, here somebody else goes, stripping me down again."

First it was Blake, Cheyenne, and Cree, then it was that article I couldn't stop reading, and then those pictures of Ace and Blake. Scandal after scandal that Ace wanted me to ignore, like I was born into the same world as him. He didn't understand that I didn't have years of experience battling the opinions of strangers.

Marcus sits on the bed next to me. He hasn't sat in that spot since the day Dr. Evanston told us Mama needed chemo and radiation.

"Then why the fuck he not here covering you up?" he asks, lifting the gun and pulling his car keys out of his basketball shorts.

He tries every morning but I can't play his drunk voice messages to Marcus. That's another one of our secrets that's not supposed to leave home because they're worse than the late night videos.

"Tell me where you wanna go, baby, so I can make it better. I'll take you and Mom anywhere in the world. You don't have to go back to campus if you don't want and I won't play ball if you don't want that either. Mom told me you ain't getting outta bed. I know it's hard, but the first step is to just get up. I'll come pick you up. You want me to do that? I'm sorry 'bout all this scandalous ass shit. I lo—I just want you home."

How am I supposed to fight that deep, slurring ass voice waiting in my notifications every morning?

Hot tears cover the rims of my eyes. I swipe at them before they fall.

Marcus raises up with his gun. "Fuck this shit. I'mma pull up on him—"

"No!"

It comes out before I can justify the reasons it *shouldn't*. It wasn't nobody but Ace. He was still being a control-freak when he hadn't even been in our house in days.

"If you touch him, I swear to God, I will *fuck* you up."

The rest of my words come out between hot breaths because Ace makes me angsty after he does stupid man-shit.

He makes me cry for him, want him when I should hate him, and he makes me want to consider giving him a chance to make everything better like he said he always would, but I'm stuck.

"I'm not playing with you, Marcus. Don't touch him."

He frowns real deep at every word. I've never threatened him—*ever* and there were a million reasons I could have.

His mouth inches up and then settles into a smirk as he lowers the gun. "He said you would be like this."

"Who? Ace?" I sniffle.

"Yeah." He smiles bigger. "That dumbass cocky ass nigga."

I see the inside jokes they've created in his smile—all the time they spent together in our driveway without me is in it.

"You talked to him?"

"Nah... not since all this... shit happened." He waves his arms. "He told me this back when the semester first started."

"We barely talked back then." My eyes flicker up to his and I see Marshall in them because shit's going left at home.

"A man don't have to have a long drawn out conversation with you to decide if you it for him. Sometimes it just takes a look... and trust." He nudges my chin and then swipes a wild tear trickling down my cheek. "Guess he got you to trust him, after all."

"Is that how you got Chelsea so throwed in the head? That's why she trusts you with her life even if you got a new girlfriend?"

I let out my first laugh in days. It's raspy and painful, like my vocal cords needed to be reminded of their purpose.

He doesn't laugh like usual when her name comes up.

Instead, he drops his head with his mouth cocked to the side and sits his gun on my nightstand. "Nah...she trusts me with her life because she knows that everything I do is for *her* best interest."

"Even breaking things off with her?"

"There's certain things I can't give her that she deserves —like a normal life as a college student. She can't have that if she chasing me around the city while I work to take care of you and Mama. Trust ain't always easy. Sometimes it feels good and sometimes it feels like shit, but if you trust somebody *for real*, you gon' follow their lead whether it feels good or shitty."

"Sound like you been talking to Ace and Mama too much," I mutter.

It's just how Ace explained it on his bedroom floor when I didn't understand that any of the things he told me were intentional, and what Mama was talking about when I cried in her lap like I was ten.

"That's my brother—even if I owe him a fade. We don't gotta talk to be in each other's heads. And that's my Mama. She experienced this world before me and you. She'll always know better than us." He tosses his arm around my neck, pulling me into his side. "So, now what you gon' do with all this trust he built up between y'all? You need to decide."

CHAPTER TWENTY-SIX

Ace

On days where black spots fill in the gaps in my memory, the toilet is my best friend. Mom used to say it's where I had my "come-to" moments—with my arms curled around the lid, my stomach folding in pain, and my forgotten memories pouring into the bowl. The toilet is where the tiniest pieces of life try to push through those black spots and jog my scrambled memory.

"Blake said all is forgiven between you two," Pops says from my bathroom doorway. "His eye's healing, but he's concerned about you... and about Lourdes."

A dry heave wracks my body and I cough up another chunk of vomit from deep in my stomach. I try to breathe through it, but I don't have Mom to coach me.

"Deep breath in and deep breath out," she'd whisper, scraping her nails through my hair. *"How 'bout we ease up for a few days, Junior? What I'm gon' do if you drown one day and don't come back home?"*

"Fuck him." I cough. "The fuck he so concerned about my lady for?"

Pops laughs. "*Your* lady?"

"That's what I said, didn't I?"

"Nigga, you can't even stay dry for twenty-four hours. I can't trust you with yourself, let alone with Marshall's baby-girl. You ain't got no lady."

I hack up another glob of spit.

"You got her face on every gossip blog you can think of because you want to play social media games. That's not the type of shit a man does for his lady."

Remember how I said alcohol was funny? I forgot to mention how ignorant it was too. Phat isn't here to stick my wrist into her middle and fix my cuff links and Mom isn't here to stand between me and Pops to keep the peace, so we're left to our own vices. It's not the first time. I can't remember all the knock out drag down battles we had back in LA, but I know Mom does. Bloody knuckles, busted lips, and bruised skin didn't mean shit to either of us.

"Well, the best part about her being *mine* is that I'll take care of it. The fuck is you worried about it for?" I heave up one last mouthful of spit while gripping the sides of the toilet so I won't drown like Mom fears. "I always take care of mines. You wouldn't know shit about that."

"Obsession don't equate to care!"

I pinch my eyes shut and try to coach myself through deep breaths, but it's impossible with him in my space. "How the fuck you even get up here, anyway? I told Lourdes to stop leaving her key in your truck."

He chuckles. "You can't erase me from your life. That's not how this works."

"Mom said I can do what the fuck I wanna do and my lady said I can get whatever I want. Neither one of 'em ever steered me wrong. If I wanna erase you from my life, I can do that. Ain't that what you trying to do with Mom?"

That's the ignorant shit that sends his voice surging throughout her condo.

"That's the goddamn problem!"

I peel my eyes open and turn around to look at him.

"*She* let you do what you want and have what you want without repercussions and look where you're at today—bent over a fucking toilet before every game and calling yourself trying to court my best friend's daughter. I told him I'd protect her from men like you and Angie drops her in your lap like she's playing with fucking Barbie dolls. It's sick."

I squint, searching for the human that Gus swears exists within him. It's hard with Mom's spirit existing in the fibers of the walls though. I hate him for me and for her, no matter how hard Gus tries to convince me I shouldn't.

"Oh, for real? What kinda man am I?" I mutter.

He dodges my eyes. When he finally looks at my face, he concentrates on my wet lips.

"I'm asking you a question."

"I'm not going there with you tonight."

"Nah, let's go there. I wanna hear all about the fucked up men you promised your *best friend* you'd keep his daughter away from since you the world's greatest mother-fuckin' friend. You ain't no friend. You think you a friend just 'cause you call his son once a year? You ain't check up on Lourdes or—or offer to get help for CeCe." I suck in a deep breath. "You ain't even check on her when you knew she was fighting the same fight as Mom!"

"I told you I didn't wanna go there, so you best take heed to my warning, young man."

I bend over the toilet, laughing. "Now it's young man? What happened to the nigga you said I'd always be? Bet all them people that worship the ground you walk on don't know how you talk to your only son, huh? They don't know how much you left me and Mom and it makes you fucking crazy that I love her so much. You should tell them about all the time you missed with us... an—and how at the end of it all, it was just me and her on that couch out there! Just us!"

Now, his eyes are wild and wet.

He steps forward, crossing over the towels scattered on the bathroom floor. "Listen... get yourself cleaned up, alright? I gotta get back to campus to meet with the boys before the game. I'll send Gus back—"

"No! Answer my question. What kinda man you think I am? Huh?"

"Junior..."

"Don—don't call me that shit. Just answer my question!"

I hate come-to moments because everything's more intense in them. I can hear each crack in my vocal cords and see every tear on Pops' cheeks. All of it makes me more desperate to numb it all.

"Answer me!"

"I can't!" His voice shakes the walls of the bathroom.

It has all the pent up shit he's held on to since he decided Houston was best for what was left of our family.

I shake my head, pulling myself up from the side of the toilet. "I hope you get the balls to tell me exactly what you think of me one day. Maybe I'll finally understand why you favor a bunch of strangers over your own flesh and blood."

I gurgle up a tequila-filled hiccup. "I can clean myself up. Go check on your boys."

AS SOON AS I stretch my legs out of Pops' truck and walk onto the yard, the eyes are there like they've been ever since Planet Ace exploded. They're behind sunglasses, books, in peripherals, and under hats. The whispers are the worst. I hear bits and pieces about me and "the freshman girl from the bookstore." All of it makes me want to go curl up in bed with Phat.

I'd let her hover over my lips and talk shit about how dirty Earth is and how much more *elite* home was.

I can even hear her: *"You see why I don't fuck around on Earth? It's a dirty ass place."*

She'd even call me by my new name.

"See why I like to stay home, baby?"

I grip my ball, taking long strides while looking forward. It's the only worthwhile thing I learned off the court at UCLA in the days before Mr. Palmer told me I had to go.

"Chin up, look forward, not backward, and smile, Ason," Mom would say every morning over FaceTime. *"People can say a lot of shit about you, but they can't ever say they saw you with a frown on your face, no matter what the circumstances were. I ain't never been the type to believe that I raised a perfect man, but I know I raised you with some sense."*

As soon as I tug my headphones to pull them over my ears, I catch Brandy's hazel eyes on me from her spot in front of the cafe.

She narrows them at me.

"Fuck." I groan, focusing on the manicured bush behind her.

It's too late though.

She marches in my direction with her curls whipping behind her from the light fall breeze.

I look in every direction but hers when she bounds up to

me, crossing her arms like a woman scorned. "Phat coming back to work? Tell her the professional thing to do is give a two-week notice since the rest of us have been covering her shifts."

I jerk my head back at the wild ambush until I remember how shit works down on Earth when you don't live up to the imagined idea people have of you in their heads—especially the imagined idea that jersey chasers have.

"I don't know." I shrug. "Shit, call her and ask her."

"Oh, so you're still playing this little game like everybody on campus hasn't read the article and saw those pictures from your dad's gala?"

I bite into my lip and roll my eyes toward the HPE.

Thanks to Gus, I'm an hour early for our game and right on time for Brandy to unleash everything she's been holding in. Phat ran away from home and she thinks I give a fuck about a two-week notice.

My shoulders hunch up in a shrug. "So you read a bull-shit article? Okay."

"Bullshit article?" Her lip curls. "Oh, so it's like that?"

"It was always like that."

"You know, I thought you were different."

"Man, what are you talking about?"

"It's sick of you to play with people's feelings."

Her eyes soften and there's an aching in my chest because even if she reminded me of the shit Mom hated about LA, Mom would still tell me she was a lady and to treat her like one.

"Look, Brandy...I didn't mean to—"

"Lead her on. I get it."

I frown. "Her?"

"Yeah, *Phat*."

My mouth falls open to cut between the rest of whatever bullshit she has to say until she leans in closer to me.

"Have you been drinking?" She balls her lips to the side. "You know what? That's not even important right now."

She shakes her head like the smell isn't oozing out of my pores and keeps talking.

"I mean, we all know she's not model-material, but God, Ace, did you have to embarrass her like this? The poor girl hasn't been on campus in days. You're supposed to be her host-brother. I know things are different from what you're used to, but to flirt with her, have it exposed, and then be so callous afterward is kind of harsh, don't you think? Shouldn't you be cleaning this up? *And* you punched your agent? Are you crazy? All of my friends are asking me about this stuff and it's only the beginning of the season. What other scandals do I need to worry about?"

A burning heat creeps to the ache in my chest at the red flags she keeps casually chirping out—model-material, exposed, scandals. Phat isn't there to throw my obsessiveness for her around to control the vibe or my words, so a loud laugh croaks from the back of my throat.

Her eyes jump. "Did I say something funny?"

"Are you fucking crazy?"

"Excuse me?"

"Are you mental?" I ask, shaking my head. "Actually, don't even answer that shit. I think I already know the answer."

The color drains from her already pale face, but it doesn't make that aching in my chest come back. Apparently, 1942 and my first heartbreak don't give a shit about Mom's life lessons about perfect girls and their enemies.

"Are you calling *me* crazy?"

I scoff. "You know, I knew a lot of girls like you back in LA."

"Like me?" She flings her head back. "What kind of girl do you think I am?"

"The saddest fucking kind."

A wannabe WAG.

She had laid all the red flags out for me in a neat line. I wasn't on the fence about which sect she belonged to anymore.

"They're some of the most selfish, crazy bitches, Ason, but they'll ride for you in ways you'd never imagine. Not because they're loyal to you though. They're loyal to their image and the lifestyle you can give them. Don't ever let them get close enough to you that they even have a chance to ride for you. Nip that shit in the bud as soon as you feel it," Mom hissed, shaking her head at another wannabe WAG I brought around her: Cheyenne.

She was like LA, like Brandy, and was the antithesis of the perfect girl Mom promised I'd find. She didn't even show up at our front door on my arm. She showed up on Javier's with me hanging behind them as their third wheel after they fucked at a party, but Mom could spot a jersey chaser from a mile away: *"That's supposed to be Javier's girl, but she looking at you like she's yours. Take care of that, Ason."*

"I'm sad, but you've been leading me on for months? Doing all the shit guys do when they're interested." Brandy tosses her arms up, frowning. "Stopping by the bookstore daily?"

"You and Lourdes almost always work the same shift, so you be there when I drop in for her or you just conveniently pop up when I'm trying to steal her time."

"Coming to my apartment?"

"Lourdes went to her first party without me. How else was I supposed to waste three hours of my night while she realized that the places I take her to are better than any college party? I didn't even kiss you and I had her back with me at home before midnight because she knows better." I shrug.

The dots connect in her eyes. "Don't stand here and act like you weren't trying to at least fuck me, Ace."

She throws out the accusation as a last resort, but my tequila fueled mouth is already ready for it.

"Why would I *fuck* you when I can go home and make love to Lourdes?"

"Ma—make love?" she stutters out.

"Yeah. The men you dated never taught you the difference between the two?" I raise my eyebrows.

The shock on her face isn't satisfying enough. I want more.

"I wish Lourdes was here to hear all this. Maybe she'd understand why I like to keep her up under me. It's too many women like you walking around trying to pollute her brain with shallow shit. In fact, if she was here *right* now I'd make her tell you how much fun I have dressing her up even though she's not model-material—your words, not mine. I even taught her how to spend my money when I'm not around, but she's real funny about that. All she ever wanna do is buy shit for me and her Mom."

"Nice speech." She laughs, clapping. "And it's too many men like you walking around, playing games. You always lead on unsuspecting girls? If I knew your type was fat ass freshman, I wouldn't have wasted my fucking time."

"I guess the cat's out of the bag—I'm that *fat ass freshman's* nigga, not some made up host-brother and if you knew anything about me for real, you'd know she's always been my *only* type. On my Mama, you the type of bop I fuck and forget, but I couldn't even be bothered to do that with your fake nice-nasty personality. Find somebody else to play with because Lourdes is the nice one—not me."

Her pale face turns red. "*Fuck* you, Ace."

There's no real closure and I don't feel bad about it when she stalks away from me and back toward her waiting friend in front of the cafe.

All the nasty tequila induced words I blubbered out to her will get regurgitated to her friend and then become mangled versions of their original selves. It's how all my falls went before this one—Cheyenne's accusation, Mom's death, and my forced transfer to Lockwood. Nobody ever bothers to get the truth. They just keep absorbing the outrageous words that got twisted along the way before they got to them. They won't care that Brandy was never nice at all. She was just nasty and plotting on my comeback while the other jersey chasers on campus were still processing what happened with Cheyenne back in LA.

Gus was right.

This was just another fall for me to withstand, but I didn't know how to get back up, because Mom didn't have time to tell me how to get the perfect girl back if I ever lost her. I didn't have a contingency plan for fleeting little ladies.

Lourdes

THERE ARE two parts to Ace—maybe even three. Since we've been apart, I think I've absorbed all of them.

There's soft Ace who makes me regret questioning my trust for him. Last night, he didn't send me a video of Planet

Ace. He just sent a text that reminded me of what I'd been missing while I was gone.

> One of One: You running. If what we have is real, you'll let me catch up to you and take care of everything that's wrong. That's my responsibility as your man and as my lady you gotta trust me baby.

I read that last part a thousand times. I wanted to ask Mama if that's how it worked with men. Did they always claim women without asking how we felt about it first? Were their bold declarations supposed to make us light-headed with a stomach full of wild butterflies even when we're running from them and all their problems? I couldn't ask her any of it though. I couldn't even ask her how Marshall made it official with her. Her brain was too stuck to even remember that she was married once.

"It's cold." She groans from beside me in bed.

"I turned the heat up. It's only seventy outside."

"Turn it up higher."

"I can't. I'm already sweating."

Her bald head peeks from under her blanket and I wish I had the second part of Ace—the strong one. That one knows everything about Mama like what medicine she should and shouldn't take, what food she should eat, and deep down I know he'd know why she's been hot for two days even though her brain keeps making her think she's cold.

I pull the throw blanket Lucy crocheted from the edge of the bed and drape it over her wet body. "How's that?"

"It's alright..." Her voice drifts off.

It's been doing that a lot—drifting in and out while I lay next to her watching ESPN, TMZ, and trying to keep my hands busy so they won't keep trolling the internet for that article I couldn't escape.

I turn back to the TV just in time to catch Shannon Sharpe grinning at the camera.

"There's something rumbling down in Texas, Skip. Something *big*," he rasps.

They flash an old picture of Ace behind Shannon and Skip. He's smiling on the court in his blue and yellow jersey, gripping a basketball in his hand. It's the old Ace I didn't know. The one who still had Angie.

I sit up against the cold brass bars on Mama's head-board, waiting on Shannon to finish what he started.

"We need to talk about Ason Williams Jr. or lil' AWII, as I always liked to call him," he adds.

This is the third part to Ace — the one the world can't get enough of—especially sports reporters.

Shannon pats his broad chest and wrinkles his eyebrows like he's trying to come up with the perfect words to describe the wonder that Ace is on the court.

"I mean, talk about *not* missing a beat. It's been two years since we've seen this kid and he's still dominating. Three games into the season and he's putting up NBA numbers... but he's doing it at an HBCU... on a team that ain't made noise in years. Thirty points, twelve rebounds, ten assists. This kid is still something else, Skip. He *is* still something else. The athleticism, the grit, the authority on the court. Watching him is like watching his Pops. It's some-thing special. We talk a lot about generational talent, but can we honestly say we've seen generational talent as good as this?"

Skip Bayless looks down and pushes his ear piece up before tugging at his suit jacket. All of those innocent things make my stomach hurt because I know what's coming.

"Shannon..." He squirms in his seat. "I can agree that the kid oozes pure talent. He's athletic, he has grit, *but* there's an important conversation that needs to be had here and I want to be mindful of how I address this situation because it's—it's delicate."

This is the part I hate.

Watching overpaid, well-dressed characters dissect one part of Ace is as addicting as scrolling down my Twitter timeline.

"How much more off the court bad behavior will we continue to ignore from this kid simply because of his athleticism and who his father is? For years we heard nothing from him except one-off incidents like smoking weed or accounts from strangers talking about their random run-ins with AW's son out in LA. The kid refused to talk to the media—"

"Let's be clear, Skip. He still doesn't talk to them. Everything we're fed about him is pieced together from reporters or leaked to the press and let's *also* be clear that this young man lost his mother last year, who I'm sure was a huge pillar of strength in his life."

"Her name is Angie," I mutter. "And she was, you dumbasses."

Talking to a television is hopeless. They can't hear me explain to them that Angie was more than a pillar of strength. She was Ace's world.

"I completely understand and empathize." Skip holds up his hands. "You're right. But let's not forget the Bruins suspended him indefinitely *before* his mother's death. So this behavior pre-dates that. Yet he somehow made it as a walk-on at Lockwood, no doubt thanks to his father. He gets there and right before the season starts, we're bombarded with *more* bad behavior."

He raises his eyebrow. "Punching his agent? The guy that has the potential to get him to the NBA despite his bad reputation? I mean, this kid can't stay outta trouble. I wanna say, 'poor little rich kid,' but this feels like something deeper, Shannon—"

Loud knocks on the front door interrupt Skip's rant.

I suck my teeth like Gus. "That messy ass nigga ain't nobody's agent."

One side of my brain wants to hear how Skip will villainize Ace, while the other side is at capacity. It can't absorb anymore outside opinions about Ace without his reassurance that he's nothing like the world says he is because I'm *still* too busy running from all that trust Marcus said he worked so hard building for us.

"The door..." Mama huffs.

"I'm going... I'm going. I'll bring you some juice when I come back."

"Nuh uh. I already gotta pee." Her teeth chatter against each other.

"You haven't drank anything all day." I push up from the bed, rolling my eyes. "You gotta drink something."

And eat too, but I didn't want to fuss about it. Ace's elite combo wasn't working so good anymore because that's how shit is on Earth—one bad thing happens right after the other.

Mama's been hot for two days and I'm having my first real fight with a man I hate and like—a man who says he's mine.

"No. Ju—just take me to pee after you get the door."

"Okay," I whisper, keeping my eyes on her while backing out of the bedroom.

When I round the corner to the entryway, Bryson's curly head peeks from between the crack I left in the blinds.

He doesn't smile when I yank the front door open and push the screen.

"What you doing here?" I ask, eyeing his slides and grey sweats. "Don't you have a game?"

"I'm not going. I came to check on you."

"Well, you checked and I'm good." I pull at the knob on the screen, but he sneaks his fingers between the crack.

"Don't be like that, man. I'm missing my game to come see about you."

"I ain't tell you to do that."

"It's been weeks, Phat. *Weeks.* We ain't never beefed this long and you ain't never been down this bad—especially not over a dude who really don't give a damn about you."

"Yeah and you never abandoned me at a party or lied on me but there's something about college that got you smelling yourself."

I skirt around his dig at Ace. He sounds like all those faceless people on Twitter. He didn't know *shit* about me and Ace.

"I told you I didn't lie on you. Come on." He pokes my cheek and some of the ice around my heart thaws. "I'll take you to get bear claws. The cool cup lady was closed."

After being holed up in the house with a delirious mama for days, even the simple things that make me smile sound grand—all the bear claws, cool cups and pokes to my fat cheeks.

I suck up more of the outside air while Bryson waits with his hands shoved in his sweats. For a second, I want to forgive him and forget about the wedge that college and peer pressure drove between us, but as usual, my brain and body aren't in sync. They're fighting each other for control.

"What about your game?"

"What about it? I know you ain't been in there staring at

the walls. Your man is all over TV and the news. Him and his daddy got what they wanted. It's no point in me going to a game I'm not gon' play in."

"'My *man*? What they *wanted*?'" I raise my eyebrow. "What you talking about?"

"Come on. Don't stand up here and act like you don't know what this whole thing was about? All this performative bullshit is to get him back in the spotlight." He scoffs, looking up. "The black girl, the black college, the underdog bringing a losing team back to life. Don't tell me you actually believe he's your man? It's all a media stunt and don't give me that bullshit about Coach knowing your daddy like Marcus does. Coach ever ask you anything about Marshall?"

My body isn't like putty for his rosy cheeks anymore. For the first time in a while, he's not thrusting a cool cup at me through the door, begging to talk. He's just here with a pale face and his chain glittering under the setting sun, calling Ace *my man* in the ugliest way, like it's impossible for a guy like him to want a girl like me. He sounds like he did that day we watched Ace swagger into the bookstore.

I chuckle. "This what you came here for? To complain about not getting any playing time and shove your conspiracy theories down my throat like the rest of the world? You wanna complain about Ason more?"

"Oh, it's Ason now? What, he called you to brag about starting the past three games to get you back on his side? You know Chelsea told me you and him wasn't talking."

"Seriously, Chels." I huff to myself, rolling my eyes. "Brag about starting? Ace don't brag about dumb shit like that."

I can't help myself. What we have on Planet Ace is sacred, but the words pour out just like all the other ones concerning him. Ace doesn't brag about basketball. He brags about Mama eating all her food, about me adulting without him, about Marcus' dumbass going to work, and about Angie being Angie. For a boy that looks like he's handling the world in his hands when he's playing basketball, he hardly even talks about it.

Bryson's Adam's apple jumps as he swallows. "So you think starting is dumb?"

It is compared to the life shit going on off the court, but it's another thing I can't say to him. Mama's always saying I can't project my problems onto other folks.

"No—I'm just say—"

"You know, that's all I wanted this semester was to keep my starting position and to have fun in college with you."

"I didn't mean it that way."

"You sure about that? We been best friends since the sandbox and this dude blows into town and all of a sudden you can't even look me in my face anymore? I'm *sorry,* a'ight? *There.* I'm sorry that he has the money and clout I don't have. I'm sorry. You can tell him I finally said it so he can get off my head."

I pinch my eyes shut, shaking my head.

"You still don't get—"

A loud, nasty *thump* cuts right into the middle of our argument.

"What was that?" he asks, pulling the screen door from between my loose fingers.

Mama.

I thought I belted it out loud, but Bryson's wrinkled face tells me it all came out in gibberish instead.

"Fuck."

That word flies out of my mouth with all of its syllables shooting in different directions. It came out clear and crisp, with all the vowels and consonants floating through the air. I take off behind them.

"Phat! Wait!" Bryson yells from somewhere behind me, but I'm gone.

I can't wait because all the floating vowels and consonants were beating me to Mama.

The hallway leading to her room is the longest it's ever been. One foot in front of the other isn't enough. I need to fly. I raise my feet as high as they'll go, but it still doesn't feel like I'm moving fast enough. The end of the hallway is the hardest part. The walls close in and push me closer to her bedroom door.

I try to prepare my eyes and brain for the worst, but I didn't give Ace time to teach me that before I left him.

"Mama?" I cough out, scraping my fingers against the doorframe.

Her words come out in deep moans while I try to fly again, but it's useless without wings. She's there in a balled up heap on the floor with her nightgown tangled around her waist.

"Mama!" Bryson yells, knocking into my shoulder from behind.

He passes me up, running to her slumped body and crouching beside her.

He looks up with wet cheeks. "What do I do? Do I call Marcus or—or Ma? Mama, can you get up?"

Sometimes I forget he's just a boy, like I'm just a girl. We ain't lived enough to trust our own judgements and girls like me don't need to fly. We need to trust.

I run to the bed and snatch my phone from the edge. I fumble over it until I get back to that text message while Marcus keeps bugging me in the back of my head, asking what I'm gonna do with all this newfound trust I have in a man.

"Lourdes?" Ace rasps into the phone when he answers. "What's wrong?"

I let out garbled chokes between tears while I kneel beside Bryson and start rolling Mama's soaked nightgown off her pale legs.

"Ason... I... Ason. I came in and she was... I know you have a game—"

"Slow down. Take a deep breath. *Open your mouth.*"

I suck in as much of the stale hot air in Mama's room that I can muster and then it all pours out in embarrassing chunks like that night in the driveway.

"She fell. Mama told me she had to pee but Bryson was at the door so—so I went to answer it and I guess she got up to go by herself and—and she fell. I heard it."

Static from the phone buzzes in my ear while I wait for the eruption—for him to tell me what I should and shouldn't have done like Marcus.

I pull Mama in my lap, holding onto my breath and the buzzing static.

"Okay, baby," he replies. "Bryson still there with you?"

His tone won't change. It's like I'm not even hyperventilating.

"Yes!"

"Okay," he whispers. "Keep being good for Mom and let me talk to him. Can you do that for me?"

"Uh, huh. I—I can."

"A'ight, well, give him the phone."

"But I need you."

"You *have* me. Put me on speakerphone so you can still hear me. Okay?"

When I pull his calm voice from my ear and stab at the screen, the world seems warped.

I push the phone into Bryson's blurry chest and keep being good for Mama, like Ace says. It's the only thing in my life I've ever tried to do perfectly. I keep listening for his voice in the melee of Mama's ragged breaths and Bryson hovering over my back.

"Bryson..." Ace calls out. "All bullshit aside, I need you to do me a solid, brodie."

"O—okay."

"I want you to listen to what I'm about to tell you and then hang up with me and call 911. You understand?"

"I—"

"You can do it. I know you can. Do you hear me?"

"Yeah—yeah. I hear you."

"Do *not* let Lourdes call 911. You do that."

There's rustling on his end of the phone, and I think I hear Coach Williams yelling in the background, but he sounds far away.

"When the ambulance gets there, call me. Call me and tell me what hospital they're taking Mom to. They're only gon' let Lourdes ride, so you gotta get that shit down before they leave with Mom because Lourdes... she's... she's..." He sighs. "Baby, I'm coming."

CHAPTER TWENTY-SEVEN

Lourdes

The doctors in the emergency confuse me more than Dr. Evanston does. They speak in sprints with their sentences running together and they ask lots of questions but refuse to answer mine.

"She's got some hyperpyrexia going on. How long has she been running a fever?"

None of them are old like Dr. Evanston. They look too young to be sporting their white coats, and they stare into my eyes like I'm doing a shitty job of taking care of Mama so I try to remember if I took her temperature between Shannon and Skip's rants.

"I—I don't know," I stutter out. "I think my brother said she was hot a couple days ago?"

The white boy pauses and looks up at me, running his fingers through his short blonde hair. "Well, yeah, she's on fire. So she's been this hot for three days?"

"I don't kno—"

"Sir! You can't come in here!" a nurse yells, looking up from the needle she poked in Mama's arm.

The room we're in is like a cage. I twist my hand around the rail on Mama's bed, hoping it's Marcus so he can explain to this white boy that we didn't leave her burning up for three days on purpose. We ain't neglectful like those folks they see on the news. Ace always says I'm doing my best.

I wait for Marcus to yell and tell her that's his "fucking Mama," but then I remember he got up and went to work this morning for the first time in a week.

"That's my mom," Ace replies. "Ms. Lisa, at intake, said I could come back here."

I try to turn around, but my body won't move because my brain's yelling at it, telling it that if it moves enough for me to see his face, I won't survive.

The nurse's round face relaxes, and she waves him in like she invites strangers into patients' rooms all the time.

"Sorry, hun." She smiles. "Come on in. We're trying to get Mom taken care of."

"I understand."

I smell him first.

It feels like it's been so long since I got a whiff of his earthy scent because separation is funny like that.

I feel him next.

He hovers over my shoulder and drops his hand on Mama's head, stroking the few hairs that survived chemo and radiation. She hasn't opened her eyes since the EMTs loaded us onto the back of the ambulance so she can't smile up at him and call him "son."

I want to touch him so bad that my fingers tingle.

He looks up at the white boy, eyeing his white coat and

stethoscope pressed to Mama's chest. "Are you the attending or a resident?"

He sounds so sure of himself and the words he's using— words I don't understand. He squares his shoulders and looks at everybody in the room like he owns the hospital and he probably could.

"A resident. I'm Dr. Morris," the boy replies. "But you can just call me Andy. Gnarly game last night, by the way. I caught it at my buddy's. He's from SoCal. He talks about that buzzer beater against Villanova all the time. He was there."

"Oh yeah? What's his name?"

Andy's eyes dart around while he skirts around Mama's bed in Jordans that I notice for the first time.

"Donald. He's been following you since you were at Pittman—we both have. You're sick, man."

His tone volleys up and down, and it isn't accusatory anymore. For a minute I think he forgets he's a doctor and I forget there's still a swarm of basketball fans that worship Ace on Earth no matter what he does. The internet and news outlets have a funny way of distorting things.

"'Preciate that, bro." Ace folds his bottom lip under his teeth and keeps stroking Mama's head.

The tingling in my hands gets more intense. Now they want to grab at his Lockwood athletics shirt so I can bury my face in his chest. He's so calm that it's contagious and my heartbeat slows.

I inhale to get another whiff of him while I wait on his next breath and word.

"After you take care of my mom, I want you and Don to come see me hoop. We play Tech next. My lady will hook y'all up with the specifics."

Andy's white face glows like he's thirteen and my

stomach folds because I *feel* thirteen. He looks over at me, connecting the dots, but I don't have time to act shy because the man I hate and like has doctors fawning over him. For the first time in a while, I forget about Cheyenne, Blake, and sports reporters and melt into the calming force that's Ace.

"That would be *sick*, man. Wow."

I scoff, swiping at my wet cheeks with my tingling fingers, trying to get their shit together.

"Cool. Can you explain what's going on, Andy?"

"Oh, for sure—for sure." Andy nods, taking a deep breath.

The death stare he gave me when I asked why Mama wasn't opening her eyes isn't there anymore. He's excited to explain why Mama won't move.

"So I was telling your girlfriend that Mrs. Hines has a major case of hyperpyrexia. Her body temperature is exceedingly high. It's a good thing she got here when she did because this can be deadly. We're running tests and the nurses are getting the IV drip going for her. She's super dehydrated, man, and it looks like she's got pneumonia. All signs are pointing to sepsis."

Deadly? Sepsis?

The calmness I embraced melts away.

"I try to make her drink something every day." I frown, looking up at Ace. "No, I—I didn't take her temperature like I should have, but I didn't mean for any of this to happen. What's sepsis?"

It feels right explaining to Ace what happened. He's the only one that gets it. Andy and his SoCal buddy didn't know shit about taking care of Mama.

"Baby..."

Hearing that pet name pour out his mouth in front of people makes me needy and full of want. I want to touch him, taste him, and hear him until I'm nauseated from being overwhelmed by him.

We stare at each other until my vision gets blurry with tears.

Andy clears his throat. "I was reading her chart and saw that she's living with metastatic colon cancer. It's unlikely—"

"You didn't do anything wrong," Ace cuts in, swiping a wild tear from my cheek. "Do you understand what he's saying?"

"No," I garble out, whining and hoping it'll make him pull me into him, but he won't fold.

His hand falls back to his side.

He looks over at Andy. "I like you, bro, but my lady don't understand none of this shit you talking about and she's scared."

Andy nods, pounding his hands together and inhaling a breath full of stale hospital air. "Ms—"

"Lourdes," Ace says. "She never hit a buzzer beater against Villanova, but her name is more important to you than mine will ever be. Start asking your patient's family members their names. It's a sign of good bedside manner."

If this is the type of responsibility Ace was talking about owning as my man, I don't think I ever want to go back to boys. Apparently, men know how to calm chaos and command rooms without even raising their voices.

Andy takes another deep breath, splaying his hands toward me. "Lourdes, I know you know your mom has cancer."

I nod, rubbing another tear from my eyes.

The nerve of that word to show up again.

"She's on chemo and radiation treatments." He slaps his hands together, inhaling a third deep breath. "While those treatments are great for treating cancer, they wreak havoc on her white blood cells. These blood cells exist to fight off infections in the body."

"Without those white blood cells, her immune system can't fight off an infection like pneumonia and it turns on itself. So, she becomes vulnerable. When this happens, sepsis sets in—the fever, confusion, sleepiness and pain are all symptoms. The pneumonia didn't cause the sepsis though. It's caused by her body's overwhelming response to the pneumonia."

Somewhere between his words, I grabbed Ace's hand because trust is a motherfucker. It makes me never want to come to another hospital without him.

He squeezes the tips of my fingers, stroking my nails. I look at him out of the corner of my eye, searching for any sign of confusion on his face, but it's relaxed.

"Explain to her it's not her fault," he says, keeping the same foot of distance between us.

"It's not your fault. Your mom is *so* vulnerable right now from the colon cancer and all the treatments that something small that wouldn't impact me or you could be deadly for her."

"Thank you," I choke out.

They're the only words that can encompass five years of frustration from doctors talking at me and not to me.

"I want you to be prepared for the future, there are ways to get ahead of this. I can get the social—"

"I can do that," Ace cuts in. "I can explain it. Please don't bother them about that."

Andy nods with his lips balled down. "For now, we're going to get her admitted and moved to our intensive care unit."

Ace drops my hand and pushes away from Mama's bed, taking long strides to Andy across the room.

Down on Earth, a man like Ace rushing toward him would've put fear in Andy's heart, but I think he's up on Planet Ace too—just temporarily. He smiles as Ace claps his hand into his and pulls him in.

"I'm proud of you, bro," he mutters, but the words bounce along the walls of the small room and me and the nurse hear them.

Andy's smile turns soft because Planet Ace really *is* wild. It's the only place where a basketball player could tell a doctor he was proud of him and almost bring an ER nurse to tears.

HOME IS WARM.

"Ason..." a feminine voice whispers. "You sure you don't want me to get the cot for you to put her on?"

It's so warm that I never want to leave—not even when other women's voices wake me up from a deep sleep. I know it ain't nobody but Nurse Shelby. That's how she introduced herself as soon as they let us into Mama's new room in the ICU—*"Nurse Shelby from Arkansas."*

She sounds like Daisy from Dukes of Hazzard, but she's black with box braids and looks so young that I wonder how she's even in charge of Mama's care. Even though she looks young, she talks to me like I'm even younger than her.

Ace bounces me closer to his chest and presses his lips against my face. "Nah. She ain't gon' sleep on a cot, Shelby, but I'll ask her, anyway."

"Well, you know best, Mr. Man. Lemme get y'all a blanket then. I'll bring back the visitation forms for you to fill out too...*oh* and some juice. You look like you need a lil' something. I'm sure it's been a long evening."

"Okay," Ace mutters against my face, shifting on the pullout chair next to Mama's bed.

"Be back."

Nurse Shelby likes Ace. All the nurses do. Even the white ones. The black nurses go out of their way for him while the white nurses are more subtle—they fling their blonde ponytails when he's filling out paperwork for me and Mama and they lean in real close to him as if they can't hear him when he speaks, but Ace speaks with purpose so I know they're lying. I'm learning more and more that Earth is a place I'll never understand, and maybe that's why Ace didn't want me to get lost here.

I shuffle closer into his warm chest and pry an eye open to make sure Mama is still laying in her hospital bed next to us with her pale skin and eyes closed.

"Lourdes, you wanna cot?" he asks, shaking me by my waist.

I groan back and try to claw my way deeper into his skin, but it's impossible to get there. God probably knows how ridiculous I look trying to lay claim to a man I was just running from this morning.

Ace didn't yoke me up and pull me onto his lap. I climbed in it when Nurse Shelby bat her falsies at him over Mama's IV for the third time. Angie was probably laughing with God and telling him her silly lil' wannabe daughter-in-law was being obsessive out in the open for once—even when her son had done stupid man-things that made me question us.

"Marcus is almost here," he says, dragging a finger across my face. "Bryson text you and said he called him."

"Okay."

"You want him to bring you some food?"

"No."

"You wanna sit here? I can stand up."

"No."

I wanted stupid and immature things. They had nothing to do with Mama and everything to do with him because he was taking care of it all like he said he would. The day had ripped my voice out of my throat and dangled it over my head. Deep down, I think he knew I couldn't get out much more than "no" and "okay."

"Alright, Mr. Man, I'll put your apple juice over here." Shelby breezes back in, talking fast and sliding the juice on a rolling tray by the only window in the room. "She can have five visitors, but they can only come in the room two at a time."

She slaps a paper against her hip and cocks her head to the side when she notices my eyes are open. "Oh, the doll's awake. You wanna fill this out for Mom?"

I roll my eyes up to Ace, but he's already opening his mouth until the room door flings open. When Marcus pushes inside, Nurse Shelby forgets about the visitation list.

"Mama?" he chokes out. "What happened?"

His deep-set eyes have a layer of wetness resting on their irises and his feet won't stop shuffling. Ace scoots forward and takes a deep breath so he can fix another thing that's wrong. He pulls the words I want to say from my dry throat and throws them out.

"She fell at home today when Phat went to let Bryson in the house. We think she was trying to go to the bathroom by herself. The doctor's saying it's sepsis. She been running a fever for about three days now."

"How the fuck that happen?"

"It's the chemo and the cancer. She can't fight off shit she used to."

Marcus accepts his short answer and I'm glad for it. I can't take another in-depth explanation of everything that's wrong with Mama.

"Is—is she gon' wake up?" he asks, tearing his eyes off Mama and looking at us for the first time since he bulldozed his way into the room.

His eyes rake across Ace's arms cradling me, and my fingers curled around the neck of his shirt.

"For sure, brodie." Ace nods. "God don't make no mistakes."

It's a good lie that Marcus needs to hear. I already saw the truth in Andy's eyes in the emergency room because he was still learning about that good bedside manner. He didn't need to break it down for me. It wasn't no guarantee Mama would wake up, but I'm following Ace to the end of Planet Ace again, so I swallow the lie too.

Nurse Shelby lets out a soft hum and thrusts the visitation paperwork out toward us. "You feel up to filling this out or should I give it to—"

"Nah, I got it." Ace shakes his head, beckoning her to us. "Marcus, me and Phat gon' get up outta here and—"

"Huh?" Marcus' brown face turns ashen.

"Lourdes needs a break. She needs to eat, to shower, to sleep."

"Man...." Marcus blows a breath, swiping his hands down his face. "I can't stay up here. I—I don't know what to do."

My slow beating heart amps up at the thought of leaving Mama with Marcus. The last time Granny left Marcus in a hospital with Mama, he left and never came back.

Nurse Shelby's head ping pongs back and forth between us, even though she said only two visitors were allowed in the room. She twists over to Ace, pulling the rolling table in front of him, and sitting the visitation paperwork next to the apple juice.

My tired eyes don't know who to focus on, so they jump around to everybody—even Mama, even though she's not awake.

Ace slides his arms from under my legs and grabs the pen Nurse Shelby's dangling in his face. He reads the paper, mouthing the words while me and Nurse Shelby stare at his pink lips.

"I love you, Mar," he says, scribbling onto the paper in slow strokes. "I respect you. I value you. We have our moments and shit, but I would *never* disrespect you on purpose. You're the closest thing I ever had to a brother."

Ever since I could hold on to memories, Marcus has been the only man in me and Mama's lives. Mama didn't believe in keeping other men around long enough for us to remember their faces, names, or have a say in the way we lived, but Ace is here now and he's not even Mama's. He's mine.

"What you tryna get at?" Marcus asks.

Ace lifts his head up and hands me the pen. "Put your granny's information down. I'm sure she'll be here as soon as Marcus tells her what's going on."

"Hold up. I just got here. You need to answer me. I asked what you was tryna get at."

I press the pen onto the paper, but it won't move because it's the only thing I've been responsible for since Ace popped into the emergency room. For the first time in my life, I forget how to spell Granny's name.

"I'm not tryna get at nothing. I'm *telling* you that today

ain't a day for you to put Lourdes in a grown-man position."

"I—I just worked a twelve-hour shift! I just got all the texts and calls from Bry. I just found out about all this. I ain't even sat with this shit yet, man."

And neither had I. I hadn't sat with Mama's diagnosis since the day we found out about it. I never had the time.

"Lourdes been working twelve-hour shifts since I met y'all," Ace replies, widening his eyes. "She found her on the floor. She rode with her in the ambulance. She was next to the gurney when they rushed her in. She saw it all—too much, if you ask me. She won't ever be the same after today and I won't ever compare my situation to yours, but I laid up in the hospital with my mom for three days, Mar. *Three days*. I sat in the same clothes because a motherfucka' was always putting me in a grown-man position when I was just a kid. You hurting her feelings again, man, but I'm not going for that shit today."

I've never seen fear in Marcus' eyes, but I see it for the first time today, floating behind the wetness that won't go away.

"How the fuck you gon' tell me what to do with my sister?"

"Out of everything I just said—that's what you took and held onto? That I'm trying to tell you what to do with Lourdes?"

"Don't. Don't try to play me right now."

Nurse Shelby clears her throat. "I think he's trying to say that the baby just needs a break. It has been an awful long day for her."

Just like five years of pain materialized in Marcus' voice, it manifests in my body while I try to remember Granny's real name so Nurse Shelby can leave.

"*I* need a fucking break." Marcus scoffs. "Y'all don't

care about how I'm feeling."

My body is hot like Mama's because even when she's sleeping, we're still conjoined twins. Little wet dots soak into the paper underneath the G that I didn't remember writing.

Ace smacks his lips and I feel all my words getting ready to pour out of his mouth again. I see Nurse Shelby's hand hovering over his forearm like she knew how to comfort *my* man. I hear Angie asking me why I was still holding onto my thoughts like a little girl when she knew how loud I could get about her good girlfriend and her son.

"On me, you being a selfish ass motherfucka'—"

"That's enough," I garble out in a hoarse voice while scratching an R onto the paper.

I'm not as loud as Angie wants, but the sound of my voice shuts Ace up, and that's what matters.

When I look up, he and Marcus are still battling with their eyes, but they aren't stupid enough to keep going when I have Angie in my ear.

I turn to Nurse Shelby and her hovering hand. "My brother Marcus will stay here with her for the night. He can finish this."

I tap the paper, sliding to the edge of Ace's lap while narrowing my eyes at how close her fingertips are to his skin.

"You can call *Mr. Man* if anything serious happens. We'll be home all night." I sniffle, swiping at my face and then scribbling my phone number on the top of the paper.

I NEVER HEARD Coach Williams curse.

"What the *fuck* is going on?" he blares through the

speakers of Ace's truck while I stare at the lights bouncing off the high-rise. "You can't just walk out before a game. Have you lost your goddamn mind?"

I never saw Ace hollow either.

He drums his fingers on the steering wheel and stares up at the red light.

"You left. Sanchez didn't even show up. I had to play Marquise. Bless his heart—that boy ain't got nobody's point guard IQ! Do you know how much pressure he was under to perform? This is the type of impulsive shit I'm talking about!"

When the light turns green, he slams his foot on the gas and I jerk forward, running into his hard arm he throws out in front of me.

I never realized hospitals put people under spells until mine lifted as soon as I walked out into the parking lot and inhaled the brisk night air. I stood next to the truck and watched Ace yank his t-shirt over his head like all the sickness from inside had crawled into its threads. His Superman facade dimmed as soon as we closed ourselves inside the truck and I got a good look at him for the first time since I left him in that parking garage with glass at his feet. Pale caramel skin and red eyes.

Cree won't stop beeping in while Coach Williams goes on about how bad Ace did his teammates, all because he missed one game against a team that wasn't even in their conference. I wait for Ace to tell him that their one loss wasn't for bullshit, but he's staring at the closed gate at the parking garage's entrance.

I yank open the middle console and rifle through papers until I pull a key fob out that looks like mine. Coach Williams eases into a panic about how the world will perceive another one of Ace's mistakes.

"They ain't gon' shut up about this shit tomorrow. Don't think they don't know something is up. They gon' speculate to hell," he rambles. "You been putting up NBA numbers and now you're suddenly missing."

A little chuckle eases out while I press the button on the fob and let the garage up. I didn't mean for it to come out, but after watching Mama taking those labored breaths on her bedroom floor while Shannon and Skip speculated to hell about Ace, Coach Williams' worries were funny.

"This is like Cheyenne-gate all over again, but worse. Now they're just picking at what's left of you because you fucked up and brought these gossip happy reporters back into our lives. We ain't gotta worry about her money-hungry family threatening to go to Gayle fucking King crying about what you did to her while *my* wife is laid up at home dying this time! No, now it's all about you *again*. I listened to Marcus and brought you home because I knew you needed folks and then Blake promised me he could make this NBA shit happen, but no matter what I do, you just won't be a man. You're too busy parading around with Marshall's babygirl when I promised him I'd keep her away from boys who would never mean well for her—especially one who can't even remember what he's done most days because he's always got his head in a tequila bottle."

We roll into a parking spot.

Coach Williams' heavy breaths fill the car.

I can't hear anymore, so I breathe out like Ace did next to Mama's hospital bed in the emergency room. "Baby..."

He flings his head over to me and my limbs have that same feeling from when Nurse Shelby looked at him like he was it for her.

"Are you okay?" I ask.

He's too empty to answer me, so he blinks. His long

lashes flutter on top of his red eyes and I reach out to touch them to settle that yearning in my body.

"Lourdes?" Coach Williams rasps.

"Coach Williams."

"I—I didn't know you were there too."

"Yeah...you never do."

After today, I'm knee deep in Ace's Kool-Aid and I don't want to be rescued from drowning—especially not by a man who thinks Ace is still a boy after everything that happened to him on Earth.

"I didn't mean for you to hear all that."

"But you meant for Ace to hear it?"

My tone is calm. It'd been that way since I had to let Nurse Shelby know she wouldn't get shit out of Ace, but an answer from me when she called.

"Babygirl, I'm just disappointed in him, that's all. He has to learn how to communicate with me. It's something me and him struggle with but that's neither here nor there and none of your concern. He has to understand that he can't do whatever he wants. He can't leave right before a—"

"I needed him."

"I understand there's some puppy love going on and you have a crush, but that doesn't excuse the fact that he le—"

"My mama is in the hospital. Who else was I supposed to call? You?"

"CeCe's in—in the hospital?" he stutters out.

"Yeah..." I swipe at Ace's closing eyes and wipe at his dry cheeks. "She is."

"I'm *so* sorry, babygirl. I didn't know. I—if you need me, I'm here."

"I don't."

I didn't need rescuing from the only person who meant well for me.

CHAPTER TWENTY-EIGHT

Ace

I forgot how hospitals make my brain work. They always convince it that every germ from inside the walls hitched a ride on my clothes so I have to crawl out of them as soon as I step outside. I'm scared the hospital did the same to Phat, so I send her to the shower as soon as we get off the elevator and stumble inside. She begs for me to come too.

After two and a half months, I've turned her into a beggar—a "you better still have your ass here when I get out since you won't shower with me" type beggar. She said it with her finger pressed into my chest like I was brave enough to go anywhere without her now that I had her back.

I think she's a lady for sure now. She checks nurses for flirting with me when CeCe's in pain, she presses Pops about me, and I know she'll fuck me and Marcus up if we ever argue about family business in front of strangers again.

I fall back onto the couch with a glass of 1942 in my hand and my body melts into the cushions until the water stops whirring in the bathroom and her feet pitter patter across the floor.

"Ason?"

At first I think I'm dreaming like all the other times I heard her in here. Then I remember the desperation in her voice when she called out for me for the first time in two weeks.

I swallow the burning tequila and pinch my eyes tighter. "Yeah, kid?"

I was never sober enough to come up with that contingency plan while she was gone, so I'm coming up with shit on the fly now that she came back—I have to respect her new boundaries, take shit slow, and keep her calm. I'll only touch her if she asks. I'll be less impulsive and more stable. It all sounds like some shit Mom would suggest, but I don't have her reassurance that it'll work.

"Open your eyes," she whispers.

I pry them open and she's there, naked, gripping a Magnum between her fingers.

"Baby." The word comes out my mouth as a statement instead of a question just like hers did in the car.

I swallow, tightening my hand around the glass. "Where you find that?"

"In our room."

Our.

That shit makes my stomach go wild and my dick grow even though I should talk her down, but she's determined. There's a fire in her eyes and I can't fault her for it. Kids like us with mothers like ours have seen the beginning and end too many times to live without that fire, but sometimes we need somebody to put it out.

She saunters up to me, easing between my legs and snatching the glass from my shaking hand.

"You not mad at me no more?" I inhale my soap from her skin as she leans over me and sits the glass on the console table behind the couch.

"I am," she mutters. "But you're gonna make it better, because that's what you always do, right? You make it better —whatever it is."

She drapes her legs over my lap while I swallow every word she mutters. I savor each one and the confidence weaving between them. All the breath leaves my body when our chests collide and I just can't help myself.

"Tell me what you want from me," I choke out, scraping my fingers through her braids. "I'll give you anything you want to make it right."

Our chests push in and out together. She breathes for me in harsh rasps, like I'm inside her.

"How many days?" she asks.

"How many days, what?"

"How many days have you lived that you don't fully remember?"

I would've taken any question but that one, but I can't run from it. Gus says I gotta stay solid for her no matter what.

"I'd be lying if I said I knew."

"Even days you spent with me?"

"Never. I remember every single time I laid eyes on you," I gasp, pulling back to look at her face. "You know better than that."

It was one of the few things 1942 let me keep. There aren't any black holes that swallow her face. I see those eyes every time I close mine and I hear Mom saying she told me I'd find her.

"Do I really?"

Her little fingers crawl down my abdomen and I let her

have her way. She shoves my shorts and briefs down until I'm naked like her.

"You know it all," I grunt, wrapping my hand around her chin while she fumbles with the condom.

"I didn't know how bad Mama had gotten or what to do," she whispers, glancing at me while pulling it open.

"But you did what you were supposed to do. You called me and I came, didn't I?"

"I didn't know about that article."

I see the confusion on her face and the hurt from having her first adult relationship play out for the world. Fixing it would mean telling the truth—all of it. Even if she won't like my answer.

"I knew about it since the day after Splashtown."

She flings her head up and her lips open, but my words pour out before she can try to talk herself out of us again.

"I was trying to protect you from it because I knew you weren't ready for that, but takers like Blake don't care about how precious you are, so he held it over my head. I thought if I could convince you he was alright, you'd say 'fuck it' and follow me to the end for real. Then I wouldn't have to worry about the world running you away from me, but you too solid to let somebody like Blake in our lives no matter what he promises to Pops."

A shaky breath rocks her chest and she hiccups.

"And Cheyenne?" She whispers while she handles the condom like it's a delicate piece of fabric, doing everything exactly the way I taught her to—rolling it over the head of my dick, pinching the tip, and pulling it down. "Why would you let a girl like her close enough to destroy you on such a special ass day?"

"I didn't." I shake my head and try to forget my memories from that day.

It wasn't even that many, but I wanted all of that shit gone—even the ones with Dough.

"Everybody was there—Cree, Javier, my teammates, and all the people that invited themselves into my life so they could leave with something they didn't have before. She wasn't there for me, baby. She was there to take, just like all the rest."

My fingers find their place between her lips while she lifts and then eases onto the tip of my dick.

"Now you know it all." I mutter with a sigh. "Does that fix it?"

She can't answer because I'm knuckle deep inside her throat so she shakes her head. She's not satisfied that I still can't tell her with absolute confidence that I can fight through the black spots from that day and figure out what happened with me and a girl I tried to stay far away from after Mom's warning.

We both stare at the last few inches of my dick we want inside her. Her moans strum against my fingers while she tries to answer me with her words, because *that's* how good I have it.

"Take the rest for me." I thrust my hips up to help her along the way until I'm buried so deep inside her that my body goes still.

I don't think we're making love anymore. I don't know what to call it but whatever it is hurts too good. We're locked in with her legs wrapped around my waist and my free hand scraping across her stomach like it's been years since I felt it. It ain't been shit but two weeks, but separations hit different in our world.

Hot tears trickle down her cheeks and splash against my fingers that she won't let go of. The frigid air blasting from the vent above us strokes our sweaty skin while I try to arrange the words in my head to flow just right for her.

"You said you wouldn't leave me."

Stupid me. I was dumb enough to think I could get out the right words, knowing damn well 1942 wouldn't ever let me do that.

"Did you lie to me? Who taught you how to lie like that when we make love?"

All the simp shit I kept bottled inside while she was gone keeps pouring out when I'm supposed to be fixing us.

"Sunny called to check on you. She said she got new powders in and wanted to test all the colors on you. I told her you weren't feeling good, but I promised her I'd bring you by," I ramble. "And Gus wanted to pick you up for class the other morning, but I told him 'no' because I knew you were still tripping about what people think... about you... about me."

She tries to move her hips against mine, but I hold her in place. "They both miss you... but not as much as I do."

I yank my fingers out of her mouth, staring up at her with her braids billowing over her bare arms just like the day I first seen her naked.

"Tell me you ain't miss me. Tell me you don't want us anymore and I'll stop trying to catch up to you. Tell me you good on us, baby. *Tell me* you ain't fuck with my head tonight just to get up and leave me again tomorrow."

If she does, I won't survive it. It'll be like Mom leaving all over again.

Her face screws into a frown that makes my heart thump in wild spasms. I focus hard on her round lips and cat eyes so I can stamp this part of today in my memory just in case.

A deep groan gurgles up her throat and in all my years

on Earth, I never had a woman burst into chaotic, snot-bubbling tears while sitting on my dick, but she does it with no problem. They pour onto her chest while she pulsates around me. I didn't think something so strange was possible, but here we are.

"I can't." She claws at my chest before burying herself in my arms. "I can't."

After the chaotic tears, something else happens that I don't understand. Deep, heart-pounding gasps bellow from the back of her throat and I really need to find the perfect words, but they just won't fucking come.

"I can't tell you any of that shit!"

Her voice bounces off the walls while I rack my brain for something—*anything* to fix this, but just like her, I can't. I'm desperate, so I try anyway.

"Why not?" I rake my fingers back through her hair while cradling her body. "You said I could have anything I want, and this is what I want. I want you to tell me why—"

The rest of my words get caught in a black hole because she's screaming some other worldly shit that makes Planet Ace stop spinning.

"I can't tell you be—be—cause I *love* you!"

Our sun gets hotter.

Our moon shines brighter.

Our words look like picture perfect sunsets.

I don't long for white sand beaches in Malibu anymore because Phat feels, tastes, and sounds sweeter when she finally lets go of all the outside opinions from people down on Earth.

Love.

She loves me.

"You think I left you? How? How, when I came running back home because you're the only person who gets it! I love everything about you—even the fucked up shit. I know *you*, Ason. I know *all* of you."

She knows me.

All of me.

How can something as simple as that statement feel as good as love does?

I'd be lying if I say I know the exact words that come out my mouth after her confession, but she loves them whatever they are. I hear it in the "I know, baby" she coos out.

Afterward, we become tangled together in a way that makes it impossible for her to leave this time. Her back stretches to the ceiling while I pull her hands behind her and grip them between mine.

"Look at me," I hiss. "Look at me when I'm talking to you."

She stares at me, waiting with eyes I can't forget, no matter how much I drink.

"You're the only thing I've ever tried *so* fucking hard to do right. I just want to protect you from dumbasses like Blake and stupid reporters that think they can tell our story better than us. I wanna take care of you because I know how grimy bitches can get just because they want what's yours, and I wanna keep you because I finally found you after searching my whole life. You answered your own questions. You don't need to know it all because you know me. *Me!* You trust me enough to follow me to the end no matter what, right?"

I get my answer when she stops sobbing and starts swirling her hips against mine. There's no direction to our lovemaking. It's chaotic, boozy and as perfect as she is.

Lourdes

FOR THE FIRST time in my post-virginal life, I wake up angry for no good reason after making love.

I hate the light God shines through Ace's big ass windows. I hate the jack hammering from the construction on the high-rise next door. Nurse Shelby called to tell us that Mama still wasn't up and I hated that, too. I hate how much love makes my brain spin and I *hate* Earth because people there can't see what I see in a man that's made of gold. Now I have beef with everybody there—especially the ones closest to him that let so much avoidable shit happen to someone who didn't deserve it.

"Cree... I'm straight. Get on the plane," Ace garbles around his toothbrush from in front of the TV. "I got like ten minutes before I have to wake Phat back up and head to the hospital and you wanna spend it being weird because Pops called you on some buster ass shit 'cause I won't answer his calls."

He's the only thing I didn't wake up hating. How could I? He's shirtless with tattoos dripping from his skin, and he doesn't wake up mad at the world even when he should.

He wakes up with bright skin, a gloomy smile and begging to kiss me good morning. It all makes me want to stare at him from under the sheets for as long as he's on Earth bickering with Cree.

"No, I'm not watching *SportsCenter*." He reaches over and grabs the remote from his dresser, changing the channel right in the middle of Stephen A. Smith's sentence.

Nobody on ESPN was "speculating to hell" about the Lockwood Lion's unusual night without their star point guard, despite what Coach Williams thought. The world still went on because Lockwood wasn't UCLA or the Lakers organization.

"Pops sent you to spy on me? I thought we agreed you'd stop doing that?"

Cree rants on the other end of the phone in Spanish and my body gets tight. I don't know who has the guiltier conscience—her or Coach Williams. It seeps out in their words.

"Nah... I ain't drinking nothing. I'm good."

He was too busy inside of me to drink anything except his name from my lips this morning, and I like it that way.

"Brunch? Didn't you say you had to be back for—for ole' girl's boutique opening or something? What you need to talk to me so bad for? I told you I gotta go check on Phat's mom."

"Ole' girl" is Cheyenne and brunch is Cree's gateway to assessing Ace since I decided to come back into his life. She wants to make sure I'm taking good care of her "brother" like she does, even though she doesn't have to. She has other commitments back in Los Angeles that she won't go tend to, like a future sister-in-law that grins while they sit courtside and a real brother who has the world in his hands by default. *She's* the thing that's wrong because I think she's a taker like all the rest of the people that were on that boat with Ace.

She's the last one standing. There's nothing left for her to hold on to in Ace's life, but she won't let go and she's the biggest cause of my irrational anger because I'm being Angie's lil' wannabe daughter-in-law again. I thought the craving for her acceptance would fade, but it just gets stronger because I can't get Ace's quivering response to my confession out of my head: *"I loved you before you even knew what love was."*

Love.

I fling the sheets off my head and sit up. "Baby."

It comes out as a statement and not a question, just like all the other times, because there's nothing left to question anymore.

He turns around with the toothbrush dangling from his mouth.

"I'm hungry," I add, coaxing him down from his wide-eyed response to me popping up from the bed.

"Okay... we'll stop and get something on the wa—"

"No. I wanna meet Cree for brunch."

"But I wanna stop by the house and get Mom some clothes for when she wakes up today."

"I'll give you my key and tell you what to grab."

His eyebrows wrinkle, and he twists his lips to the side while eyeing my face. "Mhmm. Okay. I'll drop you—"

"I can Uber there."

"Uber? Gus can take you and bring you to the hospital after."

"No. I'll Uber to the hospital too."

"I don't like this." He glides to the bed, resting a knee next to me with his toothbrush dangling out of his mouth. "You need to go see your mom."

He's serious, but I am too. Mama would support my irrational anger. She'd understand that Angie didn't plan for Ace to be a lone wolf on a planet that didn't get him. Angie always meant for it to be me and Ace against the world, and she knew that even from thousands of miles away.

Cree chimes in from her side of the phone in loud Spanish. She sounds ready for us to meet and play sisters again like the world wasn't crumbling around me and she wasn't carrying around the answers to some last-minute questions I had before I sent her back to Los Angeles on that plane she keeps avoiding.

"We'll make it quick. I just need some time to myself before I go back to that hospital."

A part of it is true and makes me feel better for telling half-truths. I didn't suddenly conquer my fears of hospitals and clinics. It was just buried underneath my adrenaline yesterday.

He nods with his arms crossed while I eye his night-stand behind him where Angie waits patiently from that picture Cree thumbed the night of the gala. She wants to see what her lil' wannabe daughter-in-law will do to fix all the things for her son that she didn't have time to.

"Okay." He sighs. "But don't be long, for real. She's waking up today and I want her to see us when she does."

Of course he did. He was a mama's boy for an eternity—even for a mama he adopted as his.

Ace

CECE LOOKS LIKE MOM.

Her lips are dry and cracked like Mom's were the last time she told me she loved me, but she's not awake to rasp out those same words.

Marcus peels his red eyes open when my shoes squeak across the floor in her hospital room.

"'Bout fucking time." He shifts around in the recliner, stretching his arms to the ceiling and kicking the empty Popeyes bag next to his chair. "Tell Phat to bring me a Coke from the vending machine downstairs."

"She's at brunch."

"At brunch?" His eyes bulge. "Fuck she doing eating at a time like this?"

"The same thing you were doing." I nod to the Popeyes bag, closing the door. "The doctor came by yet?"

"Yeah, he ain't say much though."

"You didn't ask questions?"

"Man, as long as this lil' machine keeps beeping up here next to my head, I ain't got no questions for these folks."

"Hm." I scoff. "It's a lot you could've asked, but I ain't about to argue with you about it while Mom laid up like this."

"Yeah... whatever, nigga."

Brothers are as tricky as little ladies, but they don't fold the first time they're tested—they keep standing through beefs, awkward silences, and tug of wars over the ladies they love.

"You gon' sit down or what?" He rolls his eyes, tapping the heel of his boot on the floor. "Got your back to the door like a duck."

"You gon' leave or what? Thought you needed a break like the buster you are."

His eyes sink into slits and he eyes me up and down while that beeping he's so worried about fills the dead space between us. "Fuck you."

My cheeks tingle when a smirk dances across his lips. Sometimes I wonder if Marshall and Pops talked as much shit as me and Marcus did and if it was normal to feel even closer afterward.

"You survive the night?" I ask, walking to CeCe's bedside and tugging at the side of the sheet she's wrapped in.

"It wasn't like I had a choice."

"You *had* a choice. We all got choices. We don't always make the best ones, but we all have them."

"A'ight, Pastor Williams."

"That didn't come from no pastor. Mom used to tell me that shit all the time."

"That's what she told you when Coach kept putting you in all them grown-man situations?"

Brothers are as confusing as they are tricky creatures. Of all the things going on in our family, that's the only other thing he took from my dirty hospital rant yesterday, but it felt good. People never listened hard enough to understand that the most simple shit you share is the most painful most of the time.

"Yeah..." I mutter. "That was one of the last few things she told me before the end."

Those days were a blur. We were enmeshed, and I didn't want to peel myself apart from her—not even when Pops hopped off his jet from LA and hauled ass to her hospital room just to wave his "husband" privilege around to the staff, demanding shit I had already taken care of.

"It really took him three days to get to her?"

"Three and a half." I snort. "Shit, not much can come between a coach and his playoff bound team, right? Not even his dying wife."

"*Fuck*, man."

"Mom said he had a point to prove to the world. He needed them to know his name was synonymous with perfection, even with a disappointment for a son and a sick wife."

Marcus grunts out an "mhm" like I smacked him in the face with the truth about his idol. It didn't feel as good as my thirteen-year-old self hoped it would. I used to dream about tarnishing dudes' favorite player.

"You know, I used to be kind of jealous of you," he says, leaning on the side of CeCe's bed, staring at her cracked lips. "I was so little when Marshall died that just the thought of you being able to call out for your Pops and him being alive to answer would get me tight. I'd read all his articles and see the pictures of you and him and I used to wonder how it felt for you to not have to talk to your daddy in your head all the time."

"You wanna know how it feels?" I laugh to myself. "It feels like I can't breathe sometimes—like I'm a puppet that only exists for him to control in his perfect world. Phat always joking that I live on another planet and I never realized how true it was until I met her. It's the only place where I can just breathe without the pressure. That's how it feels to talk to him."

The vital sign machine beeps louder because I know CeCe hears us. It was the same with Mom. I swore she heard my begging deep down in her shell of a body, but just like that mega-church pastor said at her funeral, her "job on Earth was done and what a good job it was." There was nothing I could say that was good enough for her to turn back from God. She never believed in keeping him waiting.

"Can you breathe now?" Marcus rasps.

I study CeCe's thin eyebrows and peaceful expression.

"Nah. I lost my breath on the way here, but I'm not trippin'. It'll come back as soon as Phat done hiding out from scary hospitals at brunch. When I see her and Mom together again, it'll come back. It always does when I'm with them."

When I look up from CeCe, he's staring at me. His eyes are different today. They're full. Fear isn't dancing along the edges of his irises anymore.

He pulls his eyes off me and grips the Popeyes bag, scooting forward in the recliner.

"Where you going?" I ask.

"Chelsea..." He holds up his phone. "She say her and her granny wanna pray for us. It sounds like you need some time with Mama anyway. Hit up Phat and tell her to hurry her ass up."

He chuckles, pushing up from the recliner and stretching his arms to the sky. "Brunch... since when she eat brunch?"

We laugh together, and he reaches out, smacking the back of my head. "I'm proud of you, you dumbass cocky ass nigga. I'm proud of you for showing up for me, for mom, and for your girl. Talking about I'm the closest thing you got to a brother—shit, I'm your *only* brother."

For a moment that breath I'd been waiting for sneaks out a little, and I'm not searching for *those words* from Pops anymore.

CHAPTER TWENTY-NINE

Lourdes

"I'm sorry about your mom." Cree tilts her head with a sad smile.

"Thanks."

After five years, my response is automatic. It hangs out on the sidelines of my brain to throw out so other people can feel better for having to address the obviously uncomfortable topic of Mama having cancer.

"I'm glad you found your side of the closet." She smiles bigger over the rim of her mimosa, tracing my neck with her eyes like she's thinking about that romantic Kibbe shit again.

Prime Selection isn't the type of lit brunch spot I scroll past on Instagram's explore page. It has the qualities of a place me and Mama would drive past in River Oaks and gawk at—skinny white stay at home moms, valet parking, and lots of luxury cars in its parking lot. It all sounds and looks as ridiculous as me having a side of a closet in a million dollar penthouse when I didn't even own a car, but I knew if I asked for one, Ace would get it. Mama ain't tell me how scary it would be to wield that much power over a man.

I glance at the silky buff colored two piece set I slid into when Ace left. "Yeah... I found it."

It fits perfect. I didn't have to do anything but comb my fingers through my braids after I put it on. I guess that's what Ace intended when he picked it out and hung it on "my side of the closet." I had a lot of stuff there I didn't know about—purses, shoes, and heavy winter coats, even though he says it never gets cold in Texas. It's a bunch of shit I imagine him buying when he's running from that candy addiction.

I clear my throat, searching for the most neutral words to add. "It was a lot of stuff there."

"Oh yeah. It was a mess before. I love my bro, but he can't organize for shit. He had your sneakers still in the boxes. Hiding Chanels from the world is blasphemous."

I raise my eyebrows. "Is it?"

She laughs hard and then takes another slurp of her drink. "You know, that's my favorite thing about you. Bitches back home be so fake and would've just agreed, but you always keep it a hundred."

Her accent jumbles up some words, and I even hear Ace in her. It resurrects more of the irrational anger I thought I left in my Uber. I can't see her as the girl grinning on Ace's arm at Pittman Academy's prom while searching for Willow Smith or the girl dressing me for my first gala while fawning over my body. I just see her on that boat with Cheyenne and the other takers.

"Does your sister Cheyenne keep it a hundred, too?"

She chokes, pinching her eyebrows together. "Excuse me?"

"Cheyenne. She's your sister-in-law, right? Or Javier got cold feet and decided not to propose?"

I don't want to talk about Chanel sneakers or my side of Ace's closet. There wasn't enough time for it. Especially not when she'd already wasted two years of Ace's life by being an inadvertent taker.

"I—I don't think we should talk about that," she stutters, eyeing the crowded restaurant like Ace would pounce on us from the fake ivy hanging from the ceiling.

"*That?*"

"I mean them."

"No, you were right the first time." I swallow my nerves. "I wanna talk about that night on the boat."

"Well, I don't." She looks down. "You look at the menu yet?"

It's the first crack in her nice facade. It ripples across her face as she picks up the heavy menu off the table. I don't bother picking up mine because I didn't plan to stay long enough to eat, no matter how many times Ace reminded me it was the most important thing for me to accomplish today. This isn't that type of girls' day out. Not when Mama was still laying in the hospital and a part of Ace was still dead inside. This needs to be quick.

"I don't have an appetite."

She rolls her eyes. "I make you lose your appetite or something?"

"Only when you're not keeping shit a hundred like you claim to like."

Cree is a lot like Brandy—confident that I'll bend to her wants and sure enough that I won't have the balls to confront her about the slick things she says, but something's different with me now. It didn't happen to me overnight, but it happened little by little, just like that bandaid I told Ace about.

She huffs and slams the menu shut. "Did one of those dumbass reporters contact you to ask questions about something that's dead and over with? Where's this coming from?"

I could tell her it comes from falling in love, from seeing your Mama hot and almost lifeless on her bedroom floor, from seeing the boy you wanted to crawl into torture himself every day for something he knows he didn't do deep in his gut.

"How do you do it?" I ask as our waiter strolls up, pushing his sleeves up.

"You guys ready?"

Cree opens her mouth, holding a finger up, but I stop them both.

"No, come back. We're still deciding."

The waiter tilts his thin top lip up and shrugs while Cree glares at me.

"As you wish," he says. "I'll be back to check in on you two."

"Really? I ain't ate since last night."

I shrug. "You can eat when we're done."

She *really* hates that response. Her shoulders bunch up to her ears and the off the shoulder blouse she's wearing falls down her milky shoulder.

"Done with what? You invited yourself here to ambush me about something you don't even know nothing about."

"You invited me."

"I invited *Ason*."

"Oh, you ain't know we was the same?"

Sometimes I wish we exist in the same body so I can

remember the things he can't and remind him he's still one of one, no matter who lied on him.

Cree laughs so loud the party next to us looks over the rims of their glasses at us. They eye our little round table shoved in the corner next to the kitchen.

"Please, just a month ago you were damn near convulsing at the thought of me insinuating y'all was together. Now you got an article on TMZ Sports, new clothes, and thirty thousand Twitter followers and you suddenly, Mrs. Williams. Girl, please." She flings her limp wrist. "Clout really be having you bitches geeked up."

Now she's nasty. There's no more nice left in her, but I don't care.

I laugh too, pushing the menu as far away from me as it can go. "I'm gon' pretend like you ain't talking out the side of your neck right now because I know how much Ace likes you."

"Yeah, *whatever*."

"Answer my question."

"What goddamn question?

"I asked 'how you do it?'"

"Do what, Lourdes?" she frowns, shaking her leg so hard that the table follows its up and down motion.

"How you keep them all separate—Ace, Javier, and Cheyenne? I saw you with her on the jumbotron at the game after you left my clothes at his place."

"I lie! Are you satisfied? I lie to them. If they knew that I was still friends with Ace, how would it look?"

The truth of how she feels is in the way she arranges her words. It's the tiny things that Ace and Angie have taught me to pay attention to because people never spell things out. I have to read between their words and actions.

"They think I have some high paying client here, but

really it's Ace. I—I can't hop on the 105 and race to his condo to check on him or—or pick him up from the bathroom floor after a bad night anymore. I had to get on a fucking plane to come meet this girl who he said would take care of him just as good as I do because he says she looks like the girl of his dreams... and has the same name his Mom was obsessed with."

Her eyes are wild and big and angry like I asked for her firstborn, but I guess it must have been exhausting stretching herself between so many lives and then having to explain it all.

"When she died, he fell apart and wasn't nobody there to put him back together but me. I couldn't leave him. He was too fragile, but I couldn't leave Cheyenne either. She said it happened and who was I to challenge it? I couldn't blame or shame her. My brother loves her and I have to respect that."

The last of her words sound like a mantra somebody drilled into her head over and over. It doesn't even sound like it ever came from her brain but from somebody else's and she has to keep reminding herself that Cheyenne deserves that respect.

"What happened that night, Cree?"

"I don't know. I wasn't in that cabin with them," she hisses back.

"I'm asking *you* what *you* remember from that night."

Tears fill her eyes and for the first time since I woke up, I have an "oh shit" moment. I'm messing in estranged relationships, police investigations, and opening doors people want to keep closed, but I can see the weariness on her shoulders that there's one door she's been dying to open—she just never had anyone nudge her toward it.

"He's always getting on to me, telling me how I should

be nice to you," I mutter. "I never got it until now because I was confused and I still am. I just wanna make sense of all this for him... and especially for Angie."

I owe it to her and all the mothers like her who would never be able to do something so important.

The tears stream down her face and she looks over at the nosy party next to us, studying them like they did us.

"Sometimes I still dream about that day." She swipes at her face. "Aunt Angie sick in Ace's cabin all day while he's getting fucked up because Uncle Ason still hadn't shown up. Javi trying to keep Chey's attention on him and not on Ace."

Her eyes dart back over to me. "It was always like that —always."

I swallow the details of that night without asking which part she's referring to. Somehow, I know she's talking about all of it.

"What else do you remember?"

She narrows her eyes and then looks away again. "I remember Ace disappearing for hella long, but nobody noticing except me because everybody was wasted by then. I was too, but I told you Ace was fragile—even before Aunt Angie died, he was. I remember running up, down, all around that boat looking for him until somebody told me they saw him wandering over to the promenade."

"Was Cheyenne there with him?"

"No," she chokes out. "No, she wasn't."

"Tell me what you saw."

"Phat...no. I—I don't think—"

"Tell me." I reach over and grab her hand like Granny does mine when she wants to feel what I'm feeling.

It's hot and moist with sweat that sticks to mine, but I squeeze it anyway. I squeeze it hard until she spills the rest.

"Ace was dangling off the side of the boat with Dough holding him up by his waist. Sometimes I question myself and whether what I saw was real because I know it's no way that Ace would leave us like that—especially not with Aunt Angie so sick, but he was there with the wind whipping his shirt around talking to Dough like his body wasn't halfway off that ship. Our brains are real funny, you know?" I squeeze her hand again, losing myself in the blue of her eyes. "I was for sure it was an accident, or—or just him playing around until I watched the Grammy's this year and saw Dough up there with the same look on his face, talking about that day like it hurt him just as bad as it hurt me to find them like that. He ain't come out and say *it* though—it's like we're all waiting on Ace to say it. To tell it in his own words."

I think I see Ace, Dough, and that boat swirling in her eyes. The warmth from her hands makes me feel like I'm there in Malibu, swallowing the same air as him while he tries to find me over the side of that boat.

"He told you, didn't he?" she mutters.

I can't answer because I'm too far gone now—too in love with a man that's impossible to hate. I'm supposed to keep our secrets close to my heart—even the painful ones he admits while diving inside me.

A speck of wetness falls against my blouse and sinks into the fabric.

I pinch my eyes together, trying to shake the reminders of his voice out of my head and finish what I started. "And what happened after that?"

She sucks in a deep breath and pulls her hand back. "Dough performed again. He performed for a boat full of fucked up college kids while I brought Ace to his cabin and put him in bed with Aunt Angie. The next morning, Uncle Ason showed up, and we all left."

"Cheyenne too?"

She nods and my irrational anger comes crawling back.

"So, when did it happen?"

"When did what happen?"

"When did he rape her?"

Her mouth hangs open, and I get it. The more I learn about that night, the less cautious I need to be. It's just a big game of *Blue's Clues* with people who had a thousand different versions of what happened on a night that changed Ace's life and the situation isn't delicate anymore. I promised him an hour, and we were going on two while Mama might've been prying her eyes open like he promised Marcus.

"I don't know, okay? I wasn't with her all night—or him. I didn't even hear about it until two days later when it hit the news. That's how we all found out. Even Javi. When she left the boat the next morning, I didn't see anything different about her, but that doesn't matter a'ight? People try to act normal when things like that happen. There's shock...trauma—"

"Cree... fuck all of this politically correct bullshit. You look me in my face and tell me if her and Ace were in the same room, which way would your heart beat—with her or with him? Look me in my face and tell me Angie raised a man that would do that. Tell me if a man who gives so much of himself to people he cares about would ever do such an ugly thing."

"I..." she breathes out.

"Call her," I urge, leaning forward. "Call Cheyenne."

"Are you fucking crazy?"

"I am. Call *her*."

Irrational anger makes me crazy and impulsive and unstable. It makes me reach across the table and grab her phone so I can go back to Mama and Ace.

I shove it toward her face. "Do it."

THE NOSY PARTY that sat next to us inside Prime Selection keeps staring when we stumble onto an empty curb outside. The oldest one twists her neck and leans back into her chair to look at us like Cree didn't slap a hundred-dollar bill on the table to cover the one mimosa she ordered.

Cree eyes my phone, hanging out of my hand. "Are you going to record this?"

"Yeah."

"That's illegal."

I shrug, staring at the blank voice memo. Legalities were the least of my worries.

Cree rolls her eyes and digs through her purse. She pulls out a joint and lights up like she needs to be high to gain the courage to do something she should've done a long time ago. I don't need to consume anything because God and Angie settled my twisting insides.

When she unlocks her phone, I learn everything there is to know about her and Cheyenne's relationship. She's saved as "Cheyenne Smith" and she lives in Cree's contact list, not her recents, despite them sitting courtside together just a few nights ago.

As soon as the phone rings, we shove our heads together and I hold my phone up to catch whatever comes out of their mouths.

"Cree?"

The first time I hear her voice is worse than the first time I saw her. She sounds like privilege.

"Hey Chey...how're things going?" Cree sucks a toke of her joint.

"The grand opening is in like three hours and I'm going to flip my shit if Javi gets an attitude with me one more time. Seriously. How hard is it to pick up the catering from Catch? So many influencers are coming. I'm literally losing my shit, babe. Where are you anyway?"

We look stupid sitting on the curb with our faces smashed together and my phone up to hers, but I don't care.

I nudge Cree in her side and she bucks at me while rolling her tortured blue eyes.

She chokes on a cloud of smoke. "I'm—I'm in Houston."

"Houston? What the fuck is in Houston? Are you still fucking that mysterious high paying client?"

Cree takes another long toke and then looks up at the sky. "Ace. Ace is in Houston."

She blurts it in one big gust.

The only sounds left between them are the static on the phone and the valet staff shouting in Spanish. We move closer together, pushing our heads into each other until our foreheads touch. Cree closes her eyes.

"Oh." Cheyenne huffs. "You're fucking Ace?"

"What? No!" Cree shakes her head.

"Oh, I was for sure going to say he's so not your type. How is he, anyway? I saw him on Insta with his new girlfriend."

She laughs at the last part. Her voice is relaxed and easygoing with that privilege still controlling everything she says. She talks like she didn't destroy his life.

"He—he..." Cree stumbles over her words until I nudge her again. "Wait, you're not mad that I'm here?"

"Babe, he's old news. It's been two years."

I'm not Tarana Burke, Cheyenne, or an expert at how victims should respond in these delicate situations, but I'm a human in love that knows when something's not right.

"Old news? What do you mean?"

"I mean like nobody's checking for him anymore. He plays for a freaking no-name school, he's punching agents, and dating some basic ass black girl who probably can't afford the lipo she desperately needs."

She's talking like a scorned ex-lover now.

Cree tries to lean away like a good big sister would, but I want to hear it all before the world does. I want to be the first to know about something for once. I want to know it all before Blake Harvey can use it for his own gain, before Coach Williams can use it to justify his disappointment in his own son. I want to digest it before I can play it for Ace.

Cree blows out deep breaths with her joint dangling between her fingers. "Are you faded?"

"I'm completely sober thanks to Mom. She's here, hovering as usual. Anyway, why didn't you tell me you were down there? I would've taken you off the guest list."

"I didn't realize you'd be so okay with me being here, considering what happened."

"What happened is water under the bridge. My curiosity was killed already, alright? Unfortunately, the rumors about him were true."

"Rumors?"

"C'mon, sissy. Don't act like you didn't use to hear about him only fucking the ghetto bitches from Crenshaw and the mini Michelle Obamas that hung out in the BBRC on campus. He's sexy, but a complete asshole that likes to remind you of what and who he likes. One time he told me his dick only belonged to black girls."

She laughs even harder at that, as if it were hilarious that Ace could only be interested in black girls. She laughs like her privilege has turned plenty of boys like Ace away from us.

Her words are hard to swallow. I want to call up Blake and ask him if this is how the most protected species in America thinks. Are they always so shallow, ignorant, and casually racist? Would they always prey on Ace and try to climb their way into our world? Would they always want to destroy us?

"Chey..." Cree breathes hard, tangling her hand in mine and bringing her phone closer to mine. "I want to ask you something, but I want your permission before I ask."

"You're being weird."

"I'm—I'm not trying to be. I just had a mimosa on an empty stomach, so I'm a lil'... queasy."

"Makes sense," she chirps. "Stop being lame and ask me. You know I'm like a complete open book, even though Mom and Javi hate it."

"Right..." Cree nods, squeezing my hand. "I—I—did something really happen between you and Ace at his party in Malibu that summer?"

The wait feels long and drawn out because I'm in my head trying to digest all of what she's shared so easily about herself and the Ace I didn't know before.

"So I'm for sure not supposed to talk about this because his crazy ass lawyer made me sign an NDA when he found out I was going to give an exclusive to Gayle King, but you're Javi's sister so..." She sighs. "Between me and you —*nope*."

She says it like we're asking her to borrow her favorite lip gloss.

"Me and Javi were still in that weird talking phase, so I

wanted to shoot my shot at Ace one last time, but your brother's pretty persistent. He caught me sneaking out of Ace's cabin that night in Malibu. It wasn't shit in there, but his mom sleeping, so I left. How else was I supposed to get out of trouble when Javi kept questioning me about it?" She giggles. "I heard Ace was loaded as usual and climbing off the side of the boat that night anyway, but you know how rumors are—won't know the truth unless you get it from the source. You should seriously ask him about that."

CHAPTER THIRTY

Lourdes

I don't feel like I'm racing across town with a pot of gold in my purse. I feel like I'm carrying a bomb across the city in the backseat of my Uber with Cheyenne's voice inside it.

The tears staining Cree's face as my Uber pulled up to the curb outside of Prime Selection are a perfect representation of how my insides feel. I don't think Cheyenne's confession was as satisfying as we thought it would be. The only satisfying sound I remember accepting was Cree's "hermana" when she told me she loved me after Cheyenne giggled her way off the phone. I believe her emotions behind the word now. We're the sisters Ace wanted us to be, and she trusts me to take care of him *for real*.

I'm not angry for no good reason anymore. I'm not happy that Cheyenne is a liar. I'm empty because I don't know how to tell a man I love I don't know why a girl ruined his life one summer night for her own selfish reasons.

This bomb makes my purse heavy.

I want to play the recording out loud for myself and my Uber driver, Ahmad, to dissect, but he's not Chelsea. He's a stranger that doesn't know any of us, but he's a black man and maybe he's come across a Cheyenne who thinks he's disposable in her privileged life. Maybe he's got a Mama like me and Ace's or friends like Chelsea and Bryson, who can't see beyond their freshman year of college. Maybe he's got a Coach Williams as a daddy who can't give him the love he's always crying for.

"Miss?" he asks, looking at me in the rearview mirror. "You going to Methodist?"

"Uh, yeah." I nod, curling my fingers around my purse strap. "You can just pull right there."

I gesture to the front entrance that me and Ace floated out of last night. It feels like it was years ago and I feel like a different person now. Instead of playing the recording for Ahmad, I grip my purse under my shoulder and climb out of his Kia.

The elevator ride to the tenth floor is blurry with random people in scrubs and long-faced families. I don't remember where Mama's room is, but my voice is too raw after two days of swallowing bombshells to stop and ask for directions.

My sandals slap against the floors while I pick up my pace, floating through a sea of doors that look the same. Room A103, A104, A105. None of them have familiar faces sitting inside when I peek through the windows. I roam through three different units on two different floors before I recognize Nurse Shelby's box braids hanging down her back while she sits behind a computer in the nurse's station in Unit 4B.

Suddenly, I remember that room B102 is Mama's. It's

next to the bulletin board with all the pictures of the nurses stapled to it—all the "Shining Stars of Unit 4B." It's the only room in the back corner of the unit and the front of her door should've been empty but there's a broad backed man standing there. When he turns his head, I get a glimpse of his caramel face. The familiarity makes me walk up to him.

"Coach Williams?" I ask.

He whips his head around like he's caught, and I follow his line of vision through the window.

Ace is there with Mama, and Marcus is gone. His lips are moving, but Mama doesn't open her eyes like he promised Marcus. No miracles happened while I argued with Cree at brunch. Somebody even folded the clothes he was sure Mama would put on and sat them on the edge of her bed. He leans over the side of it like he does at the house —resting his chin on his hand like Mama is awake to answer the questions he's always throwing at her about me.

Coach Williams stares through the window again and right when he opens his mouth, Nurse Shelby's country voice cuts him off.

"Hey... there you are." She smiles, twisting toward me with another glint in her eyes. "I hope you don't mind. I told Mr. Williams he could go on in. Somebody added him to the visitor list, but he says he's been waiting for you."

"But it's three of us."

"No worries at all, doll."

She's even nicer today than she was yesterday, but I think our family drama is Unit 4B's entertainment this week. They got eye-candy, sports legends, jealous girl-friends, weird family dynamics, and two people playing tug of war with each other's hearts.

"Thanks."

She nods and twists back to the nurse's station, where

she sits behind a different computer. This one faces Mama's room.

"It's been a long time since I saw CeCe." Coach Williams smiles. "I ain't wanna just barge in there, you know?"

It's the first time me and him are face to face after the mess bubbling between me, him, and Ace. It's all unexpected—her name flowing out of his mouth again and him studying Mama and Ace through her room door's tiny square window. Even his smile is unexpected. It's full but sad. All the unexpectedness is on point for the *Twilight Zone* type of day I'm having that started with my angry for no good reason feelings.

"Last time I saw her was at Marshall's repast. I never saw a grieving lady cook a pot of greens with a baby on her hip until that day. I remember wishing I was as strong as she was. I couldn't even get out of bed to get Ace to his grandmother's that morning while Angie helped at the viewing."

"What took you so long to come see her? We been in the same house since that repast."

He swipes at his bald head. I see Ace in him for the first time—in his muscular shoulders and chiseled jawline. They both stand like they've seen all there is to see in the world.

"By now, I think you know that I'm not like Junior. We're two different men."

Ace runs his fingers on the back of Mama's hand and Coach Williams lays his against the door.

"Junior is the type of man that can walk through fire and won't ever let you know he's burned. You just realize he's been scathed in other ways—in his words and eyes. He can take a lot and survive. In the end, he's always the last one standing though."

"And why would you think Marshall wouldn't want me to end up with a man like that?"

He looks at the floor and runs his hands down his sweats. "Because me and Marshall talked about you so much when you were in CeCe's stomach—about his hopes, dreams, and plans for you. He wanted you to find a man with the same heart as his."

I try to picture Marshall with his broad nose and almond eyes, holding the world in his hands just like Ace does every day. I see his face without Mama helping me remember his features for the first time. The thought of him makes that bomb in my purse a little lighter.

"They have the same heart. I can feel it," I mutter. "You just can't see it because you think Ace is so strong that he can go at life all alone—even without you."

"You think that?"

"Blake Harvey called him a lone wolf and I guess that's what he was when Angie died. A sad, lone wolf. Men who can walk through fire still need someone waiting on the other side though."

Coach Williams' sad, full smile falls like it's the first time he's ever thought of Ace's lonely existence back in Los Angeles. "That's all I was trying to give him here—a family."

"He needs you too, every day. Every single day. Not just us. There's a lot of no-good people out there that love lone wolfs."

I reach out and squeeze his forearm before reaching around him and pushing open the door. "You don't have to say everything right. That's the worst thing you can do. Just work at it little by little. Angie knows your heart."

When my voice carries across the room, Ace peels his

head from his hand. There's relief in his eyes, even with Coach Williams trailing behind me.

"You said an hour," he rasps. "You just missed Andy. He came to check in on her even though she's not on his service anymore. He says he talked to her new attending and they might increase the dosage of her antibiotics."

The bomb in my purse ticks while the machines around Mama beep and Ace and Coach Williams avoid eye contact. It's like two strangers meeting for the first time.

"Okay." I smile, walking toward him and scraping my fingers through his hair. "It's okay. I won't leave again today."

"Junior?" Coach Williams booms from behind me. "You mind if I sit? I wanted to check on you guys."

When their eyes touch, it's a sad connection. Their roles are reversed for once. Ace is the coach in our family—the provider, the pilot, the stable one. He keeps us in line. Even Marcus.

"I figured you'd be with the boys," he replies.

"I told them we had a family emergency." Coach Williams slaps his thighs and eases into the extra chair somebody dragged into the room even though Ace never agreed he could.

Ace scoffs while I squeeze between him and Mama's bed, easing on his lap. He grabs me and the stress he's been holding is in his stiff arms.

"Since when do you believe in family emergencies?" he asks.

"Since Lourdes told me she needed you and you went running out of that gym. I ain't been able to sleep since."

The silence between them is loud.

Sitting between an angry father and son and a sick Mama while holding a bomb in my purse is worse than walking through that fire me and Coach Williams talked about.

"Is that why you came?" Ace asks. "To ease the guilt?"

"Guilt is a heavy word, don't you think?"

"Nah, it's never too heavy for a man like you."

"I didn't come here to argue."

"Then what you here for? To surprise an old friend after running from her for almost a lifetime because she reminds you of everything you abandoned?"

I glance over at Coach Williams, raising my eyebrows as high as they'll go to remind him of the little by little I mentioned. I forgot to tell him that Ace and Mama got as thick as thieves during his absence and today might not be a day for little by little miracles.

"I came to support you... and your friends... and my friend."

"Well, I don't need your support anymore. When I needed it, you didn't have any to give if it didn't feed into your agenda."

"If I didn't support you, you'd be sitting in somebody's cell. Don't sit up here and tell me I don't support you when you know I'd give my last for you."

"How many times I have to tell you I don't want your last, a'ight? Go give it to Javier and all them other boys you be so proud of for *just waking up*."

"Don't do this to me, Junior. Don't do this." Coach Williams shakes his head and that bomb in my purse ticks louder.

"They never had to wake up to the world hating them, but you so goddamn proud of them because they didn't come from you and didn't tarnish your perfect legacy."

"That's not why I tell them that, and you know it."

"Fuck this—"

"Stop," I blurt, gripping Ace's face between my hands. "Stop it."

The loud silence comes back, but I'm sick of it. I'm sick of *it* and the bomb in my purse.

"I need—I need to show you something, Ason," I stutter, letting go of him and yanking the zipper on my purse.

"What's wrong?" he gasps out, forgetting about Coach Williams and all the shit that keeps them apart.

His voice makes me move quicker because I have all of his attention, even through arguments and hospital chaos. It's no wonder I want to crawl into his body.

My hands shake as I pull out my phone and my fingers slip across the screen while I pull up half the reason for their arguing.

Their strained relationship existed before Cheyenne, but she magnified the cracks in it, making them spread further and further until there was no way they could ever be put back together. But I'm hopeful, so I press play.

There's shame, grief, anger, fear and sadness in Ace's eyes when Cheyenne's nasally voice blasts throughout Mama's room.

His fingers dig into my side. "What's this? Did Cree send something to yo—"

"'Houston? What the fuck is in Houston? Are you still fucking that mysterious high paying client?'"

He reaches over me to grab the phone, but I dig my nails into his hand and yank it into my stomach.

"'How is he, anyway? I saw him on Insta with his new girlfriend.'"

"Lourdes, what did you do?" Ace's chest pushes into my back while he breathes out harsh breaths that make Coach Williams push forward in his seat.

I finally see the finished product of Cheyenne's ruining.

His eyes get big and wild the more she talks. Now I know why it took him so long to even say her name out loud. Her existence hurts him so bad.

"'I mean, like nobody's checking for him anymore. He plays for a freaking no-name school, he's punching agents, and dating some basic ass black girl who probably can't afford the lipo she desperately needs.'"

"Turn it off right now." We wrestle over his hand while Coach Williams holds his up to us. "What if Mom wakes up and hears this?"

"Let it play, Junior. Let it play. Let it play."

He chants the words with deep breaths between them.

"'I'm completely sober thanks to Mom...'"

She keeps talking and everything I didn't feel in that parking lot with Cree comes hurling through my body while Ace holds me around my middle, bracing himself for another fucked up thing to happen to him on Earth.

"'So I'm for sure not supposed to talk about this because his crazy ass lawyer made me sign an NDA when he found out I was going to give an exclusive to Gayle King, but you're Javi's sister so...'"

"'He caught me sneaking out of Ace's cabin that night in Malibu. It wasn't shit in there but his mom sleeping, so I left. How else was I supposed to get out of trouble when Javi kept questioning me about it?'"

Now, her confession feels like it should. My chest fills with warmth when Coach Williams charges out of his chair toward us. When Mama wakes up, I can tell her that for the first time in my life I saw two grown men cry—deep, soul-stirring, heart mending cries that shake a hospital room.

Tears fill my eyes and Coach Williams wraps his blurry arm around Ace's neck. I want to shake Ace and tell him how fucking ridiculous it is for us to wallow over Coach

Williams' pride in other boys when the look on his face is worth more than any "I'm proud of you" will ever be. It's pure like he's meeting Ace for the first time since he came out of Angie's womb.

Ace pulls his face from my chest. His tears stain my buff colored shirt. I swipe at them just like I did on his balcony and fight against those deep, heart-pounding, gasping for air fucked up panic attacks that make me forget about my own tears.

The air in the room gets still again, and he sounds exposed, like he did last night when he told me he loved me.

"I'm sorry," he gasps.

And he's still apologizing for a thing that never happened. A pretend crime that came from a girl's imagination.

I want to crawl into him again, but I can't, so I settle for his lips, pressing mine into them as hard as I can while he trembles underneath me.

"That's enough," I coo into his mouth. "No more torturing yourself. We finally made it to the end."

"So what happens now?" he asks, red-faced and raw, with Coach Williams hanging onto his neck.

I don't have the answer or know the right thing to say, so I follow Mama's advice.

"You go back down to Earth for a lil' while. There's some people that miss you there, but don't stay too long. I need my pilot back at home because that's what happens at the end of it all, right? You come home—you come home to the only Lourdes you're supposed to love, just like Angie wanted."

I was wrong about little by little miracles. Today is a day for them, but they're not little. They're strong, like Coach Williams' arms around Ace's neck. They're heavy, like my lips on his face. They're as big as Ace's heart that keeps holding onto Angie, and they're loud, like the raspy breaths that cut through Ace and Coach Williams' sobs.

We all pull away, looking at each other's mouths, but the raspy breaths keep coming until I glance over at Mama's wide brown eyes staring at us.

"Mama?" I squeak out.

CHAPTER THIRTY-ONE

Ace

Six Months Later

Reporter's voices sound worse when I'm asleep.

"This is a Cinderella story for history books. Lockwood State is the lowest seeded team *and* first HBCU to dance their way all the way through the Sweet Sixteen, Elite Eight, and in true Cinderella fashion, they've made it back home to the Final Four here in Houston. Although basketball is a team sport, a lot of folks might argue that our hometown team has a special point guard to thank for their success. We got the rare chance to talk to a few sources close to Ace Williams better known as *The Kid,* depending on who you ask. And get this, he's going to be late to the Lions' open practice before tonight's semifinal game because his girlfriend's mother has her last round of chemotherapy and he *is* amped—"

"History breaking! Record setting! Awe-inspiring! The world wants to know—is *The Kid* finally headed to the draft after his record-breaking performance in this year's big dance? Listen to what his dad had to say in our exclusive—"

"Shannon, have you ever seen anything like this? The kid's in the middle of a defamation trial while playing the best basketball of his life. He's flying back and forth from LA to whatever city the team's playing in. This makes me question AW's decision making as a father to a kid as troubled as Ace. He's still grieving and rehabbing his tarnished reputation. There are a *lot* of things coming to light in this trial—"

It's like a never-ending loop of voices floating through my dreams while I try to squeeze in five more minutes with Mom. Muffled girly voices sneak under my blanket as I squeeze my eyes tighter and fight to hang onto the cloud she's sitting on.

"How does it feel?" Chelsea asks.

It's too early for reporters, FaceTime calls, and for Chelsea to dissect her and Phat's every thought, but they don't care. They never do. And I never complain about it.

"How does what feel?"

"To see your man on TV every day."

Phat blows out a quiet strawberry. "Annoying. Sometimes I watch it on mute so I can see his face without their corny ass voices. He looks so good in 4K."

Chelsea snickers. "Granny said he looked sharp in his suit last week."

"Duh. I picked it out. Cree wanted him to wear a black pinstriped suit. Marcus ain't never wore black to court."

"*Oh-kay,* Miranda Priestly."

They giggle together and force me to peek from under the blanket.

My baby isn't a baby anymore. She wears dainty La Perla pajamas to bed and Mom's silk scarves that she found in my nightstand one day, around her braids. Thanks to Cree, she has personal shoppers at Mom's favorite places who she gossips with more than she shops from. She's met The Dream twice, likes to golf with Pops because I don't, and thinks we have to make love before every game, no matter how much shit Pops crams on my schedule.

She stares up at the TV with a mountain of pillows behind her back as if catching the six o'clock Saturday morning news is normal for a college aged girl.

"Is he gonna let you go to court with him next week since it's the last day?"

She purses her lips and rolls her eyes while shrugging. "No."

I smile.

Chelsea wants to know everything that happens in our house—even delicate things like my irrational fear of Phat being in the same building as Cheyenne.

Cheyenne's name doesn't taste bitter when I say it anymore. Instead, it feels like a swarm of butterflies fluttering through my throat and out of my mouth because Phat's granny told me that butterflies symbolized rebirth while dabbing drops of cinnamon smelling oil in the loafers I wear to court every week. Phat picked those out too and I'm not allowed to wear a different pair, no matter how much Cree begs her.

"Did you ask if you could—"

"No, and I'm not, so stop suggesting I do."

"Dang, okay. What does he think's gonna happen? You gonna jump her in the courtroom or something? Her prissy mama gon' curse you out for blowing up their spot?"

No. Something worse will happen.

"Have I ever jumped on anybody?"

"No—just Bry, but he doesn't count. He deserved it."

Chelsea snickers. "Did you see him and Paris on Insta? That's my line sister and I love her to death, but you know she's a lil'... *touched*. I tried to tell her he had a whole roster but she won't believe it. Ever since the team started winning, he thinks he's a God or something knowing good and well he be riding that bench."

Phat's cheek lifts, and she curls up on her side. "Nah... I ain't see it."

"Are you on another husband-fueled social media cleanse?"

"Maybe."

Chelsea can't wrap her hyperactive brain around the things I do to maintain Phat's sanity because the world is obsessed with us, just like Blake Harvey predicted before him and his 911 left town. There're social media fan pages dedicated to us and some just for her. They post our every move, dissect her outfits, claim me even though they don't know me, and sometimes they lie. When I decide our house is on a social media cleanse, Chelsea says I'm acting like an "overbearing husband" because Phat won't tell her she loves when I shut Planet Ace down.

"I told you, you could log into mine to lurk—"

I push my hand from underneath the blanket and grab the phone from Phat's loose grip.

"Aren't you supposed to be volunteering with your line sisters at the food bank before you meet us at the clinic?" I ask, pushing the blanket off and smiling at her braces filling up the screen.

"Dang, Phat. You could've said something." Red creeps along her cheeks. "My bad, Ace. I ain't know you were back already. How was the weather in Cali?"

She scratches at the pink scarf around her head and tries to control her wide eyes. It's the same expression she had when she caught me with my lips on Phat's outside CeCe's hospital room.

"I didn't have time to feel it. Phat don't let me."

"Hmm... I bet." She smirks.

I didn't care about the calm breeze blowing through the palm trees or hitting up Roscoe's before I hopped on Pops' jet. As soon as court let out, her voice was the first thing I wanted and got while I loosened my tie.

"Where you at, baby?" she'd ask in a low hum as if I was kicking it back in my condo there and not fighting for compensation for my damaged rep in a stuffy courtroom for five weeks.

"Well, I was just kidding, Ace. I completely support social media cleanses. You know when I was pledging—"

"Bye Chelsea." Phat's finger beats mine.

She presses on the screen and ends the call while flinging her body on top of mine.

My cologne is stitched in her pajamas and the scent from the walls at CeCe's lives in her braids. She smells better than the calm Cali breeze. My hands jump from her ass to her face and cup her cheeks while her fingers stroke my chest.

"Are you jet lagged?" she murmurs, grinning.

"Am I ever?"

"No... and that shit worries me."

She swipes a finger under my eyes and squints like she's checking to make sure she doesn't have to put her foot down somewhere in my life—with Pops, Quame, Cree, basketball, or when Mom is real heavy on my heart and I try to sneak away from home for a minute.

"You need to sleep on the plane instead of watching film."

"If I did that, I'd be cheating myself."

"Taking care of yourself is *not* cheating yourself."

"I thought we talked about what you need to worry about?"

"Here you go." She rolls her eyes and then drops her lips over mine.

"Didn't we agree no attitude before nine? It's too early for you to be mad at me. I got a lifetime to rest, kid."

She drops feather light kisses across my lips and pries my mouth open. Her tongue sneaks inside, swiping against mine even though she *still* didn't know how to kiss and hated that I wouldn't teach her how.

"You act right while I was gone yesterday?" I mutter around her tongue.

"I paid Jazmine's invoice, both mortgages, and ordered groceries for both places. I even helped Mar's aggravating ass pick his classes for the fall because this sorority is consuming Chelsea's life, just like we said it would."

We laugh together in quiet huffs while the sunlight peeks into our bedroom and settles against her face.

"I don't know if she's more obsessed with it, or Marcus. Mama said to let her have her moment, but if I have to hear her complain about learning their new stroll or how they're wearing their hair this week, I'm gon' scream."

I drag my finger down her nose. "Mom's right. Let her have her moment."

Her eyes veer off and scrape against my chest. "She has a point, you know?"

"Who? Mom?"

"No, Chelsea. People are wondering why I'm not there with you. I see it in the comments online and hear people whispering on campus like I ain't cry and beg to go with you."

She had another one of those snotty-nosed, blubbering

crying fits while I was inside of her before the trial started and now I know what Mom meant when she talked about how her heart wouldn't leave Pops no matter what happened. Phat sewed her heart to mine so tight that she even wants to experience the aftermath of Cheyenne-gate.

"It's none of their business. You don't have to prove your loyalty to a bunch of strangers. You did more than enough already."

She shifts her weight forward with her eyebrows crawling together.

Mom would hate me if I had her relive Cheyenne admitting to being a taker over and over on the stand. Quame got paid good money to make sure she'd never see the inside of that courtroom in LA.

"Yeah, but I started it and I wanna finish it."

"It's already finished."

"You ain't won yet." She slides her hands across my shoulders, kneading her fingertips into my skin. "The jury still has to decide on Monday morning."

She pulls her lips under her teeth like she always does when I come home with the weight of the courtroom on my shoulders.

"It don't matter what decision they come to," I mutter. "We know she lied."

There're some days I chant the words over and over to myself while tearing up our kitchen for all the Don Julio bottles Phat put out for recycling until she gets home and sees me—like really sees me—*for real*. Then we make love until I remember I don't need those bottles to exist anymore, but it's hard. Even after Quame's team blasted Cheyenne's confession across America, it was still hard.

"Quame says it's nothing for us to worry about," I add. "We're good."

She groans. "Is the jury all white?"

"Baby..."

"Ason..."

I press my fingers into her thighs. "Relax. You're exactly where you need to be. We planned for this. You take care of home and I take care of the rest."

She swallows and nods while I tug at her camisole. "You lead, I follow?"

"And where do I always lead us?"

She stoops down, covering my lips with hers and breathing the thousand questions into my mouth that she's been holding onto.

"Back home where it's safe," she mutters, pulling back.

I tug at the camisole and she pulls it over her head without fussing, because this is the only time we'll have to indulge in my only pregame ritual. The hour right after the six o'clock news is sacred. CeCe doesn't have any appointments scheduled. Pops can't blow me up to pick through my brain about plays, and our place is the quietest.

I fold my arms behind my head while she rolls her shorts off and slides mine down. Between my heavy blinks, she steals a Magnum from my nightstand and tears it open.

The TV hums in the background with more voices speculating about our life because Planet Ace was on another husband-fueled lockdown. No Twitter. No Insta. Just us.

I close my eyes while she rolls the condom over my dick and sinks onto me.

She's soft and warm and sometimes I wish I could live inside her.

"Home is the best place for you to be during all this. I don't want you to know what that courtroom feels like and I don't want you to hear the shit I did back when I was lost—back before I came to you. Do you hear me, baby?"

She chokes on a grunt, with her eyes rolling into the back of her head even though I can't move.

"Thanks to me, she has money for a lawyer as good as ours," I gasp out as she pulls her legs up and rocks against me. "But not for much longer, a'ight? Before you know it, it'll be your money and you'll be picking out your favorite charity for us to donate it to because we don't even need it. How that sound? Hm?"

A loud screech barrels from her gut as she nods, with tears welling along her eyelids.

I lift my hips to help her paralyzed body move. "Look at me when I'm talking to you."

The way her eyes snap back into place in their sockets makes my breath hitch in my throat. "All those people you so worried about don't even have the same problems you got. They don't know what the air tastes like from the fifty-sixth floor, they never hit a hole-in-one on the Fazio course, they won't be planning a gala for the next six months, and they for damn sure don't know how to take care of our home. So explain to me why you so worried about what they think?"

"Ason?"

"I'm listening, baby. I'm always listening."

"I—I..." she stutters out through my grinds.

"You what?"

"I—I—I *love* you."

"I know." I slap at her thigh and laugh. "Now stop letting strangers in our house."

Lourdes

NOW THAT I'M in love, I talk to Marshall more.

I don't need Mama to fill in the missing pieces of his life and I don't need to drag his backpack around to feel connected to him. I see his face in the burst of maroon in the stadium and hear him in every man that screams for Lockwood with his chest.

Today is *exactly* like the reporters said it would be— History breaking. Record setting. Awe-inspiring. An all-black team prancing around in America's big dance because Marshall's old best friend wouldn't let go of a dream Marshall didn't get to fulfill.

Our cheerleaders grin into the hundreds of cameras moving around. Their makeup looks painted on and they laid their edges perfectly for the biggest day of their cheer-leading lives. In fact, it's the biggest day for anybody who ever stepped foot on Lockwood's campus and fell in love with it. This morning Stephen A. Smith said Ace was the Lions' savior, but Ace said he was just full of shit. I didn't tell him that Marshall said the same thing in my dreams one night.

"Are you blind?" I scream, shooting up from my seat. "That was a foul! There was contact! Number two fouled him!"

Ace's lip sneaks under his teeth while he glides toward the ref. He sits his hand on the ref's shoulder while winking at me.

Even in a football sized stadium crammed with thou-sands of people screaming for him, he always finds me in my spot right behind the team's bench. Sometimes I hear Marshall laughing at the secret language me and Ace concocted, even though I don't remember how it sounds. I know he'd be happy that the one thing Ace didn't have to fight me on was basketball.

The HPE was the first place I ran to when Mama got discharged from the hospital, and it's where I'd been ever since. Coach Williams liked to joke that it was *my* house. I guess that's why I never felt all the curious eyes burning holes in the side of my face when Ace found me before and after each home game or when random visitors like Dr. Andy popped in to see Ace in his element.

Ace talks to the ref, sweeping his hand out. He pleads his case and apologizes for my outburst, while keeping his eyes on me. After he finishes, he squeezes the ref's shoulder and points toward me.

I ease back in my seat while Mama laughs, leaning into my side. "I think I know what that means."

She's weak and woozy, and me and Marcus argued while loading her wheelchair into the back of Gus' truck, but she promised Ace she wouldn't miss this day.

"Yeah, it means she better sit her ass down before they kick us out," Marcus mutters around a mouthful of popcorn.

The refs huddle at the score table and watch the replay. Afterward, they decide what I'd already been trying to tell them—there was absolute *unequivocal* contact.

Ace claps, walking to the free throw line.

"They can't kick us out." Chelsea grins in her pink sweatshirt, leaning over Marcus. "We're with Coach Williams."

"Shittt." Marcus snorts. "These folks don't care who we with. She better shut up. I can't miss my bro win his second national champion—"

"Take your time, baby!" I yell, as Ace swipes his hand across the back of his shorts and looks at the ceiling like he's talking to Angie.

I hope he's telling her how we almost didn't make it to his last game this morning, but she probably already knows. Mama ringing the bell at her last chemo appointment, their semifinal win, and his defamation victory shook him worse than any hangover ever had and in some ways I'm still Angie's lil' wannabe daughter-in-law so I didn't know how to pull him out of the spontaneous funk that all of those good things caused.

We made love as soon as he got in from the airport and I picked out the charity I wanted to donate Cheyenne's money to while he went to their last open practice. Afterward, he came home and slept for the first time in a long time. While he slept, I cleaned up, attempted to cook dinner, and then tried to shake him awake, but he still wouldn't get up. Mama told me to give him time, so I gave it to him until I had to pull him out of bed to play the second most important game of his life.

"Come on, Ason." Mama rests her head against my shoulder and brushes her sparse hairs against my skin while the stadium quiets.

Ace takes a deep breath and bounces the ball like there's not two minutes left on the clock and they weren't two points away from being tied up with Gonzaga in the second half. I asked him once what he thought about at that free throw line.

"Nothing," he said. *"Pops always told me that Marshall said the best thing to think about at the free throw line is absolutely nothing. So I don't."*

Today's different though. He's thinking and talking to Angie at the free throw line, despite Marshall's advice.

He pulls up with his eyebrows furrowed and then takes the shot. The ball goes in like we expect. His spontaneous funk makes his shoulders droop after he makes another and ties the game up, but it's like I'm the only one in the crowd that can see the weariness on his face.

The rest of the team takes turns slapping his back and then they get back at it, but Ace moves slower this time.

"He's tired," I mutter, glancing at the clock while he brings the ball down the court.

"He good," Marcus replies, leaning forward. "Let him cook. We talked this morning before he left LA. He said he was good."

The funny thing about love is that I can even translate the most basic ass words Ace says. After hearing that white jury remind the world that Cheyenne was a liar, there's no way he was just *good*. Good meant he was tired of carrying the world on his shoulders and now he's tired of carrying it in his hands.

"He's tired, Mar. I see it."

It was in his sighs while he slept and in his kisses when I pulled him out of his sleep, but he's so good at what he does, the ball still looks like the world in his hands on the court.

He darts in and around the defense with ease, gliding into the paint and bringing the ball to the hole while drawing another foul. Afterward, he lands on the court with a nasty thud.

Coach Williams squats and squints at him.

"And one! And one!" Marcus yells, shooting up from his seat. "That's my nigga! That's my brother!"

The stadium screams louder, even though he doesn't hop back up. LaQuan hovers above him and yanks him from the court.

I try to read their lips but I can't make out their words. They talk fast, with sweat sliding down their frowning faces.

"What the hell they talking about?" Marcus groans.

When they finish, Ace goes to the free throw line and looks at me again, but I don't have time to read his eyes before Bryson's curly head darts between us.

"What the fu—Bry! Move!"

He keeps his head in front of me and eases from the bench, so I scoot forward in my seat. I crane my head over Marcus and catch the ball swishing through the hoop.

Ace and LaQuan keep going at it as if there isn't just one minute left in the game. They stop long enough for Ace to gain control of the ball and call a play, but their discord trips them up and Gonzaga's center snatches the world from Ace's hands. He barrels down the court with it and slams the ball into the hoop. The dunk shakes the stadium and our three point lead dwindles to one.

"Oh shoot. Oh shoot," Chelsea chants, grabbing at Marcus' hand.

"Time out! Time out!" Marcus yells.

Ace nods his head from the court and signals a T to the ref. It's our last timeout and everybody's anxious body heat engulfs me.

The team huddles together while the sea of maroon keeps the energy high in the stands. I block out their screams and scoot to the edge of my seat, trying my hardest to hear what's coming out of Ace's mouth in the middle of that huddle.

When he mushes Bryson underneath his armpit, my heart stutters. It feels like that day I try to forget sometimes and I can hear him telling Bryson, "to do him another solid" because he was tired and they were brothers whether he liked it or not just like he told him outside Mama's hospital room one day.

"What the fuck is he doing?" Marcus mutters, hooking his arms behind his head. "What the fuck is he doing?"

He chants to himself while Ace shakes Bryson by the neck and talks in his ear.

At the end of their timeout, it's clear what he's doing.

"Oh no, please don't tell me they're going to put him in. Oh, no." Chelsea breathes hard. "Phat, say something."

I don't have to say anything because the crowd's confused grumbling does it for me. Everybody wants to know why Coach Williams would put the starting point guard in who hadn't started since the first game of the season. Bryson averaged five points and ten minutes a game off the bench.

His body stays stiff as Ace walks him to the edge of the court, chirping in his ear.

"*Phat,*" Chelsea hisses again.

Mama snaps her fingers at her and shakes her head. "He knows what he's doing."

I don't know if she's talking about Ace or Bryson, but it doesn't matter, because Bryson's already on the court. At least this time he tucked his jersey in and tied his laces.

Ace squats on the sidelines and Mama reaches out and grips my wrist.

Bryson's eyes get big as soon as he looks out into the stadium and sees a million eyes staring back at him. Ace slaps at the court and shouts until he gets Bryson's attention. He digs his finger into his temple.

"Pick your head up," he mouths.

Bryson nods with his mouth hanging open.

"Come on, Bry," Marcus says. "Don't hide from it today. You got this shit in the bag."

The first ten seconds is the longest because Bryson is cold from spending an entire season riding the bench and complaining to me about it. He stumbles, turns the ball over, plays some of the most lackluster defense that makes

Marcus scream into his fist, but none of it makes Ace shut up from the sidelines—not even when Gonzaga makes another two pointer and steals our lead.

"Pick your head up, Bry!" He claps. "Pick your fuckin' head up, brodie!"

I shoot from my seat, clasping my hands together. "Head up, Bry!"

Gonzaga's point guard attempts another shot from the paint, but LaQuan blocks it and Marquise picks up the ball. He passes it to Bryson. He's got the last ten seconds to make up for the first, and I hear Marshall in my ear, pounding his heavy hands together with Ace.

There's no time left on the clock, so the game moves so fast that my head spins. Bryson bounces the ball faster than I've ever seen him and Ace talks louder, but the stadium's screaming drowns out his voice. I just see the last of his words shooting out his mouth like they did during their first practice.

Whatever comes out makes Bryson so confident that he pulls up from the three point line with the last two seconds of the game resting on his shoulders. He hasn't made a three pointer all season.

He falls back on the court from the energy he used to take the shot and the shot clock dwindles down with the ball swirling in the air.

Instead of holding their breaths, the stadium screams louder because Ace controls them too—telling them to get on their feet with his arms while the ball keeps gliding in the slowest trek to the basket I've ever seen.

It hits the rim and twirls around it while the buzzer sings. Now it's my turn to hold my breath for Coach Williams' team that hadn't lost a game since Mama woke up in the hospital.

The ball twirls while the stadium vibrates with screams. It twirls while Bryson pushes his arms on top of his head. It twirls while Mama pushes herself up to get a better view so she can report back to Lucy, who couldn't take off work. It twirls until Marshall gets tired and nudges it with his big finger from up in Heaven because there was no way all his boys who *almost* had the it factor would lose in a once-in-a-lifetime moment like this.

"He did it!" Mama screams, clamping her frail hands over her mouth. "It went in! He did it!"

There's one thing those reporters forgot to mention in their description of today. They didn't say how breathtaking it would be to see Coach Williams' losing team run out onto that court with their fists in the air and confetti fluttering around their heads. They didn't even warn me about the tears that would come after Ace dodges everybody and dashes toward me.

He climbs over chairs and into the stands and picks me up. As soon as he makes it back onto the court with me in his arms, his biggest fear swarms us with cameras and microphones. I don't even get a chance to taste his lips because they want what's mine. They want his thoughts and to capture his first expressions and they're banking on Jim Nantz to get it for them.

He grips Ace on his forearm while the camera zooms into us. "You did it again, Kid. You did it."

Jim Nantz's skin is paler than on TV and after so many years of calling NCAA games, his hair is thin around the edges. White America's relief is on his weathered face as he shakes Ace by the shoulder and then thrusts his microphone at his lips without warning.

"I'm here with Ace Williams. Talk to me about those

last few moments of the game. What were you telling Bryson Sanchez from the sidelines?"

Ace swipes his face and pulls me in at the waist, dragging his wet hands under my shirt as if he needs to feel my skin to get through this moment.

He looks at me and smiles while he strings his words together in his head. "I told him it didn't matter if the ball went in or not, all that mattered was that we were proud of him for waking up this morning—that's the only thing that matters today, that we woke up and showed up for something so monumental despite all the obstacles constantly being thrown our way."

The first time he talks to the world, the stadium gets so quiet I can hear his sharp breaths on Jim Nantz's microphone. He sounds clear, crisp, and just like Los Angeles despite not practicing.

I reach up and swipe at the sweat dripping down his red face.

This moment will be at the top of everybody's timelines before the team even puts their hands on the championship trophy. The world will pick apart his hand resting on my ass, my bedazzled shirt with his last name and number on the back that Cree made, and even the way he introduces himself to them for the first time with me wrapped around him like a safety net because he's so damn scared of them.

"This morning, we saw you walking out of a courtroom in Los Angeles and now we've just watched you play the second most monumental game of your basketball career. All of this happening in just one day. Talk to us about how you feel after such a victorious day personally and professionally."

His eyebrows furrow and he takes longer to string his words together this time because Jim Nantz is taking advantage of his own once-in-a-lifetime moment. He's the first reporter to dangle a microphone in front of *The Kid's* face and get him to talk in it.

I sneak my fingers up the back of his Jersey and stroke his skin to calm him while the stadium waits in silence. I peer around him and catch Bryson's wide eyes on the cameras, lights, and me with a grin on his face.

His eyes get wider when I toss my hand up for him to come to us. Ace follows it out of the corner of his eye and there's a "thank you" in the gentle squeeze he gives my ass.

"With all due respect, Mr. Nantz, this day isn't for me. This is a first for my team and the biggest moment in their basketball careers. I want you to talk to Bryson Sanchez about how he feels after that fire buzzer beater. Today is for my brothers and my girlfriend's dad, who played for Lockwood. He didn't live to see this moment, but I know he's looking down on us, pumping his fist for Lockwood."

He looks up in the stands at Mama grinning with Marcus and Chelsea wrapped around her and blows her a kiss that Marshall laughs at in my ear.

EPILOGUE

Lourdes

Dates with Ason Williams Jr. are as opulent as I always thought. I can't decide which ones I like best though. There're the dates that happen after monumental occasions or the just because he feels like it dates. Both always end with me being drunk off of life, if that's even possible.

"Getting another view of your city?" he asks, mushing his face into my neck.

After twenty-one years of being rich, he isn't fazed by the same things as me. It doesn't matter how many rooftops he whisks me away to, the downtown skyline never gets old. I don't smell the air on the Pacific Coast or hear the waves pounding against the shoreline in California, but it doesn't matter because somehow he makes Houston exciting just the way it is.

"I can't decide if it looks better at home or up here," I reply, tilting my neck so he can nip at it.

Loud R&B music floats from under the patio doors of the restaurant and sneaks into our reserved space.

His tongue pokes out and soothes the places his teeth sank into. "I thought you knew it looks the best from our bedroom. It's the perfect backdrop."

Heat creeps up my neck while I blink away the reasons he thinks that *I* think that. For some reason, all the light that God shines through our floor to ceiling windows hits me in his favorite spots as soon as the sun rises in the morning. There's no more jumping up and down on his dick forever because I've had enough practice to do it with my eyes closed, with the city behind me, and with that light basking around me in our bedroom.

I twist around in his arms and smile at his sneakers and shorts and the empty table set for three. "Don't start talking slick. We can always get outta here."

He chokes out a loud laugh and pulls me into his middle. "Then what am I gonna tell my good friend that flew all the way in tonight to meet you?"

"Tell them we had something to take care of."

"Hold up now, you can't make that call—only me."

I laugh, tossing my head back. "This better be Obama or something. I'm missing a free Dave and Buster's trip. I whoop Bryson's ass in air hockey at least once a year."

"Chill. I'll bring you to whoop his ass after dinner. I told Pops to get a damn woman and to stop using you to plan shit for his team."

"But I like planning *shit*. Don't be jealous because we cool like that."

"I can be jealous if I want to." He smirks. "He better take Mrs. Anderson up on her offer and let me have my peace."

"Ason!"

"What?" He laughs. "He always got you tied up with

something. Fuck I look like at Dave and Buster's with dudes I see every damn day?"

There's a glint in his white smile when he talks about the team. The truth is, they love him and he loves them. LaQuan dry heaves anytime somebody mentions Ace leaving them for the league, but nobody knew anything about Ace's post-college life—not even me, and I'm his.

We were a week out from our monumental win and on unplanned celebratory date number six. The first five were a blur, and I didn't know how he could top private flights to cities I've only ever saw on television and dinners in obscure restaurants whose names I couldn't pronounce. Sometimes I feel like he's building me up to let me down, but Mama says men like him were for a lifetime. I guess she's right because I feel it when he's buried deep inside me and promising me forever in his own way.

He takes my cheeks in his hands and squeezes them. "Let me spend the night with you, baby."

"You spend the night with me every night."

"Yeah, but tonight is different."

Different sounds loaded with mystery when he says it, but not the good mystery that keeps me on my toes. It sounds final.

"Mr. Williams?" One of the brunette waitresses pokes her head through the patio door.

She looks like all the other girls roaming around the restaurant in unsuspecting swanky clothes and light makeup. When they call him "Mr. Williams" it sounds like they're talking to James Bond.

"Your guest is on his way up. I'll get you guys started with some sparkling and flat water."

"Okay," he mutters, looking at me. "Thanks, Dana."

She smiles at us and eases back inside. All waitresses

smile at Ace because he holds onto their names as soon as they announce it to our table and leaves outrageous tips even on the rare occasions the service is subpar. I'm sure it's another good thing Angie taught him.

"Oh, this is for sure Obama. Wait until I tell Marcus my man knows the POTUS." I wiggle my eyebrows until the serious expression that "different" brought onto his face disappears.

"You hella stupid." He snorts, pulling me into him. "Act right for me tonight or no dirty ass Dave and Buster's."

"Don't be lame. I promise I'll keep my smart mouth in check as long as whoever it is don't be talking slick shit—"

"Kid?"

My tongue gets caught on the roof of my mouth.

I know this voice.

I've listened to it rap millions of verses. It's the only other voice besides Ace's that can shut me up. It's smoother than it is on wax and if I stay conscious throughout the night, I'll try to commit it to my memory so I can describe its vibrato to Chelsea.

"I heard you a Houston nigga now. How that happen, Twin?" Dough laughs.

Even his laugh sounds good and full, like there's no other place he'd rather be than laughing on a rooftop in Houston with me and Ace.

Ace takes my hands and laces his fingers through mine. "Still wanna dip on me and hit up Dave and Buster's?"

"No—no," I stutter, swallowing the nerves that come with meeting somebody like Dough for the first time.

"I thought so." He smiles, turning around and keeping me hidden behind him.

Maybe he knows that this "just because" celebratory

date might be the one to send me up into the sky with Marshall and Angie.

My sweat settles between our palms, and I rock back and forth on my heels. If Cree was here, she'd pinch my arm because creasing Chanels is just as blasphemous as keeping them hidden from the world.

"You know you never explained that I wouldn't wanna go nowhere else when I found my way back home," Ace says to him, laughing.

"Nah… see, I left that part out 'cause I ain't wanna scare you, but I guess I could've warned you that no other place feels as good."

My stomach rumbles with the butterflies that didn't use to exist there because they're talking about me—little ole' me that has the world at my fingertips ever since I fell in love with a man I couldn't hate.

Ace tugs me from behind him and I choke on a butterfly's wing when I see the cause of my sudden need to hyperventilate. Chelsea said it was the tattoos that had us hypnotized and God, I wish I could tell her how crisp they look underneath the lights strung across the restaurant's patio.

He holds out his hand toward me. "Come 'ere."

Ace nudges me at the small of my back and I inch toward his butterscotch hand.

I grab it, and he squeezes it tight.

"Clo' couldn't come because flying makes her nauseated right now, so it's just you and us tonight, baby sis. I wanna hear all about this rehab shit my brother been texting me about."

I belt out a sigh and whip my head around. "Rehab?"

Ace's lips ease up, and he stuffs his hands in his pockets. "I told you I'd always fix it—even the hard stuff."

Ace

POPS DOESN'T BELIEVE in fancy rehab facilities off the coast in Malibu, just like he doesn't believe in losing.

"I see things ain't changed much." He takes a slurp from his thermos and leans forward, squinting at the grey brick building.

It's so early that a rooster crows from the front yard of the house next door. My engine hums, covering the voices from the people walking across the parking lot. They all have salt and pepper heads and styrofoam cups of coffee.

"You sure about this?" I ask, twisting my keys out of the ignition.

"Would I ever let you do anything I wasn't sure about?"

"You really want me to answer that?"

We look at each other and laugh so hard that his eyes crinkle together like they did when Phat slid a McDonald's pancake in front of him at our kitchen table this morning.

"Marie knew Angie well. They were classmates. I can't think of any other person who could want the best for us than her."

I nod, tugging my lip under my teeth.

Getting out and walking toward that building is harder than lacing up my shoes and running onto Marshall's court with Phat holding her breath in the stands.

Pops claps his hand against the back of my head. "We got this."

Us. We.

That's what those reporters neglected to mention when they talked about Pops "letting" me play through the tournament after Cheyenne blabbered my darkest secret to the world on the stand in the courtroom: *"Yes, I saw him get so drunk that he wouldn't remember anything he said or did, but it was strange because none of us could even tell he was drunk sometimes. My fiancé, Javi, said it was normal for him to get blackout wasted. It was like his thing."*

Quame said it was her way of getting in one last kick to my reputation before she faded into obscurity where she belonged. So me and Pops decided I would ball in the big dance just in case it was the last time I ever did. Now that it was done, the records were broken, and they hung my name next to Marshall's in his renovated gym, it was time to face the music or like Phat said this morning over breakfast: *"Time to rip the bandaid off, baby. No little by little today."*

Pops takes another slurp from his thermos with a smack. "Marshall would say you finally made it to the end of your story. You overcame all the internal and external obstacles life's thrown at you."

"Couldn't let the day end without another Marshall quote, huh?"

"Never. He was wise beyond his years."

"You think that's what CeCe liked about him?"

He smiles big when I say CeCe's name and I don't blame him. She makes us all smile these days—especially when she's got Mom's name on her lips.

"I think she liked that, among other things." He chuckles. "Her and Marshall were supposed to be forever. I always believed he was supposed to coach the boys' team at Lockwood eventually and she was supposed to stay at home with the kids, but..."

"But what?"

"Life happened like it always does." His mouth drops into a serene smile while he stares at a grey-headed lady shooing a dog away from the building's front door. "He played his last game on that court at Lockwood and collapsed. The world just ain't felt right since."

He takes another slurp while the dog scurries across the parking lot.

I try to lift my hand to grab the door handle, but it's too heavy.

"Meeting should start soon, huh?"

I nod and try again.

"Marie's biggest pet peeve is tardiness. She taught for twenty years. There's nothing she can't stand more than a late kid."

I lift my heavy hand again and curl it around the handle. Pops pushes his door open at the same time I push mine. There's only a few feet between my truck and the building, but it feels farther.

I get out and take a step, and then another.

"Hey, Williams," Pops calls out from behind me.

I turn around and smile at him, leaning against my truck's hood.

"I'm proud of you, young man." He lifts his thermos in the air. "I'm so damn proud of you."

I swallow his words. They settle in my chest and reassure me I'll never want for them again.

THE GREY BUILDING is just as bleak on the inside. I'm the youngest person sitting in our circle, but nobody cares because I'm Marshall and Angie's son. The people here remind me of how pretty Mom was in school and ask if Pops likes being back home. Nobody talks about why we're spending our Saturday in an empty rec center on the Northside until Ms. Marie urges each of us to stand one by one and introduce ourselves.

I don't know how to do that until Mom's old friend Joe claps me on the shoulder to help himself out of his chair.

"Good morning," he drawls. "I'm Joe and I been an alcoholic for twenty somethin' years now."

Their eyes rove from him and his stained Wranglers to me.

I stand up and clear my throat to knock away the nerves from so many eyes staring at me in a cold, sterile room, but the phlegm keeps coming back.

I fight through it and gurgle out. "My name is Ace..."

Ms. Marie's warm eyes stroke my face and she smiles like she knows there's more that's been stuck in my chest for a long time. She twirls her finger to nudge me along and all of her jewelry clinks together.

I look at the Jordans Phat left for me by the door this morning. It's easier talking to them rather than a room full of strangers until Ms. Marie snaps her fingers and makes me tear my eyes from my shoelaces.

"My name is Ace..." I start again. "And I'm not addicted to reporter's voices, basketball, or even girls. I'm just an alcoholic and this morning my girlfriend told me it was okay that I am."

~The End~

ENJOYED THE STORY?

If you enjoyed the story, please consider leaving an honest review on Amazon and Goodreads. It helps other readers discover my work and opens the door for amazing opportunities.

ACKNOWLEDGMENTS

Beta Readers: Mie, Ayanna, Genel, Terra, Lisette, and LaCorrie.

Thank you for your time, flexibility, attention to detail, respectful honesty, and willingness to help. I could go on and on. I will forever cherish our in-depth discussions about these characters and your willingness to trust me with your personal stories. Thank you for getting it, reading with care, and accepting the story for what it was.

Allegra: You're crazy if you thought I was leaving you out of this. Thanks for always cheering me on and recognizing that when I'm quiet, it just means something is cooking.

Jenine: Thank you for providing your priceless expertise and creating a safe space that allows me to feel comfortable sharing my work. I'm still working on that whole patience thing, lol.

Shaun Chadwick: I'm still going.

Antoinnette Kates: As always, your emails come at the best times. Thank you for your kind words. As long as I have amazing readers like you, I promise I will never stop.

Husband: Thank you for always being willing to answer my endless sports questions, being so engrossed in the stories I come up with, and making sure I never play myself when it comes to the art I create. I might fuck around and let you read this one, lol.

Granny: At the end of it all, he treats me like the lady I am. I promise.

ABOUT THE AUTHOR

Rae Lyse is a Texas-based romance author who enjoys reading and traveling. With a background in social work and a love of romance, she seeks to blend the two by crafting love stories about some of the most complex characters.

ALSO BY RAE LYSE

The Sun Series